WHERE EAGLES DANCE

A Saga of Early California

Marian Sepulveda

ISBN: 0990582744
ISBN: 9780990582748

Published by www.AquaZebra.com
Web, Book & Print Design
Cathedral City, CA

Library of Congress Control Number: 2016937882

First Edition
First Printing, May 2016

Printed in the United States of America

DEDICATION

To the inhabitants of early California, both human and animal, who shared a very special place and time in this state's history. It is through our stories that we remember and honor them.

PREFACE

Welcome to the world of the 1850s. The wagon trains, Indian attacks, a lone survivor, and her tale of life among the Kumeyaay Indians.

Parts of this story are actual history, the Butterfield Overland Mail, the history unfolding in California and in a country divided by the issue of slavery, and the looming Civil War.

I have walked a fine line between actual historical persons and the needs of my fictional story, so I shall endeavor to clarify. The character of Abigail Bristol, is, of course, totally from my imagination. Her time with the Kumeyaay Indians is fiction. While there actually is such a tribe, my account of them is from my imagination.

The character of James Cassidy, I so wanted to name for his actual historical figure James Ruler Lassitor, but didn't want to offend any remaining descendants. James Lassitor was station master at Vallecito, in what is now the Anza Borrego desert. I changed its name to Seven Springs.

Note: You can still visit the restored stage station at Vallecito, where there is also a primitive campground. And, there might be seven springs, depending on the earthquake activity.

As for John Jay Butterfield, son of John Butterfield who was the guiding genius behind the Butterfield Overland Mail, he actually was involved in the startup of the mail run, as I have depicted.

Though my account of his life with Abby is purely from my imagination. I tried to change his name…but couldn't seem to do it. I hope his descendants won't find my version of his life uncomfortable.

On the first run of the Overland Mail, Waterman Ormsby, a reporter for the New York Herald, rode all the way from Tipton, Missouri to San Francisco, along with John Jay Butterfield, and sent dispatches back with the east bound coaches. My quotes from his writings were taken from the book that was later printed of his dispatches. They are his actual words.

The incident with the Indians and the stage coach happened at a later time with another coach, but I changed it to the first run. Many of the hardships on that first run are actual history, as are many of the events depicted in California. The research into this era, some of which concerned my late husband's Spanish ancestors, was fascinating. The character of Vicenta Carrillo, was actually Vicenta Sepulveda Carrillo, my husband's great, great aunt…and much of the account of her life and that of her husband, Ramon Carrillo are actual history.

ACKNOWLEDGMENTS

I would like to thank Ted Seastrom, who encouraged me to finish a saga started 30 years ago. And thanks as well to my sister, Virginia Foster, without whose enthusiasm and copy editing I couldn't have come this far.

1

June 1852

Abby ran as fast as her short legs would propel her, through brush that scratched her face and her faded gingham dress. Her long red braids flopped against her back, her worn shoes were little protection against the desert rocks. But she had to keep running. To stop was to die, or worse. Her mother's terrified whisper echoed over and over in her mind.

"Run, Abby! Run like the wind until you are far away, then hide! Don't come back until after dark. Promise me!"

"I pr...promise!" the confused ten year old said, then, when her mother told her to, she slipped from under their wagon and ran, leaving behind the sound of guns firing, of chilling war cries, and pounding hooves.

Her heart was pounding so fiercely she couldn't have heard the sound of pursuit, yet she sensed it. She could almost feel the whip of an arrow into her back, expecting at any moment to be felled. Instinct made her switch directions often, using the tall brush to conceal herself.

Ahead of her, she saw her only hope, a large clump of mesquite. A tiny opening in the lowest branches told her it was used by the wild desert animals. At this moment no fear of animals could equal her terror of the painted warriors who had swooped down on the wagon train.

Abby had heard whispered stories about what the Indians did to those who survived an attack to be taken prisoner. She didn't want to spend the rest of her days as an Indian slave, if indeed the warriors permitted her to live.

She was at the end of her endurance, her knees turning to rubber, her lungs burning with each labored breath. Diving at the opening, she wiggled on her belly as the sharp thorns of the mesquite ripped her dress and scratched deep into her arms. She barely felt the pain, heard only the war cries of the warrior tracking her.

Terror drove her deep into the clump until she reached the trunk of the tree and the bare sandy area that surrounded it. There she huddled, shaking, panting, and unaware of the tears streaking her face. She listened to the sounds of a horse circling the mesquite, the frustrated cries of the savage.

If not for this sanctuary the warrior would surely have caught her, yet she still didn't know if she was safe or if he would find a way to penetrate the thorns and drag her out. Smothering her sobs in her torn skirt she was like a terrified animal. The long, razor sharp thorns of the mesquite kept her enemy from following. She could hear him trying to fit through the same small opening she had used, could hear the harsh sound of his breathing, the snarl of anger when thorns ripped his flesh.

Time ceased to have any meaning. She kept her face buried in her skirt, too terrified to see if the savage would reach her. Eventually she was aware of silence. Her breathing slowed but she was afraid to move, afraid he was out there, waiting.

The sand at the base of the tree had been dug out by animals searching for the coolness just below the surface. Abby burrowed down into that coolness, her throat parched from the desert heat and from running. Her thirst grew stronger with each minute that passed. She prayed for darkness. She prayed to awaken and find herself back at her uncle's farm, the smell of biscuits baking, the sounds of her cousins setting off to do their chores.

She tried not to think about her parents still at the circle of wagons. The force of Indians who attacked was so large the settlers were badly outnumbered. They'd been warned that a renegade band often came up from Mexico to attack poorly protected wagon trains. Inexperience on the part of their leader caused a delay in forming a tight circle. By the time they were ready to make a stand the Indians were all around them, their blood-curdling cries sending shivers down the spine of the bravest men. As long as Abby was praying, she prayed for a miracle.

Darkness came. Abby had listened to the clucking of the quail for quite some time. There was no alarm in their chatter. Finally it was thirst and hunger that drove her from her shelter.

In the darkness she hoped she could find her way back. Her mother wouldn't let the wagons go on without her.

The silence was eerie. Now and then came the rustle of a night creature scurrying away at her approach. The screech of an owl brought terrifying visions of gruesomely painted warriors swooping down, until she realized it was a familiar sound. Her relieved sigh sounded loud in her ears. She listened for the familiar sound of voices. Samuel Walker, their wagon boss, had a booming voice that lashed the inexperienced drivers to keep up the pace. Right now, even the complaining voice of Jake Talbot would be like music. Nothing was ever to his liking. It was either too hot or too cold. He was too far back in the train, or too close to the front.

The smell of smoke first alerted Abby that she was close, but it was the silence that made her cautious. Tall brush kept her from seeing very far in front of her, and the faint moonlight was just enough for her to make out the large hazards. She moved without a sound, slowly, step by step.

There was no warning when she stepped into the open and surveyed the smoldering ruins of the wagons. Bodies were strewn around the burned out hulks. Her gaze turned away from the bloody, hairless heads. She couldn't even cry, her shock went beyond tears.

Even before she located her wagon she held no hope. She would not have her miracle. Her beautiful, blonde mother lay in the sand. The bullet wound in her temple told Abby it was her father who chose not to let her be taken captive. An arrow protruded from his back as he lay sprawled beside his wife, like lovers in an embrace.

At least they had been spared the scalping knives. For a long time she stared at them, willing them to move, willing them to be alive. Finally, realizing others might have survived, she began a search, counting the families and the children. Finding dead children was the worst part, but equally frightening was the inescapable fact some of the women and children were missing. A shudder shook her slender body knowing how close she had come to sharing that fate.

It was obvious some of the men had survived long enough to be taken captive, then slowly killed in the savage's brutal form of torture. She couldn't bear to go near them, but couldn't escape the scent of blood and death that lingered in the air. A smell she would never erase from her mind.

Once she completed the grisly inspection, finding no one left alive, she began to search for food and water. The water barrels on each wagon had been smashed and burned. None of the food supplies escaped the fire or been taken by the savages.

Her toe bumped something in the sand. Reaching down she uncovered a canteen, buried in the scuffle. A quick shake told her it was nearly empty. There was just enough to slake her thirst for the moment, but she slung it around her body anyway. Her mind was already preparing her for the task of survival.

The scorching heat of the day had turned to bitter cold. Wrapping her arms around herself was meager relief. A smashed trunk that escaped the fire produced some boys' breeches and several shirts that would fit her. She shed her tattered dress and slipped into the unaccustomed warmth of long pants and a long-sleeved shirt. A small, rough blanket would serve to carry anything else she could salvage.

She felt like a ghoul as she searched among the dead boys for shoes that would fit her. Her own would never survive even a day in this rugged terrain. Robbing the dead seemed like a sin, and briefly she wondered if she wanted to live at all. Wouldn't it be much easier to lay down beside her parents and join them in death? Only fear that the raiding party might come back looking for her in the morning kept her from seriously considering it.

Once she had shoes and two thick pair of socks to warm her feet, she selected a hat and tucked her red braids under it. With her slender form she could easily pass for a boy, a disguise which no doubt would be safer.

There was one chore left. She didn't have the strength to bury them all, but knew she had to do that much for her parents. She couldn't leave them to the animals.

The first touch of the sun's rays on the barren ravine found Abby kneeling in the sand next to a rock covered mound. She had seen enough of such mounds along the trek to know to protect their remains. It had taken her all night to dig a hole deep enough to hold both her mother and her father, to wrap them in scorched blankets and drag them to their final resting place.

She wanted them to be together, touching, knowing they would have wanted it that way. From her mother she had taken a gold locket with miniatures of both her parents, and from her father she took the sharp hunting knife he kept hidden in his boot, strapping it around her own thin leg.

Painstakingly she carried rocks to cover the grave, and erected a charred wooden cross marked with their names, crudely lettered in charcoal; Michael and Ellen Bristol. Their dream of a better life in the West had ended in tragedy. One of Ellen's final acts had been to save the life of their only child. So far, Abby was alive, but for how long she could remain so was something she didn't even want to consider. She only knew they were a long way from any habitation.

Before long she would have to make a decision about what to do, but for the moment she could only murmur every prayer she knew, hoping God would be satisfied and accept her parents into his safe keeping.

The sun's rays warmed her back telling Abby she had stayed too long already. Her hunger and thirst had turned into a gnawing in her belly. Then came a sound that turned her blood cold. Her grief had caused her to linger, and now she sensed it was too late.

It took a tremendous amount of will to force herself to look over her shoulder. The figure of an Indian was outlined against the brilliant back light of the sun. Instead of being mounted on a war pony he stood tall and menacing, though she couldn't make out his face.

Strangely she didn't panic. She considered making a dash for the brush but this time she knew she'd never make it. Her enemy was too close, and he was not alone. If she was fortunate he would kill her and leave her here with her parents.

For one brief moment she turned her attention back to the grave, patting the mound of rock and saying her final goodbye. Then she stood up to face the warrior, her green eyes flashing with defiance.

No, she thought, it would do no good to run. She was too weak from thirst and hunger to have the strength or endurance to escape. She wasn't afraid to join her parents in death. At the moment it seemed preferable to the alternatives. She just hoped he would be quick about it.

The half-naked man did no more than stare at her, unmoving. Several things registered in Abby's mind. This man's bow and quiver were slung over his shoulder, his knife sheathed at his waist. He made no move toward either one. There were no horses in sight, even though behind him was a small band of Indians, including women and children. They looked to be carrying all their possessions. Dogs raced about the traveling band, sniffing at the dead bodies.

Some of the boys were driving a few head of cattle.

Most shocking was the fact the young boys wore no clothes at all, and seemed quite unconcerned about being naked.

Obviously they were not the same ones who had attacked the wagons. The man in front of her shifted his position, bringing Abby's attention back to him. This was no young man now that she could see his face. He was middle aged, heavy through the middle but well-muscled.

She refused to cower under his direct gaze. She was more afraid he wouldn't kill her, that her fate would be even worse. It occurred to her that she was wearing boy's breeches and a hat that covered her long hair. He probably didn't realize she was a girl.

A movement among the ruins of the wagons took her attention. Several young Indians were moving through the wreckage salvaging anything that might have been overlooked by the marauders. Abby tried to summon up anger but it wouldn't come. She seemed strangely benumbed. The young men looked thin. They searched out blankets and tools the attackers hadn't wanted; hoes and pick axes.

The man in front of her made a motion with his hand. Abby had to force herself not to back away as he took several steps closer. Again he motioned for her to join the others, speaking words that had no meaning to her, but his tone revealed no menace. No friendliness either.

Her choices were few. Being alone on the desert frightened her more than the prospect of going with these people. The weakness she felt told her she wouldn't last long in this hostile land.

Gathering her courage she stepped past him, walking hesitantly toward the others. She felt his presence as he walked behind her. He smelled strongly of odors she couldn't name, like smoke, and musk, and more. The step she was taking was irrevocable as she studied the others, shivering with the knowledge these people were more alien than any she had ever met. They couldn't communicate, and she couldn't escape if they chose not to let her go.

Most of the group showed little interest in the remains of the wagon train, as if it were nothing unusual. Their gazes showed curiosity, not hostility. The big man was beside her now, directing her to a family group. Around her Abby saw five children, ranging in ages from an infant to a girl about her own age. The black-eyed girl was wearing a type of net slung around her body with all her possessions inside. The infant was tied to his mother's back on a cradle board and looked to be sleeping peacefully. The others all wore the same net to carry things.

The older woman said nothing as the man turned to Abby and motioned for her to stay with that group. Without another word he strode away.

With open curiosity, the black-eyed girl looked at Abby. Her hair was cut short at her shoulders, her dress made of some light weight cloth, which told Abby these people must have traded with white men at some time. The girl's sandals were made of plant fibers, and her seashell necklace had intricate carvings.

2

A bby was awakened by the activity in the camp. She listened for the usual sounds, the clinking of harnesses, the snorts of horses, the creaking of wagons, the bawling of the cattle they drove along with them. But nothing was familiar. Memory came back with a flood, bringing with it overwhelming grief. She would never hear those sounds again, would never awaken to her mother's call.

Tears scalded the back of her throat. She hadn't allowed herself to cry before, and now was not the time. Not in front of the Indians, they might see it as weakness.

Sitting up she saw it was late afternoon, and the People were erasing all signs of their brief camp. They had slept during the heat of the afternoon and were ready to move on. Feeling refreshed, Abby joined her new family, even though she was still feeling the empty rumbling of her stomach.

Briefly she considered staying behind, or slipping off into the desert, but saw nothing to be gained. She didn't feel as if she was a prisoner. No one watched to insure her compliance. Even if she wasn't ready to give them her trust, she was smart enough to realize she needed them. But, at the first hint of trouble, she would slip into the brush and be free within minutes.

She wondered how far they were traveling as they continued across the desert, avoiding the well-traveled immigrant trail. Sooner or later, someone would come across the remains of the wagon train. They would know someone had survived to bury two people. Maybe her uncle would come for her.

For a moment Abby allowed herself to daydream about be-ing reunited with her uncle and his family. Uncle Jacob would, of course, do his Christian duty and take her in, and never would she be allowed to forget she was living on his charity. She shuddered at the thought of what her life would become. Without her parents to intervene, Uncle Jacob would turn her into little more than a slave, the same as he had his own children, and his wife. Among the so-called savages she saw more joy and laughter than Joseph permitted.

The sound of a child's giggle gave a measure of relief to Abby's gloomy thoughts. She had no family now. There was no way she would allow Jacob to take her back to Illinois. For now, she was too young to be on her own. Perhaps these people would help her find a white family who would take her in. Yet, wouldn't they try to reunite her with her only remaining family? Her mind refused to contemplate her future. For now, it was enough to be alive.

As the sun dipped toward the horizon Abby could make out a low range of sand colored hills before them. They looked as bleak and barren as the open desert. Perhaps that was where they would stop for the night. She was hot and thirsty, but when she saw the others didn't drink from their meager supply of water, she was de-termined she wouldn't either. What was their secret? How could their mouths not be as dry as hers?

The dark-eyed girl pulled some bean pods from a mesquite tree, placing them in her net. One pod she broke open to get at the peas inside. Abby watched her put them into her mouth and suck on them. She saw others doing the same thing.

At the next mesquite, she picked pods as green as the ones the girl had selected, put some in her shirt pocket and broke one open.

The hard green peas she put in her mouth, expecting them to be bitter. But they weren't. She was aware of moisture coming into her parched mouth and of a faint lemony taste. It was obviously a way to conserve water.

The sun was settling on the tips of the distant mountain peaks by the time they reached the hills. Abby followed her new family, utterly weary now, wanting only to lie down and sleep. As they entered a ravine with steep rocky sides, several men scaled the ridges on either side to keep watch.

Desert scrub gave way to the vivid green trunks of palo verde trees and desert willow. The growth became denser, indicating the presence of water. Abby prayed they'd reached a camping place. Her legs turned rubbery, too weak to hold her. If she sank down onto the warm sand she was certain she wouldn't be able to rise again.

She swayed with weakness, dully registering the fact that the women and girls were removing their nets, emptying contents onto the ground. Rocks were moved into a circle, and the sticks and limbs collected in the desert were laid beside them.

One of the men made a fire with a flint while women began to prepare their clay pots for cooking. There was animated chatter all around her.

Forcing her shaky knees to support her just a few steps more, Abby selected a shadowed place beside a large rock and sank into the sand. She sprawled into an exhausted sleep before she could even remove her canteen or unwrap her blanket from around her body.

It was the sound of laughter that brought her awake. She felt muddled, groggy. How long had she been asleep? Darkness had fallen, the eerie dancing shadows of the fire lit up the camp. Her mouth began to water the moment she caught the scent of food.

Turning her head she almost jumped out of her skin to find an old man with gray hair leaning over, studying her. His face was so close she could feel the warmth of his breath, smell the musky odors of his body. It wasn't necessarily offensive, only strange and frightening.

"Kyu! Come," he said, "We eat."

"You…speak English," Abby said, scrambling to her feet to follow him. Even the weakness in her legs couldn't stop her at the mention of food.

"Learn from priests," he said in a broken speech pattern that showed he didn't use the language often. "Live in San Diego, when boy. Learn. No like. Come back."

Abby's eyes seemed to grow larger as the man led her to the side of the fire where the men were sitting. The young, dark-eyed girl handed the old man a small clay bowl which he then filled with something from a large pot by the fire. It smelled heavenly. There were stories about Indians eating rattlesnakes and other abhorrent creatures, but hunger was a powerful incentive.

When the girl handed Abby a similar bowl she followed the old man's example, serving herself. Instead of sitting with the other men, the old man moved away from the fire to some rocks. Abby sensed she was expected to follow.

The old man sat cross-legged in the sand. Following his example, she sat near him, dipping her fingers into the bowl. All her previous conditioning on table manners rebelled at the experience and she almost giggled at the thought of his response if she were to ask for a fork.

Ducking her head to hide the momentary, half-hysterical urge to laugh, Abby sucked the stew from her fingers, finding it warm and delicious, dipping back in for more bits of meat.

Rabbit. She hadn't expected anything so delicious.

Aware the old man was watching her she didn't care. Half-starved she held the bowl close to her mouth and shoveled the food in as fast as she could chew and swallow. He ate more slowly.

"I am called Pion," he said finally, his speech coming easier with practice.

"I'm Abby," she said without thinking. She was filled with momentary panic until she realized he wouldn't know that was a woman's name.

"Ah-bee," he repeated slowly, savoring the strangeness of it on his tongue.

She expected more questions but they didn't come. When they'd finished eating, he showed her how to clean the bowl with sand. This wasn't new to her, she'd done it often on the cross-country trek where water was in short supply.

Pion took her back to the fire so she could return her bowl to the dark-eyed girl.

"Moyla," he said, motioning toward the girl. Then he pointed to Abby. "Ah-bee," he told Moyla.

Abby became aware a number of the men in camp were looking at her. One young man of about eighteen came closer to touch the red hair peeking from under her hat. Knocking his hand away, Abby forced herself not to show the sudden panic she felt. Instead she glared at him.

Another young boy came up behind her, and before she realized he was there, he playfully swept the hat from her head. Abby froze in horror as her red braids dropped down to her shoulders.

A sudden silence fell. Abby was afraid to breathe. What would they do to her now?

"Firehair," Pion said in wonder, repeating the word in the Indian's language.

Another man reached out for Abby's hair. She steeled herself, too frightened to knock his hand away. His eyes reflected only curiosity as he stroked her head. Another man stepped closer to feel the soft texture of her hair, then another. She tried her best not to cringe, not to scream or run as the stroking of hands went on, only aware of the women coming forward when she heard their chatter.

The men began to make jokes about the strange color of her hair, bringing laughter all about her. Frantically she opened her eyes and looked to Pion for help, seeing only the merry sparkle in his eyes. His smile gave her courage to look into the faces surrounding her. There was no cruelty reflected there, no menace.

Realizing how groundless her terror had been Abby was unable to stifle a giggle of half hysterical relief. Clamping a hand over her mouth she tried in vain to silence it. The others seemed to find her girlish giggles funny and laughed all the harder.

For Abby it was a great release to laugh with them, to give vent to the intense emotions she'd been holding inside. The Indians wouldn't respect her tears, but they didn't mind her laughter, even if it was tinged with hysteria.

Over the next few days Abby became Pion's shadow. Since he spoke her language he was the logical one to teach her their ways and their language, finding her quick to learn.

During the day, as they walked toward the mountains, Pion would take her off into the desert to show her how to find food. When they rested in the heat of the day, he showed her how to weave the long fibers of the yucca into a net of her own.

"We are Kumeyaay," he told her on a hot afternoon while they sat in the shade of a desert willow, and Abby tried to imitate the tight weave Peon showed her. "We have lived in this land since the beginning. Amaayahaa give us this as our home."

"Do you always live in the desert?" Abby asked, a deep frown marring her brow as she struggled to make her fingers work the stiff fibers.

"Mow. No. We live here when Father Sun is cool. When He hot we go to the mountains."

"Is that where you're going now?"

"Hah, yes, we gather food here for many suns to take with us. I show you how to live in this land so you not go hungry. A white man dies of thirst and hunger when all is here. He looks but he cannot see."

"I want to learn," Abby said fervently, sensing it was knowledge she would need to grow up without her family. She glanced at her teacher, noting the still powerful muscles of his barrel chest and his arms, in spite of his years. His face showed the lines of age, deep grooves marking his cheeks and brow, yet his body was strong, and his back straight. She wasn't used to seeing men almost naked. Pion, like the other men, wore a breech cloth made of woven grass, deer hide or cloth. The children wore no clothing at all. She winced to think what Uncle Jacob would say. She could almost hear his booming voice calling them heathens and savages. "Godless! Doomed to the eternal fires of Hell!"

Shaking off her thoughts, Abby noted how the muscles of Pion's thighs and calves stood out. On his feet he wore sandals made of plant fibers. In his net, he carried only a few items, including a gourd, with a stopper, for water, fibers for her net which he had been collecting as they walked, and a long section of bone Abby hadn't seen him use as yet.

One thing she was quick to grasp was the difference in the People's approach to survival in the wilderness; the fact they didn't destroy anything needlessly. They took fibers from a yucca, leaves from the sage for their tea, tubers from the sand, or parts of a cactus, but they never took enough to kill the plant. She knew what a white man would have done. He'd have uprooted anything he wanted to use with no regard to those who came later.

At first she'd been concerned when he carried no food. But she never went hungry. He fed them both from roots and seeds.

"Do you have children?" Abby asked.

"My woman die long ago. My son live on white man's ranch. My daughter took husband from Yuma tribe. She live with his people."

"Do you miss them?" she asked in childish innocence.

Pion gave a shrug. "I accept. I visit them. They come to our camp." He gestured in the general direction of the rest of their small band. "These are my people. As long as I can hunt and gather food, I stay."

Abby was afraid to ask where he'd go when he could no longer do those things, not certain she'd like the answer.

"You wear too much clothes," he told her. "Too much heat."

Abby felt a deep flush stain her cheeks. Pion noticed and chuckled. "To be Kumeyaay you must shed the white man's ways. Is it not your intent to stay among us?"

Abby stared up at him. "How...did you know?"

Again he chuckled, his dark brown eyes twinkling merrily. "You watch. You learn. If you go away, you not care to come with Pion and weave your net." He gestured at her crude attempt to copy his net, but he didn't make fun of it.

Abby's fingers began to move again, gaining skill. "I do need to stay," she admitted, suddenly afraid they would send her away. "Will the People let me?"

"It is strange you not wish your own people."

"My mother and father died a few days ago." It was hard to say the words, to realize it was final, irrevocable. "My only family now is an uncle. I...don't like him. He talks of God all the time...he makes me feel wicked." The rest she couldn't put into words.

Pion gave a grunt to show he understood. "Not good man for young girl. We make Kumeyaay of you. Hahro and his family will let you sleep at their fire, but once we reach our village in the mountains, it is the elders who will have the final say."

"Who is your chief?"

Pion shrugged. "We not have chief, only elders. Wahss speaks for them."

Abby wondered if he was the squat man who had seemed to stare holes through her, who seemed to see no humor when the others laughed. What would she do if they didn't allow her to stay? Where would she go? "Is he the one who didn't want me to come with you?"

"Wahss afraid white man see white boy and think we had taken him. It very bad to let you stay. Now we know you girl, not boy, even bader."

"What about you?" she asked, not having considered how her presence would endanger her hosts. "Do you think I should go away?" She realized she had come to like this old man who was so patient with her.

"I think what will happen will happen. I be uncle. I teach you."

"Why not Hahro if I am to live with his family?"

"He is younger man, needed to feed his family, to teach his son. We help by gathering food."

"What about Moyla?"

"She learn from her mother."

"Then why do I learn from you?"

Pion laughed at her constant questions. "Kwer kwer too much. You learn by watching." After a few minutes he answered her question. "You are different, Firehair. Enyaa, the medicine woman spoke of your coming to us. There is much you must know before you go back to the white man's world."

Abby's mouth dropped open. "Who is Enyaa? How does she know this?"

"Enyaa is keeper of our medicine ways. She knows things we not question."

"But...how can she know that I'll want to go back some day?"

"It is enough she says it is so. You have purpose, little one. It is not to be part of the People forever. Amaayahaa has brought you to us to guard and to teach. I fear you must learn your lessons well."

Abby felt a strange shiver go through her at his words. Could this Enyaa actually peer into her future and know what lay ahead. She'd heard that some Indians sought visions, some of which turned out to be remarkably accurate.

Pion wasn't used to her constant chatter so she resolved to keep quiet and learn by watching. To her, Pion would be an uncle, though any comparison between him and Uncle Jacob was too bizarre to contemplate. They were total opposites.

When their rest period was over, Pion slipped Abby's partly woven fibers into his own net then showed her how to gather agave...

though she knew this was only done by the men. Already she was being accorded teachings not given to a woman, and took Pion's teachings very seriously.

Tall stalks of agave grew out of a clump of bayonet sharp spears. To Abby the stalks resembled giant asparagus, and she wondered if they would be as delicious as they looked.

She was too short to reach over the spears, so she could only watch as Pion took the bone tool from his net and slid the sharpened end down to the base of the lone spear, severing it. Lifting the stalk free of the bayonets he lay it across Abby's arms. The fresh scent of it already had her mouth watering.

She'd had little lunch. Pion ate nothing at all. She was learning the People only ate twice a day, except for children and pregnant women.

When he cut some stalks with blooming flowers, Abby gave a start when bees fled from the severed stalk, sounding annoyed. Pion watched the direction they took, and she guessed he was thinking of wild, sweet honey.

Her lesson continued as he showed her how to gather apples from the cactus. Now, in late spring, the desert was alive with color. The agave blooms were golden yellow, reaching proudly into the warm air. Cactus blossoms ranged in color from a vibrant red to saffron yellow. The desert willow put forth fragrant, delicate lilac hued blooms on drooping limbs that reminded Abby of a weeping willow.

There were glimpses of the illusive quail and occasionally the speedy retreat of a chaparral cock. Often a jack rabbit would freeze in place at their approach, then bound away in giant leaps. The smaller cottontail would simply disappear into the brush.

That night, as Abby lay in a lean-to made of palm fronds, arrowroot and sage, she felt safe. Moyla was only a few feet away, as was Moyla's mother Opachuk and the baby. Hahro and the boy, Weatuk, slept on the other side of the fire. She let her mind go over the things she'd learned. It was almost as if she were still going to school, only instead of learning to do sums, and about the constitution, she was learning to survive in a hostile land. When she thought of it, Pion's lessons made more sense than Mrs. Kincannon's.

Learning to track prey, learning to find water, these were lessons that would keep her alive. Practicing penmanship was boring, especially when Jamie Plummer would pinch her or tug on her braids. More than once Abby was sent to the corner for punching her tormentor.

At first she had been embarrassed to sit at the front of the room listening to derisive giggles, but eventually she came to enjoy it, allowing her imagination free rein while the others worked on their assignments. What wasn't so enjoyable was the extra work to catch up. Yet, often the teasing of the other kids was tinged with respect. Jamie was a bully. Abby was the only one who refused to cower, even if it resulted in punishment.

Lying in the sand, in the middle of the desert, she felt a thousand miles removed from her former life. But she wasn't sorry to leave it behind. Her uncle had begun to make life intolerable for the entire family, as if he, singlehandedly, had to save them all from imagined sins.

Her father hadn't the will to oppose his older brother. Instead he chose to leave, enduring Jacob's harping on the terrible thing they were doing by deserting him, choosing instead to live among the godless.

Abby closed her ears to the memory of his booming voice which often followed her into her dreams. When Jacob learned of the massacre she was afraid he would come to verify their deaths. What if he learned she was still alive? She shivered in instinctive fear. These so-called godless heathens seemed gentle in comparison. She refused to believe they were wicked simply because they didn't know the white man's God. She couldn't imagine Moyla being sentenced to hell's fire because she had never been taught.

Moyla was now her sister. From her, Abby would learn the ways of the Indian women. She was learning to grind seeds, mix the meal with water then cook the resulting biscuit in the ashes of the fire.

Thoughts of her parents still brought an overwhelming sadness. Difficult for her to believe they were gone forever. At times, when she was alone, she found herself talking to her mother, seeking advice. In talking, would come the answer she was seeking. Whether it came, somehow, from her mother, or out of her own mind, she didn't know.

3

Abby peeked through the sweet scented sage at the hot pool on the hill below. Moyla crowded closer beside her, hardly able to control her giggles.

"Be quiet," Abby scolded. "They'll hear us." She had long since mastered the language of the Kumeyaay. Lying on her stomach she wiggled deeper into the brush, making no sound.

Below them, on the side of the hill, where hot water bubbled out of the ground into a large bathing pool, the young men of the camp were laughing and joking as they lay naked in the soothing waters.

Normally Abby wouldn't have been driven to peek at them, there was no need. She knew how men were built. Young male children ran without clothes until they were half grown. It was only one man who interested her. The Yuma warrior who came with Pion's daughter and her Yuma husband. He was called Night Wolf, and already he had a reputation as a bold and wily hunter, for all his seventeen summers. One day he would make some maiden an excellent husband. Abby sensed Moyla's gaze was directed at another visitor, also one of the Yuma.

"Ah, he is a handsome one," Moyla conceded, watching the rippling muscles of Night Wolf as he dove into a pool of hot water. He rolled onto his back like a sleek otter, shaking his head to soak the thick black hair that hung past his shoulders.

Abby watched in fascination, her heart beating faster in response to his powerful movements. He was from the land of the great river and obviously knew how to swim. His relaxed floating on the bubbling pool stirred her envy as well as new feelings she couldn't name.

None of the other young men made her shiver just to look at them. Ever since this man had first come to their village several summers back, she had found herself staring whenever he was near. Like any proper maiden she would lower her eyes whenever he looked her way, but she sensed he watched her too. She was always aware when his gaze was on her, aware of a prickly heat along her nerve endings.

Even with her eyes closed she could have described the burnished copper of his skin, the strong muscles of his arms and back. His face was finely chiseled, as though out of the granite of the mountains. His nose was long and noble, his chin strong, sometimes stubborn. His flashing eyes were as black as the night, with thick eyebrows and unusually long lashes. He was a beautiful man to look upon, and many of the maidens hoped he would notice them, maidens older than Abby and ready for marriage. For herself, her ceremony of womanhood would not come for at least another year.

"Be careful, Firehair," Moyla teased, "You will end up in his ewa." Moyla's expression fell, her teasing changing to a frown. "No, I would not like that! You would go away to live with his people."

Abby put her arm around her sister, careful not to rustle any of the leaves to betray their presence, giving her a quick hug. "Have no fear, sister, I will not live in that man's ewa. He is pleasant to look upon but he is not for me."

Even as she said it, Abby knew it was true. She suddenly felt childish lying here in the brush, spying on the young men. Silently she wiggled out of the tangle and walked away from the laughter at the pool. Moyla caught up with her.

"Why did you change your mind?" Moyla asked, "You wanted to watch him."

Abby sighed, trying to explain even to herself. "It was silly. I am not a child to sneak about."

Moyla giggled. "No, we are no longer children. Soon we will take husbands."

"And you already have your eye on one," Abby teased her. "And, I think maybe he has eyes for you."

"Just as Night Wolf has eyes for you," Moyla teased her right back.

Abby greeted that thought with mixed feelings. It saddened her to think of leaving her adopted family, yet in her heart, she knew someday she would have to. She was of the white world. Her heart was there even though she had chosen a different path for now.

At the same time, she respected the ways of her chosen family. Over the years she had seen many puberty ceremonies in which girls became women, seen them tattoo their faces to make themselves more desirable, and were soon chosen as wives.

Moyla eagerly designed the tattoos she would wear, but for Abby, Enyaa, the medicine woman, said there would be no such markings. The woman seemed to know that Abby's time with the Kumeyaay was growing short.

"Why do you look so sad, sister?" Moyla asked. "You must want a handsome warrior like Night Wolf for your man. He will provide plenty of meat and give you many strong babies."

A surge of longing went through Abby at the thought of children. She loved to play with the little ones, longed for one of her own. "I would like babies," she admitted. "But if I marry a man from the tribes I would stay here all my life. I have tried to guard my heart so this will not happen....but there is something about this Night Wolf that calls to me."

Moyla giggled again. "You want to share his ewa," she teased. "There is nothing wrong with that. I would share the ewa of Little Otter if he asked me."

"And if you had his baby?"

Moyla smiled wistfully, "I would be very happy. Wouldn't you be happy to have Night Wolf's baby? You can take a baby if you choose to leave us."

Abby shook her head, a sad smile on her lips. "No, sister, the whites would never accept me with an Indian baby. They look down on women who have lived with Indians, thinking them tainted in some way."

"But babies are to be loved. Even white people love them."

"If they are white," Abby said, with unerring wisdom. "I remember stories I heard as our wagons came across the southern states where white women had been taken captive. Those who were eventually freed were often shunned as if they were whores."

"Whores," Moyla scoffed. "You have explained what that means but I see nothing bad. It is up to the woman to decide when she will give her body. To one, or many, that is her choice."

"In many ways your people see things clearly. More so than the white man, who view the relationship between a man and woman as shameful unless it is done to create a child."

Moyla snorted. "That is stupid."

"I know, but it is the way many white men think...not all. And the women mostly think the same way."

"Then why do you want to go back? Why not stay with us? Have you not been happy here? Be Night Wolf's woman."

It was tempting, yet Abby knew it was not what she must do. During the years of her growing she was always aware that one day she would have to leave her sister, her Kumeyaay family. She loved them all. The parting would be so painful she had tried not to think of it. Now it was imperative. Something was telling her to return to her own people just as soon as she was old enough to decide her own path.

The two of them walked into a thick stand of oak trees, moving away from the camp and the hot pools. Abby looked down at her plain much washed gingham dress. How shocked her mother and father would be to see her dressed so. The dress was thin, hanging loosely on her reed-like figure. She was barely starting to develop breasts. About her neck she wore a beaded necklace she had made herself, working out the intricate design with Enyaa's help.

She dressed the same as the other village girls, and over the years, her light skin had been darkened by the sun to the color of golden grass, the fiery red of her hair, which she kept braided, had darkened to a rich auburn hue. Her body had become lithe and quick as she learned how to survive on her own. That knowledge was written in the way she moved. Her father's knife never left her side, hidden on the inside of her thigh. But she had never had reason to draw it in self-defense.

Occasionally she had been threatened by a rattlesnake, but it was rarely necessary to kill it. If she could retreat safely she would do so. If she was forced to kill, she would take it to Enyaa who used the rattles in her potions and loved to eat the meat.

4

September 1857

Abby's mind wasn't on gathering acorns, but on how glad she was to be back in the mountains. In the desert they moved about frequently to harvest what the arid land had to offer..., but she preferred the cool valleys of oak and pinyon, the lush grass of the meadows, and sound of the wind in the trees.

It was early autumn and ripe acorns lay upon the ground. By now, it was automatic for her to check each one for worm holes or rot, selecting only the best for her basket. She and Moyla had become separated by their task, each finding their own area to harvest.

She hadn't been aware of the sounds of the birds and insects until they stopped. It was the utter silence that alerted her. Without thinking she moved into the concealment of the brush. Setting down her basket, she moved deeper into the shadows, hoping Moyla was doing the same.

If she were hunting she would have her bow, but while gathering acorns it would be a nuisance. Her fears grew stronger as she approached where she had last seen her sister. A muffled cry came to her, one that brought her knife instantly into her hand.

Pinpointing the direction of the sound she moved cautiously, the feeling of danger screaming along her nerves. Moyla was in trouble. The sound of low, harsh words came to her.

It was neither English nor any Indian dialect.

She was able to distinguish two male voices and muffled protests that could only be from Moyla. The scent of horses caused her to test the air to be certain she was downwind from them. Otherwise the animals might betray her presence. What could she do against two men? Then she saw them. One had Moyla on the ground, holding her down, a handkerchief tied over her mouth to muffle her cries. Her dress was pushed up to her hips. The second man was standing at her feet, hurriedly removing his vest and shirt.

From Pion's description these had to be Mexicans. The black hair, the dark skin, and the clothes they wore... Their intent was obvious. They had eyes only for Moyla, their glazed looks telling Abby exactly what they intended.

The man shed his gun belt, laying it across the fallen tree. Abby's gaze went instantly to it. Her knife would be useless against two of them, but with a gun, that was something else. Her father had taught her before they had started on their long, cross-country trek.

Slipping her knife back into its sheath Abby's gaze went to the two horses grazing some distance away. She could spook them, but that would alert the men. They would draw their guns and then she could do nothing.

A part of her watched Moyla's struggles with cold detachment, vitally aware of the rapid beat of her own heart as she drew in a deep, steadying breath. Her head was clearer than she ever remembered. For the two jackals preying on her helpless sister she felt no sense of pity or mercy. They deserved none.

The excited laughter of the two men covered any sound she made as she moved directly behind the one who had unfastened his gun belt, leaving it carelessly draped over the tree trunk. She heard his growl of passion as he forced Moyla's legs apart and knelt between them.

Struggling fiercely, Moyla was no match for the far stronger men. Knowing they were too intent to notice her, Abby moved swiftly, slipped the pistol from its holster, cocked it and fired a shot into the air. She cocked it again as the two men froze in their tableau of attempted rape.

The one holding Moyla's arms looked up into the barrel of the gun, eyes widening in fear. The one trying to mount Moyla froze, knowing only someone was behind him with his gun.

Abby slowly raised the gun barrel toward the man holding Moyla down, her cold glare and the cavernous barrel of the pistol caused him to release his captive instantly, his frantic words no doubt begging for his life.

Moyla's swift movement carried her away from the men before they could react. Abby didn't want to alert the man with his back to her that she was a woman. Her shot had succeeded in spooking the two horses, leaving the men on foot.

Moyla was panting in reaction to her close call, her mechanical movements betraying the effect of shock as she gathered her fallen basket, carefully replacing each spilled acorn.

Abby motioned Moyla into the brush and silently the girl obeyed.

The man facing her must have signaled to the other as she saw a change in the kneeling stance of the one with his pants around his ankles. Realizing they were about to make a move, she stepped back and to one side. To come at her, the men would have to climb over the thick limb, something the one wasn't capable of in his present predicament.

At the same time, she became aware of the one facing her, was slowly inching his hand toward his pistol. Abby thrust her pistol out, pointing it directly at his head. He froze, and as her gaze hardened into a murderous glare he eased his hand upward, away from his gun.

Using the barrel of the pistol, Abby motioned for the man to stand up, the quick movements included his friend. The message was relayed and slowly they got to their feet, hands raised to keep her from getting nervous enough to pull the trigger. She motioned for the one to drop his gun belt as the other one turned slowly to look at her. She heard his quick intake of breath.

As the one began to reach cautiously for the buckle of his gun belt, too cautiously, Abby sensed they were getting ready to try something.

Again she pointed the gun upward, only not as high as the first time, and fired, the bullet whizzing between the two. Both men jumped visibly, and even as she cocked the gun again, the man frantically removed his gun belt, letting it drop to his feet. The half-naked man nervously tried to cover himself with his hands.

Abby motioned for them to walk. The man's eyes widened, pointing to his trousers, his words babbling meaninglessly. Again Abby raised the gun threateningly. His hands shot into the air and again he tried to follow his companion with pitifully slow, mincing steps but with an urgency spurred on by fear. She felt cold satisfaction at their terror.

What they couldn't know was that Abby was already afraid the shots could draw more men like those. She'd already taken a big chance, but knew she couldn't have controlled the two men with anything less than abject fear.

When the men were far enough away, she released the hammer on the gun carefully. With a burst of mischief, she grabbed up the discarded clothes and gun belts and ran off into the brush. Just the smell emanating from them, the dirt and sweat was enough to make her soon abandon them. She could probably have kept the guns, but the noise made them too dangerous.

She ran easily now, knowing the brush would hide her. The Mexicans would be too busy retrieving their horses and guns to look for her and Moyla now. Night was coming, an even greater incentive for the two men to leave the area before irate Indians came after them.

Moyla was waiting for Abby by the giant oak. They exchanged only quick, relieved hugs before Abby ran to her abandoned basket. Then, together they ran like fleet deer, keeping under cover. They didn't go directly to the village, but were careful to lead any possible trackers in the wrong direction first.

Later, when Moyla recounted the tale of Abby's daring rescue, and how she forced the one man to walk away with his trousers about his ankles, the people of the village howled with laughter. It was understood that the young woman with hair of fire was different, therefore she was capable of great feats of courage. No one seemed surprised by her actions, but respect for her grew.

At an age where most Indian maidens were married, Abby showed no interest in young men or in being married. And, while the young men regarded her with grudging respect, none of them wanted her for a wife. She lacked the proper qualities of submissiveness and dedication to wifely duties. Though she contributed her share of work in the preparation of food, she also hunted with her bow, which no other woman was allowed to do. Rarely did she return empty handed.

A few days following the incident with the Mexicans, Abby was sought out by Enyaa, whose name Abby now knew meant Sun Woman. In spite of her years, Enyaa still walked straight and tall, possessing the vigor of a woman half her age. Her hair was streaked with gray and worn loosely about her shoulders. Her black eyes still held the ability to quail the strongest man, or gaze off into some inner spiritual world no one else could see. She was the medicine woman, the healer. She knew the ways of the herbs.

Abby was sitting alone in the cleansing hot waters of the bubbling pool close to the village. She was surprised when Enyaa came to the pool, shed her dress and joined her in the soothing water. If any of the women were to come to bathe and saw them together they would have left quietly, knowing this was a matter of great importance.

"I remember the day you came to us," Enyaa said, her eyes closed as she leaned back in the shallow pool, steam rising around her in the cool autumn air. "You were a white child then, knowing only the ways of your people. Yet, you came away with us, leaving your parents buried in the desert. You left your white life behind to become one of the People. It was a choice on your part. We would have taken you to a white village."

Enyaa gave a soft laugh at the memory. "At first we thought you to be a skinny boy with strange, fire colored hair. That first night when we camped and one of the boys knocked your hat off, we found not a boy but a defiant maiden, one ready to take on the whole camp if necessary."

Abby's discomfort grew as she listened to Enyaa's recounting of her first hours with the Kumeyaay. It brought back the fear, the grief, the terrible fatigue and hunger.

"I have watched you since," Enyaa went on. "In my vision I have seen that you will be among us for only a brief time. You have become one of the People, but, in time, you will return to the world of the whites. You will leave us, yet you will always be with us. You will never forget the Indian is your brother."

Enyaa was silent for a moment, to allow her message to be absorbed. Abby knew what the woman said was true. In a corner of her mind hadn't she always known that one day she would leave?

"Even old Pion felt these things," Enyaa said, her voice changing to a near chant, as if even now she was seeing a vision. "He took you as his niece to teach you. There was much you needed to know, more than just a young maidens duties. You are part warrior, a thing proved by your bravery when you first came among us, and again when you saved Moyla from the jackals.

"Your skill with the bow, your keen eyes and hearing, these you have developed while in our village. One day, it will save your life."

Abby tried to imagine such an event but the mists of time blocked her view of the future. She envied Enyaa's talent to see beyond the mist. Few were given that gift.

"I have spoken to Wahss, Hahro and your mother. I wish to take you to sleep at my hearth. I will teach you the ways of the medicine woman."

Abby felt a thrill of excitement. This was a great honor. "I am honored, Sun Woman, deeply honored that you would choose me… but if I leave the village, as you say I will, who will be healer then?"

The old woman gave a long sigh, her eyes opening to regard Abby who leaned forward to catch her words. "That thought has troubled me too, child. It delayed my decision. I'd thought to teach Moyla, your sister, but she has not the ability to learn. Soon she will take a husband. She will be a good wife. That is her path. I have seen a future for you of things I do not understand. I see the ocean with large canoes floating on it. I see a white man's village with wide paths and square dwellings close together."

Abby shivered, awed by the glimpse of the future.

"You will wed more than one man, but you will have children by only the one who will be your great love. I see storms and trials as well as happiness and joy. I have seen you with a child that is not your own." Enyaa subsided, her eyes hooded as if she didn't wish to reveal more. "In that life, the art of healing will be of help to you. You will live in places where few know these things. You will heal, you will save lives, but it is to the People that your greatest gift will bear fruit."

Abby wanted to remember every word, words that whirled around in her head. It sounded too much like a dream. How could she experience all the things Enyaa was telling her? Yet she would learn because she needed to. On occasion she had helped Enyaa with her herb gathering after the old woman showed her how to recognize them. Already she knew the art of selecting the tenderest leaves of the sage and wild mint. In spring she had gathered the elderberry blossoms and later the fruit. She'd gathered the bitter leaves of the chaparral and the fruit of the chokecherry.

"Before we begin, we must purify your body," Enyaa said. "You will come with me to the sacred pool of white water. We will fast and pray."

"Yes, grandmother," Abby agreed, barely able to suppress her excitement.

The following day Abby and Enyaa left the village for the steep, rugged canyons. Even though it would be cold at night, Abby was permitted to take nothing but the deerskin dress she wore. In the net Enyaa slung around her body was little more; no food, no water. Streams were plentiful along the way.

Moyla waved goodbye to her sister with a sadness in her eyes. Both maidens knew Abby would not be the same when she returned. She would be apprentice to the medicine woman, no longer truly a sister, nor one to share family, hearth and all a young maiden's dreams.

5

For two days Abby and Enyaa walked into the mountains, surviving on what they found along the way, on nuts, seeds and roots. Abby deferred to Enyaa's knowledge in selecting each item she ate. She was so excited by the trek she had little appetite anyway.

On the evening of the second day, they were well into the mountains, walking up the rocky floor of a steep canyon. Abby spotted buff colored sheep moving across the face of cliffs which seemed impossibly dangerous, their movements swift and sure. A stream cascaded down the floor of the canyon, tumbling over rocks, sometimes forming small, clear pools. The taste of the water, as well as its warm temperature told Abby that further up the canyon it bubbled hot from the ground.

She wanted to ask Enyaa what she meant by "white water" but Pion had long ago taught her the way of the Kumeyaay. Her questions would be answered in time.

Enyaa was a strong woman for all her fifty six summers. She walked the steep trail without stopping to rest, leaving Abby to follow along as best she could. The canyon narrowed to a barely discernable path between the stream and the sheer rock walls reaching hundreds of feet above them. The faint trail only showed tracks of animals. It was a place unknown to the white man. Sacred to the Kumeyaay.

They walked in the creek when the trail grew too narrow, climbing over great piles of slippery boulders. The sun could only penetrate the shadows when directly overhead.

Abby could no longer enjoy the feeling of isolation and adventure, she was too busy selecting her footing so the stream wouldn't sweep her away. There was little danger of drowning, the water wasn't deep, but bruises would be unavoidable.

Curiosity made her glance ahead now and then but all she could see was the narrowing of the canyon until the stream touched solid rock walls. A cascade of water barred their way, tumbling over a fifty foot rock cliff. It was obvious that a section of the canyon wall had crashed down to block the stream before forming the waterfall.

Surely this would end their trek. Abby paused to wipe the sweat from her forehead, expecting Enyaa to stop too. Instead, the older woman crossed to the far side of the stream and began to search for handholds on the wall of the canyon. Then, partly in the water, partly clinging like one of the big horn sheep, Enyaa began to climb. To slip here would mean more than a few bruises.

Abby looked back the way they had come, seeing no sign of their passing, only the rock strewn stream bed. She doubted anyone would attempt this difficult trek unless they knew what lay ahead, something Enyaa obviously did. She had no more time to wonder. Enyaa was half way up the cliff and Abby had yet to start. Drawing a deep breath she began to follow Enyaa's painstaking path, searching out hand and toe holds. Turning back never entered her mind.

Her deerskin moccasins acted like grips on the slippery rock, but she still had to proceed slowly. One misstep would send her tumbling onto unforgiving rocks. Ignoring the sweat streaming down her face, she selected each toe hold, testing to make certain it would support her weight. Enyaa was no longer in sight. Abby marveled that the older woman had the strength for such a climb. Her own arms and legs were aching with the exertion of pulling herself from one hand hold to the next. It occurred to her they could never return this way. It would be impossible to climb down. But she'd face that problem when and if she came to it. Right now, it was all she could do to keep her footing.

Spray from the cascading water soon had her dress soaked and hanging heavily upon her. Night was coming…another daunting thought. It would be cold this high in the mountains.

Abby's arms grew tired, her legs shaky as she hauled herself up to the next level, again marveling at how quickly the older woman had accomplished the difficult climb. It was that thought that kept her going, which kept her from looking down or thinking about where she was.

Ahead was an outcropping of rock. She couldn't see what lay beyond. As she strained for a hand hold and started to push up with the failing strength of her legs, Abby felt a hand seize the back of her dress and haul her up bodily until she lay sprawled on solid rock, her legs touching only air but her cheek pressed to the coolness of safety. Panting for breath she wanted only to lay there and sleep.

Afraid to open her eyes, afraid of what she would see lay ahead, she heard Enyaa chuckle as if knowing her thoughts. Perhaps she, too, had once felt the same.

Raising her head, Abby gazed first at Enyaa who was sitting nearby, looking amused. It irritated Abby that Enyaa showed no sign of fatigue, and made her all the more determined not to give in to her own. Next she looked up stream to where the canyon took a sharp turn to the left, and grew slightly wider.

The roar of the waterfall beside her kept speech impossible, but at least they wouldn't have to walk in the fast flowing water.

Enyaa began to pick her way among the rocks next to the rushing stream. Abby almost groaned aloud, wanting to stay where she was until her legs felt stronger. Reluctantly she pushed herself up. Surely it couldn't be much farther.

The boulders came in all sizes, lying about as if tossed by some careless hand. Abby was too busy watching her footing to do much looking around. Enyaa seemed to grow stronger as they neared their destination.

A sharp turn in the canyon sent the bubbling water churning in protest, splashing against the rocks in a tempest barely contained. The walls of the canyon widened considerably after that, and the water became tamer. Abby barely spared a glance at the sheer walls rising around them, too tired to care.

Enyaa made her way toward the right hand face of the canyon, toward a jumbled outcropping of rocks. Flowing from those rocks, Abby could see a small stream joining the larger one, only it seemed to come directly out of the cliff. She sensed they had reached their destination as she stopped beside Enyaa.

A startled screech from nearby brought Abby's gaze into the shadows of the opposite wall some forty feet away. From her years in the wilderness she recognized the sound even before she saw the great bird on the ground, flapping its mighty wings in an effort to release its dead prey. It floundered, unable to let go, unable to take off. Abby was drawn to the fierce looking creature, unaware that Enyaa made no move, only watched.

Abby approached cautiously, not wanting to frighten the bird. She sensed it was female, and from her solid reddish hue knew it was the mistress of the skies, the golden eagle. One claw was somehow trapped by her intended prey, an old raccoon, but there was no submission in the eagle. Tipping backward with her wings to brace her, the eagle's one free leg came up like a weapon, talons clicking wickedly.

"Do not fear me, mother eagle, I will not harm you." Abby moved closer with slow steps. If the bird were to sink her needle-like talons into her skin they would go all the way to the bone. Infection was likely to result. Somehow she must free the bird which had become trapped by its own prey.

A quick glance around revealed nothing she could use. Her fingers brushed her deerskin dress and almost before she was aware what she intended she pulled the dress over her head.

Stepping closer to the giant bird, it lay on its back, its beak open, wings flared. Her yellow glare was unblinking as her talons reached out threateningly. Leaning forward with her dress in one hand, Abby reached out with her other hand to distract the bird. As the bird's fierce gaze followed her open hand to meet that threat, Abby dropped the dress over the bird, making certain the deerskin was trapped in the grasping talons.

Abby then pinned the bird to the ground. It struggled a moment, unable to see. Gradually the eagle's movements ceased, but the talons didn't release their death grip on the dress. Kneeling beside the trapped bird, Abby drew her knife from the sheath strapped to her thigh. The dead raccoon was so heavy the eagle had not been able to fly with it.

Careful not to cut the eagle's leg she cut away fur from the dead raccoon's head. Somehow the bird was caught in the skull, one talon piercing an eye, another an ear canal. Gently she pried at the talons but was unable to free them. They were locked. It was a bloody job, slicing away fur and skin. A ridge of skull bone was the cause of the locked talons. Picking up a rock, Abby had no choice except to smash the skull, trying not to think about what she was seeing as she pried away fractured bone with the tip of her knife.

After several minutes of chipping, Abby laid down her knife and tugged on one of the talons. Suddenly it came free, clutching frantically for new prey. Abby barely escaped its grip.

Seeing the leg and talons were undamaged, Abby drew her dress away from the eagle's head. Yellow eyes blinked then stared at her, talons still clutching the dress. For a moment Abby's gaze was held by the furious glare until the great bird realized she was no longer held prisoner by either the dress or the raccoon. When Abby made no move, the bird loosed its hold and stood up, wings flared to make her appear larger.

With a final glare at Abby, the great bird hopped onto a boulder, the fan of air from the great wings stirring her hair. Fixing Abby with another yellow glare, she took a quick look around as if gauging height and distance before making a great leap into the air, giant wings beating powerfully. Abby felt the rush of the wind, almost felt the brush of the wing tips as the eagle gained altitude until she caught an updraft and seemed to soar up and out of the canyon as if by magic.

Breathing a sigh of relief, Abby watched the majestic queen of the sky disappear. A movement drew her attention to Enyaa who was cutting into the still warm carcass of the raccoon, draining blood into a small gourd she carried. From the ground she gathered two primary feathers the eagle had lost in its struggle. Without a word she turned toward the place from which the side stream flowed. After slipping into her dress, Abby followed.

Though she still couldn't see any opening, Abby stooped as Enyaa had under an overhang, squeezed by a boulder, and suddenly found herself inside a cavern. With a gasp of shock she felt surge of unreality at the color of the rocks. At the back of the cavern, on a rocky shelf, water bubbled up in spurts, steam rising. This was no ordinary cave, Abby could feel it in the very air.

Awestruck she moved silently to where Enyaa stood in a small patch of stark white sand. The woman lay down her net and removed her dress and moccasins. When she was as bare as the day she was born, Enyaa held out her hands toward the misty region behind the bubbling water.

Without being told Abby knew she was to do the same, removing her dress and moccasins.

"Father Mountain, it is I," Enyaa spoke. "Woman of the Sun. I have brought a child worthy of your notice. You have seen how she freed your sister, the eagle. It is a sign of her medicine. Accept her as one of your own."

Enyaa began to chant, eyes closed, her hands raised toward the unseen spirit who dwelled within the cave. Abby stood in silence, waiting for a sign that she was to be accepted. Perhaps it was only her mind playing tricks but she could feel the presence Enyaa was calling forth. The hair at the back of her neck began to bristle. Spirits were not always benign. They were powerful beings who needed to be appeased.

She watched as Enyaa dropped the two eagle feathers into the pool, and a mist began to drift over them like fog. Closing her eyes as it enveloped her, Abby felt the sacredness of this place. She attuned her thoughts to it, accepted it, and in doing so, felt she too was accepted. Automatically she raised her hands toward the unseen power.

Her fingertips began to tingle, startling her. It took an effort not to draw back, but to stand, naked, open. She forced herself to relax and let it happen. She wasn't frightened, sensing there was no evil in its touch.

The tingling extended along her arms, reaching her shoulders and spreading down across her breasts and stomach. It seemed to reach into every corner of her body, filling her. Her body vibrated with a joy such as she had never experienced. Then, suddenly, her mind was free of her body. She had leapt upward through the solid rock of the canyon, great wings beating as they lifted her up and up, out of the narrow canyon, into the face of the wind.

Her feathers were golden fire as she soared higher and higher toward the flaming brilliance of the sun. She had no fear. She belonged to the sky. Her giant wings caught the wind currents that bore her ever higher. The sun was living flames above her yet there was no sensation of heat. The giant ball of fire filled the sky. She was aware of nothing else...wings ablaze, flames streaming from her feathers.

Lifting her face toward the great giver of life Abby could feel herself being drawn ever upward until she was one with the sun. Its vast power filled her, vibrated through her. She was powerful beyond measure.

Reluctantly Abby opened her eyes, not wanting to return from the sky. She had lost track of herself, had no idea how much time had passed. She was lying on white rocks, aware now of crystallized minerals under her bare skin. Half of her was submerged in warm water as Enyaa leaned over her, chanting, fingers dipped in blood drawing a design on Abby's chest.

She felt unearthly, strange, her senses heightened. Enyaa finished the design then touched a dot of blood to Abby's forehead. Next she drew lines resembling the talons of an eagle on each cheek.

"You are sister to the eagle," Enyaa spoke reverently. "You have been accepted by the spirits of the eagle, and by Father Sun. You will be called Eagle Woman and your medicine will be powerful."

Abby couldn't explain what had happened to her. It was like a dream, yet it started when she was wide awake. She couldn't shake the feeling she had soared through the sky, wingtips on fire, yet she was not burned; had bathed in the cool flames of the sun.

"It is not unusual for the old ones to take days or even weeks to accept a medicine woman. By freeing their sister, the eagle, you have made your place among them. They will permit the teaching of the Old Ways, the ways of healing. Tomorrow we begin."

Abby was given nothing to eat that evening. She was taken from the hottest of the pools to the cooler ones as Enyaa taught her the songs of purification. Together they chanted through the night. They didn't sleep until the first light of dawn touched the mouth of the cave. Only then was Abby allowed to lay on the sandy floor, using her dress for a pad. She was instantly asleep.

The cave was warm, clothes unnecessary. For two days Abby and Enyaa fasted and prayed. Abby learned the old songs, listened to the sacred legends of the Kumeyaay. Before she could invoke the healing power of the herbs, she must learn the names of the spirits who made the potions work. Herbs alone would not heal.

From the eagle feather Enyaa had retrieved and the raccoon pelt, Abby fashioned her medicine bag. She added a sacred white rock from the cave, first asking permission of the cave spirits. Into the pouch she added red sand scraped from a crevice in the canyon, and a nugget of sky blue turquoise given her by Enyaa. It was a flawless stone, brought from some faraway place by Enyaa's grandfather, and lustrous in the manner of a stone handled so often its surface became highly polished.

On the fourth day they asked permission to leave the cave. Enyaa bowed toward the glowing corner of the pool. "We thank you for your shelter, great one, we go now to complete our quest."

Donning their dresses, the two left the cave, heading deeper into the canyon. Following little more than a game trail, Enyaa led the way up the side of the rock wall. Abby was weak from lack of food. She plucked anything edible as they walked, noticing Enyaa did the same.

They climbed slowly, conserving their strength. It took most of the day to reach the top. Here they foraged for the rest of the day gathering chia and berries. The only thing Enyaa would not permit Abby to eat was the flesh of an animal.

That night they slept in the shelter of a thicket where they cut branches to cover themselves and gathered pine needles for their bed. Abby slept snug and warm, the scent of pine sweetening her bed. Enyaa close beside her.

Early the next morning they continued their trek through the mountains. After days of fasting and walking Abby felt lean and strong. Climbing had strengthened her legs, yet there was another strength she could feel, one that came from inside.

6

A week and a half later Abby and Enyaa returned to the village, welcomed by a chorus of greetings. Abby was aware of the way the People stared at her, even her own sister. She had no way to see herself as they did. Her girlish chubbiness had melted away, leaving a lean erect woman, with a glow of confidence in her eyes. Her red hair was marked by white wings at her temples. Her medicine power obvious.

Abby moved into Enyaa's ewa. The learning of the medicine ways had begun in the wilderness as they gathered the herbs and plants to bring back with them. It would continue in the village with Abby assisting Enyaa whenever she was called upon. She learned the birthing of babies, the healing of fevers, sore throats and wounds.

The stories of Firehair quickly spread beyond the village, and her new name, Eagle Woman. She was spoken of in other villages in the area. It was at the village of the Kupa she learned first-hand how the whites were treating the Indians of the mountains.

If the Kumeyaay had escaped the notice of the whites it was because their village sites were remote and not on what the whites considered the best grazing land for their ever increasing herds of cattle.

Abby and Enyaa visited several local villages, and what Abby saw almost broke her heart. The once proud people were living in poverty. They barely had enough to eat, yet weren't allowed to hunt on the white man's land, even though that land had belonged to the Kupa for centuries.

Any land with hot pools or rivers was jealously guarded by the white man, and when the rains didn't come, there was never enough water for the Kupa. The concept of irrigation, once taught by the Spanish Fathers, had long since been forgotten on land that had once provided for all.

"The white man's treaty promised us cattle, flour, clothing," Tomas, one of the elders told Abby. Though the man had been wary at first, he came to accept Abby as a medicine woman, seeing beyond her light skin to the goodness in her heart. "We were promised many things, even teachers for our children."

"We sign treaty," Jesus spat. "We move to this place where nothing grows and agree to stay. We honor the treaty and now we starve. The deer have gone. We must go far into the mountains to hunt, yet, when the white man sees us he thinks we want to steal his cattle."

Abby was appalled. She couldn't believe her own people would do such a thing. Yet the stories in each village were similar. The Kupa's were fortunate to live close to a generous white man called Juan Largo, Jonathan Trumball Warner. From time to time the Kupa were allowed to kill one of his steers for food. Other villages weren't so fortunate.

A number of villagers trailed after Abby when she went to inspect the crops that had been planted but had not thrived. The corn stalks were wilted and dry. The even rows of her childhood on Uncle Jacob's farm were nonexistent here. There were weeds everywhere among the beans and green chilies, which barely clung to life.

"We have no rain," Tomas complained. "Our crops die."

Almost without thinking she grabbed a hoe abandoned among the weeds and began to form long even troughs for water, pulling weeds as she went. The men laughed derisively and walked away. The women with hungry children watched, and soon they too took up hoes or pulled weeds.

Ignoring the skeptical looks of the men who were searching the sky for signs of rain in a cloudless sky, Abby walked up a grassy rise to a flat meadow where the San Luis Rey River flowed. It was a small river, barely more than a stream compared to the mighty rivers in the East. Yet, during parts of the year this one overflowed with snow melt.

From the rise, she looked down on the crops, her gaze resting on the low area. Why hadn't the men seen this? They were too busy complaining about how they had been cheated by the white man. When she went back to the men and explained what had to be done, they laughed at her. Such a thing could not be done.

Abby glared at Tomas, her green eyes blazing with anger. "Then why don't you just lay down and die? If you won't help yourself that is what you deserve!"

Though her hard glare never wavered Abby knew she was treading on soft ground. Indian men did not like to be challenged by a maiden. Even one who had been given the Indian name of Eagle Woman. She saw the answering fire in the eyes of four men. Tomas looked as if he was about to strike her when his wife pushed her way through the angry men to Abby's side.

"They can starve if they wish," she said, casting a contemptuous glace at the men. "I have babies to feed. Show me what to do, and I, and the women will do it."

This time it was the women to whom Abby explained what must be done. She showed them a place in the upper waters of the San Luis Rey River where they could cut a ditch to divert a portion of the water to a low place.

For the youngsters it was a great game to gather rocks to place around what would become a pond. Once Abby showed them what to do they scampered about for rocks. The men watched with skepticism, pretending to deride their efforts, yet watching every move. Abby showed the women how to fashion shovels of bark then led the digging of the channel herself.

Enyaa was busy with a woman about to give birth, and could only watch Abby's efforts from afar with amusement. Tomas was overdue for a lesson in humility.

It took two days to complete the ditch. In that time, the men merely watched, but derision soon turned to watchfulness. Even the most thick-headed among them could see what was coming.

The sound of a new-born babe had brought cheers from the women. Enyaa signaled from the door of the ewa that both mother and child were well. The new life made it all the more important that the mother have adequate food to nourish her child.

Abby had selected a plank of bark to act as a dam. Everyone in the village gathered as she looked down the deep channel they had dug. Expectantly the women lined the banks, the men still pretending not to be interested, yet watching from the corners of their eyes as Abby lifted the bark from its place at the mouth of the channel. Little by little a portion of the river water surged into the new path. It sped down the hill. A gasp went up from the people as the pond began to fill.

Tomas laughed at their foolishness. It would all seep into the ground, he said, disappear. Abby said nothing. She stood guard at the river making certain they took only a portion of the water, so the white man would not know, and come to stop them.

All day the pond filled until nightfall when Abby stopped the flow by damming their channel, allowing the river to resume its full flow. Now it was obvious to the men what Abby had done. The crops weren't far from the pond. When she took a stick and dragged it along the ground to where the next smaller ditch would go, she told the women what seeds to buy in the white man's store.

It would soon be dark so the remaining work was left to the following day. The scent of cooking food wafted on the evening breeze, and though there was little enough of it, spirits were high. The men became caught up in the enthusiasm of the women. Tomas, seeing that he alone was still deriding Abby's plan, began to take some of the credit, saying he knew all along it would work. Abby said nothing. She had given the people something to hope for. They would no longer be totally dependent on the word of the white man or the whim of the weather.

Abby settled back into the ways of her village. Since her people were mostly healthy there was still time for her to spend with her sister and to hunt. She was now Eagle Woman. Pion called her a warrior woman, teaching her all of his skill before he had passed to the land of Amaayahaa two summers previously. She had learned well. Her sharp ears could detect an approaching horse and rider long before they could get close enough to spot her.

Along with her sister, Moyla, Abby went through the rites of womanhood, and they were now considered ready for marriage. Moyla's chin bore the dark tattoos which her mother and Enyaa pressed under the skin with the sharp point of the yucca. Moyla was proud of her bravery through the painful process, proud of this sign of her womanhood. Together she and Abby had lain in a shallow pit and been buried to the neck in warm sand. The other women sat around them, shielding them from the sight of the men, teaching them a woman's duties in the words of their songs. Songs handed down by wives and mothers to the young women, generation after generation.

Abby's face had not been marked. As a medicine woman she was not considered marriageable except under special circumstances. A fact that fit in with Abby's own plans.

On a warm afternoon in early spring, Abby and Moyla were on their way to the deep pool in the river to bathe when they heard a sound that sent them scurrying into thick brush. Their movements stilled as they became part of the forest; silent, unmoving.

The sound came from the river, a sound of creaking saddles, which could only mean white men. Abby watched from her hiding place as three riders came into view. The first two were large, rugged, bearded men, who looked at home in the wilderness. It was the last rider who made Abby's mouth fall open in astonishment. She would know that flaming red beard anywhere. Jacob, her uncle.

Was he looking for her? The thought was frightening. What if he rode into the village asking for her? What if someone told him she was alive, that she was here? Even after all these years an instinctive fear welled up inside her. She could see the uncompromising set of his jaw as he followed the others, a glitter in his dark eyes. The years hadn't mellowed Uncle Jacob. If anything they had made him harder. And they were headed toward her village.

Abby was unable to move until the men were well out of sight. She wasn't even aware she was shaking violently, instinctively afraid.

"Sister, they are only white men. They did not see us," Moyla insisted. "There is nothing to fear."

"I know one of them," Abby managed to say, trying to still her quaking.

Moyla looked mystified, then suddenly her eyes cleared. "The one with the beard of fire."

"He is my uncle, the one I told you about."

Moyla's eyes grew large. "He has come to take you away!"

Abby felt a surge of love for her little sister. Though they were the same age Moyla was shorter and heavier, her mind not as lightning fast as Abby's. "He can't take me away if he can't find me," Abby said with determination. "Come, we have plans to make."

Moyla was always ready to do as Abby wanted, always ready to play, or walk, or swim. The two were closer than sisters, close in a way only those who survive in the wilderness could understand. Close in a way in which the survival of many depended on the skills of each.

Moyla slipped into the village alone. She didn't want the strangers to see her. The white men's horses were tied outside

Wahss's ewa. Gliding closer she could see the three white men sitting on the ground with Wahss, Hahro and two others. She knew enough of the white man's language from Abby to understand most of what was being said. Obviously they wanted something, their gifts lay on the ground in front of Wahss as he was the elder of the People.

Moyla heard one of the men, not the one with the fiery beard, say they were looking for a white woman. Her heart jumped into her mouth, fearful that Wahss would betray her sister. He had never had any love for the white woman, and this could be his chance to be rid of her once and for all. When Hahro quickly denied knowing of any white woman, Wahss was given no choice but to go along. Wisely the People pretended to understand little of the white man's language.

Moyla was proud of her father. He knew Abby's feelings about her uncle. The one quick look Moyla allowed herself of the man made her understand. There was a fire burning in his eyes, an obvious distaste for the People in the set of his mouth as he let the other men do the talking.

As was their way, the women prepared tea for the visitors. The elders went through the ritual of offering it to the visitors along with food. From the shadows Moyla watched the man with the fiery beard lift the tea to his mouth but there was no sign of swallowing. She watched him set the bowl behind him and carefully dump out its contents before he raised it to his mouth again.

Moyla was outraged. Everyone drank the tea of the elderberry, even the Spanish. This man was ignorant and rude.

The narrowing of her father's eyes told her he hadn't missed the act either and was offended. She noticed while the other white men did the talking, the red-bearded one's eyes darted everywhere. He looked over each ewa, each person.

Knowing her sister would be worried and afraid to come near the village until she knew for certain they were gone, Moyla kept watch. The white men seemed anxious to leave and barely swallowed the dried meat and flat cakes before they were on their feet and moving toward their horses. Moyla heard the promise of horses and cows if anyone heard of the red haired woman. They could send word to the Bristol Ranch in Temecula.

Only when they were gone did Moyla come from her hiding place. Her father looked relieved to see her alone. "Where is your sister?" he asked.

"Hiding until the men go. She was afraid you would tell them she is here."

"We told them nothing until we could talk to Eagle Woman to learn of her desires in this matter. Now that I have seen this uncle, I do not like him

"Shall I bring her into camp?"

Her father shook his head. "I do not trust these men. Take her food and stay away until after dark. The one with the fire beard will not give up easy."

7

It was long after dark when Abby crept into Enyaa's ewa. Moyla had come into the village ahead of her to make certain the way was clear. Even when she lay snug on her bed of salt grass and pine needles, covered by a blanket of woven fibers and rabbit fur, Abby was unable to sleep. Maturity had brought her a better insight into her uncle's character. She doubted he would give up.

Enyaa told her one of the young men had been sent to follow the white men, to make certain they left the area. No doubt he would not return for several days. Laying on her back, Abby tried not to disturb Enyaa with her wakefulness, listening to the older woman's soft snores. She had no one to talk to, no one to tell what was in her heart. She was afraid of being taken away by her uncle, afraid of falling in love with Night Wolf and being held here forever, a prisoner of her love.

Inside her was a nebulous feeling. She didn't know what she would do when she left this place, but a restlessness was telling her the time was near. As she stared into the darkness a feeling of sadness overwhelmed her. She could never be like Moyla, content to live among the People. There was a shadow in her heart that would soon send her out into the world to seek her destiny.

During the years with the People, Abby had kept her language alive by teaching it to others. It was a knowledge designed to help them in the years ahead. She knew first-hand the numbers of immigrants who were coming to this land; knew of the seekers of gold, though the rush was mostly over. Now the lure was free land.

On that long ago wagon trek with her parents, Abby had listened to the talk of the grown-ups. She learned what had happened to the Indian tribes in the east, as well as those on the vast plains; heard the voices of intolerance. From those still remembered stories she knew the fate that awaited these gentle people. Some whites understood that not all Indians were warlike, but most lumped all Indians together, feeling only their extermination could make room for the white man. In places where red man and white man clashed, it was inevitably the Indians who lost. Retaliation by the whites was swift and deadly.

Abby wondered if there was something she could do from the white man's world. Once she was established in one of the nearby towns, safe from the reach of her uncle, she would work to help the Indians. That thought finally let her mind relax and allowed her to drift into a fitful slumber. Her dreams were filled with the sadness of saying goodbye to all she loved.

In her dreams she was again the great golden eagle, gliding on the air currents. Below her was a place she didn't recognize, a white man's adobe dwelling surrounded by mesquite, desert willow, and a heavy growth of brush that indicated much water. She sensed rather than saw her mate above her and became caught in an up-draft that carried her swiftly upwards. Her mate folded his wings in a dive toward her, plummeting with heart-stopping speed. Abby knew just when he was close and rolled over onto her back. Her golden mate flared his wings to end his dive, his talons locking with hers as she extended them upwards. For a moment they twirled to-gether in space in the ritual mating dance of the eagle.

Then she slipped out of his grasp and righted herself on mighty wings. Her mate stayed close, dancing with her on the wind.

Late the following afternoon as Abby was finishing her chores for the day, Hahro sought her out. She walked with him into the trees.

"Little Deer returned a short time ago. The three white men are visiting each village in the area asking for you. They offer horses, cows and trade goods. So far, none of the villages have told them anything, but it will only take one greedy man to bring them back here. What does the white man's law say of such things?"

In many ways the white world seemed so remote to Abby that she had to think back with only the perception of a child. "I think the law would say that because I am under the age of eighteen, my only relative, my uncle, would have complete say over me. He would take me to live with him."

Her father gave a slow nod, his dark eyes thoughtful. "I do not trust him. He is like the snake that slithers along, hiding under rocks, sneaking about to find his prey."

Abby thought how much she loved this man who had at first frightened her so badly. It was laughable now. She knew he would never hurt anyone, and his assessment of her uncle was no doubt correct.

"Little Deer also learned the man has been here before in past years asking questions about a red-haired white girl," Hahro said.

A sudden tightening in her stomach shattered Abby's feeling of safety. Over the years her people had come in contact with others, her presence was known. She could never again take for granted she was safe here, not when Uncle Jacob was offering a reward. It was only a matter of time before some greedy or desperate man betrayed her. The sadness in her father's eyes told her he realized it too.

Weeks passed with the village constantly watchful for strangers. Word was passed to other villages whose people knew of Abby's presence among the Kumeyaay, letting them know she wanted to stay with her adopted people, that she had no wish to be found.

The Indians of the area were already distrustful of any white man, but especially this one with the beard of fire. They had never seen such hair and regarded it as a warning. None could miss the zeal that burned in the eyes of Jacob Bristol.

Abby passed her sixteenth birthday. Night Wolf was expected to arrive soon with Pion's daughter and her family. Her reaction to the news was one of excited anticipation. Inside her was a growing awareness of strange new feelings when she touched certain parts of her body, feelings that were kindled just by thoughts of the handsome Yuma brave.

Night Wolf was now nineteen summers, old enough to take a wife. Abby was afraid he would ask for her this time, and afraid she wouldn't be able to say no. Hahro knew of her feelings, yet he and Enyaa both had the power to make a decision for her. If Hahro accepted Night Wolf's bride price, she would be honor bound to marry him.

Jacob Bristol was seen in the area a second time, searching more diligently. He had obviously received word of Abby or he wouldn't be back. The People were constantly on the lookout.

For that reason, the stranger who rode into the village of the People had been spotted long before he reached it. Abby was sent into hiding in the brush.

Hahro was wary of the large stranger who greeted him in his own language as he stepped down from his horse, then tied it and the pack animal he was leading to a tree. He brought a present of a knife made of steel, presented it to the Elder, Wahss, as a token of friendship. Hahro could see it was a fine blade. The stranger knew a bit of the language but seemed pleased to find they spoke adequate English.

The white man was invited to sit with the older men. His black beard hung like a bush against his chest, his hair long and untidy. His trousers were of a hardy twill, black boots scuffed from hard work. It was his eyes which were so striking, gray like a stormy sky, and intent. Not in the fanatical way of Jacob Bristol, but in a manner that missed little of what went on around him.

"I am called Cassidy," he told them, accepting a bowl of tea and drinking deeply, without hesitation. "I live at the place called Seven Springs. I have a store there and cattle." Wahss was familiar with the oasis and nodded his understanding.

"I live there alone," Cassidy went on. "There is much work for one man, yet not enough for two." His gaze shifted to several of the women who were watching from a distance. "I need a woman to cook for the wagon people who come through and want to buy a meal. Soon the Butterfield Overland Mail will be stopping several times a week. I need a woman who can work hard, who is not lazy. I will be glad to call such a woman my wife."

"Have you no white woman to take as wife?" Wahss asked.

"Most white women want to live closer to town, or other ranches. Seven Springs is remote. Sometimes there are raids on my stock. I need a woman who is strong, one who is not afraid to live in the wilderness."

His gaze darted over the women who were gathering and whispering, sensing the stranger's interest in them. Cassidy hoped to find one who was half-way attractive, but he'd be satisfied just to have one who wasn't lazy.

"If you do not have such a woman here, perhaps you can send me to another village that might."

"What bride price will you pay?" Wahss asked.

"I will return with two cows, a horse, and two more knives like the one you have now. I also have in my pack blankets and pots for cooking, as well as cloth and beads."

To Wahss that seemed an enormous amount to pay for a woman. For a moment he was silent, trying to think what woman in the village might suit the white man, which one might be content with such an arrangement. "This is something we must discuss," he said finally, fingering the sharp blade of his new knife. "Perhaps there is such a woman here."

Cassidy finished his tea and stood up. "I'll go wash up at the river and see to my horses. I'd be right pleased to spend the night."

"You are welcome to do so," Wahss informed him.

As the big man untied his horses and led them to the river, Abby watched from her hiding place in a nearby oak tree. He wasn't as big a man as her uncle, yet he reminded her somewhat of Jacob. This man was large through the chest and arms, with the look of a man who worked hard, sturdy as the wide-trunked oak. She wondered what he was doing in their village. Possibly he was a spy for her uncle.

While the horses drank Abby watched the man hang his black hat on his saddle horn and strip off his shirt. Underneath he wore a torn gray undershirt. Stooping next to the gently flowing water he scooped his hands full, splashing it over his face and hair. She gazed in fascination as beads of water dripped from his long hair and beard.

He seemed in no hurry, moving leisurely as he spoke softly to his horse and unsaddled him. He rubbed the animal down with a handful of grass, then let him wander off to a patch of lush grass while he removed the pack from the other animal. The patch of grass the horse chose happened to be close to where Abby was hidden, half way up her favorite oak tree.

She ducked behind the thick gnarled trunk, concealing herself among the leaves when the second horse joined the first. The pounding beat of her heart annoyed her. He would never know she was there, but it frightened her to realize the man was settling down as if to stay for the night. To her, any stranger could be a spy for her uncle, and the thought of Jacob riding into the village to fetch her made her wish she could flee into the mountains. Jacob would most certainly expect her to be forever grateful for being rescued from the heathens.

The man left the horses and walked back into the village. Abby didn't dare remain in the tree in case he came back to bed down for the night. Silently as a falling leaf she slipped down the tree, her bare feet making no sound as she made her way around the village, to dense brush where she could better conceal herself.

Once she saw the man stop and look back. The broad brim of his hat concealed his eyes so she couldn't see where he was looking. For a moment she froze, knowing only an Indian could see her in the dense growth. After a moment he turned and entered the village.

Cassidy schooled his face to show nothing as he lounged a short way from the tribal males, waiting for an indication that they had finished their discussion. Wahss motioned for him to join them. More tea and corn meal cakes were brought by the two women. He took a quick glance at each one, thinking them too old to be offered as wife. He wondered about the concealed figure he had glimpsed briefly in the brush. She was well hidden but he would swear the girl had red hair.

"It has been decided," Wahss told him. "That you may remain in the village for the night. You may sleep in the ewa with the young men, or sleep by the river, as you choose. In the morning we will have an answer about a woman."

Cassidy wished he could ask about the young woman he had seen, but knew he would get no answer. He was well acquainted with the ways of the local Indians. He'd worked with them at Warner's Ranch when he was younger, had visited some of the Rancherias as the Spanish called their villages. If he sometimes lost stock to Indians he knew it was not by these people, who had few horses and seemed not to care to own them. They had always been on foot and that was the way they preferred to travel.

When Cassidy returned to his horses to settle them down for the night, he let his gaze scan surreptitiously for the hidden figure, but he sensed she was gone. Perhaps he would see her in the village later. He would eat with the Indians then bed down here on the soft grass by the river.

8

Moyla found Abby at the hot pools. She, too stripped off her dress and joined her sister in the water. Abby chose to sit near where the water bubbled out of the rocks where it was the hottest, but Moyla preferred the cooler water at the opposite side. It took the young girl a few minutes to adjust to the heat before she could submerge herself.

"Our father wishes to speak to you," Moyla said after several minutes of enjoying the soothing heat.

"Is the white man gone?" Abby asked, remembering the size of him. He was a giant compared to the Indian men.

"No, he is allowed to stay at the village tonight. Father wishes you to come to the big acorn tree so the white man won't see you."

Abby knew well the tree Moyla meant. It was the grandfather of all the oaks, with great towering branches which yielded a tremendous harvest of acorns each year. Unbidden came the thought of how Indians viewed time. If Uncle Jacob had sent that summons, he would expect instant compliance. Hahro would not expect such haste.

Floating in the steaming water, Abby let her thoughts drift to the young Yuma warrior who would soon be visiting. Her naked body surged to life with feelings she didn't welcome.

Looking down, Abby saw her entire body was almost as dark as her face from the time she spent in the mountain sun, though not nearly as dark as Moyla. Her nipples were pink tipped and at the junction of her thighs was a patch of fiery hair, brighter than the hair on her head.

Not liking the direction her thoughts were taking, Abby rose from the water, deciding to answer Hahro's summons. She wrung the water from her long, burnished hair, leaving it loose about her shoulders to dry. Already it reached past her breasts because she didn't singe her hair at the shoulder the way Moyla and the other girls did.

She slipped into the dress that Opachuk, her mother, made for her when she became a woman. It was a white woman's material, but sewed so it fell straight to her knees, decorated with many-colored beads in front. Her sandals she had made herself of yucca fiber. Humming to herself Abby moved through the warm mountain air, thinking how fortunate she was to live in such a wonderful place, wishing her life would never change.

Yet, she knew it would, knew her destiny lay elsewhere, and one day soon it would take her away from all she loved. Trying to force such thoughts from her mind, Abby wondered about Hahro's summons, if it had something to do with the white man's presence.

"You wished to see me, father," Abby said, finding Hahro seated under the great tree whittling a piece of oak, fashioning it into the figure of a coyote.

"Yes, my daughter. Sit."

Abby folded herself onto the bed of leaves in the shade across from him. Though she was curious about why he had chosen this spot to meet, she didn't ask, showing her respect for him with her silence.

"A stranger has come into our village, a white man."

"I saw him," she said.

Hahro gave no sign that he heard her. "He lives at a place called Seven Springs, which we pass by in the desert. We often camp nearby and find water there. He needs a woman to help him. He has come to seek a wife."

Abby felt her heart leap in alarm, her emerald eyes betraying her fear. Hahro gave a gentle smile. "There is too much love in my heart for my child with the fire hair to speak for her in such a matter. It is something you must consider carefully. Soon Night Wolf returns. It has come to me that he will ask for you as his wife."

For some minutes Hahro continued to whittle unconcernedly, while Abby tried not to show her impatience by fidgeting. She was well used to Hahro's slow way of spinning out a story or imparting important news, as if he enjoyed the drama his delay caused.

"It has long been my feeling," he went on, "that you do not wish to be his woman, nor that of any of our young men. But knowing a maiden's heart, you might find it difficult to say no when he asks for you." He gave a soft chuckle. "Even if you did refuse, I doubt he would take that for an answer. He would woo you more strongly than before."

Abby knew he was right. Night Wolf would not easily be distracted from a path he had chosen. It made her view the stranger in a new light.

"I know, daughter that it has been in your heart to return to your own people. That is where you truly belong. We have given you all that we are. No daughter of my own blood could have pleased my heart more. Though you will always have a family here among the People, once you leave us we will not be able to protect you. I have heard that white men look down upon any woman who has lived in an Indian village. If you go from here into a town there would be questions about your past," he was silent for a moment letting her absorb that.

"If you go with a man like Cassidy, you will meet people who pass through your outpost, but will have little time for questions. You don't have to consider it a permanent home, this Seven Springs. In time, you could leave…or you may be able to work your plan through this man."

Abby was silent, absorbing his wisdom. "Leaving is not so easy in the white world, father. Marriage is for life."

"That is a foolish custom. People should be free to choose, and to change their mind if happiness does not come."

Tears surged at the back of Abby's throat. She lowered her head, blinking furiously to hold them back. The thought of leaving her family was more than she could bear. Even trying to look at the situation dispassionately her heart refused to be schooled. Leaving these people would hurt as much as losing her parents six years ago. At least with Hahro, Opachuk and Moyla, she could return to visit.

Hahro's words were true. She would not find welcome in the white man's world. Until she was older and had gained respectability, she needed the protection of a man. If she accepted Night Wolf, her destiny would be sealed. If she accepted the one called Cassidy she would be taking the first step on her way back to her own people.

"What if he does not want me?" Abby asked.

Hahro threw back his head and laughed, a sound what warmed and embarrassed her all at the same time. "You need only look into the water, daughter, to see the beauty that is in you. Do you not notice how the young men look at you overly long?"

Abby had seen the looks, the hunger in their eyes. If she had returned their looks she might have had many offers to lie with them. This was accepted among the People. But her own inner hunger had been slumbering until it was awakened by Night Wolf. It would grow stronger when he arrived and she could again look on his handsome face and his strong, muscular body. She was afraid to trust herself with him when her heart wanted to accept him.

A cold shiver went through her. Hahro was right. Her only recourse was to be gone when he arrived.

"There will be a feast tonight in honor of our guest," Hahro said, seeming to sense the direction of her thoughts. "You will look upon this man. We have said he would have his answer in the morning if one of our women wishes to go with him. None of the others will go. If you accept him, you will leave when the bride price is paid."

Abby hadn't even considered the bride price. Whatever price was offered would be of help to Hahro and his family.

"I will look on this man and I will tell you tonight of my decision."

It was after dark when Abby returned to the village. From the concealing darkness she watched the stranger, watched how he reacted to her people. He didn't show the barely contained distain of most other whites. He accepted any food given to him and ate without hesitation, complementing the woman who gave it to him. Saw the women blush at his praise.

Cassidy wasn't a bad looking man, even with his great shaggy beard. Most of the white men she chanced to see in recent years also wore beards, as had most men on her wagon train. In this harsh land, shaving wasn't the easiest thing to accomplish. A beard was also protection against the sun.

The meal gave way to dancing. Abby noticed her people seemed glad for an excuse to celebrate, to show off their skills before the stranger.

It was a cool evening. Many of the women wore their best deerskin dresses. In a moment of daring, Abby slipped into her ewa and changed into hers. She fastened a beaded band with eagle feathers around each braid, and hoped she looked pleasing to the eye. She wished Enyaa were here to advise her, rather than off visiting a nearby village. She felt shy of the stranger, not certain how she felt about the possibility of going away with him.

Once more she thought herself well hidden in the shadows until Cassidy lifted his head and gazed in her direction. His eyes were like those of the eagle whose realm they all shared. She could feel his searching look. He had seen her today, she knew that as surely as she knew he sensed her presence now.

A dance started where the woman chose her partner. Taking a deep breath, Abby stepped from the shadows and walked toward the fire; toward Cassidy. She saw his eyes widen in surprise, his lips moved to form words that looked like "God Almighty!"

Even before she reached him he was on his feet. He accepted her offered hand and let her lead him into the dance. In the Indian way, they danced side by side, circling the fire, hands crossed in front of them. There was only the sound of drums, flutes, and the chanting of the older men…the crackle of the blazing fire.

Inside Abby could feel her oneness with the dance. It had never felt this way before. Always it had been a mechanical performance. Now she felt the fire burning all through her, felt the touch of the stars and the full moon lighting the valley of the oaks. Beside her, the tall man moved with the same ease, unembarrassed to be included in the dance. It wasn't a time to speak, they only moved to the ancient rhythm of the drums and their own heartbeats.

Abby was unaware of the knowing smiles following them. It was obvious to all that the white man had found his woman. Moyla's smile was filled with a poignant sadness.

When the dance ended, Cassidy tried to guide Abby to his place by the fire. Suddenly, overwhelmed by the enormity of what she was doing Abby jerked her hand from his and fled into the darkness. She ran silently, like a deer, not stopping until the sound of drums faded into a dull, heartbeat like throb.

9

bby was not denying Cassidy, only the decision she was being forced to make. There was no going back. It was unlike her not to face the decision squarely, yet this was a dramatic turning point in her life. It meant leaving the only home and family she had known for the past six years, going into the unknown with a man she didn't know. In front of the others she had chosen him. It should be cause for celebration, yet her decision was not made out of love, but out of necessity.

She could not bring herself to return to the village. In the cool of the silver moonlight she moved silently as a shadow through the trees, asking the gods of the valley if she was doing the right thing. She listened for an answer.

A rustle in the grass alerted Abby to the presence of her sister. Moyla ran to her, clinging to her, tears streaming down her cheeks.

"You have chosen the white man!" She choked on the words. "You will leave us!"

Abby hugged her back, needing the comfort she offered. "It is time," she said choking back her own tears. "I must go before Night Wolf returns."

"He will be angry! It has long been known he would ask for you."

"I know," Abby said softly. "But that can't be. This man offers me a way to return to my own people."

"But I will miss you, sister," Moyla choked back her tears. "We have been best of friends. My family will miss you."

"I will miss you too. Your mother and father took me in until Enyaa took me to her hearth. No family could have been dearer to me," Abby said, folding her legs to sit in the grass under the large oak tree. "And, sister, when Little Otter comes with Night Wolf, you will be his woman, and go to live with his people. We would be separated anyway."

"No!" Moyla nearly collapsed to sit beside her. "You were to go with Night Wolf and we would still be together with their people."

Abby let out a long sigh for what could have been.

"And you don't know this stranger! This white man!" Moyla argued, tears streaking her cheeks.

Abby nodded in agreement. "I have watched him. He respects our ways. He is not like my uncle and the two who came with him."

"But you don't know…"

"No, I don't," she agreed. "But this is the path I must take."

Moyla nodded in reluctant acceptance. "But promise me one thing, sister," Moyla said, clutching Abby's hand. "If this white man is not good to you, come to me with the Yuma."

"Yes," Abby agreed, knowing that was always an option. "I will come to you if I do not like him or this place he takes me."

Cassidy rode out the next morning with a feeling half of disappointment, half of elation. He hadn't seen the red-haired woman-child again. He was still stunned by his luck in finding a white woman in this wilderness. Someday she was going to be a real beauty, and unbelievably she had accepted him as her husband. Why was she here? Surely these people weren't keeping her as a slave or a prisoner. The Kumeyaay didn't believe in that. Certainly she had been free to come and go as she wanted.

He could only wonder what made her run from him. At first he was certain she had rejected him, yet this morning came word of her acceptance. He longed to see her again before he rode out to collect the bride price at the Carrillo Ranch. In two days' time, he would return to claim his bride. He doubted she was much more than a child. As a rule, Indian girls married very young, soon after their ceremony of womanhood at fifteen. He guessed his bride to be no more than sixteen.

Questions welled up inside him. Did she speak English? Was she the one who taught the village to speak that language? How long had she been here? Had she been with any of the young men? He knew the Indians had different customs when it came to sex. The young girls were not permitted to marry a man of their own village, but they could lay with them if they were careful not to let a child result. Virginity was not prized as it was by the white man.

Cassidy also knew it wasn't going to be easy living with a woman who had lived with Indians. For himself, it didn't matter. He would just as readily have accepted an Indian wife. But it would matter to those who came regularly to his store. Those who passed through wouldn't know of her past, which would make it easier. He hoped this young woman had a lot of courage. She was going to need it.

Didn't the fact she had come to him from the shadows and chosen him for the dance show she wasn't shy? Her gaze had held his, flashing green fire in the darkness as she led him into the circle. He could still feel the pulse of the drums and her lithe body moving next to his. He wanted her with a fierceness that made him growl with impatience. He was determined to get this trip over with and return for her before she changed her mind.

By the end of the third day Cassidy was back at the village. One of the young men met him on foot, helping him drive the three cows he had promised. The horse he led behind him. In the bulging pack on the animals back were cloth, knives, iron skillets and a large iron pot, things the entire camp could use. These people were like one large family. It wouldn't do to single out the girl's father for all the gifts. The milk cow would benefit them all.

Cassidy was welcomed by the entire village. They swarmed around him, eager to see what he brought. He looked for the girl but didn't see her. Yet, he sensed she was close by, watching.

When night came, several of the older women came to Enyaa's ewa to prepare Abby for the marriage ritual. Opachuk, too, brought colorful beads to entwine in her hair as it hung loosely about Abby's shoulders.

Chanting the ancient songs, they rubbed Abby's body with scented oils before her deerskin dress was draped over her body, and Enyaa added beads and eagle feathers. As if sensing her thoughts, Enyaa handed Abby her father's knife, which she strapped to her thigh, even as the other women gasped in surprise. They would not question the medicine woman.

Abby gripped Enyaa's hands, her eyes questioning this step she was taking.

"I know child," Enyaa said, trying to reassure her. "This is a big step for you. Yet we have always known this day would come."

"He frightens me," she whispered, still clutching Enyaa's hand.

"He is known to our people and no one speaks ill of him," Enyaa said. "You can only trust your own feelings."

"I will miss you, grandmother."

"And I you, Eagle Woman," Enyaa said with a reassuring smile. "Remember all you have learned. I will send with you the herbs you will need in your new life."

Unable to delay any longer, Abby faced the opening and was glad for the company of the women as she stepped outside.

The feast had begun, a celebration of joy and sadness. It was during the dance, just when Cassidy had given up hope of the woman joining him, he saw several older women come out of one of the round dwellings. Behind them, in the same deerskin dress he'd last seen her in, came the red-haired woman. She was even more ornately dressed then the night of the dance, in eagle feathers and beads.

The women led her to him, her eyes lowered. She appeared shy, frightened, and very young. Cassidy swallowed hard, his pulse beating faster at the sight of her. Her hair was gloriously loose about her shoulders, but he longed to dress her in gingham and see her as a white woman. He cautioned himself to give her time to adjust to being white again. He didn't know how long she'd been with the Indians, sensing it was for a long time. She seemed very much a part of the village.

As the girl was seated at his side, her eyes remained downcast, giving him time to notice other things about her. Her back was straight and strong. Her hands showed she was a worker. The unusual white wings streaking her otherwise reddish hair intrigued him, making her seem almost unearthly. She was going to suit him just fine.

He was barely aware of the different cadence of the drums in the start of the marriage dance. As far as Indian custom was concerned, he would be considered married when he took her to his bed that night. Her Indian father called her Firehair, another had called her Eagle Woman, and as much as he wanted to ask her what her white name was, he sensed this was not a time for talking.

Abby kept her eyes downcast as was customary for the women of the People. It was a sign of her obedience to her new husband. She wasn't certain how obedient she could be in actual fact. It depended on the man. She hoped he wouldn't be cruel like her uncle, that he would be kind like her real father, and like these gentle people she had lived with all these years.

No longer was she small and helpless. Even now she could feel the pressure of her father's knife pressing against her thigh, yet even with its comforting presence she was still frightened. This man could look down upon her because she had lived with Indians. He could treat her like a slave.

Abby hoped the dancing would go on all night. Cassidy wanted it to end so he could take her to his camp by the river. He'd been offered the use of one of the ewas but he preferred the open, the feel of the wind on his face, the sound of the river flowing by.

When he'd eaten all he could, he stood up, intending to take his new wife into the darkness. The look of fear and dread that flashed in her eyes made him change his mind. Instead he led her into the circle of dancers, seeing the relief that erased the fear from her eyes. Even as he moved about the fire he could feel the tension in her. She reminded him of a wild colt, one that needed gentling. Some men believed in breaking a horse by riding it until it was forced to accept man as its master. Some tried to treat a woman the same way.

For all his rough ways, Cassidy was well aware a woman wasn't a dumb animal. From his observations of the people passing through Seven Springs on the immigrant trail, he suspected those who fared the best were couples who were more or less on even footing. There was a sense of partnership when he was around them, not the usual dominant male syndrome evident with so many. A woman was capable of love and gentleness as well as fiery blasts of temper and nagging. Cassidy had fears of his own, yet he knew there was more to be gained from cooperation than coercion.

For a time they danced, shuffling their feet to the rhythm of the drums. As others moved along with them, Cassidy sensed their approval. Only one young woman did not look happy, and that was Hahro's Indian daughter. She sat with her mother, watching them with a sad expression.

Finally there came a time when Cassidy sensed he would meet no resistance even though he could feel the fast beat of her heart. He wondered if he could find the words to soothe her fears. For once he felt inadequate to deal with a situation.

When they reached the far side of the fire, Cassidy broke from the circle and led her into the night. He was aware of the swift intake of her breath. From behind them came good natured teasing. The young woman's hand was withdrawn sharply from his. He'd been a long time without a woman. This one was so lovely he wanted more than anything to take her straight to his blanket. But he was aware her cooperation was important to him in the years ahead, when she would be beside him every night.

"Let's go for a walk," he said, trying to still the fast beat of his own heart. He was glad the weather hadn't turned cold yet. It would soon enough. Right now, the cool breeze felt good against his face.

Abby tried to still the frantic beat of her heart. He only wanted to walk, why was she so frightened of him? She knew why. In the eyes of the People she was now his wife.

"My name is Jim," he said in a mild tone. "But most folks call me Cass, short for Cassidy. What's yours?"

"…Abby," she said after a moment, not having spoken that name in a long time.

"Abby. Abigail? Abigail what?"

"Bristol," she answered, then wondered if she should have told him. Her uncle was still out there looking for her. Suddenly she almost laughed. Jacob couldn't take her away now. She was a married woman…No, on second thought, he wouldn't recognize her as being married unless the marriage was performed by a minister.

Cassidy misread the fear on her face. "Don't be afraid, Abby. I'm not a hard man. I have a nice place at Seven Springs where I raise some cows and sheep. There's a small store for the wagons that come through, and for the few settlers who live in the area. I've got an adobe house that's warm in the winter and cool in the summer. There's rabbits and quail to keep fresh meat on the table, though I don't always have time these days to go out and hunt."

Abby let herself be mesmerized by the deep timber of his voice. He was taking the time to talk to her, to tell her about himself. It seemed a good sign.

"There's always people passing through so it's not lonely like some places. I fix the meals mostly, but I ain't the best cook in the world. I'm hoping that's one of the ways you can help."

She could feel his expectant look, even in the darkness, as they waked along the river. "I know how to cook the Indian way," she said.

"I can teach you what I know," he said wanting very much to touch her, but knowing it would put the look of fear back in her eyes. "And the ladies passing through will no doubt give you some pointers too."

"But…" She wasn't able to put her fears into words. How would those good people treat her knowing where she'd been these past years?

"There's no reason they have to know," he said, reading her doubts. "We just tell them you're a new bride and never learned much from your mother. Make up any story you want to."

"Yes,….I guess I could."

"A few people will know, such as my friends near Warner Ranch. You'll like them. Vicenta and Ramon Carrillo are from one of the old Spanish families, very hospitable. We'll be going there tomorrow. A priest should be there by the time we arrive."

Abby stopped abruptly, her eyes full of questions. Cassidy turned to face her, giving a shrug that made his massive shoulders rise and fall heavily.

"I know the Indians consider us married now, but the white folks won't. It would be better for both of us if we make it legal and make certain everyone knows. That way, in spite of you living with Indians, they won't dare say anything. But if someone does, you let me know. Understand?"

Abby's eyes widened in surprise. "I…thought…"

"That I'd treat you like a squaw?" he asked with a soft chuckle. "There's a lot of men who would. I'm not one who happens to think Indians are dirty and poor, they just have a different way is all."

Abby felt marginally better, and began to walk again, aware as he fell in beside her that she was still afraid of this big man physically. His shoulders were so wide, his arms and legs strained the clothes he wore and it was obviously all muscle. This was a man who was not afraid to work.

For a time they walked without talking. When they reached the fallen oak, Cassidy leaned against it, facing the bend in the river with a view of a brilliant silver moon framed above the distant mountains.

Abby stopped a distance away, afraid to be too close to him. The thought he was going to marry her the white man's way made her feel better. She would be respected as his wife. Jacob couldn't touch her. Why, after all this time, did she still fear her uncle? The fact that he was looking for her, that alone was frightening. She had been close enough to see the look on his face, knew what her fate would be if he found her, the punishment she'd receive to cleanse her from the contamination of living among heathens.

"What you scairt of?" he asked seeing her strange expression.

She looked away from his steady gaze. "Just…someone I knew once," she hedged.

"A white man?" he asked, curious about her past.

She nodded but didn't answer.

"How long you been with these people?"

"Since I was ten."

"Ten. No wonder you remember your language so well. You taught it to the Kumeyaay, too, didn't you?"

She nodded. "I knew they were going to need it. It's harder for the white man to cheat them if they understand what's being said."

"How'd it happen?"

She knew what he meant but it was difficult to form the words, to remember the day she had tried to block from her memory. "Our wagon train was attacked."

"Your parents kilt?" The sympathy in his voice helped her to nod and get through it. "And these people took you captive?" he asked in surprise.

She shook her head. "No, they found me afterwards. The attackers rode horses. Renegades most likely."

"Why did you stay? Wouldn't they take you back to your own people?"

"They offered…many times. I didn't want to go."

Cassidy's mouth fell open in stunned surprise. "Didn't want…" He broke off, several things registering at once, her fear of someone in her past, and her name…he knew he'd heard it before. "Bristol!"

Her gaze flew to his, seeing his sudden intense scrutiny. "Of course! You're the niece he's convinced is still alive. Why wouldn't you want him to find you?" Even as he asked the question he knew the answer. He hadn't liked the man the minute he laid eyes on him.

"He's a bully! A bible thumping, fire breathing, self-appointed messenger of God!" she hissed.

"Oh, lordy," Cassidy murmured. "I know the type. There's only one view of the world and religion and that's their own."

Abby relaxed a little, seeing that he understood. "He'd have taken me to his ranch and put me to work like a mule, same as his wife and my cousins. They don't have any say about anything."

"Whew! No wonder you hid out. Did you know he's been lookin' for you?"

"Yes, I saw him a few weeks ago."

Cassidy nodded as the situation suddenly made sense. "That's one of the reasons you accepted my offer, isn't it?"

Abby saw no reason to lie and nodded. "He's offered the Indians a reward for me. As long as he knows there's a red-haired woman living in the mountains, he won't give up."

"No, I don't much expect he would. But as my wife he can't touch you," Cassidy said with a humorless smile. "He has a ranch near Temecula. We'll see to it he knows where you are and comes for a visit." Abby's frantic look made him smile reassuringly. "Don't you worry none, little lady, I don't take kindly to anyone messing with what's mine. We let him know where you are, and how things stand. After that, he won't bother you no more, that I promise."

With that promise, Abby was tempted to throw her arms around him and kiss him she was so grateful. She restrained herself knowing the gesture would be misunderstood. Fear of Jacob had been so strong all these years that it was difficult to realize she could soon be beyond his reach. That fear wouldn't release its grip easily. There was always the fear Cassidy wouldn't stand up to Jacob, that her uncle could take her away. She'd do anything to make certain that didn't happen. Anything!

10

Cassidy decided it was time to change the subject, telling Abby about Seven Springs and his home there. He told her about the Butterfield Overland Mail which would be starting in a few months, that Seven Springs would be a stage station, how he had to have everything ready; the stock for changing horses, supplies for preparing meals for passengers. Seven Springs would be a meal stop.

It all sounded so strange to Abby. For the past six years her daily activities concerned gathering food and helping prepare it. She'd learned how to tan deer and rabbit skin for clothes and leggings. She made robes of rabbit fur and bead necklaces.

When Enyaa required her help, she gathered plants for healing, and helped when she was called to neighboring villages. During this time, she had no idea what was happening in the white world. Didn't even know who was president. So she asked Cassidy.

"A man named Buchanan, James Buchanan. Good man. A southerner. Seems to be doing a right admirable job. Rumor has it he's a friend of John Butterfield, which is one of the reasons Butterfield got the contract for the mail. Buchanan's southern ties are also the reason this god-forsaken route was chosen, putting mail coaches through the South even though the route is a lot longer. Butterfield's son John Jay has been through Seven Springs a number of times. He's in charge of the section of the road between Yuma and San Francisco." Cassidy shook his head. "Gotta hand it to him, he's got one of the toughest stretches. Not much water. They've had to dig wells, build stations, and sometimes even build the road. Seven Springs is one of the few places in the desert that already had both a building for the station, and water."

"Who helps you at the station now?"

"There's a man named Wesley, Peter Wesley, who wanders in from time to time. He don't want money, just supplies. He lives somewhere in the hills but won't take no one there. Strange cuss. Seems he don't much like people," Cassidy gave a sigh. "I gave up trying to figure him out a long time ago. He won't talk much about himself. Other than him, I get a drifter now and then or an Indian wanting to work for whiskey, which I won't do. I don't sell spirits to them neither. Now, what with the stagecoach coming through, I need someone I can count on."

"And you chose a woman for that?" Abby surprised herself with her daring question. Normally she would not question the judgment of a man, but this man seemed to have a sense of humor, and he wasn't treating her as if she was an ignorant savage.

Cassidy gave an appreciative chuckle. "You should have seen my mother. She worked side by side with my dad and never complained. Then, at night, I'd hear them giggling like a couple of kids when they were in bed."

A stab of pain went through Abby at the memory of her own parents, of their laughter together, their private looks and jokes. She remembered how they lay together on the hot desert sand, not to be separated even in death. She quickly shook off such thoughts, thirsty to hear news this man could tell her.

"Sides," Cassidy went on. "It's time I took a wife, but asking a white woman to live in a God forsaken place like Seven Springs, with the prospect of Indian raids, and who knows what kind of riff raff passing through, well, I didn't have much luck. I figured an Indian woman would be a better worker then most white women anyhow. So I left Wes in charge and came here." His grin turned lopsided. "I sure didn't figure to find a white woman living here, and liking it."

Eventually Cassidy led her to his blanket roll, opening it for them to sit on. As the night took on a chill he covered them with another blanket, but didn't try to touch her.

Abby couldn't remember talking so much, or being so interested in what another person had to say. She had six years of catching up to do. It felt strange to share a blanket with a man, sit close and know he had the right to touch her if he wanted. And relieved when he didn't. No doubt he was waiting for the sanction of the priest.

Sometime during the night Abby fell asleep with her back against a tree. Cassidy was braced by his saddle. When she awakened, at the first rosy glow of daylight, Cassidy wasn't beside her. Looking toward the river she saw him with his shirt off. His back and shoulders were brown from the sun, corded with bulging muscles. She almost giggled as she wondered if the rest of him was as brown.

When he stood up and turned toward her, his face was buried in a towel, and she let her gaze take in the dark thatch of hair on his chest, avidly following it down to where it disappeared under his trousers. He was different from the Indian men who had very little hair on their faces and bodies. Cassidy, with his long bushy beard was foreign looking to her. She had always looked at white men through the eyes of a child. Now, she was looking at her husband through the eyes of a woman.

Soon she would know him in the most intimate way possible, but she could summon no eagerness. Curiosity, perhaps.

He looked up, catching her thoughtful gaze. He grinned. "Morning, Abby. You ready to get goin'? I want to reach the ranch before nightfall."

In her mind Abby was already gone from this place. Her goodbyes had been said. Her sadness at leaving lingered in her heart, yet another part of her was eager for what came next. Her heart had already flown to this unknown place called Seven Springs, which would soon be her home.

Unable to do more than nod her agreement, Abby began her preparations to leave. While she washed up in the river, he began to pack the bed roll and supplies on the backs of both horses.

"Do you ride?" he asked when she came closer to watch.

"It's been a long time, but I used to ride on my uncle's farm. He just had work horses though."

"You'll soon get the hang of it again." Reaching into a pack he drew out some clothes; a woman's split riding skirt and a blouse. "You might find these cooler and easier for riding."

Abby fingered the texture of the material as she took them from him. She'd been wondering how she'd ride in her deerskin dress, which would soon be too hot. Even her every day dress would ride up, leaving her legs bare. For some reason she felt shy about him seeing her that way.

Without a word she slipped into the brush and stripped off her dress. It felt strange to put on the clothes of a white woman again. The split skirt fit loosely, and fell almost to her moccasins. Her fingers were awkward fastening the buttons. Even that simple task had become difficult from lack of practice.

It was a totally different woman who stepped from the brush, rolling her deerskin dress to take along. Gone were the beads and eagle feathers from her hair. She was aware of Cassidy's gaze sweeping over her in a leisurely fashion, from head to toe.

"I'll be danged," he said softly. "You look like a different lady. With your hair down like that no one will ever know where you been."

Abby hoped he was right. He handed her a hat with a string that tightened under her chin. It was uncomfortable but it made Cassidy grin all the more. "Just wait till my friends get a look at you," he said almost to himself. "They just might die of envy. Most of them thought I was crazy to go off searching for a wife."

Abby's vocabulary was increasing just talking to the man. She'd stopped learning her language years ago, but it was amazing how fast it came back, even if it did sometimes feel strange on her tongue. The words she had taught in the Indian camp were simple ones. Talking to Cassidy challenged her mind and her language. To her surprise she was beginning to enjoy his company.

He gave her a quick lesson on how to ride, how to adjust her stirrups, and which side of the horse to mount from. Gingerly she swung her leg over the saddle, finding herself sitting high above the ground, a little intimidated by the size of the mare. Cassidy's bay was even larger.

"She's a gentle one," he reassured her as he mounted. "You won't have to do much, she'll follow Big Red."

Abby looked toward the Indian camp, seeing only a few people stirring. In the Indian way she didn't wave. Her heart felt heavy as the mare followed Big Red across the river. In this part of the country, rivers were nothing like the ones she remembered from the trip west. Many of those were deep and wide. Crossing had often been dangerous. The Colorado River was the last of the great rivers on the southern trail. Ferries had carried the wagons across at a place called Yuma Crossing.

Here in the mountains the rivers were little more than streams, running their course from the snow clad peaks in the high mountains, or from underground springs, to the Pacific Ocean hundreds of miles to the west.

Ocean was only a word to Abby. She'd never seen one, only drawings. From the family home in Illinois, the Bristol's had traveled to St. Louis, where a wagon awaited them. Supplies were purchased, sturdy oxen to do the hard work, with a spare set hooked to the back to share the load. Cattle, sheep, goats and mules were being herded along with the entire party, with several sheep dogs and the young boys to help drive them.

From St. Louis, they had crossed the mighty Mississippi River, and what seemed at first to be an exciting adventure began. All her memories of the wagon trek were stirred as she rode behind Cassidy, letting her mind drift back to the wild country she'd seen; the rolling plains, the rugged mountains. By taking the Southern route through parts of Texas and the territory of Arizona they didn't have to worry about the steep slopes of the Rocky Mountains.

Things might have been different if they hadn't had so much bad luck along the way.

Again she wondered if any of the missing women and children had ever been found. In her years with the Kumeyaay, she realized some of the stories told by the whites of Indian atrocities were highly exaggerated, at least as far as any Indians she had come in contact with. True, marauders might take women and children captive rather than kill them, but as a rule the women weren't molested. They became slaves and were more likely to die from hard work and a poor diet than from torture or rape. A male from the tribe might even take a white woman as his wife. Their lives were hard, but they didn't suffer the indignity of sexual abuse.

Once they left the valley of the Kumeyaay behind, Abby never looked back. Inside she was both frightened and excited. How would she be accepted at the ranch? How would she like being married to this man?

Though he tried not to appear too eager, there were times when she saw the burning hunger in his eyes and knew what it meant. She doubted he would allow her to spend another night chastely at his side. If only she could feel for him the same warm, melting sensation that stole over her whenever she thought of Night Wolf.

From the high valley they dropped down through a natural pass between peaks. On either side of them rugged slopes grew thick with pine and pinyon. Abby remembered visiting there with her people gathering pinyon nuts. She knew these mountains well, knew the general location of the Carrillo ranch, though it was a place her people avoided. Near the ranch was a small village of Indians related to the Kumeyaay, the place where she had shown the people how to form their own pond for irrigation.

Pion had told her stories of when the Spaniards came and built their missions. He told her they invited Indians to come and live with them and learn about their God. The people hadn't minded at first. They had room in their hearts for many gods. But the Spanish insisted they throw out all the others and believe only in theirs. Some did. Some only pretended to.

It wasn't long before the Indians realized they had become slaves to the white priests. They worked hard at whatever tasks the priests set for them, and often at night, the Spanish soldiers came into the rooms of the Indian girls to lie with them. They didn't ask the young women if they were willing. They came anyway.

If an Indian grew tired of the Spanish way and tried to return to his family in the mountains he was pursued by the Spanish soldiers and dragged back to the mission. He would be whipped in front of the others as a warning. If he survived the punishment, he would be locked up until he was well enough to work again.

Pion said it was a bad time for the Indians. Some were able to escape. Others stayed and were absorbed into the way of the Spanish. They learned the Spanish language and labored for their priest masters.

Abby thought it a sad story. Seeing it from the side of the Indians made her feel differently about the stories she'd heard as a little girl regarding the Indian tribes of the east, the way they'd been killed. Exterminated like vermin. Either that or forced onto reservations.

Jacob had always been vocal about those he called heathens. Once Abby was old enough to be aware of his bigoted ways she no longer accepted everything he said as truth. Seeing her father's tight expression during Jacob's tirades she withheld her own belief. Later she and her father would talk it over in private.

Very early this instilled in her the knowledge that grownups weren't always right, that she should try to find her own truth, not blindly accept that of others.

Pines gave way to oaks and then to open meadows of lush grass. In some, cattle grazed, lifting their heads to placidly study the two riders. As Abby and Cassidy entered a broad valley of oak late in the day, she knew they were nearing the ranch.

To the west she recognized the mountain peak the village of the Kupa lay under. Cassidy stayed along the base of the hills, heading toward a path of dark vegetation that told Abby where the San Luis Rey River lay.

Cassidy pointed out to her the direction to Seven Springs from here and the San Felipe Valley that they would be following to reach it. When he paused at the top of a hill, Abby stopped beside him, her gaze following his to the adobe ranch house almost hidden against another hill, surrounded by cottonwood trees. The ground that sloped away from the house had been cleared of brush and was lush with rich nourishing grass. Cattle stretched as far as she could see.

11

The ranch had a thatched roof with a long overhang for the front porch. It was a long, low adobe with a thin curl of white smoke rising from the chimney. A barn sat a distance away, made from timber from the nearby mountains. Abby could see the bustle of activity; riders moving purposefully about the yard, and in the corral next to the barn were many fine looking horses. It was a sight she had not seen in many years. A young boy waved to them from the yard then ran into the ranch house to announce their arrival.

A sudden hard lump formed in Abby's throat. She wasn't ready for this. She needed more time. Feeling Cassidy's gaze on her she couldn't meet his look but sensed his concern.

"They don't bite," he assured her. "Don Ramon and Dona Vicenta have been my friends for a long time. Out here, neighbors are few and far between. Whenever I go to Temecula or Los Angeles they'd be insulted if I didn't stop for a visit. They call their rancho El Valle de San Jose, have herds of cattle and sheep, and a house full of young 'uns. Fortunately they learned English from Vicenta's oldest, Jose, who went to school in Los Angeles. Now, he's living here and helps run the rancho."

Big Red didn't need any urging, his ears stood straight up as he sensed the end of their journey and started down the slope. Abby held the mare back, feeling her strain at the bit in confusion. Panic seized Abby. She wanted to flee into the hills. These people would be cruel to her; their ways strange after all these years.

Fear paralyzed her as she watched her husband's back grow smaller as the distance between them increased. Though he didn't look back, he had to know she wasn't following. With a feeling of helplessness Abby knew her life was changing and there was nothing she could do. It was too late to go back. Almost without realizing it, her hand eased on the reins, allowing the mare to break into a trot to catch up to Big Red.

What if they don't like me, Abby thought. Her mind was quick to answer….so what if they don't. You aren't going to be living here. You'll see them from time to time is all. Maybe I won't like them.

Several Indian workers stopped their work to stare as if they recognized her. There were also a few Mexican workers with their close fitting pants and large sombreros who Cassidy waved to and called by name.

When Cassidy pulled up in front of the casa he turned to give Abby a reassuring look. He dismounted gracefully for such a big man, then held the mare's head while Abby swung down, feeling the weakness in her knees, partly from apprehension, partly from being unaccustomed to riding.

"I will see to your horses, Senor Cassidy," one of the vaqueros said.

"Gracias, Eduardo."

The front door of the casa opened and a brown-skinned man came out, followed by his beaming wife. "Amigo!" the man enthusiastically. "You made good time."

The two men shook hands then all eyes turned toward Abby. She couldn't stop the heat that came into her cheeks at their scrutiny. She took off her hat and fingered it nervously. There was no wariness in their eyes, much to her relief, only welcome.

"Ramon, Vicenta, I'd like you to meet my wife-to-be, Abigail Bristol."

"It's high time you were taking a wife," Vicenta scolded good-naturedly. "My dear, mucho gusto! We are most happy to meet you. Please come inside."

Abby stepped into the cool interior of the adobe ranch house. Tears came to her eyes when she saw the colorful rugs, upholstered chairs and a few religious pictures hanging on the walls. A large fireplace promised a cozy warmth on winter days, and white lace crocheted doilies adorned the arms of most chairs, and the back of the sofa.

"It's lovely," she murmured. Vicenta put her arm around Abby's shoulders.

"Welcome to our home, mi casa es su casa. Come meet our children."

The wide-eyed giggling group of youngsters stared at Abby's red hair, something rarely seen.

"This scamp is Ramon, tell the senorita how old you are."

The boy giggled. "I'm nine," he announced

"Maria Ygnacia?" Vicenta prompted.

"I'm eight."

"Encarnacion is too shy," Vicenta said of the dark-eyed scamp hiding behind her older brother. "She's seven. Florimedo is six, Alfreda is five, Felicidad is two. And, though he isn't here right now, my oldest is Jose Antonio Yorba, he's twenty-one. He helps the vaqueros and keeps the accounts for the ranch."

"Mucho gusto," Abby managed, one of the few Spanish phrases she knew. She was enchanted by the handsome brood, and couldn't help wondering if she'd ever have a family such as this. It was a daunting thought.

"Now scram, you rascals, come back in time for dinner." With a burst of laughter and sounding like a stampede they charged for the door, greeting Cassidy as they went out. Abby saw the tender look on Cassidy's face and it made her feel guilty for taking Enyaa's potion.

"Come," Vicenta said. "I will show you to your room."

Abby felt the comfort of the older woman's gesture and knew she had found a friend. Down the back hallway Abby was shown into a rather large bedroom. The furnishings were surprisingly nice considering the remoteness of the ranch. There was a large high boy with the rich, dark sheen of walnut, several small tables, an armoire, and a double bed with tall posts at each corner. A hand-made quilt covered it. It seemed so familiar, like her home long ago. Abby felt overwhelmed.

"For now, Senor Cassidy will use another room," Vicenta explained. "But we have more quests coming. They all want to meet you. This evening, in the chapel, you will be married by Father Estudillo. Are you Catholic, dear?"

Abby shook her head. "We were Lutheran."

"No matter, you shall have a proper wedding."

Abby looked down at her one outfit, knowing it wouldn't be proper to be married in.

Vicenta clucked like a mother hen. "Don't you worry, we have seen to everything."

She went to the armoire and opened it. Inside was a handmade white dress with lace inserts in the sleeves and in the long skirt. "Our daughter Adela was married in this dress. I know she would be happy to have you wear it. I have also hung some of her dresses for you which she can no longer wear. With a bit of alteration they should fit you. You are about the same height, but my Adela is plumper."

Abby looked at the dresses in surprise. "You're giving them to me."

"All except the wedding dress. Adela would like to keep it for her own daughter. The others are yours with pleasure."

"I…I don't know what to say."

"Say nothing, querida, Senor Cassidy is a good friend. I want us to be friends, too. You are fortunate to have such a man."

"Am I?" She felt foolish as soon as she said it.

Vicenta smiled her understanding. "I was scared too. I loved Ramon but still I thought about running away and hiding rather than meet him in the chapel." She gave a soft chuckle. "I'm glad I didn't give in to my panic. We have had a good life together, and were blessed with healthy children. God has been good to us." Her smile softened. "For you it is different, eh? You have not had time to love this man. He is a stranger to you. But he is a man with ambition. He will not always live at Seven Springs. For now, it suits him. He makes money there. For you, perhaps it is a good place to start, away from the foolish tongues of people who can only see the Indios as savages. We have come to know them, especially the ones who live near the rancho. They have not been treated well by the Spanish or the Americans. We do not wish to see them pushed out of their village, they've been pushed enough."

Vicenta's attitude made Abby grateful, her smile was warm. "Did you say you have a chapel here?"

"It is the way of the Spanish. In the ranchos one room is usually set aside for worship. On Sunday morning people from the area, even the Indios will come to hear Father Estudillo when he is here, or if he is not, one of the younger priests from the San Luis Rey Mission.

"I have heard of San Luis Rey," Abby said, sitting on the bed to test it, the first real bed she had seen in years. "The Indian man who taught me once lived there."

"At one time they had many, many Indio neophytes, but the ways of the Spanish are fading. The missions no longer function as they once did, to teach the Indios."

A young Indian girl came to the door and spoke a few words in Spanish to Dona Vicenta.

"We have a bath ready for you," Vicenta said, taking a robe from the armoire. "Come along with me. Then you shall have time to rest before the ceremony and before dinner.

Tonight we will have a feast such as you have never seen."

Abby let herself be led to a room, little more than a closet actually, where a large metal tub had been filled with warm water.

Feeling the grime of the trail all over her clothes and her hair, Abby began to undress. Her privacy was respected and she was left alone. She brushed out her hair with the first real hairbrush she had seen in a long time. With her hair hanging far down her back she stepped into the tub, letting out an ecstatic gasp as she sank into its perfumed warmth.

Tilting her head back she dipped her hair to wet it, then leaned against the sloping back of the tub to enjoy a soak. She realized what was happening. She was being seduced by the pleasures of civilization, seduced away from the people who had been her family and her protectors for the past six years. She was grateful to the Kumeyaay. She never wanted to forget the lessons she had learned, especially from Pion and Enyaa, and of the trek to the sacred place.

She still missed the old man who had been her first teacher. Though he had been gone for several years, she would miss him all her life.

Soap was a luxury. She scrubbed her skin until it was pink and glowing, then washed her long hair. It wasn't as easy to manage in the tub as in the river…where soap had come from the root of the yucca.

Purposely she refused to let her mind dwell on what would happen after the ceremony. Later this night, when she returned to this bedroom, Cassidy would be with her as her husband. Strangely she couldn't think of him as Jim, or even Cass. He was Cassidy. She shivered with the knowledge it would soon be her name too. Abby Cassidy.

In the robe Vicenta had provided Abby returned to her room while the Indian girl, Maria, collected her dusty clothes to wash. On the wall was a highly burnished piece of metal used as a mirror.

Abby went close, drawn by her wavering image. Leaning close she put a hand on her face as if to be certain the image she saw was really her own. She had grown so much, changed from a skinny red-haired child to a young woman with hair that was more auburn now, with golden highlights from days spent in the sun, and two streaks nearly white radiating from her temples.

She'd seen her image in the still pools of the river but it was not as clear as this. Her face was that of a woman. At sixteen, she looked older.

Among the Indians, many of the young women were married and had one or two children by her age. She would have to be careful of that by using the ways Enyaa had shown her to keep from conceiving until she knew Cassidy better, until she knew if she wanted his child.

Her leisurely inspection of her image was interrupted by Maria bringing a tray. The smell alone was enough to make Abby's mouth water. Her first civilized food.

The tea smelled sweet, like sage, but before she drank, Abby went to her bundle of belongings and took the powder Enyaa helped her prepare. She poured the right measure of ground leaves into her tea and sipped. It was hot and delicious.

Taking the cover from a small plate on the tray, she found unfamiliar food. There was something made of dough, filled then baked in an oven. Vaguely she remembered her mother making something similar. Also there was a small portion of beans with cheese on top and a tortilla with butter. Abby hadn't tasted butter in years.

She hadn't meant to eat it all, but suspected she would be too nervous later. The dough was filled with a mixture of spiced meat, raisins and cinnamon. Using a fork was awkward. She would have laughed at herself if she wasn't afraid someone would hear. It made her thankful Vicenta was giving her this time alone, letting her learn to be civilized again.

When the plate was clean, the tea gone, Abby lay back on the soft bed gingerly, seeming to sink into it. Most likely the mattress was stuffed with chicken feathers just like on Jacob's farm. She meant to close her eyes only for a moment and was asleep instantly. The excitement of the past few days had taken its toll.

Abby awakened at the opening of her bedroom door. Vicenta and Maria came in, their broad smiles telling her it was time to dress. A flutter of fear went through her. Why was she doing this? She didn't even know the man she was binding herself to in the most intimate fashion.

But it was too late to run, and there was no place to hide. Even her mountain home was no longer safe from Uncle Jacob. If he knew she was there he might return with soldiers to take her away. Some of her people could be hurt. Jacob would have no feelings for them. In his eyes they were godless, therefore unworthy of mercy.

Abby forced her mind away from thoughts of Jacob. She might as well try to enjoy what was happening. A girl only married once. If she was fortunate it would be the type of marriage her parents had. Yet, she knew the two of them had fallen in love almost from the moment they met. She had no such strong feelings for Cassidy. She wanted to feel them, ached to feel them, but when she looked inside herself, they weren't there.

"You are a beautiful bride," Vicenta chatted as she began to fix Abby's long hair. It was shining with golden fire in Vicenta's expert hands. With the help of tortoise shell combs she drew some of Abby's hair to the top of her head, leaving the back hanging in long fiery curls.

When it was finally time to dress Abby was so nervous she could hardly stand still for the corset, pantaloons and petticoats. She felt as if her breath was being choked off as she was laced into the white, whale bone contraption. It was torture yet she giggled as Vicenta urged Maria to pull it tighter.

"Enough!" Abby gasped. "I won't be able to breathe!"

Vicenta was finally satisfied. Next came the frothy white dress, slipping over her head and falling to her bare feet. In sudden dismay Abby wondered what she was going to wear for shoes. Indian sandals or bare feet would be laughed at. She had no wish to humiliate her husband-to-be.

"No need to fret," Vicenta assured her. "We have just the thing I think will fit you."

From the closet Vicenta took a pair of slightly worn, white, high button shoes. Abby pulled them on over her silk stockings, finding them a little large. But that wasn't a problem. Vicenta stuffed cloth into the toe until they fit perfectly.

Time passed quickly. Abby was patted, brushed, turned this way and that until at last Vicenta was satisfied. The Spanish woman led Abby to the mirror and let her gaze on her own image. Abby stared. That couldn't be the same woman she'd seen earlier. This one had hair piled on top of her head, wreathed with a garland of fresh white flowers. The gown clung to her torso, accentuating her small, firm breasts. She could barely feel the pins Vicenta had tucked out of sight to ensure the fit.

The vision that stared back at her looked exactly the way she pictured a bride. Only a few days ago she had been wearing a shapeless dress and beads, her feet most often bare.

Which one was she really, the savage or the blushing bride?

A knock on the door told them it was time. The sound of guitar music filled the ranch house. Abby felt her heart beating wildly as she was led through the door. She tried to answer the beaming smiles of the two women but it wavered and trembled. In the hall, Ramon, Vicenta's husband dressed in his finest black broadcloth Sunday suit, waited to escort Abby to the chapel.

She might have laughed at the sound of the guitar is she hadn't been so scared. To her it sounded like a prayer, a prayer that she be happy, that Cassidy would be a good husband.

The chapel was only a small room. As she entered she saw there were more people than she expected, sitting on straight backed chairs and benches. All eyes turned toward her as she moved slowly on Ramon's arm. At that moment she was glad to have him to hold onto. If not, she might have fled from those curious stares.

To keep from thinking about them she looked to the far end of the room, to a small alter with lighted candles on either side, to the older man in an ornate robe, and lastly her gaze settled on the man who was staring at her as intently as the others, the man who would be her husband. She could see his chest swell with pride. He wasn't ashamed of her.

The dark suit he wore didn't fit well. It was a bit short, the shoulders tight and the material straining to accommodate his bulk. In this back country people made do. No one would give it a second thought. It was enough that they tried to go through the proper motions.

The look in Cassidy's eyes set an enormous burden on Abby's young shoulders. She saw the pride and admiration, the possessiveness. If only she could be the wife he wanted.

The words barely made sense to her as the priest began to speak in Latin. It was a foreign ritual. She responded when prompted, went along without a will of her own. There were responses at times from the people in the room, startling her. Finally there was a quick, chaste kiss from the man who was now her husband before he took her by the hand and led her from the room.

In the hours that followed, Abby met so many people she couldn't possibly remember all their names. She was wished happiness and many children. Her cheeks were kissed, her hand pumped, until she was weak with relief when everyone was called to dinner.

The children were fed separately at tables on the front porch. The grownups filled their plates buffet style and sat wherever they could. Abby and Cassidy were given places of honor at the dining room table. Ramon Carrillo, their host, and several neighbors sat with them.

Abby was glad when the men's attention turned to politics and away from her. Her face felt stiff from smiling, her voice becoming hoarse from talking more than she was accustomed to.

Across the table from her was a man named John Rains, who owned an adjacent land grant. He was in the process of building a rancho at yet another location which he called Rancho Cucamonga. At the moment he and his wife were making their home at the

Rancho Chino. Abby learned he was a gringo who had married a Spanish woman, one who had inherited a vast land grant upon the death of her father. And, as was the custom, the husband had full control over all of her properties. Rain's wife, Merced, was in the kitchen helping Vicenta, along with many of the other wives.

"They're taking bets," John Rains said. "On whether Butterfield will be able to roll the first stagecoach out of St. Louis by the deadline. That's only two months away."

"Which way you betting, John?" Cassidy asked.

Rain's weathered face was youthful when he smiled, his long, dark brown beard bobbing as he spoke. "If the entire route is being handled with the same competence young Butterfield has been showing in this area, then there's little doubt."

"Yeah," Cassidy agreed. "He's made Seven Springs his camp several times while working on the road. This is one of the roughest stretches on the route, here and part of Texas and Arizona territory. Its thirteen hundred miles of nothing. I think they'd have been smarter to use the overland route, thru the Salt Lake maybe."

"President Buchanan is a Southerner," Rains said. "He wanted to help out his fellow Southerners by sending business their way. Not only that, but by using this southern route they miss the dangerous mountain passes of the Rockies that close up in winter. This route will be open year around."

"Young John Jay said they'll be using your ranch for a stop, too," Cassidy said to Rains.

"Yep, it stands to reason. We already take in travelers and feed them at Rancho Chino. With the coach stopping we'll get the latest news from the East, even before Los Angeles and San Francisco."

Cassidy knew his friends political ambitions, ambitions he wanted for himself, only not in the same area. Cassidy's interests lay in San Diego, not San Bernardino and Los Angeles as Rains did.

"What do you think of the talk about some Southern states wanting to secede from the union if a Northerner is elected president in sixty?" Cassidy asked.

Rains laid down his fork and leaned toward Cassidy, an intent look in his eyes. Abby could feel the interest of all the men around the table.

"As long as Buchanan is in office it's just talk. But he's only got a few more years. Our next president won't be a Southerner, you can bet on that. Too many Northerner's don't like the idea of being part of a union that supports slavery. I think they'll overwhelm the South in the election, and if they do, there's a good chance it will mean war. The South is too entrenched in their way of life. They couldn't afford their grand life style if they didn't have free labor to support it."

Cassidy was nodding his head as Rains spoke, as if John were echoing his own thoughts. "What will happen here in California?" Cassidy asked. "You're closer to the talk than I am out at Seven Springs."

Rains shook his head in a way that said he didn't like to think about it. "We have people from all over the country here, from the states and territories," Rains said, picking up his fork again, but his mind was on his subject more than the food. "We got them from the North and the South, some with such fierce feelings on the subject that it can only mean big trouble for California. There's already talk of what our governor would do. One of the suggestions is to secede from the Union and form our own government, our own separate country."

Cassidy stared at Rains to see if he was joking. "You're serious?"

"Damn right…excuse me ma'am," he said to Abby with barely a glance at the bride, then warmed to his subject. "It's a darn interesting idea for the governor to proclaim himself emperor or president. You just watch. If war comes, California will erupt within itself. There's too many strong, outspoken men who don't mind letting people know just what they think, and too many others who don't think the same way who'll remember what they said."

"If war does come," Cassidy said thoughtfully, "That would be a good time to be in the business of raising beef. It takes a lot of meat to feed an army."

A man across the table gave a snicker. He was a rancher from Temecula who had been passing through and decided to stay for the wedding. His name was Frank Manners. "How you going to get cattle from here to there? That's a few thousand miles with little in the way of grass and water."

Cassidy's grin was rueful. "Yeah, I thought of that too, but Texas is a Southern state, you know. There could be fighting closer than you think."

"What's all this talk of fighting?" Vicenta demanded, bringing a plate of steaming enchiladas to the table. "There should be talk of dancing and fiesta. What bride wants to hear of war on her wedding day?"

Cassidy looked at his new wife, a smile lighting his face to see how lovely she was, to see envy in the faces of the other men. "You're right, as usual, 'Chenta. It's a darn good thing you already got a husband or I might a come a'courtin' long time ago."

Vicenta took his teasing good naturedly. "You don't fool me, James Cassidy, it's my cooking you love, and if Abby wants, I will teach your lovely wife how to cook your favorite dishes…but not all of them, or we'll never see you again."

Everyone around the table laughed. Vicenta's husband pointed to his round belly. "You see this?" he said. "This is what happens when you marry a good cook. Take my advice, Cassidy, don't let 'Chenta teach your wife or soon you won't be able to sit on a horse."

Cassidy chuckled. Everyone knew as well as he that life was hard at Seven Springs, there was little chance of his growing a belly like Ramon's, no matter what he ate.

Cassidy passed the plate of enchiladas to Abby, holding it while she helped herself. With all the food, and her nervousness, she wasn't able to eat much, but she wanted to taste what Cassidy seemed to enjoy. It made her think of her new responsibilities in preparing his food. All she knew was the Indian way. She smiled hopefully at Vicenta, wanting very much to learn.

Vicenta gave her a wink then went back to the kitchen, return-ing with another platter heaped with hot tortillas. Some of the oth-er wives came in with bowls of things Abby didn't recognize, but the men dug in without hesitation.

Abby tasted the enchilada tentatively. It was a pleasant taste, a little spicy, with shredded beef wrapped inside a flour tortilla along with chopped onion, olives and spices. The red sauce was tangy. As Abby relished the strangeness of the food, she wondered if she could ever learn to make it. It seemed beyond her small abilities.

From what Cassidy told her, one of her duties as his wife would be to prepare food for the emigrants passing through if they wished to buy a meal, and for the stagecoach passengers. If she remem-bered correctly, in Illinois, her family had eaten a lot of beef and pork, a lot of potatoes, and lots of fresh vegetables from their own garden. She'd have to see if there was a garden at Seven Springs. If not, she needed seeds to start one of her own.

When dessert came, Abby was certain she couldn't eat another bite. Already her stomach was protesting her nervousness and the strangeness of the food. But she took one look at the rice pudding, at the apple and cherry pies, and somehow found room for just a bit of pudding. The long forgotten taste of cinnamon and cream brought back painful memories. Tears formed in her eyes and she lowered her head over the bowl so the others wouldn't see. A bride was expected to be happy on her wedding day.

A moment later she banished the ghosts as the sound of music came from outside. Vaguely she could recall similar music on the wagon train. On Jacob's farm, no music was permitted, even her at-tempts at singing hymns had brought stern looks from him.

The Kumeyaay had expressed feeling in song, in chanting. She had felt her own spirits soar at the joyous sound. Seeing her bright eyes shining with interest, Cassidy took her hand and led her out onto the porch. Immediately seats of honor were cleared for them.

Under a large cottonwood tree a group of workers, one with a guitar, one with a trumpet, and another with a fiddle were creating a lively sound that had the children whirling about in dance. Before long some of the adults joined in, and Abby watched in fascination as they performed dances that were strange yet familiar. On the trip West there had been dancing a few nights, a similar type of circle dance.

In the shadows of the deepening night, Abby saw several Indians watching the festivities. They were dressed as ranch workers in clothes that didn't look quite natural on them. The people on the ranch were a mixture of American, Spanish, and Indian.

Abby liked Merced Rains even though she didn't have much chance to speak to her. She had lovely dark eyes that embraced everyone she met. Even her husband's gaze followed her with a soft, loving look. The same way Ramon did with Vicenta. Abby hoped in time she and Cassidy would share that same feeling. So far, she felt very alone and very frightened. The white dress kept people at a distance. She was a new bride, this was her wedding night, and it was not a time to intrude.

A small ceramic jug was making the rounds among the men. Even Cassidy took his turn. Abby remembered some of the men of the wagon train doing the same. After a while they would talk too loud, sometimes slurring their words. They would dance crazily, or walk funny, until finally they went to sleep, sometimes in the strangest places. The wives would merely collect their man, often with the help of others to take him off to their wagon. Her father had never been one of them.

Pion had talked about how the white man's whiskey was ruining the Indians who tried it. One drink never seemed to be enough. The taste fired their blood, making them useless for any type of work, including providing for their families. Pion's face had always shown worry when he spoke of it, so Abby watched with apprehension as the jug came around more frequently.

One of the merrymaker's urged Cassidy and his bride to dance. Abby was vastly relieved when Cassidy begged off, saying it was one thing he'd never learned to do. Finally it was Vicenta who came to her rescue. "Pobrecita," she clucked. "Come, you are tired. These hombres will dance half the night. Maria and I will help you get ready for bed."

Abby wasn't certain which was worse, to stay or to go with Vicenta, but she went, aware that Vicenta nudged Cassidy as she went by. "Don't be too long, amigo."

Abby was also aware of the eyes of most of the guests, including Cassidy's following her from the porch, making her hide her flaming cheeks. Vicenta's arm came around her, hugging her as they walked down the hall. "Pay no attention to them, little one, they are a little envious."

Maria already had the room pleasantly aglow with oil lamps, and was running her hands admiringly over the long white gown laying across the bed. Abby wondered if she was supposed to sleep in it. In the Indian camp, she wore nothing at all. Here, she decided, it was best to do as they did, to adapt to their way.

In the Indian camp there was little modesty. She remembered the time she and Moyla had peeked through the bushes at the young men frolicking in the hot pools. She knew the shape of a man's body, an Indian body. She wondered if white men looked the same. It was a stupid thought. Of course they were the same, except Cassidy had more hair on his body. His face was covered with it, and from what she had seen of him without his shirt, his chest was also a thick, curly mat.

Numbly she allowed Maria to undress her and help her into the white night gown, feeling the scratchiness of it as it slid down over her body. The sleeves were long, reaching all the way to her wrists, the high neck ending at her throat with a row of small buttons down the yoke, and a blue ribbon tied just above her breasts.

Vicenta was chattering about her life with Ramon, how much she had come to love him, and about their life at the ranch. Abby only half listened, relieved that she wasn't expected to respond. She had to keep her teeth pressed tightly together to keep them from chattering with nervousness.

Maria brushed out her long, fiery tresses until they were gleaming in the light of the lamp. Seated at the dresser Abby tried not to look into the mirror. The pale image was not one she recognized. It was the face of a white woman, a thought that brought a sense of mourning for the loss of her Indian self.

No, she denied abruptly, her eyes suddenly taking on a fire that had been lacking in her all day. She wouldn't let that part of her die. She was called Eagle Woman, and her medicine would one day be as powerful as Enyaa's, this she felt in her bones. She must never lose that identity, even if she had to hide behind the image she saw in the mirror.

Enyaa's face came to her, her teachings, the strange things that had been revealed to her. Words about her future, and the time when she would need all her skills as a huntress, and as a healer. Enyaa had seen her future, though what little Abby had been told left her feeling puzzled. The fact that part of the prediction had come true should have made Abby feel safe and protected.

When she was young she had thought most men were good, that only a few were renegades or liars. Pion had instilled in her a healthy mistrust of the motives of men, especially white men when it came to a pretty woman…men who would fill her head with sweet words, give her pretty things. He cautioned her to always be wary of such gifts. They were never without cost as many a pretty Indian girl learned when she accepted gifts from Spanish soldiers.

Those men came to their rooms at night and took what they wanted. If the girl didn't submit they used force, and such men were never punished. The good priests looked the other way.

Pion also warned her that the fact she had lived with Indians could leave her vulnerable to such treatment at the hands of white men.

Abby wondered why his words came back to her now. She knew what Cassidy wanted from her, but he had made her his wife. That gave her a certain amount of prestige within the community of the whites. Officially and legally she had the man's protection.

At the dinner table she had seen the respect Cassidy commanded. He was listened to when he spoke, the same as John Rains. As his wife, she would be accorded the same respect.

12

"Ah. How lovely you look," Vicenta said, her dark eyes sparkling merrily. "Your husband will be enchanted. Come, Maria, let us leave our lovely bride to await her husband."

Even Maria's smile was full of knowledge of the way between a man and a woman. She bid Abby a shy good night, followed by Vicenta's hearty one, and Abby was at last alone.

Fear rushed in on her. Soon Cassidy would come. What would he be like? She had seen many sides of him. He was one man in the Indian village, quiet, competent, very much at home in the wilderness. He was another man on the ride to the rancho, speaking to her as an equal, not as an ignorant woman.

She had enjoyed listening to Cassidy talk. He was more like Pion, ready to help her learn. At this moment she wished she could seek the wisdom of her mentor. She had missed him every day since he had been gone. She remembered the last days when the old warrior knew his time was short. He'd asked her to come to his ewa and sit with him.

His breath didn't come easy as he lay wrapped in robes, his face gray, his eyes sometimes looking to some far place Abby couldn't see.

"You have been like a daughter," he told her. "You have learned well. When the time comes, you will know it, and you will return to your white world. This is not your place, child. Do not try to make it so. If you marry one of the People you will only make him and yourself unhappy." For a moment he had struggled for breath, his words came slowly and from deep within him. Abby could only hold his shriveled hand and choke back her tears, knowing he would scold her for them.

"You have needed us these years you have lived among us. We have protected you and taught you our ways. You must never turn your back on those ways, even after you leave this place. Your heart will always be with the Kumeyaay."

Abby absorbed his words knowing they would be the last he ever spoke to her. She did not want to let him go. She still needed him. He must have felt that in the way she squeezed his hand.

"Do not grieve, daughter. The time we had has been good. It has given me much happiness."

"It has given me much happiness as well, grandfather," she told him, calling him that for the first time. She saw his faint smile as if it were an effort. "How can I let you go?"

His brief grin faltered. "You cannot stop death from coming. Do you not see him standing there in the corner?" He raised his hand to point. Abby shivered and looked in spite of herself. She saw nothing but the shadows of approaching night, but she shivered again as Pion's eyes seemed to see what she could not. "With him is my father, a great chief before the coming of the Spanish. He tried to drive the soldiers from this land, but there were too many. He knew they would devour us, push us aside."

Pion moved as if to rise and go to those shadowy figures but fell back again, his breathing even more labored. "I am glad you are with me, daughter, as I go to the Spirit world. Do not be sad for me. I go to a good place. And, on some distant day, we shall meet again. I knew you had a special destiny, and that I must safe-guard you for that day." He gasped for breath. "Do not be afraid of your destiny. Meet it eagerly. You are one of the chosen."

"Chosen, grandfather? For what?"

For a moment he didn't answer and she thought perhaps his spirit had gone. The blue tinge around his lips frightened her.

"I do not know." His voice was barely a whisper. "Only that it is in some way connected with my people. Perhaps you can do for them what we cannot do for ourselves. Keep them safe, child. Walk with Amaayahaa."

His words faded and Abby knew that he slept. His breathing began to ease gradually but the blue around his lips grew more pronounced. She knew he was dying, felt life leave him even as her hand gripped his, trying to somehow hold him to this place.

In the end, she accepted that he was ready to leave, to be with his father. His body had become a burden, one he now had shed. The ewa grew silent. Abby allowed her tears to fall, knowing he was beyond seeing them. Her eyes were drawn to the corner as if she felt a presence there. In the shadows of the smoke of the fire her eyes played tricks on her. She saw a shadowy form enter the smoke where another hand reached out to help him through. Pion was gone from this place. Forever. Without thinking she began to sing the song of mourning.

Abby jumped when the door opened and Cassidy came in. Shyly she stood up to face him, seeing him stop to stare at her, a strange fire burning in his eyes. He began to remove his clothes with such haste Abby was frightened.

"You're so beautiful," he murmured as he pulled off his shirt and sat down on a chair to pull off his boots. "So soft and so pretty."

Abby was unable to move, watching him unfasten his pants and slide them down, stepping out of them. His undershirt followed. Abby saw again his muscled chest, his massive shoulders. She knew there was strength there and she was even more afraid.

He came to her wearing his socks and a pair of strange looking undershorts. They came almost to his knees and fit loosely. For a moment it looked as if he wanted to overwhelm her with his strength and his need, but seeing her wide, frightened eyes he took a steadying breath.

"Don't be afraid, Abby," he murmured. "I wouldn't hurt you. You're too pretty. You're my woman now. All mine. The others can only dream about having someone like you."

She smelled the sour scent of whiskey on his breath as he began to kiss her. He wasn't rough, he was trying to be gentle with her, but Abby didn't know how to respond, her mouth unyielding under his. After a moment he drew back and chuckled at something she couldn't understand. "Those Indians must not have taught you how to kiss."

"Why would they teach me that?" Abby asked, puzzled.

"Maybe they didn't know how. Open your mouth a kittle," he coaxed, them brought his lips down on hers again. This time Abby's mouth softened under his and she heard his low groan.

"Oh, that's much better."

His breath was coming faster, as if he'd been running a long ways. Abby thought it strange, as was the look in his eyes. There was a fire there, a hunger she didn't understand. His mouth grew more insistent, his hands began to move over her body. Her first impulse was to push away those seeking hands then realized she could not. He was her husband, and this was what men did with their wives.

A moment later he was tugging at her gown, raising it up, stopping only when he realized there were buttons to unfasten. His fingers worked clumsily at them in his haste. When they were free he gave a satisfied chuckle then lifted the gown once more. With flaming cheeks Abby raised her arms so he could slip it over her head.

Cassidy tossed the gown across the room, unheeding as it crumpled to the floor. Abby wanted to go to the lovely garment and pick it up yet knowing Cassidy wouldn't allow her to move. His gaze was devouring her full, rosy peaked breasts, then traveled avidly down her golden body to the bright triangle. It was all she could do not to shrink away from him when he weaved unsteadily on his feet. His massive hands reached out to draw her naked body hard against him. The urge to struggle almost won out over what she knew was her duty as his wife.

Some of the Indian women spoke of their enjoyment of their husbands touch so it couldn't be too dreadful. What made her nervous was the feeling he was somehow losing control; especially evident in his ragged breathing, the feverish haste with which his hands moved. He lifted her and bore her back onto the bed, his powerful body coming down on top of her. Her arms went around his bare back automatically, and though he still had on his smalls, she could feel a hardness pressed against her, the grinding of his hips.

With a groan of impatience he rose up on one arm and quickly dispensed with the only restriction between them. Abby felt his hard, pulsing maleness probing between her thighs. His groan of some strange anguish made her tense up as his strong legs pushed her legs apart so he could lay between them.

His lips were hard and bruising as they captured hers, leaving her too afraid to feel any response. She knew he was out of control and unheedful of her fear.

When he rose up on one elbow preparing to enter her she could feel the tension in his body, see the intent, feverish look in his eyes. It only tightened the tension within her own body, instilling a dread of the moment when his body joined with hers. The Indian women whispered how it hurt the first time so she was partially prepared for the first searing sensation as his hardness pressed into her. He wasn't patient with her, too intent on his own pleasure to realize he was the first. He disregarded the firm resistance of her body and bore in harder.

Abby's body convulsed at the sharpness of the pain but she refused to make a sound. She wanted to scream for him to stop, to push him away, but she dare not. Tears of pain gathered in her eyes as his cries of pleasure filled the room.

Outside, the sound of music and laughter filled the night air. Abby wished she could be out there with them. Any place would be better than this, with the big man sweating and thrusting, his hips rising and falling with primitive pleasure. The pain eased. The act became easier to endure.

Abby let her mind drift from reality, back to the Indian village and to the handsome warrior Night Wolf. Would it be different if he were her husband? Would he be as mindless to her pain? Would it always be this painful, or as the women whispered would it be easier next time. Next time! How often did a man want to do this? All she could do was hope it wasn't often.

It was a long time before Cassidy's cries of pleasure rose to a peak, his head thrown back in what could almost have been pain, but Abby knew it wasn't. His body throbbed for a long moment, then he fell forward onto her, spent. She was aware of the scent of his sweat, the weight of his body as his harsh breathing eased. Moments later he shifted his body to lie beside her, his head turned away. He didn't say anything. Didn't ask if he hurt her. Within moments his low snores filled the room.

Her eyes bright with unshed tears, Abby was afraid to move, afraid to awaken him. Her body ached, throbbing with pain and wetness. Touching herself there she knew the dampness was blood and something else. She felt used, demeaned. For her there had been no pleasure, only revulsion. She'd expected more, much more.

Suddenly remembering the ways of keeping a child from coming Abby sat up Indian fashion on the bed. For a time she remained in that position, trying not to think, but her mind refused to be still. This was the bargain she had made to return to the world of the white man. This was something she had to know, a new facet of her education.

After a time, when Cassidy's snores told her he was sleeping soundly, she slid from the bed, going to the water pitcher to wash away the blood and stickiness of Cassidy's seed on her thighs. She would be diligent in her effort to keep from having his baby. For some reason she didn't want to be tied to him forever, though she knew the marriage ceremony did just that. She'd made a promise to love, honor and obey. Love? Perhaps it would come. Honor? She could do that. Except for this incident he seemed a fair man. Obey? That word brought a reluctant twinkle of humor into her eyes. She'd have to see about that. She wasn't always so good about obeying, which a few times had gotten her into trouble with her Kumeyaay family. Even Moyla drew the line at some of her escapades and would leave Abby to her mischief. Hahro and Opachuk had been very tolerant of her. They hadn't tried to make a meek Indian maid of her. She sensed Pion's hand in that. She was allowed a freedom most maids didn't have. Perhaps Pion and the others knew one day she would need all her wits, all her courage and cunning to make her way in the white world. A world that would attempt to shun her.

The fiesta continued for several days with neighbors camped about the ranch. Vicenta and Maria and Merced were constantly in the kitchen. Abby was not expected to help but insisted as a way to keep from thinking about being alone again with her husband. She was glad Cassidy wanted to take part in the games the men played, the horse races, the roping and throwing of the cows, the knife throwing.

Both the newlyweds had to endure the good-natured teasing about their wedding night, the knowing smiles. Abby never let on she was disappointed in that side of marriage. When Cassidy turned to her in the darkness of their room she didn't refuse him, neither did she feel the pleasure he did. At least there was no sharp pain as there had been the first time, only a discomfort from her dry, unprepared body.

Several times Abby caught Vicenta's appraising look, and she would always smile, but somehow she didn't think she had fooled the older woman. Vicenta knew the spark just wasn't there for her.

Abby learned to make some of the Spanish dishes Cassidy enjoyed, the enchiladas, the refried beans which would be one of the staples at Seven Springs, and even how to make tortillas. It wasn't as easy as it looked, she realized, as she watched Maria toss the dough in her hands, working it into a large thin circle.

Abby grew to relish the taste of tortillas warmed over the fire, slathered with freshly made butter, and rolled up with meat and beans inside. She was glad for the work, glad to keep busy. This life was new to her, these people different, so emotional compared to the reserved dignity of the Kumeyaay. The bombarding of constant chatter, the wild play of the children, the noise of the vaqueros with their rodeos, at times made her want to flee to some quiet place to regain her mental balance.

Yet, too, Abby saw these people were more like her. She had always been like a bolt of pure energy in the Kumeyaay's placid world.

On the fourth day, the visitors began to drift away. The ranch turned quieter. Cassidy took Abby for a ride into the oak forest, showing her where hot water bubbled from the ground and formed a river. It reminded Abby of the quiet pool she'd bathed in many times near the Kumeyaay village, and she wasted no time in stripping off her clothes.

Cassidy was more modest, taking a long careful look around before he followed suit. Abby dove into the deepest pool, created by the placement of the rock dam. The place had obviously been used by many others for the same purpose.

The water was hot on her naked skin, creating a sensation of pleasure that made her want to close her eyes and throw back her head as she smoothed her hair back from her face. She didn't see the look of naked longing that came into Cassidy's eyes as he came into the water more slowly, watching her. Her look was purely sensual, one he'd never been able to elicit from her in their marriage bed.

When Abby did glance at Cassidy she saw that his lower body was white compared to his torso. In the darkness of their bedroom, when he made love to her, she'd hadn't been able to see him all that clearly.

Cassidy was somehow larger, more solidly built than the Indian men. He was very much a man. He would be a good protector, a woman should feel fortunate to have such a strong man to provide for her. She laughed at his gasp and grimace at the heat of the water. They were close to the source where the water was hottest. She splashed water on him to help him adjust more quickly. With a yelp of surprise he splashed back. It then became a battle with great bursts of water filling the air, thoroughly drenching both of them. Their laughter rang like that of children at play.

To quell her expert, and more accurate splashes, Cassidy covered the distance between them and grabbed her arms. Abby's struggle was playful, but she saw the gleam come into his eyes that told her she had aroused him. Already she felt the insistent pressure against her belly.

"Every time I look at you I want you," he murmured. "You're so pretty. Sometimes I have trouble remembering you're my wife, and I can have you any time I want." His voice was husky against her cheek, his hands moving up her arms, over her shoulders then down her satiny back, molding her hips against his.

Abby was disappointed that her time to bathe had turned into something else, but she no longer dreaded the intimacy with him as she had at first. It was something she could do without giving it much thought, though she was vaguely dissatisfied because she never experienced any of the pleasure he did.

"I never knew you hadn't been with the bucks." It took a moment for it to dawn on her what he said. "I never knew 'til the next morning that I was the first."

She knew he was referring to the blood on the sheet. He seemed pleased, but she had never been tempted, not until she saw the Yuma brave Night Wolf. He was the only one who made her heart beat faster, who made her day brighter just by looking on his face.

Cassidy's hand stroked her small breasts, then one hand trailed down her flat stomach to possessively cup the flaming mound. He seemed fascinated with her body, gazing at her intently, his eyes glowing with pride and heat. Suddenly he lifted her into his arms so effortlessly that Abby gasped, feeling small and helpless as he carried her to the grassy bank. He lay her down on the sweet, cool grass then slowly stretched out beside her, his hand stroking her breast.

He made love to her more leisurely here, caressing her sun warmed body, kissing her in places no lips had touched before. It was pleasant. She smiled at the feelings he aroused in her, an almost maternal feeling. He still wasn't able to take her with him to the pinnacle he reached when their bodies were joined. When he could hold back no longer he threw back his head and grunted his pleasure.

It never lasted long, for that she was thankful. She knew she had pleased him, but he hadn't been able to touch her desires. She would have to settle for that. He was good to her, wanted to please her, and if he realized it wasn't as good for her he didn't talk about it.

Cassidy lifted his considerable bulk from her and lay on his back, hands under his head. He looked content.

"Tomorrow we'll go to Seven Springs. I've been gone too long as it is. Wesley gets antsy after a while and wants to get back to his mountains."

"Wesley?" she questioned. "He's the one who looks after your place when you're gone?"

"Yeah. He's a strange cuss, got no use for money. When he helps out all he wants is supplies. He lives in the desert or the mountains somewhere, won't say where. He don't want no one snooping around. Just wants to be alone."

"Does he have a woman?"

Cassidy shook his head. "Nope. Doesn't seem to have much use for 'em. Sometimes he talks to the men passing through, but gets all tongue-tied when there's women around. I got the feeling something happened to him once, that's why he's out there."

"But you trust him," Abby stated, knowing he'd never leave the man alone with his store and his stock otherwise.

"Oh, yeah, I trust him with everything I own because I know he doesn't want it. He works hard when he's there, then just vanishes without a word with the supplies I give him."

Abby enjoyed their time by the river, playing in the water and making love in the open. It revealed a side of Cassidy she felt certain few people ever saw. He revealed a vulnerability to her, a need to have her affection and her friendship.

In the days at the rancho Abby had picked up a smattering of Spanish. She had already learned some of the language from Pion, who had learned it from the missionaries. She had an ear for languages and retained what she learned. Her English was coming back to her with constant use. New words were added to her vocabulary.

In a way she would be sorry to leave her new friends. John and Merced Rains had left the previous day to visit other friends in the area before returning to their home at Rancho Chino. Vicenta had been like a mother to her, patiently teaching her to cook, talking to her in Spanish.

It was not yet dawn the next morning when Abby was enveloped in Vicenta's embrace.

"Take care, my Chiquita," she said softly. "If you ever have need of a friend, Ramon and I are not far away." The concern in the woman's eyes spoke volumes.

"Thank you for everything, Vicenta, I'll miss you." They hugged again. Abby kissed Ramon on the cheek as Cassidy led up their horses along with two pack horses laden with supplies.

Cassidy shook hands with Ramon and gave Vicenta a big hug before he helped Abby onto her mare and mounted himself.

"Take care, amigos," Ramon said. "Vaya con dios."

"Come back soon," Vicenta called as they rode out, her eyes vaguely troubled. Then softly, under her breath she murmured, "Be happy, piquena."

13

The trail was easy to follow. Ruts were worn into the ground by countless wagons over the years. Soon the sound of stagecoaches would echo across this silent land. As they crossed into the neighboring rancho, Cassidy told Abby it belonged to Jonathan Warner, whom the Indians and Spaniards called Juan Largo. The place bore his name, Warner's Ranch. Warner was a strapping gringo, Cassidy told her as they rode. He'd married a woman who was the foster daughter of Pio Pico, a former governor of Alta California. Originally Pico had owned the rancho where Ramon and Vicenta now lived. Depredations from the Indians of the area many years earlier had driven him out. Later, he sold the land.

Warner was an astute man, Cassidy went on, becoming a Mexican citizen in the days before California became a state. This entitled him to own land, and his petition to the governor had granted him this giant rancho in the hills.

Cassidy told her Warner's was also a store and would be another stagecoach station for the overland mail.

The trail turned east, past Warner's adobe rancho and into a long, downward sloping valley. Cassidy told her if they had continued south they would eventually come to San Diego.

The San Felipe Valley road followed a meandering stream. Now that she was adjusting to riding, Abby could enjoy the alertness of her mare, and picked up tips on how to sit a saddle from her husband.

On the hills flanking the valley, she pointed out deer to Cassidy. Under a greasewood bush she showed him a red tailed hawk with its kill, a cotton tail rabbit, quietly ripping it apart with a razor sharp beak. On the dead limb of a nearby tree sat its mate, its yellow stare following every move of the two riders as it waited its turn to feed. Cassidy marveled at her sharp eyes. As good as he was at spotting game, she was better.

"How are you at hunting?" he asked after she pointed out a healthy looking coyote crossing in front of them, a large raccoon locked securely in its jaws.

Abby smiled. "I have put much meat on the fire of my family," she boasted. "Pion taught me."

Cassidy nodded. "Good. I don't always have time for it. Sometimes I git tired of beans, salt pork and dried beef. If you want to hunt, it will put more variety on our table, both for us and for the people passing through."

At first Abby thought Cassidy was a generous man to feed all those strangers. It wasn't until later she learned he sold the meals. From his conversations it soon became clear he was a man who wanted a lot of money. It was a word that came up often in conversation; how much his cattle and sheep were worth, the horses, the mules, the store goods.

If it was important to him, it would be important to her. In the white man's world everything was purchased with money. Even prestige could be bought, Cassidy told her. She listened and remembered. The lessons were starting anew.

It was late afternoon when Cassidy cut back to a marshy area at the lower end of the valley.

"We'd best camp here for the night, even if we do have a few hours of daylight left. Once we reach the desert there won't be much grass for the horses or water for us."

Abby didn't mind. It was a beautiful place. Birds chattered and flitted through the marsh grass and reeds. Several mud hens glided silently across the water. The vivid turquoise sky had only a sprinkling of fluffy white clouds. For a moment she paused to enjoy the view. Green mountains towered to the south west, tall pines silhouetted against the sky on the high ridges.

Looking to the northeast she saw low hills covered with chaparral, a good place for deer.

Even without thinking Abby began to gather fuel for their fire while Cassidy saw to the animals. She moved rocks into a circle on a bare patch of rocky ground. It was something she had done many times when the People were on the move. Many a night she had slept in the open with barely a blanket to cover her. She had not been cold. She had adapted to the ways of the Kumeyaay.

Cassidy tossed her a flint and within minutes she had a fire going. There were no terrors for her here. The only thing she would have to fear were any men passing through. But there, too, she could take care of herself. Her father's knife was always within easy reach.

Cassidy hobbled the horses so they could graze. Abby brewed some of the tea Vicenta had given them, adding some of the fresh blossoms of the clover to give it a sweetness. Along the stream she found watercress in lush profusion, using one of her blouses as a sack to gather enough to take along, dampening it to keep it fresh.

She turned when Cassidy came to help, nibbling on the sweet greens as he went. "No," she admonished when he pulled it up by the roots. "When you do that, it dies." She showed him how to pinch the leaves off near the base and not kill the plant.

All around the camp she saw signs of rabbits. By scouting around she found a game trail that led to the water and set one of her snares. Perhaps they would have rabbit for dinner.

It would be easy for Cassidy to use his rifle, but being alone in this country it was best not to draw attention. Along the marsh Abby gathered some of the tall grass, laying it out to dry. From this she could make baskets. It had become second nature for her to gather what nature provided. There were tubers that grew along the water's edge which she dug for their supper.

Cassidy watched with a smile of amusement. Usually he did the gathering, but his knowledge was nothing compared to hers.

On her way back to their camp, Abby checked her snare, finding a plump cottontail caught there. Her knife made quick work of him, and before the body even had a chance to cool, she had skinned it expertly, saving the pelt. She buried the entrails so they wouldn't draw scavengers, especially the coyotes which were thick in the area.

Cassidy prepared a spit over the fire to roast the meat, the sound of juices sizzling made them both ravenous. They ate a good meal without touching any of their supplies...or the food Vicenta had sent with them. Cassidy's enjoyment of the food told her he was proud of her abilities. He had made a very good choice taking her as his wife.

The next morning he added the rushes from the marsh to their packs without comment. There was cold rabbit, hard tack, coffee and watercress for breakfast. They were mounted and on their way before sunrise.

The valley sloped gradually downward as they approached the desert. Though Abby had never been on this trail, the Kumeyaay did pass nearby on their way to and from the mountains, following ancient Indian trails. As they neared the end of the valley, Cassidy turned the horses away from San Felipe Creek which had turned into a deep gorge cut into the soft sandy earth. There were fewer trees here, more of the low scrub which told them they were nearing the desert. The air was losing the mountain chill, and turning warm.

They came upon the desert abruptly. Warm gave way to heat. The rocky, sandy soil of the San Felipe Valley gave way to sand, cactus and yucca. In the past Abby had always been on foot. It was a pleasure to see the desert from the vantage point of her horse.

Scored into the desert floor, the wagon trail was easy to follow. The Indians avoided the tracks. Without a sound they could fade into the greasewood landscape until even the sharpest hunter couldn't spot them. Babies were quickly trained not to cry; not to betray the People's presence.

To the south the pine covered mountains gave way to a range of hills, only ghostly silhouettes in the twilight. From Cassidy's purposeful pace Abby knew they would be pressed to reach Seven Springs today.

The rising sun struck them full in the face as it peeked over the distant hills, turning the few clouds into hues of yellow, pink and crimson. For a time even the hills took on a pink glow, gradually assuming the normal tones of pale brown sand. Though they looked devoid of life, Abby knew that was deceptive. There were rabbits, lizards, snakes, and also ground squirrels and little desert chipmunks. Quail thrived in this place, and even now their calls echoed around them. Once Abby glimpsed a coyote, too intent on its stalking of the quail to see them at first. He froze, giving them a yellow stare, his buff and gray coat looking healthy and smooth, an indication prey was plentiful.

A low range of hills seemed to block their way. The trail followed a sandy and rocky stream bed. The horses picked their way, but even at that Abby could see an attempt had been made to clear the trail of the larger rocks so wagons could pass.

Cliffs rose around them as they wound deeper into the canyon. Lizards scurried across the rocks at their approach, a lazy butterfly flitted by. At one point, the cliffs on either side of them came so close together she wondered how a wagon, much less a stagecoach could fit. The rocks showed signs of being chipped away by pick axes.

"They call this Box Canyon," Cassidy told her. "At one time it must have looked like one. A horse could fit through easy enough, but they had to widen it for wagons. The Mormon Battalion did most of the work."

"How will the stagecoaches get through?"

"That's one of the things young Butterfield has to do yet, get a crew and go to work here. I expect him any day now if he isn't here already. Time is getting short."

"Why is that?" Abby asked, curious about anything affecting her new life.

"After John Butterfield Senior signed the contract with the postmaster general, he was given one year to send out the first mail coach. That year will be up in September." Cassidy shook his head as if he considered it an impossible feat. "Over thirty three hundred miles of nothing. In a year's time he had to widen some of the trails, even create one in places, build stations every twenty miles or so, for every "horse run" they call it, then they have to have fresh horses, food, supplies...horses and men need water, so there are wells to dig."

"There is good water here, the People know where to find it."

"Yep, that's one of the reasons they chose this particular route rather than the crossing on the Colorado River north of here. That way is mostly sand. Even though it might be shorter in distance, there's little water, no way to dig wells. In places the sand is so deep the horses could never pull a coach through it. Along this stretch it isn't so fine grained though there are some bad stretches." He gave a soft chuckle, tipping his hat back and scratching his head. "I'm not saying this way is easy. The Spaniards call this El Desierto del Muerte, the desert of death. Many a wagon train reaches Seven Springs with tales of friends and relatives buried along the trail, of dead and dying stock abandoned, of furniture brought all the way from the east left along the trail to lighten the load for the exhausted mules and oxen."

Abby could easily picture the scene. It reminded her too vividly of her own trek west, a trek that ended in tragedy. "Do the Indians still attack them?" she needed to know, wondering if things had changed over the past six years.

"It still happens," Cassidy said slowly, knowing the story of her family. "Not so often, maybe. Out here there's no law. Justice is apt to be dispensed at the nearest tree."

"And with the Indians?"

"That's a whole different thing. The army deals with that problem, usually so long after the fact it's hard to know who actually did the attacking. The Indians disappear and strike somewhere else."

"You said they sometimes steal horses from the ranches. Do they steal from you?"

"It's been tried a few times. Usually I can sense when they're in the area. It's just the way things get so quiet out in the brush. No quail calling, no birds. We bring the horses up to the station where they're easier to defend."

Cassidy guided his bay along the sandy wash, rounding a point which revealed the open desert before them, hills on either side. "But the Indians soon found out I was willing to trade with them. They come for knives, blankets, pots…all sorts of things. They bring deer meat and skins, sometimes even silver from Mexico. A couple of times I've traded for horses I'm sure were stolen."

"You took them anyway?" Abby asked startled.

"Sure, why not? I can't find out who they belong to so I can't return them. I trade 'em cheap then get a good price from someone passing through. A man has to make money where he can. It's not as if I stole 'em."

Abby supposed he was right. It wasn't actually stealing, it was only providing a profit to those who did.

It was late afternoon when they stopped at the summit of a hill for a breather. Cassidy led the horses to a water hole. Though Abby was thirsty she was too intrigued by the view of the desert below. The narrow wagon track disappeared over the edge of the cliff, so she couldn't see how it reached the valley floor.

Below them, leading off as far as she could see was the wagon trail. The valley was one Abby had crossed many times over the years. In spite of its look of desolation she knew there was life there, that it was possible to survive if you knew where water was located.

Cassidy joined her at the edge of the cliff and pointed into the distance. "Seven Springs is there, that dark place you can see against the far hills. We'll be there about night fall. It's pretty easy going once we get down this cliff."

He handed Abby some jerky and hard tack. She drank from the canteen, feeling the cool water soothe her hot throat. It had been a long ride but she didn't complain. She wondered if she'd be able to bathe once they reached the station, to rid herself of the trail dust.

"We just go to one of the springs," Cassidy told her.

"Springs? More than one? When we came by here we used the one farthest from the station."

"Actually there's seven of them."

Abby was startled. One was rare enough.

"They don't all flow at the same time. One of those survey fellas that came through here told me it's because of the earthquakes we get here. The shakin' can cause one to dry up and another to start flowing again."

"Earthquakes?" She'd felt temblors several times while she was with the Kumeyaay.

"The Indians might say the spirits are restless," he said with a chuckle. "But there's a lot of earth movement here. It never amounts to much."

Cassidy was eager to reach Seven Springs before dark. After a brief rest they mounted for the last push. The horses knew they were close to home and picked up the pace, needing no urging.

Abby followed Cassidy and his pack animals as the trail dropped over the edge. It was steep and narrow. It was impossible to imagine a team of horses pulling a heavy stagecoach up this incline. Leaning back in the saddle she let the mare pick her own way, her gaze drifting out to the far end of the valley where Seven Springs lay.

There was a spot of deeper green there, no doubt from the springs. The hills looked to be quite close to the station. They would offer deer for hunting. The land would offer much even without the supplies they carried.

The trail zigzagged down the face of the cliff, until they reached the sandy wash bed that formed the desert trail. Though she was weary, Abby wanted to know this country. She would be hunting here, and needed to know the terrain.

There were many types of cactus, their fruit drying up with the passing of spring. There was the ever present greasewood, desert willow, and now and then a palo verde, ocotillo and the edible stalks of the agave and mescal. Several times rabbits bounded away at their approach, both the rangy jack rabbits as well as the smaller cottontails, whose fluffy white tails vanished into the brush.

She saw the tracks of raccoons and coyotes as well as quail and the chaparral cock, sometimes called a roadrunner. As they neared Seven Springs, Abby could see the hills to the south were topped with pine, while the closer hills showed enough vegetation to support deer. This promised to be an abundant place.

Topping a rise as they neared the station, she looked off to the left, close to the pale colored hills and saw wagons and cooking fires. Her first impulse was to hide, a reflex ingrained in her in the past years. She felt shaky inside. Would they know just from looking at her how she had lived these past years?

Cassidy sent a curious look their way, unaware of her inner turmoil. "Usually the settlers' camp by the springs," his tone was thoughtful. "Must be greenhorns, though I don't know how they could travel this far and still be that green."

Ahead of them Abby could see the thick growth that indicated the location of the springs. They were almost on top of Cassidy's home before she made out the adobe building. It blended in with the color of the landscape, pale but sturdy, the windows shuttered with thick planks of wood in case of attack. The building was much larger than she expected.

Cassidy let out a shrill whistle that changed to a chirping at the end. Immediately a figure emerged from the open doorway near the chimney. Abby saw a tall, spare man throw back his head to regard them as they rode up. His worn pants were held up by suspenders, his shirt looking as if it had seen too many washings and was about to dissolve into rags. Around his neck he wore a faded kerchief, and instead of boots wore deerskin moccasins.

There wasn't an ounce of fat on him. His arms were only saved from being skinny by the muscles. His hair was somewhere between sandy brown and white, making it impossible for Abby to determine his age. He might have been forty or fifty. His craggy face was weathered by long exposure to the desert sun, his pale blue eyes looked as distant as the far away hills.

"Bout time you got back," he said in a voice which sounded too husky for his thin frame. "I put some extra stew on just in case."

"That'll be mighty welcome," Cassidy said as he swung down from the saddle. "It's been a long ride."

The man's gaze drifted to Abby, showing a casual interest, but she had a feeling he noticed everything about her, even though he seemed not to. He scratched his thinning hair.

"Don't look much like a squaw."

"None-the-less, I got her at a village."

Cassidy was in no hurry to tell the story, enjoying the questions in Peter Wesley's eyes. Abby sensed the teasing that was about to commence and saw Wes grin in expectation.

"She speak English?"

"Good as you…almost," he amended. "She's a mite rusty is all."

"You would be too if you'd been living with savages," Wesley said as Abby swung down from her horse, grateful to have solid ground under her again. The man's grin showed he was doing a bit of teasing of his own, that he knew full well the local Indians weren't savages at all.

"Abby," Cassidy said, relenting for a moment. "This is Peter Wesley. Everyone just calls him Wes."

Wesley offered his hand and after a moment's hesitation Abby clasped it the way she'd seen the men do. "I've been hearing a lot about you, Mr. Wesley,"

"If you please, missus, it's just plain Wes."

"If you'll call me Abby."

"Abby," Wes repeated, then slowly released her hand. "I'm right pleased to make your acquaintance. Sometime I'd like to hear all about your stay with the Indians."

"I expect we'll have the time," Abby said. "And, possibly my friends will be stopping by when they pass through the valley."

"Good, good. You two come in now, you must be starving after that long ride. I got a fat juicy rabbit stewing."

While Cassidy saw to the horses, Abby took out some of the tortillas Vicenta Carrillo had sent along. Wesley's mouth was watering when she lay them out.

"That woman makes the best tortillas I've ever tasted. All we lack is butter."

"I brought some of that, too," Abby said. "But it won't last long. I didn't think to ask Cassidy if there were any milk cows here."

If Wesley thought it strange she referred to her husband by his last name he made no comment. He seemed to be taking her measure, withholding judgment until he knew her better.

"We have a few some of the settlers left behind, too weak to go on. But they're slowly getting their strength back. We sell milk to the settlers."

"Vicenta showed me how to make cheese too, I can't make enchiladas without it."

"Oh my, I surely do think I'll be hanging around here a bit longer than I planned."

"Wes, you scoundrel," Cassidy said, stooping to enter the room. "You'll do anything to keep from eating your own cooking."

Wes's grin widened. "I'm thinking hers will be a darn sight better than yours or mine."

14

Abby found the inside of the station roomier than she expected. The main room was the largest, but was filled with supplies for Cassidy's store. It wasn't neat with shelves, but stacked every which way. The far end of the room had a small table by the fireplace. Adjacent to the main room was a smaller room with a makeshift desk where Cassidy kept his accounts. Several shelves lined the wall on which sat a jug and some chipped porcelain cups.

The room that served as the kitchen was about half the size of the main room, with an open fireplace and bake oven. On either side of the room were two small bedrooms. She hadn't looked yet to see which one she would share with Cassidy.

The floors were bare, hard-packed dirt. The adobe walls were about eighteen inches thick, and the wooden shutters of the windows open to the fresh air. It was large compared to the ewas of the People, yet Abby wondered how she'd adjust to being closed in.

She watched Cassidy toss her things into the room at the front of the building. When she finally got the nerve to look inside, she found a small room with a crude wooden bed. The quilt was in need of washing but other than that, the room looked comfortable with its four drawer lowboy and a make-shift rack for their clothes. A door led outside to the front porch.

Next to the door were several more pegs for clothes.

"You fix the place up however you want," Cassidy told her. "I ain't much at keeping the place neat, or keeping the critters out. If you look close in the corners you'll find spiders. I gave up trying to get rid of them."

Abby gave a smile. "For an Indian that is easy. Soon they will move elsewhere."

Cassidy gave her an appreciative grin. "Let's eat. The smell of that stew is making my stomach rumble."

Their plates were mismatched items given to Cassidy by people passing through, some cutlery nicked and bent. Wesley had a pot of strong, hot coffee, something Abby had not learned to appreciate. She grimaced when she sipped it…strong and bitter.

"Here," Wes said, picking up a small crock. "This will help." He spooned in honey and stirred it for her. Abby's second sip tasted much better, but still not as good as the tea she was used to.

The stew was good. There were a few tubers in it, and some wild onions. With tortillas it was a filling meal.

"You gonna plant a garden?" Wes asked, his expression telling Abby he was already anticipating its harvest.

"I brought some seeds from Dona Vicenta. Where is the best spot?" she asked him.

"Right by the spring so you can water it with a bucket. You'll have to do something to keep the rabbits out though. They'll mow it down quicker than it can grow."

"They won't be hard to outsmart," Abby assured him.

Wes grinned at her confidence, turning to Cassidy. "Know something, my friend, I think you got yourself a bargain. This little lady knows all the things a squaw knows, and more besides. Got any more like her up there?"

Cassidy knew he was only teasing. Wes didn't seem to have much use for women in general. "Sorry, I got the only one."

Abby buttered her tortilla and listened to the men talk about what had happened while Cassidy was gone. "What's that group doing camped over by the mountain?" Cassidy asked. "No one ever camps out there."

Wes scowled. "Some kind of religious group. They don't want their kids to mix with any of the others passing through. You should see the women folk hauling buckets of water from the springs. I offered to help but there was a man keeping an eye on them every minute. He stared at me as if he thought I was going to drag one of them off by their hair any second."

"Did they say where they're headed?" Cassidy asked, knowing he'd be glad when they moved on.

"Somewhere around Temecula. They want to set up their own community there."

"That'll be a good place to stay away from."

Wes seemed to know Cassidy's viewpoint on religion. "They ain't all like your pa."

Abby looked at her husband, sensing the under current between the two men. "Did your father dispense religion with a strap?" Abby asked, not surprised at his confirming nod.

"That's why I ran away as soon as I could survive on my own. If you look, you'll see the marks he left on my back."

"He sounds a lot like my uncle."

She felt the curious looks of both men. As she ate the hot stew she let her mind drift back to the past. "My pa wasn't like him, but we all lived on Uncle Jacob's farm. He treated us like poor relations, gave us all the hard chores, even my ma. She had it the hardest, working all day then having to cook for pa and me, to make all our clothes and keep them clean." Abby looked more deeply into the past. "She lost two babies while we were there. Pa knew it was from overwork. He wanted to go away and start a better life."

"How'd he get the money to leave?" Cassidy asked. "I know your uncles type. He'd keep all the money for himself."

Abby nodded, memories filling her mind with things she didn't realize she knew. "My grandparents left Jacob the farm when they died, because he was the oldest. But they also had sense enough to leave my pa some of the nice furniture and some horses and cattle. If it hadn't been for that…" her voice trailed away. If it hadn't been for that, her parents might still be alive.

Jacob's slaves, but still alive.

"It wouldn't have been much of a life," Cassidy said, sensing her thoughts. "They had to take a chance or they'd have died of hopelessness long before their time."

"I…know," she said softly. "Yet it hurts to know they never had a chance to find that dream."

"What happened to the uncle?" Wes asked to change the subject, and hopefully erase the sadness in Abby's eyes.

"He must have sold the farm and came west, after we did." She hated to think of Uncle Jacob being anywhere near. "….He's been in the mountains looking for me."

Cassidy stopped eating. "He knows you're alive?"

"I don't know how, but he does. Maybe because of my red hair. That's one of the reasons I was afraid to stay with the Kumeyaay any longer. He's offered a large reward."

"Would he come here?" Cassidy asked.

Abby gave a nod. "He would go to the gates of hell itself to get what he wanted," she said bitterly, then suddenly her face brightened. "But now that I am legally married, he cannot disrespect the law of God that united us."

Cassidy's nod told her he knew the type. It also gave him a new insight as to why this lovely creature had been willing to become his woman and leave her Indian home. She was no longer safe there.

"Any idea where he is now?" Wes asked, knowing how Cassidy's mind worked.

"I hear he has a place near Temecula."

Cassidy gave Wes a shrewd look. "I think its best we take care of that before it becomes a problem. We'll send word with the next group that comes through. We'll let Uncle Jacob know where Abby is. We want his mind settled as to the fact she's being taken care of." He turned to Abby. "That sound all right with you?"

Abby gulped, and after several moment's hesitation she nodded. Perhaps it was better to face Uncle Jacob, she had no doubt he would come to see for himself. This way she wouldn't worry about her Indian family and about Jacob's searching.

After supper Abby did the washing up from the bucket of water Wes brought in. While she was doing that, the two men went to check on the stock even though it was after dark.

Cassidy drank in the scents of the desert willow that wafted in the night breeze. He liked this place. It was the only home he wanted right now. "Been quiet while I was gone?" he asked.

"Yep," Wes replied as his keen gaze scanned the dark shadows around them. "A few wagon trains, some men on horseback...the usual. One of them brought a message that young Butterfield will be here next week. There's more than one well to dig out by Carrizo Canyon, and a couple of stations to complete. If he doesn't ride herd on those Mexicans he hired they don't get much done."

"Seen any Indians?"

"Nope. I kept a sharp eye out. Questioned anyone who came thru, even scouted the area a few times while I was hunting but didn't see any sign."

"Good." Cassidy gave a sigh. "I don't expect that to last though. Once the station is stocked with the Butterfield horses and mules we'll be too much of a temptation to resist."

Wes glanced back toward the station. "You found yourself a right proper bride. She'll be able to stand this life without much bother if she lived all this time with the Indians."

Cassidy nodded thoughtfully. "Not only that, they taught her things they don't usually teach a squaw. She knows about hunting, tracking and surviving in the desert."

"And she's right purty too." Wes grew serious. "That could be a problem with some of the riff raff that comes thru here. You'd better warn her to keep clear of the menfolk, and teach her to shoot first thing."

"I won't be having much time for that," Cassidy said as they strode down to the spring. A short distance away the horses stamped and snorted in the corral. From the distant hills came the eerie wail of a coyote. A moment later its cry was answered, the sounds blending together like restless spirits calling in the night. "I don't suppose you could stay around for a time. You're a crack shot. You could teach her."

Wes was silent for a moment. Cassidy half expected him to refuse. Yet, he sensed the man had taken a liking to his wife. Not in the sense that he was interested in her for himself, but in the fact she could accept this hard life. He was interested in her knowledge about the Indian's ways. Knowledge he could use.

"It might be," Cassidy went on. "You could teach her more than how to shoot. She ain't had any learnin' since she was about ten. No doubt she's forgotten how to read and write. It would be a big help if she learned something about keeping accounts."

"Well now," Wes conceded. "It might be right interesting to see if she wants to learn. Maybe that little lady and I can teach each other."

Cassidy's grin was full of satisfaction. "I had a hunch you'd want to know what she learned from the Indians."

Peter Wesley remained outside long after Cassidy had gone in. Through the cracks in the wooden shutters of Cassidy's bedroom he could see the flicker of a lamp. It would be strange having a woman at Seven Springs, especially one so pretty. He knew he would stay to teach her the things Cassidy couldn't. He had to make her wary of the men who came through, yet she must be very alert already from living with the Kumeyaay. There were men who roamed the hills who would take advantage of any Indian woman they found alone.

Abby Cassidy wouldn't be like a city woman, not gentle and sweet like his Sarah had been. The memory was still burned in his brain. There were nights he was certain he saw her in the moonlight, wearing her white flowing wedding gown. From habit, his gaze scanned the brush. He came out almost every night looking for her.

He tried to tell himself it was only because he enjoyed being outdoors, that he enjoyed the cool night air. But in the moments he was honest with himself, he knew why he stayed, living off the land or the supplies Cassidy paid him for his work. He would never leave Sarah out here alone.

15

A bby soon settled into life at Seven Springs. Until the stage-coaches began their weekly stops she had freedom to roam the area. Some days Wes went with her. She found him an efficient hunting companion, but he had much to learn. She showed him how to set snares for the rabbits and quail. There was wood from the hard ironwood to form bows and lots of arrow weed around the springs for arrows.

The area to the southwest of the station was abundant with game. Due to the springs seeping out of the ground, the growth was thick with desert willow, palo verde, and mesquite. She gathered tubers and roots, teaching Wes how to recognize the edible ones. A few of the agave were still in bloom and she had him cut some for cooking, choosing the ones with tender blossoms.

She taught him that mesquite was good for many things, to slake thirst by keeping the mouth moist with the green peas. As they became riper they could be cooked as a vegetable, or dried and ground into a meal. When they dried and turned red, she made a spicy sauce out of them. Horses and other stock would also eat the mesquite beans when no grass was available.

Any savvy trail boss was well aware of that.

Cassidy had accumulated a few chickens over the years, traded by settlers in place of money for needed supplies. Abby often gathered seeds for them to keep them from straying too far during the day. Mostly they foraged on their own, and when night came, they flew high into the mesquite to escape the coyotes and owls. No predator, no matter how hungry, would brave the wicked thorns of the mesquite.

Wes taught Abby how to shoot. It was something she had to learn even though she wasn't eager to do so. There would be times when the station and its stock had to be defended. It was a fact of life she dreaded to experience firsthand. She didn't know if she would be able to view an Indian as an enemy and shoot with intent to kill.

Between Cassidy and Wes she learned to cook the foods they liked, the eggs, which she searched out each day, often suffering the sharp pecks from an irate hen. Wes hollowed out a root cellar near one of the springs where the ground stayed cool under a thick stand of willow.

Here Abby was able to store some of her harvest.

There were days when she hunted alone, days when Wes stayed to help Cassidy with the job of enlarging the corral to hold the Butterfield stock that would soon be arriving. Abby hunted early in the day, using the afternoons to work on her garden and to drag dead mesquite to form a barricade against marauding rabbits and ground squirrels.

One thing the garden would make easier was the setting of snares. She wouldn't have to go into the brush to search out game trails. Outside, not far from the kitchen door she piled rocks to form an outdoor oven. On the hot summer days it would keep the adobe building cooler if she did the cooking outside. Even Cassidy and Wes helped whenever they came across large rocks, carrying them in for Abby to place.

Cassidy had no reason to regret taking Abby for his wife. She worked hard without complaining, needing no urging. She knew what had to be done. In the evening, while Abby mended their clothes, churned butter or wove baskets, Wes would read to them, sometimes from the Bible, sometimes from books he'd brought from the east.

At night Wes continued to make his bed out of doors, even though there was another room inside the station. He preferred the stars over his head, and the song of the coyotes to lull him to sleep. For the first time since he'd lost Sarah he felt a measure of peace.

Abby had been at Seven Springs for over two weeks before the first wagon train came in. Her heart went out to the weary, exhausted families and their equally exhausted stock. For the evening meal she cooked chicken, beans and tortillas, along with the last stalks of blooming agave.

She brewed tea the way the Indians did and the women especially were appreciative of having something other than strong coffee. To those women, she showed them how to gather the tender leaves of sage, and how to dry it. Those who wanted to sample Abby's cooking were charged a small amount. Many of them eager to eat someone else's cooking for a change.

One of the older ladies sat on the drooping branch of an ancient mesquite behind the station. Abby had been aware of the woman's gaze on her, an unspoken appreciation of her competence.

The woman's dress was faded and bore many patches. Her shoes were almost worn through and were stuffed with rags. Her smile, though weary, was friendly. Her blue eyes showed an easy humor and pleasant disposition. When Abby was finally able to sit down to eat, she chose a spot by her and was welcomed with a smile.

"Mrs. Cassidy, I'm Sally Borchard, I'd be pleased if you'd sit a spell. I do get tired of the same old faces day after day."

Abby smiled warmly. "I remember what it was like," she said, then went on quickly before the woman had a chance to ask questions. "Has Mr. Borchard eaten yet?"

"He'll be eating at the camp tonight. He's taking Mr. Cassidy to look at some of our sick stock. I surely thought we'd lose them all before we got here. As it is, we had to leave some of them on the trail, plumb wore out."

Abby's sympathy was with the poor animals who had to bear the burden of pulling the wagons. "It's hard on man and beast," Abby said softly, cutting into the tender stewed chicken as she spoke.

"We purely were glad to see this patch of green," Sally went on. "We've been weeks in some of the most desolate land I've ever seen. I never believed all the stories we heard. Now I see they weren't exaggerating at all. I could cry when I think of the fine pieces of furniture we had to dump along the way. Our poor animals would have died for sure if we hadn't lightened their load."

"I feel for the poor overworked animals," Abby said.

"Have you been at Seven Springs long?"

"No, only a few weeks."

"Ah, a bride," the woman cooed. "You're very young to be living out here without other women around."

"I don't mind. I like it here. It's an abundant place."

"You couldn't prove that by me. I'm just glad to have the desert behind us. I hear we'll soon be in the mountains."

"Yes," Abby nodded. "In a few days. How long will you be stopping here?"

"I imagine for a few days. Our stock needs to forage on good grass. There have been too many days when they went without any food at all, and sometimes without water."

"They'll be able to gather their strength here," Abby said. "And so will you."

Mrs. Borchard gave a weary smile. "My husband had no idea what he was letting us in for when he planned this trip. He has visions of making a strike in the gold fields. I've tried to tell him the gold strike has been over for years, and he's a bit old for that anyway, but he won't listen. He's tired of grubbing on the land for a bare subsistence."

Abby's heart went out to the woman. She had heard stories about the gold fields. Knew of men who had caught gold fever which blinded them to everything else.

"Did your folks come out for the gold?" Mrs. Borchard asked.

Abby had to still the stab of pain the question brought, hoping the woman wouldn't notice her smile had lost much of its brightness. "I think my father had that in the back of his mind, even though he told us we were coming here to farm. We lived in Illinois, the southern part. Where are you from?" she asked to head off any more questions about her family.

"From Nebraska. Miles and miles of nothing. Not a mountain to be seen. Originally we lived in New York. We raised part of our family there and part of it on a farm in Nebraska. It was a hard life. Now that we're getting older my husband would like to take it easier." She gave a soft sigh. "I don't think he has any idea of what's ahead for us in the gold fields. He only hears the stories of the rich strikes, not the ones of disease, claim jumpers, or the ones who come away disillusioned and dead broke."

Abby didn't know what comfort to offer the woman. As she finished her meal, two more people came to see if there was food left. There was just enough. Cassidy suddenly appeared to collect their money. It was something Abby had trouble getting used to. Food was for everyone. It was there to gather, to share. But obviously it was different among whites, so she reserved judgment.

While the settlers camped at the springs Abby made friends with some of the women by treating sores and coughs with her collection of herbs. She didn't bother to tell them where she had gained the knowledge, and the grateful women never asked. Sally Borchard treated her like a daughter, and Sally was the first white woman Abby had been around in six years. She was a home body, a woman used to mothering. In some ways, Sally reminded her of her mother.

On the last night of their stay, the settlers put on a farewell party, cooking over a large open fire, inviting the Cassidy's to join in. Wes had disappeared as soon as he realized how long the settlers would be there. Cassidy told Abby to get used to it. She already was. It was the Indian way. In Kumeyaay there was no word for "goodbye".

Abby sat beside Sally on a log that had been dragged there for seating around the fire.

She ate from a tin plate of venison stew and greens, a pleasant change from her own cooking.

Across the clearing a man with a guitar was singing songs for the children. It seemed so familiar Abby had to blink back tears. She would miss having the people around, and most of all she would miss Sally. The woman had taught her how to bake bread, and had given her a starter for sourdough.

Sally had also taught her how to sew with tiny stitches, how to mend clothes so that it barely showed. These were things her own mother would have taught her had she lived. A fact that aroused Sally's curiosity.

"I'm surprised, child, that your mother didn't teach you these things. My girls knew how by the time they were nine and ten."

Abby gave a low sigh of regret. "I'm sure she would have if she had lived."

Immediately a look of concern came into Sally's eyes. "Oh child, I had no idea...you didn't mention..." Her voice trailed off uncertainly.

"I know," Abby acknowledged. "I still find it difficult to talk about." She felt Sally's concern, the questions she was too polite to ask. "She and my father never had the chance to realize their dream. They didn't even make it this far."

She felt the woman's start of surprise as she went on, her voice low with remembered pain, with visions and scents of death that would never leave her. "We were attacked by Indians shortly after we crossed the Colorado River at Yuma Crossing. I'm not sure, not even after all this time, but I might have been the only survivor...though I think some of the women and children were carried off."

"Oh, my dear child!" There was genuine distress in Sally's voice. "How terrible for you. I remember that area very well, and the stories our trail boss told of the tragedy there. How did you survive out there alone?"

"I was lucky," Abby said, lost in memories. She felt certain enough of their friendship to tell her the rest of the story. "A band of Indians found me. They took me to live with them, took care of me."

Sally reacted with an involuntary withdrawal Abby didn't notice. Nor did she see the look of horror come into the older woman's eyes.

"They became my family. I stayed with them until Cass, Mr. Cassidy found me there and married me."

"You lived with savages?" Her voice ended in a squeak of outrage.

Abby gave a soft laugh, not realizing the reason for Sally's reaction. "No, they weren't savages. They were loving and kind…" She broke off then Sally rose abruptly, spilling the tin plate on her lap.

"How can you defend murderers?" the woman demanded.

For the first time Abby looked into Sally's eyes to see the disgust there. Her own smile didn't waver, though it took considerable effort not to wilt in the face of the woman's scorn.

"They weren't the ones who attacked the wagons. These people…"

"…Are still savages!" Sally cut in sharply. "Heathens! How could you live with them like a…like a squaw?" Sally spat the word as if it were the worst fate imaginable. "I hear they treat their women terrible, that they share them with anyone who comes into camp!"

The older woman's eyes filled with disgust and loathing. "You're nothing but a squaw! And here I spent all this time a'tryin' to be your friend!" Sally stalked away, her back rigid with anger, leaving Abby stunned. She couldn't believe the woman who had befriended her could change so quickly.

Cassidy had tried to warn her, so had Vicenta Carrillo and Wes. Indians were the terror of the wagon trains. People didn't like to be reminded that their lives could be snuffed out at the whim of savages, or be taken captive to suffer an even more hideous fate.

Abby's eyes filled with hurt and sadness as she watched Sally join a group, speaking rapidly, her hands moving in quick agitated gestures. Abby didn't need to hear what was said, the sharp stares the others directed her way made it abundantly clear she was no longer welcome in their camp. Her appetite gone, Abby set her plate down on the log and started back to the station, suddenly feeling depressed and alone. They didn't understand. Sally had some ridiculous ideas about how Indians behaved. Sharing women! How stupid! Maybe some tribes did, but certainly not the Kumeyaay. It was clear that Sally would never listen to the truth, and Abby had just learned a very painful lesson. One she would never repeat.

The music and dancing went on until well into the night. Abby didn't know where Cassidy was. Lonely and bored she watched the settlers from outside the station, her heart aching with the knowledge she was suddenly an outcast. She had been stupid to trust Sally. Stupid to think she could overcome the prejudice.

"They're sure whoopin' it up, ain't they?" The male voice startled Abby. She turned to see a man she'd noticed around the wagons for the past few days, one who was always grumbling about the work, yet his wife was the only one Abby ever saw doing any.

He was standing at the edge of the tall mesquite Abby had taken refuge under. He wasn't a man she wanted to talk to. The look in his eyes was shifty, not friendly.

"Why aren't you dancing, Mr. Burke?" she asked, keeping her voice cool.

His chuckle didn't do anything to ease her mind. It was almost a sneer. "I ain't much for dancin'. My wife, she can dance all night. Me? I can think of better things to do."

Abby couldn't see his eyes clearly in the darkness but she was certain what was there none-the-less.

"Seems like Cassidy has better things to do, too." His insinuation had no effect on Abby. She wasn't really interested in what her husband was doing. "He's helping the Pullman's. If it was me, I wouldn't be leavin' a purty lady all alone on a night like this." He stepped closer.

Abby resisted the urge to step back. She knew exactly what was on his mind. "Mr. Burke, my husband wouldn't take kindly to you being here."

"Likes to keep it to hisself, does he?" The man snickered again, a sound that sent a warning shiver up Abby's spine. Her heart began to beat faster. Her gaze darted around the camp to see if her husband was near.

"You'd better go before he comes back," she warned, disappointed not to see him.

"He won't be back for a while. I made sure of that. There's plenty of time for us to get better acquainted."

"That's not likely now is it, Mr. Burke? How can we get better acquainted when you're leaving in the morning?" She decided boldness would be better than an appearance of submission.

He chortled at her humor. "Look," he said, pulling something out of his pocket and moving closer. "I brung you somethin'."

It was a string of beads, the type wagon trains carried for trading with the Indians. Suddenly she realized exactly what he thought and why he was here. Sally's tale had been spread throughout the camp. Anger began to build within her like a slow fire, yet she didn't let it show in her voice.

"Beads?" she scoffed, incredulous, hoping to shame him. "You're offering me beads? For what, Mr. Burke?"

He fidgeted, licking his lips at her boldness. "Come on, woman, you ain't that dumb. What did the bucks offer you? Or did you just do it for free?" Abby could see he was losing patience.

With a soft laugh that showed anything but amusement, she felt Burke take a step back at the harsh sound of it. "You have the wrong idea."

His answering snicker was an attempt to bolster his courage. He moved closer again. Abby was aware of the press of her knife strapped to her leg. Her heart beating loudly in her chest she realized this man wasn't going to be distracted easily.

16

Burke's thumbs hooked in his belt as he took another swaggering step closer. "I hear lots of tales 'bout bucks sharin' their women."

"Did you ask Mr. Cassidy how he feels about it?" she asked coldly.

"He ain't here right now, is he? So I figure we can do us a little business and he's none the wiser."

"And Mrs. Burke? How does she feel about it? Does she like to share?"

He found that funny, laughing out loud at first then muffling the sound behind his hand so as not to attract attention. "She may not know it," he chortled, shoulders shaking with laughter. "But she shares. A man needs a change now and again. Out here that ain't easy. You're just what I been lookin' fer. You'll look right purty in these."

He held out the beads toward her. Abby yanked them out of his hand, threw them on the ground and spat on them. "I spit on your beads!"

"Have it your way," he said, his massive hands reaching out to draw her against him.

Abby slapped his hands away. "You'd best leave now, Mr. Burke while you're still able to walk away. Since you've heard stories about Indians you'll know they're fond of taking scalps.

That thick hair of yours would look mighty good on the center pole of a lodge."

Burke's hand went instantly to his hair to run a hand over it, she could see he was vain about it. "I like my hair right where it is." But she could see that she'd made him uneasy.

"There's still desert between here and the mountains, Mr. Burke. That is where my Indian family lives. One word from me…" Her gaze fastened itself on his hair, as if admiring it.

He hesitated then decided not to believe her. "Cassidy bought you from them, they don't want no part of you. What do you want since you don't want my beads? A looking glass? A blanket? I can get those."

"From your wife, you mean. Will you tell her what they're for or will you sneak them from the wagon?"

From his guilty look Abby knew that was exactly what he would have done. But he took her words as acceptance of the price. He came closer, reaching out to pull her against him.

Abby reacted swiftly, her hand snaking down to her leg in a practiced movement. The sharp blade of her knife glinted in the moonlight, the point pressed against Burke's throat. He froze as he felt it prick his skin. "Hey!"

"You come any closer, Mr. Burke, and you'll get your throat cut. That's another Indian trick, you know." Purposely she fed his fears. "First we cut a man's throat, then while he's lying there, bleeding, we take his scalp. I'm beginning to fancy yours."

"Ouch! Be careful with that! It's sharp!" he whined, afraid to move, his eyes large as saucers.

"I assure you, it's very sharp. It's a good thing you didn't open your pants, Mr. Burke," she lied outrageously, trying to keep from smiling. "Squaws take more than scalps."

As the words sank in Abby could feel his stunned horror, his gasp of fear. With a cry he whirled and ran into the darkness, leaving Abby standing there chuckling to herself.

"Nice work." The voice was so close it startled Abby, bringing the tip of her blade up to face the new danger. Neither she nor Burke had heard the man's approach. "I was about to step in but I see it wasn't necessary. That ought to keep his pants buttoned for a while."

Abby could make out the shadow of the stranger standing at the corner of the building. From the broad expanse of his shoulders, his lean wiry build, she knew he wasn't one of the settlers. His hat was pushed back on his head at a jaunty angle revealing masses of thick dark hair. She couldn't see its color. And while most men in this wild country grew beards, this man was clean shaven, showing only a one day growth of dark stubble.

His stance told her he was very sure of himself. Strangely she wasn't afraid. She could feel his amusement at her handling of Burke. She was embarrassed that he'd heard her crude threat.

"Where did you come from?" was all she could think to ask.

"I just rode in. My horse is tied out front. I guess with all the noise in the camp yonder no one heard me. I'm John Jay Butterfield. Who might you be?"

She could feel his gaze trying to bore into the shadows to see her clearly. Deciding she wasn't afraid of this man she returned her knife to its sheath, giving him a quick flash of her leg, not aware his night vision was every bit as sharp as her own. "I'm Abby Cassidy," she said curious about him as well. "We had word you were coming. I'll see to your horse."

She started for the front of the building, John Jay following.

"I take care of my own pony," he said, then with an amused chuckle. "So old Cassidy finally got himself a wife."

Abby didn't comment. She was willing to care for his horse but the man untied his gelding and led it toward the corral. In the moonlight, Abby got a better look at him. Something about him was very elemental, very male. He moved with an easy assurance, a light pantherish tread that made her aware she'd never seen a man quite like him before. The shivery awareness he created inside her was not something she welcomed. She didn't want to feel anything for this arrogant stranger.

But his face was nice to look at. The color of his eyes was hidden by the darkness, but they were widely spaced on either side of a long, narrow nose. His mouth was wide also, and looked as if he laughed often. He seemed much at home in the wilderness outpost of Seven Springs.

She knew John Jay was taking her measure too, noting how her hair was pulled back into a bun at the back of her neck. It was cooler worn that way, braids no longer seemed appropriate. The fiery hue was subdued by the pale moonlight leaving him to guess at its true color. She felt also the touch of his gaze as it swept her from head to toe, not with the same interest Burke had shown, but merely the interest of a man when he met a woman for the first time.

"You seem awfully young to be living in a place like this," John Jay said. "But from what I just saw you can take care of yourself. How did you learn that?"

Abby was feeling defiant enough that she didn't want to make excuses, didn't want to hide what she was. "From the Indians, Mr. Butterfield. I lived with them for six years, as part of a family," she said firmly. "Not as a man's squaw, as Mr. Burke chose to believe."

To her surprise Butterfield gave a low, amused laugh. "That's why you talked about scalps."

"That was only to scare him. The tribe I was with was peaceful. They didn't take scalps, they don't even count coup on their enemies. They live simply but they protect what is theirs."

"Which tribe?" he asked.

"The Kumeyaay."

"Yes, I know of them. You must not have lived very far from here."

"In the winter we camped here in the desert. We avoided the white man's road though, and the chance of meeting travelers. In the summer we lived in the mountains." She motioned toward the hills visible in the distance, even on this bright, moonlit night.

"Where's your husband?" John Jay asked as he stopped at the corral and began to unsaddle his horse.

"Burke said he's helping one of the families."

John Jay chuckled again at the thought of how she'd handled the man. "Is there any food left?" he asked, his voice sounding weary. "I've been riding all day to get here by nightfall. I missed it by a bit but I need to talk to your husband." Even to Abby that sounded strange to her; her husband.

"There's food down at the camp," she said motioning to where the music and the dancing was still going on. Pots were visible over the fire.

Her stance told John Jay her feelings about the people, his gaze shifted to her briefly, noting she made no motion toward the camp. He rubbed his horse down with the saddle blanket for several minutes then turned him into the corral. The hungry animal made straight for the grass Cassidy had tossed in earlier.

"Why don't you introduce me," he suggested.

Abby's reaction told him as much as her words. She drew back instinctively. "I'm not welcome there."

"Why not?" he asked, then suddenly he knew. "Because you lived with the Kumeyaay?"

She liked the way he named the tribe without condemnation in his tone. She merely nodded. John Jay gave a cluck of disgust. "They've been hearing too many stories, most of which becomes more exaggerated with each telling."

"Perhaps they have good reason to be afraid," Abby said. "My parents died in an Indian attack. When the Kumeyaay took me in I was scared to death of them. Afraid they'd do to me all the awful things I'd heard about. It was only by living with them that I learned different."

John Jay was silent for a moment, puzzling over the unusual creature Cassidy had brought to Seven Springs. She would survive well in this setting that could destroy a woman with less inner fiber. She was enough woman to know how to handle a man like Burke,

but child enough to be hurt by the settlers prejudice. He had a no-
tion to take her down there with him and dare them to do anything
about it. Common sense prevailed. He hadn't the right.

"Yeah," he said softly. "These past months that I've worked here
in the desert I've learned a lot about the local Indians. I learned to
be wary of the Yuma's and the Kawea's. The Kumeyaay and their
related tribes have always been known for their friendliness."

"You go on down to get something to eat, Mr. Butterfield. I'll
see to your gear," Abby said, trying to tell herself it didn't matter
what the others thought of her. "Do you want to sleep inside?"

He nodded. "I always take the extra room if it's available. Even
that makeshift bed is better than sleeping on the ground every
night."

Abby restrained the impulse to giggle. The bed, with its leather
straps, creaked and groaned as if protesting every move when she
kneeled on it to make it up. It was rigid too, but not so much as the
ground. Even the Indians used branches, leaves, or pine needles
under their fiber mats.

He moved off as silently as he'd arrived. Abby watched him,
never having seen a white man move that way. She would like to
take him to meet her Indian family, see how he reacted to them.
Her thoughts died away. Whatever was she thinking? John Jay was a
stranger. She had no business going anywhere with him.

A picture of Cassidy flashed into her mind. It was too soon to
know what she thought of her husband. She was slow to give him
her total trust, as if she were withholding judgment until she knew
him better. He treated her well enough, though he was quick to give
orders about what she need to do during the day. In spite of that, he
allowed her time to hunt and tend her garden.

The solitude of the wilderness around Seven Springs was more
of a home to her than the adobe building. She wasn't used to being
enclosed, or having someone so close beside her when she slept.
The intimate side of marriage caused her thoughts to shy away. It
was something she submitted to. Cassidy found pleasure in it so she

must consider it just another of her chores. A price she must pay for returning to the white world.

She watched the way John Jay was welcomed by the settlers, the respect he was shown. One of the women rushed to prepare him a plate of food. Abby could see that she, too, was affected by the man's handsome face, his bold masculine demeanor. Just watching him made her own heart beat faster with strange longings, feelings that reminded her of how she felt whenever Night Wolf was near. Perhaps any handsome man would make her feel that way. Cassidy didn't. Wesley didn't. Nor had any of the settlers passing through. It was a puzzle. One she hoped to eventually solve.

Cassidy joined the group around John Jay, giving Abby a chance to compare them. Cassidy was a big man, taller. John Jay was leaner, with wide shoulders that tapered to narrow hips. Something in the way he carried himself, the way he wore his gun low on his hip, gave the feeling he would make a formidable enemy. Cassidy was a bull, John Jay a stallion. That was the closest comparison she could make.

Realizing what she was doing Abby turned away. She had no right to be thinking of John Jay Butterfield, or any other man. She had pledged herself to Cassidy and she would honor her vows. She was beyond the point of maidenly day dreams. Cassidy was her reality.

John Jay wasn't around much during the following days. He rode out early in the morning, often without breakfast. If he wasn't back by supper she saved food for him. When he did ride in he would be hot and tired. Sometimes he would talk with Cassidy about the stage line which would soon be running through Seven Springs four times a week.

Two coaches would be heading west, two would be heading east. From the kitchen Abby listened to their talk, trying to imagine what the sudden influx of people would be like.

Since Seven Springs was the largest of the stations in the area, it would offer meals to passengers, or food to take along. Butterfield suggested the prices for their services but the final word would be Cassidy's.

Since Abby arrived at Seven Springs there were two men she sometimes saw Cassidy ride out to meet, away from the station. They never came close enough for her to get a good look at them. Cassidy never brought them in. They looked to be Mexican, and their gaze, whenever Abby found them staring her way gave her an uncomfortable feeling of familiarity.

After a wagon train had moved on from the springs, about a week and a half after John Jay's arrival, Abby was out on her early morning hunt when she saw her husband by the farthest spring from the station, in earnest conversation with the same two men. One was sitting a horse, the other was driving a freight wagon of a type that looked lighter in weight than the usual ones that brought Cassidy's supplies from San Diego. Abby halted in the brush to watch, too far away to hear the conversation.

As always before, after their talk, the men headed east along the wagon road. She could only wonder what the purpose was. She never questioned her husband. Often times he was silent, uncommunicative. It was a way she was used to from the Indians and didn't expect anything else.

Two days following the visit from the two strangers, Abby was hunting in the hills south of the station. It had been quite some time since she'd been able to bring down a deer, which was her quarry today. She'd ridden her horse to the base of a hill, leaving her tied, concealed in the mesquite but with a patch of grass to graze on. If she was successful, she would need the horse to carry the deer.

Moving silently through the brush she knew she was nearing a rarely used trail. It was wide enough for a wagon, and from its direction she guessed it would end up in San Diego. In the times she'd hunted, she'd seen signs of someone using the trail, but she suspected few people knew of it. The sound of a wagon first startled her, then sent her into cover.

Though she could easily have slipped away, she was curious, and wasn't surprised when she saw it was the two Mexicans, both riding on the wagon, leading a horse behind. Two mules, looking overworked, pulled the laden wagon. Now she recognized the two men, they were the same two who had tried to rape Moyla. Men who had reason to hate her. No wonder their stares had bothered her. But what dealings did they have with Cassidy?

Abby found their load of furniture unusual. Where would it come from out here? The only thing in the direction they came from was the immigrant trail. Then she remembered Sally Borchard telling her about dumping furniture along the way. It was just possible that these men went back along the trail to pick up what had been discarded. And quite probably they were taking it to San Diego to sell, making a profit from the misfortune of others.

The fascination of the white man for money puzzled her. They all seemed to want it. Conversations were often dominated by talk of ways to make more money, especially digging for gold. If it was really that important, if Abby would need it to live in the white world, then she would need to have some of her own. Whatever Cassidy took in he kept hidden, even from her. He told her women didn't need money, their men took care of them.

Sally had mentioned she kept a little money hidden from her husband. Perhaps all women did. It only made sense. Men wanted absolute control over their women, she had seen the same thing among the Indians. The man was to be obeyed.

If the two Mexicans were doing as Abby suspected, why had they been talking to her husband? Why hadn't he told her about them? From now on, she needed to be doubly wary.

When the wagon was gone, Abby resumed her hunt by moving out ahead of it. Deer would hear it coming and run away. All she had to do was find a spot and wait.

Her arrow caught a large buck square on target behind the shoulder. He walked a short distance before he fell. With a quick slash of her sharp blade she dispatched him.

"Thank you for your meat, brother," she said in the Indian way, feeling regret for taking the life of so magnificent a creature.

He was much too heavy to carry so she went for her horse, hoping no scavengers would get to the meat before she did.

On her way back to the station, Abby purposely rode through the area where Cassidy's cattle grazed. This time she saw several cows and a mule that looked to be in terrible shape. They were skinny, exhausted, and listless. They barely even looked up as she rode by. Each bore a different brand.

Frowning, she realized that a great many of Cassidy's stock bore different brands. Another curious fact to store away.

The rest of the day was spent skinning out the deer and cutting the meat for stew, for roasts, and for drying. Cassidy was helping John Jay digging a well down the trail, so she wasn't expecting him back until late. She put a chunk of venison in her outside oven to roast, then went back to cleaning the hide for drying.

For the next week, activity around the station increased as men arrived to help with enlarging the corral for the Butterfield horses. Abby worked her garden, knowing she would need fresh vegetables for the passenger's meals.

John Jay tried to be every place at once. There were stations all along the desert corridor that had to be staffed with men, horses, supplies and equipment. Abby didn't see how the Butterfield Overland Mail could meet its September deadline. There was still so much to do.

There were lines of fatigue on John Jay's face when Abby served him venison that evening. His eyes brightened when he looked at her, but soon he was deep in conversation with Cassidy and a man named Weston who would be the superintendent for this stretch of the road.

"They're still working on the well out by Carrizo Canyon," John Jay said. "It's the only one we're having a problem with. The water is a lot deeper than we expected, but by the time I come through here on that first coach, you should have everything under control."

Westin nodded. He was a chunky man with a sprinkling of gray in his brown hair. His sideburns were thick mutton chops, his gaze intense. "Don't you worry none, John Jay, when you come through everything here will be ready."

"I hate to leave before it's completed," John Jay said with a weary shake of his head. "But if I don't leave now my father will be wondering what happened, and I sure don't want to miss out on that first coach.

"You ain't goin' to drive it all the way to San Francisco, are you?" Cassidy asked.

John Jay gave a crooked smile and a shake of his head. "Heck no, I'll drive the first leg, when all the dignitaries are on board. They'll get off at Fort Smith, Arkansas. From then on we'll have men waiting who know their section of the road, since we'll be running at night too. In places the road is so hard to see we need men who know the way. I can take over when needed. But I will be on board all the way."

"Yeah," Westin agreed. "If one of the drivers doesn't show up there's got to be someone to keep the mail on time."

"Twenty-four days," Cassidy said. "It seems impossible to take that ox-bow route from Tipton, Missouri all the way to San Francisco in that short a time. Especially when there's all sorts of things that can happen."

John Jay's look told Abby he'd already thought of that. "I know it sounds impossible, but if anyone can bring this thing off it's my father. He's got more guts, more determination than any ten men I've ever known. There's no way I'm going to let him lose this contract. We've poured a pile of money and nearly a year of hard work getting ready for that first coach to roll. By damn, it'll make it through in less than twenty four days and I'll be on board to see that it does."

Abby felt a glow of pride at his determination until she realized she had no right to feel that way. With a sudden need to be alone with her thoughts, she used the excuse of clearing the table. Tomorrow John Jay would ride out. She wouldn't see him again until the first coach rolled through. And after that….she might never see him again.

As she washed the dishes she could still hear the men's voices, smell the scent of cigar smoke. She wasn't even aware of what she was doing, her senses tuned to the sound of John Jay's voice. She'd come to like his presence here. He seemed a part of Seven Springs. Lately there had been so many men, all working on the road. Things were going to be quiet again when they completed their work.

Come to think of it, she hadn't seen Wes since the men had been in the area. She hoped he was all right. But thoughts of Wes couldn't hold her attention for long. She saw only sky blue eyes that had a way of reaching deep inside her, a bold male walk that made her want to stare, a fact that made her cautious lest her husband see her watching another man.

She'd already seen Cassidy set several men straight who tried to get friendly with her. And even though she was aware that John Jay's gaze followed her, he didn't try to catch her alone as some of the men did. He didn't try to talk to her behind Cassidy's back. She admired him for that even as she perversely wished he would.

That night she lay awake long after Cassidy's snores filled their room, thinking of John Jay in the other bedroom, thinking how she wanted to go to him, to slide into his bed beside him. Just thinking about his hands on her body sent shivers of need surging through her. She couldn't imagine how his touch would be different from her husbands, yet, somehow she knew it would be.

Instead of feeling the numbness she felt when Cassidy made love to her, perhaps she would find the pleasure the Indian women spoke of. But it was too late to be thinking of such things. She was married and she would keep her bargain with Cassidy.

17

John Jay lay on the hard bed, hands under his head, staring up at the ceiling. His mind had been filled too often lately with thoughts of the flame-haired young woman who was Cassidy's wife.

He wasn't a man to make a move on another man's woman but something about Abby wouldn't allow him to be indifferent to her. He was too aware of the way her small breasts moved under her very proper dresses, aware of the way the wind would mold the skirt against her slender form. It almost made him groan aloud. Her skin had darkened from years of living outdoors. She was strong, her body would feel firm under his questing hands. It drove him crazy to think of her responding to Cassidy's touch, of her feverish passion given to another man.

He had no right to think of her like that. It was a good thing he would be leaving in the morning, a good thing he wouldn't be seeing Abby every day. He wouldn't see her again until the first coach rolled in, yet he knew he would be counting every mile along the way. He needed sleep, yet dreaded its coming.

Too often his dreams included a flame-haired woman who taunted him with her youth and beauty, and the promise of the lovely woman she would one day become. He could picture her dressed in an exquisite gown of satin and lace. He wanted to give her that, to show her this great land, his father's home in Utica New York. His body hardened, telling him what he most wanted to give her. With a low groan he closed his eyes, willing his body to relax and forget the charms of the half-savage woman child. She was beyond his reach.

In a brief moment of insanity he contemplated asking Abby to come with him, to leave Cassidy and this wilderness behind. He could picture her riding out with him, a smile of anticipation on her lips. Then he could picture Cassidy and the rage he'd seen in the man's eyes only a few times. John Jay liked the man. Technically he was an employee of the Butterfield Overland Mail. He was on the payroll. Not only that, there was no way he would steal another man's wife.

It took a moment before the outside sounds penetrated his thoughts. He'd left the shutter of his window open slightly to allow the cool air to circulate. He became aware of horses snorting and stamping. Something was out there, a big cat perhaps, but another possibility was Indians.

Quickly he pulled on his pants and boots, strapped on his gun and grabbed the rifle standing in the corner.

Abby nudged Cassidy awake. He knew from her touch to be silent. He listened, and he heard it too. Something was bothering the horses. In an instant he was up and dressed. He strapped on his gun, grabbed his rifle and went into the kitchen so he could slip out the door that would be in shadow. He found John Jay in the kitchen with the same idea. Silently Cassidy opened the door and they slipped into the darkness.

There was no moon. Staying in the shadow of the station they worked their way around the corner and along the front of the building. Their attention was focused on the farthest corner of the corral. Cassidy's sharp eyes picked out a man, most likely an Indian, trying to take the fence apart.

When he raised his rifle John Jay could see he was aiming over the man's head. To aim lower would risk hitting one of the horses.

Cassidy squeezed the trigger, sending a bullet just over the man's head. Something stirred from the side of the building nearby. John Jay turned in time to meet the attack of an Indian who had been standing watch next to the building to warn the others if the white men awakened.

In pure reflex John Jay swung the butt of his rifle, catching the man across the face. A knife dropped to the ground as the man was hurled away with the force of the blow. As John Jay swung the business end of the rifle around, the intruder scrambled to his feet and dashed into the shadows. There were shouts as the Indians scrambled for their horses. Cassidy and John Jay fired over their heads just to keep them running.

Both men were panting from the force of the adrenalin that was coursing through them, and both gave a start when Abby came up between them, a rifle in her hand. She'd seen the last part of the skirmish.

"Any one hurt?" she asked.

John Jay stooped to pick up a wickedly sharp, long, bladed knife. "No, only scared out of three years growth. Us and them."

"Let's go see what they did to the corral," Cassidy said.

Abby kept watch, following the two men. Her keen ears listening for the sounds of movement in the brush, her eyes watching for movement in the shadows. Her senses told her the riders were gone, yet she didn't relax her vigil. The two men were vulnerable by the corral.

They heard shouts from the men camping by the springs, running to see if help was needed. Abby welcomed their presence to protect her husband and John Jay.

The horses were quieting after the scare of gunfire. They milled around, but their snorts were no longer of fear. She was aware of the men examining the fence where the Indians had been trying to tear it down, but she didn't shift her attention from keeping watch.

"We got here just in time," she heard Cassidy say. "They had this rope tied on to pull the fence down. Another minute and we'd have been too late."

"Damn!" John Jay swore. "It's starting already. I can see this is going to be one of our biggest problems."

The men from the camp milled around, looking for any further sign of trouble.

"Indians?" one of them asked.

"Yeah," John Jay responded. "They wanted the horses. We ran them off."

"The excitements over, boys," the man called to his companions. "Let's try to get some more sleep. We'll be on the trail before long."

Abby listened to the grumbling of the men. Her vigil relaxed. The Indians wouldn't be back this night, but there was always tomorrow night, or the one after that. Maybe she could set some traps.

It was still dark when Abby slipped from her bed to start a fire in the kitchen. She wanted to send John Jay off with a good breakfast. It might be the last time she would cook for him, though she knew the first coach would be stopping here for a meal. That would be different. There would be others around.

The smell of biscuits soon had Cassidy and John Jay up and dressed. They poured themselves coffee while Abby cooked eggs and stirred the beans. She also prepared tender, thin sliced venison steaks. It was a good thing the men found plenty to talk about, she doubted she could get any words out, feeling unaccountably sad.

Sitting across the table from John Jay, unable to say the things she wanted to say was painful. When she caught his gaze on her she had the feeling he shared her thoughts. They would never be able to spend time like this again. Once the mail run began John Jay Butterfield would be needed elsewhere.

The first streaks of dawn hadn't yet lightened the sky when John Jay walked out of the station. The men who would be riding with him, were already mounted, his own horse saddled and ready.

"Cassidy," John Jay said, shaking hands with the big man. "I'll see you sometime around the end of September. You listen sharp for my horn."

"Don't you worry none, your horses will be ready. And we'll keep them pesky Indians away," Cassidy replied. "You ride safe now."

Abby hung back, watching every movement John Jay made, knowing those memories would have to last her. She memorized the way he wore his hat tipped back on his unruly dark hair, the confident way he sat on his horse. With her eyes closed she could picture the way he moved, his bold walk, the way his wide shoulders stretched his shirt across them. Handling a team of horses from the box of a stagecoach had given him physical strength.

She felt like crying as John Jay mounted and lifted his hand to her, his gaze holding hers for just a moment, as if he too were memorizing her face. She could do no more than raise her hand in return, then he turned away and started down the trail into the desert.

"Go with God," she murmured under her breath. Then she turned away and ran into the heavy brush surrounding the springs, unable to face anyone right now.

18

John Jay luxuriated in the bathtub, trying to soak off the trail dust of a thousand miles. He lay back in the copper tub, a cigar clamped between his teeth, his entire body a mass of aches. Tipton had never been such a welcome sight. It was there he traded his horse for the comfort of the Pacific Railroad for the next hundred miles to St. Louis.

The desk clerk at the Halifax Hotel had wrinkled his nose and looked doubtful about giving him a room until John Jay gave his name. Then things began to happen. Everyone knew of the event about to take place. History was in the making.

John Jay didn't care about history. He sent word to his father at the home of a friend, asking if he could join him for dinner at the hotel. It would be days before John Jay would consider sitting a horse again.

Every time he tried to relax he saw visions of a red-haired vixen he had no business thinking about. Firmly he put such thoughts out of his mind and reached for the large fluffy towel. Stepping out onto the rug he began to dry himself, feeling the hot mugginess of the St. Louis summer coming through the French doors of his suite.

It was a far cry from the privations of the trip from California. Most of the time he had slept on the ground. There had been a settlement or two, a fort where he found a bath, a bed and hot food, and a few completed stage stations.

What he was looking forward to most was a thick, juicy steak, something he hadn't tasted in over two months. Supplies were short along the ox-bow route. Fresh meat was what you could shoot yourself. It made him wonder if President Buchanan knew what he was doing in selecting the Southern route. A lesser man than his father would never have been able to pull this off…to open a mail route through such inhospitable wilderness.

With a towel wrapped around his middle, the cigar between his teeth, John Jay ran a hand over his thick hair, feeling it curling wetly under his fingers. A haircut was definitely in order too. He glanced at the clothes the bellman had just returned to him. They were clean, but that was all he could say for them. They were badly worn, much washed, and not fit for the hotel dining room.

A knock at the door startled him. He didn't know whether to struggle into his clothes or answer as he was. "Who is it?" he called out.

"It's me, Jay Jay."

John Jay sped to the door, yanking it open for his father. The two embraced with spontaneous laughter.

"You look skinny as a wet cat," John Senior observed, looking at John Jay's partially clad body. "I think I can count your ribs."

John Jay's gaze fixed on the valise his father held. "It's great to see you, dad. I've had a long, tiring trip, and I sure hope that bag holds what I think it does."

John Senior tossed the bag on the bed. "I'm sure you can use some of your things, and you can tell me about your trip over dinner."

"It's a good thing you brought that. Everything I have isn't fit to wear in public, let alone in St. Louis."

Within minutes John Jay changed from a scroungy looking cowboy to a handsome man about town. He wore a suit and vest very much like his father's, a shoestring tie and shoes instead of boots.

Combing his unruly curls into place he vowed to get a haircut at the first opportunity, and finally felt ready to face the dining room.

"I hope they have a lot of fresh beef tonight," John Jay said as they left the room, "I'm so hungry I could eat the whole cow!"

John Senior laughed and slapped his son on the shoulder as they headed for the dining room. The resemblance between the two men was obvious. Both were over six feet tall, with the same wide shoulders and the same walk. John Senior was a bit thicker through the middle and his brown hair was turning gray, but he was still a handsome, distinguished looking gentleman. His clothes were expensive, tailor made. His business sense had made him a lot of money. He burned with an inner energy, a trait shared by his son.

John Senior ordered wine plus an appetizer of shrimp creole which he barely touched, leaving it to his ravenous son. He watched with an amused smile as John Jay ate, until he couldn't stand the suspense any longer.

"Well, how goes the road?"

John Jay wiped his mouth with a linen napkin. "There are still some holes," he said. "By that, I mean places where the stations aren't built, others are no more than tents until the new buildings are completed. It's a slow process making adobe as they go."

"Can't they hire more workers?"

John Jay gave a lopsided grin. "There's no one to hire. There's nothing out there, dad. Why congress saw fit to designate that route is beyond me. I can understand them wanting to shift business to their Southern constituents, but most of the way there's no one out there. Many of those stations will be poorly protected and a great temptation to the Indians to avail themselves of our stock."

There was a thoughtful silence. "There's no help for it now. I've already poured almost a million of my own dollars into this project. We've got less than a month to get that first stage out of Tipton. How will the road look then?"

John Jay leaned back in his chair as the waiter removed their plates. "That first run will be a bitch!" he predicted.

"That's why I want you on it, Jay Jay," his father said. "All the way to San Francisco."

"I'm not sure I know the road all that well, but I had Emmitt Morgan with me on the way back this time. He knows that trail better than anyone."

"Too bad we can't afford to hire him, but we have our drivers lined up for each section, ones who know the trail. All you have to do is be there in case of problems."

"Think we'll have many passengers?"

John Senior shook his head. "Not the first trip. Myself and a few dignitaries will ride as far as Fort Smith. Too many people think this is a foolish venture. They're sure we can't pull it off by the deadline. What do you say, Jay Jay?" His father was the only one who called him that. Better that than "Junior".

John Jay's grin widened. There was only one answer he could give his father. "The mail will get through on time, dad, even if I have to walk the entire distance with it."

"Let's hope it doesn't come to that."

As their dinner was served, conversation turned to family matters. Mrs. Butterfield had remained in Utica, New York with the younger children. John Jay's brother Daniel, was presently buying stock and supplies for one section of the line in Texas.

"What's the news in Washington?" John Jay asked when the plates were cleared away and they sipped freshly made coffee.

John Senior gave a snort. "The usual. With the presidential election coming up in two years there's a lot of maneuvering going on. Lincoln and Douglas are debating all over the place for the Senate seat in November. There are some hot issues with the slavery controversy. By the time the presidential election gets here I'm afraid that it's going to boil down to North against the South."

"I heard some pretty strong talk as we came through Texas," John Jay said, accepting the cigar his father handed him. "Especially about seceding from the union if a Northerner is elected."

"That's hot head talk," John Senior said, with a dismissive wave of his cigar before stopping to light it, then his son's. "I doubt it will come to that."

"There's also talk that the main reason Buchanan and the Southerners he represent wanted the overland mail to take this so-called ox-bow route is so the south would be tied directly to California. If the time comes for a split in this country, they want California to be allied with the South."

John Senior nodded as if it didn't surprise him. "Which way do you think California will go?"

For a moment John Jay studied the glowing tip of his cigar, leaning back in his chair and enjoying the pleasant fullness of his stomach, the refined atmosphere of the dining room. It was a decided contrast to the way he'd spent the past ten months. "That's difficult to predict. The people in California come from all over. My guess is they'll be so busy squabbling among themselves over the issues they'll never get around to making a definite commitment."

John Senior began to fill him in on some of the in-fighting in Washington, and John Jay listened with interest. His father was well acquainted in the capitol because of his friendship with President James Buchanan. His gaze drifted to a couple just entering the dining room. The woman was in her twenties, dressed in the latest St. Louis fashion, her hair swept up under her fashionable hat. It was the color of her hair that attracted his attention. It was a deep shade of auburn, not as vibrant as Abby's, lacking the sharp fire that made hers glitter in the sun, or the white streak-like wings at her temples.

Wearing a dress like that one, Abby would capture the attention of everyone in the room. True, she was a bit rough around the edges, but she could learn to be a lady.

Aware that he was staring John Jay dragged his gaze away before her escort took offense. He found his father watching him with a quizzical half smile. "You've been on the road a long time."

John Jay grinned. "It's not that. She...reminds me of someone."

His father's eye lit up. "You've met someone?"

The grin faded into a frown and a faraway look as John Jay shook his head. "She's already married," he said trying to sound unconcerned, but not fooling his father for a minute.

"That's too bad," the older man said as he drew in a long draft of smoke then slowly exhaled it.

John Jay's humor was back as quickly as it vanished. "I don't know if it is or not. I didn't get a chance to know her all that well."

"It's a good thing, or you might have found your hide full of buckshot."

John Jay chuckled. "That's the least her husband would do. He's not someone I'd want to mess with."

The subject switched back to politics but every so often John Jay would find his gaze drawn to the woman across the room. Stuck in the wilderness of Seven Springs, Abby would never see a place such as this, never own a gown such as the young woman was wearing. She would always be half savage, not at all the type of woman he would want. Not one he could be proud of in any setting, or take to New York and introduce to his family.

His father he didn't worry about. He had the feeling John Senior would accept Abby for what she was; a warm-hearted creature who had never known the touch of civilization.

Abruptly John Jay forced his thoughts away from another man's wife. He should know better than to entertain such fancies. He concentrated on his father's words, not knowing the older man had noticed his preoccupation and was concerned.

After dinner they strolled along the main street of St. Louis. Even at this late hour there was plenty of activity. The saloons, the eateries were doing good business. The gas lights along the board walk gave a cheery glow to the night.

The air was humid and warm. A few fans spun lazily over store entrances. The air scented with spices and sea food. A number of black men could be seen going about their business, and much of the economy of St. Louis, and all of Missouri was rooted in free labor. If the plantation owners and business people were suddenly forced to free their slaves and pay wages for the same work, the grandiose life style would change.

As they walked, John Jay told his father about how things were shaping up along the stagecoach route. He'd written letters whenever he could, but often it took more than a month for a letter to make connection with a ship, and another month for the long voyage down the Pacific coast to the Isthmus of Panama. There, the mail and passengers were switched to a train for the forty mile crossing, through the stifling heat of the jungle, to where another ship waited on the Gulf side. From there, they sailed to New Orleans, and the mail made its way up the Mississippi to St. Louis.

The Butterfield Overland Mail promised to deliver mail in twenty-four days. Common opinion said it couldn't be done. The Southern Route was impossible, they said. There was nothing but Indians and rattlesnakes. After spending the past ten months on the road, John Jay knew it was mostly true. Much of the line was in remote areas. He had to hire crews to widen the road, chip away at rocks and select the best river crossings. The first run would be rough, but he couldn't wait to be on it.

It was a challenge he couldn't wait to face, and by damn, he'd bring that first mail into San Francisco in less than twenty four days. He was determined to show the entire world it could be done exactly as his father and President Buchanan predicted.

19

September 16, 1858

John Jay stepped out into the street and glanced at the angle of the sun as it moved closer to the horizon. They wouldn't have much daylight left when they left Tipton. He could only hope the train wouldn't be late, that there weren't any delays in St. Louis. But, if his father had any say, and he could be very vocal when he had cause, the train would be on time.

"Here she comes!" came a shout from up the street.

John Jay listened. In the distance came the sound of a whistle echoing mournfully across the plains. The jingle of the harnesses from inside the stable told him the team was being readied. All they'd been waiting for was the sound of that whistle.

From the buildings along the street people materialized, drawn by the excitement in the air, yet there wouldn't be the size crowd John Jay felt the event deserved. Perhaps in St. Louis the first leg by train had been given a royal sendoff, but Tipton, Missouri, with its several hundred inhabitants, didn't seem too impressed.

A flutter of anticipation went through him when the six horses were led from the stable to the new stagecoach out front. The Concord was a beautiful sight, its bright red paint and yellow lettering proclaiming the Butterfield Overland Mail.

He'd inspected every inch of the coach himself, as well as the harnesses and the horses. Nothing was going to go wrong. The one year deadline was only hours away and he would give the doubters something to talk about. He wasn't the least bit surprised by what had been accomplished in one year. It wasn't the first time his father had done the impossible.

With the rapid approach of the train, John Jay took the yellow slicker slung across his arm and shrugged into it. His father knew how to do things with a flair. The tall black boots, pants tucked into the tops of them, and the yellow slicker set apart the Butterfield Mail employees. All down the line, yellow slickers had been distributed to the drivers who would guide the coach through their territory.

"All ready, John Jay," the livery man called, holding twelve lines for him. The fresh team stamped impatiently, well aware of the job they had to do. Already they'd been on several test runs with young Butterfield. They knew his touch on the reins.

John Jay crossed the dusty street, aware of the curious onlookers. A few gathered near the train station as he climbed up to the box, years of experience reflected in his ease. The lines were handed up to him. With his boot on the brake, John Jay took the twelve lines, tracing them with his eyes all the way to the individual horses to see there were no twists which would affect his control of the team. Automatically he threaded the lines through his gloved fingers in a way that gave him individual control of each horse.

It was no small skill to manage six horses, compelling them to work in unison. John Jay had been doing it for so many years the technique was now automatic, yet he never took any step of the preparation for granted.

"Good luck, John Jay!" the livery man called as with a flick of the reins, the team pulled as one, heading toward the train station.

There was a murmuring in the street as the coach wheeled by, an imposing sight with the handsome young man in his yellow slicker on the box. When he pulled up at the station, a young man stepped forward to stand at the head of the lead horses. John Jay nodded to him as he wrapped the lines around the brake and stepped down.

Among the crowd he spotted another yellow slicker. Jared Miller would be with him on the box. John Jay noticed the casual way the man held his shotgun at his side, but he knew the man to be a quick, deadly shot, who could also handle a team when necessary.

It would have made John Jay feel safer to have Jared at his side for the entire trip instead of only part way. There would be many dangerous miles ahead. The narrow trail held many perils from the trail itself and from hazards along the way. Anything from Indians, to outlaws, to breakdowns.

John Jay moved to the closest horse when the train gave another powerful hoot as it glided into the station. The dark gelding tossed his head but John Jay spoke softly into his ear, soothing him as he rubbed his glossy coat, his gaze automatically examining the harnesses, the traces. Everything had to be perfect.

Pulling his watch out of his vest pocket, John Jay saw it was six o'clock straight up. The train was exactly on time, but it would take a few minutes to transfer the mail and the passengers.

As the train coasted to a stop John Jay caught a yellow flash jumping to the ground. His father was already calling for the mail, his eagerness to be off registering with everyone within the sound of his voice. John Senior hurried the passengers along, looking for his son who was watching him with an amused grin.

"Ready to roll?" John Senior called, barely stopping to help the passengers.

"Ready and waiting," John Jay called, looking over those who would be the first passengers. One was a young man in a striped suit who stared at the red coach with a mixture of awe and excitement. He was carrying a small satchel and looked too bookish and slender to be undertaking a trek into the unknown.

When the man spotted John Jay's yellow slicker he approached with more confidence than John Jay would have expected.

"You must be John Jay Butterfield," he said, holding out his hand. "I'm Waterman Ormsby, a writer for the New York Herald. It appears you and I are going to be the only through riders."

John Jay gripped his hand, finding a strong grip for so slight a man. "Glad to have you aboard, Mr. Ormsby. I've read you a number of times back in New York," he said, genuinely admiring the man's talent. "You're in for one heck of a ride."

"My readers will want to know about the Butterfield Mail first hand. I'll be sending back my reports from along the trail."

"Climb aboard, Mr. Ormsby," John Senior called. "Let's roll!"

John Jay watched impatiently as young Ormsby boarded the coach behind a woman with two children. There was a man his father introduced as Mr. Corbin from Washington, and also John Butterfield's longtime friend, Judge Wheeler. Whether he was an actual judge or if the title was merely honorary he never ascertained. He knew only the man was much respected and very influential. He was about his father's age, in his middle fifties, but with a spritely step as he climbed aboard.

It took another fifteen minutes for John Jay to secure the baggage into the boot in the back of the coach and under his seat. The two pitifully small sacks of U.S. Mail were stowed under his seat as well. It was too soon for people to have confidence in the overland mail.

"Let her roll!" John Senior called out to his son as he swung aboard and closed the door behind him with a resounding click. He leaned out the window as John Jay took the lines. Even though there was no need for it, John Jay went strictly for show, cracking his whip high over the heads of his team.

With an extra flick of the lines across their flanks he urged the horses to greater speed as they left town. After days of waiting they were finally under way. It was a long way to San Francisco. Beside him, Jared Miller slouched nonchalantly, his shotgun propped against the side of the box within easy reach. John Jay's rifle rested in a scabbard beside him. Both men wore a pistol on their hip.

Between Tipton and San Francisco was a lot of Indian country. They had no way of knowing how the tribes would react to this strange wagon. But for now, while the road was good, John Jay wanted to make all the time he could. The team seemed eager, stretching themselves to a steady lope.

Inside the coach conversation was subdued. In spite of the rocking motion, the rough jolts, Waterman Ormsby braced a pad of paper against the satchel on his knee and recorded his impressions:

"The road for the first few miles was very fair, coursing through small prairies, where for the first time I noticed those traveling hotels so commonly seen in the western country. These are large covered wagons, in which the owner and his family, sometimes numbering as high as a dozen, emigrate from place to place, traveling in daytime and camping near wood, water and grass at night. All along the wildest western roads these hotels may be met in every direction, enlivening the way with their camp fires at night, and presenting pictures of domestic felicity which might well be emulated in certain quarters more comfortable and less homey. We rode along at a somewhat rapid pace, because John Jay Butterfield was determined that the overland mail should go through his section on time, and though his father kept calling out, "Be careful, son," he assured him it was "all right" and drove on.

"The first stopping place was Shackleford's just seven miles distant, and we seemed hardly to have become comfortably seated in the coach before our attention was attracted by the illumination of our destination – a recognition of the occasion which seemed quite cheering after the apparent previous neglect. The team wheeled up in fine style, and we found the change of horses ready harnessed and supper waiting. Mr. Shackleford assured us he would have fired a gun for us, but he couldn't get it to go off. We took the will for the deed, however, and hustled in to supper, which was soon dispatched. After taking leave of Mr. Corbin and the others, we were off again to the next station, having been detained, in all, twenty minutes," Ormsby concluded.

It was completely dark when the coach resumed the trail. John Jay was familiar enough with this section to keep his team moving at a canter, knowing the upcoming incline would slow them soon enough. The next station was only thirteen miles away, but it was nearly all uphill.

It took an hour and forty five minutes to reach Mulholland's Station. Again, at Jared's bugle call, the horses were harnessed and waiting so it took only a matter of minutes to change teams. By this time it was so dark the road was difficult to see. Coach lamps were of little use in the dim light. Jared climbed down from the box, took one of the lamps and walked the trail in front of the team.

John Jay was impatient with the slow progress, yet knew they were ahead of schedule. It was slow going, taking three hours to reach the Warsaw station on the Osage River. Here the road was well defined once more allowing Jared to climb back on the box and the team to pick up speed. A man from the Warsaw Station preceded them on horseback with a light to show where to ford the river. Fortunately the water lever was low, reaching only half way up the wheels.

Inside the coach, no one slept though they were fatigued enough to rest. The constant rocking and bumping took time to adjust to. By the light of the coach lamp Ormsby found words pouring from his pen.

"The ride was, though rather fatiguing to a novitiate, rather pleasant on the whole. The views of prairies, the vast fields of corn, tobacco, and wild mustard seed, the picturesque encampment of the travelers, the fields of Chinese sugar cane, droves of roving cattle, the sounding of merry horns as we approached the stations, the bustle of changing horses, and the entire novelty of the scene made an impression upon my mind that will never be effaced.

"I can never forget the grotesque figures which my imagination conjured up out of the objects in the woods on this our first night out. The stories I read of bands of roving Indians, rambling through the forests to kill and steal, all rushed to my mind, and transformed each decayed tree or stunted brush into a lurking foe. Then, the music of the forest, the moonlight struggling through the trees, the easy motion of the vehicle as it rocked to and fro on the rough road, like a vessel moving on the sea, all tended to make one thoughtful of the impressiveness of the occasion. Young John enlivened the road with his eagerness to get on and to make good time, and evinced the greatest anxiety that no accident interfere with the safe carriage of the mail. There seemed to be a catching enthusiasm about the whole trip, which excited more interest – I know for myself – than I ever supposed could be mustered out of the bare fact of a common coach traveling over a common road, with a common mail bag and a few common people inside. But the occasion made all of this uncommon, and I soon got so I would willingly go without my dinner for the privilege of helping along that mail by a quarter of an hour."

In the days that followed John Jay gained more time. He kept a fast pace yet he was cautious. At some stops he greased the wheels and double checked harnesses for wear. He barely took time to eat, or else ate while he worked.

Jared Miller watched over the party with sharp eyes. At every station he would quietly check out every corner of the place, then would check the trail leading out. The mail was well protected.

From Missouri the trail took them through Arkansas, across the eastern corner of Indian Territory and into the vast wilderness of Texas. They were in Indian country. From time to time they took on a driver to spell John Jay who fell into instant sleep inside the coach. The passengers, except for the writer Ormsby from the Herald, had disembarked at Fort Smith, Arkansas.

At some stations they'd pick up passengers for short distances, but for the most part the idea of this mail route was too new. People weren't ready to accept it.

Other times, Jared Miller would slip down into the coach without its even slowing down. He would stretch out his lanky frame on one of the seats and instantly begin to snore. No matter how rough the road, the rocking and bucking of the coach didn't disturb him.

None of the men took time to shave. Before long they were grizzled looking, including Ormsby. John Jay hadn't expected the man to adjust to the rigors of the trip, only to learn the writer was tougher than he looked. He never complained when asked to go without a meal and seemed eager to do anything, even walk when necessary to spare the team.

The countryside varied from day to day, hour to hour. The coach rumbled across small, level plains, past Choctaw Indians watching their cattle, through mountain passes and along rocky canyons. Where the road was roughest, the bright red Concord coach was exchanged for the Celerity Wagon, which was lighter. It had flaps of canvas on the sides that could be rolled up to let in the fresh air, and the dust.

Horses were sometimes replaced by mules, some of them still half wild. There hadn't been time to break all the animals. There were delays while reluctant mules were roped and harnessed, with the stationmaster keeping a close eye out for flashing hooves and teeth of an angry mule.

For John Jay it was fortunate he was an old hand at handling a team. It took a sure hand and great skill to get six balky mules to pull in unison.

Three solid days the coach traveled day and night. John Jay was spelled at the reins by the other drivers, and occasionally by Jared Miller.

"I'm an old bullwhacker," Jared told John Jay with his lopsided grin. "It ain't my favorite thing, but I can handle a good team. The mean ones I leave to the experts."

On the third dark night, after taking on a driver named Wiley at Pusley's Station in Indian Territory, John Jay stretched out on the seat of the Concord for some much needed rest. He was oblivious to Ormsby's discomfort at the wild speeding of the new driver who seemed anxious to make good time. The team of horses was fully cooperative.

The moon's bright glow was often obstructed by trees, and Ormsby knew the driver had to be relying on his knowledge of the road rather than what he could see. He was also aware of jagged rocks whizzing by, and, as he hung on for dear life, amazed that the wild bounding wasn't keeping John Jay awake, while he was going to be bruised from one end to the other from bumping his head and arms.

John Jay was finally jarred awake when the coach gave a great bound that tossed him off the seat on top of Ormsby who'd been dumped on the floor.

"What the hell!" John Jay hollered as the great crashing sound told him something had broken. He was out of the coach before it came to a complete stop. "What the hell do you think you're doing?" he demanded of the driver as Jared climbed down from the box on the opposite side, a disgusted look on his face. "You been taking this road like a mad man!"

Wiley was a burley, barrel chested man with heavy suspenders holding up his pants. He looked unconcerned as he climbed down to inspect the damage to the coach. He ignored John Jay's fuming anger, but walking away from the young coachman was the wrong thing to do.

John Jay grabbed him by the arm and spun him back to face him.

"Don't you turn away when I'm talking to you!" His blue eyes were shooting off sparks of anger. "You took a damn fool chance with this coach. If you've done any damage to the Concord that delays us, you're going to be damn sorry."

Wiley didn't seem perturbed. "I know every inch of this road," he said nonchalantly. "We didn't hurt nothin'."

"That remains to be seen."

In the dark, even with the help of a coach lamp, it was difficult to make a thorough inspection of the coach. John Jay didn't trust

Wiley who seemed not the least concerned about either John Jay's anger or the delay, and double checked everything.

Waterman Ormsby stood by the side of the road unable to help with more than his silence. In the end all they found was a broken seat inside the coach, the one that had dumped John Jay.

"We got off lucky," Jared said when no further damage was found.

John Jay glared at Wiley. "No thanks to him. If I wasn't so dog tired I'd take the box and let him walk the rest of the way." With one last assessing gaze, still feeling troubled, John Jay knew what he had heard in those moments before the coach came to a full stop. It was more than a broken seat. He felt it in his bones. "I still want to take a better look when it gets daylight. Blackburn's station isn't far."

His gaze came back to Wiley, full of warning. "You take us in, and you take us in easy, you understand."

Wiley finally had the grace to look uncomfortable. "Yeah, I'll go easy."

John Jay shot a look at Jared. "See that he does."

They pulled into Blackburn's Station as the first streaks of pink touched the horizon. A sleepy stationmaster came out to harness up a team while his partner rustled up breakfast.

Once the exhausted team had been unhitched and led away, John Jay began another inspection of the coach, starting with the wheels, axels, and working his way up to the tongue.

"Holy cow!" he yelped when he saw the split down the length of the tongue. He whirled around looking for Wiley who seemed to have disappeared, perhaps sensing it was a good time to make himself scarce.

Jared came over to have a look, water dripping from his face and hair after having washed in the trough. Even to his inexpert eye he knew the damage was serious.

"We're damn lucky we made it in," Jared said, shifting his shotgun up to his shoulder.

"We shouldn't have!" John Jay said, his gaze again searching for Wiley. "This thing could have shattered completely."

The stationmaster, sensing something was wrong, came up to look. He tipped his hat back on his thinning hair and scratched his head. "How in tarnation did you do that?"

"Wiley!" John Jay spat.

That seemed to come as no surprise to the old man. "He never did have enough sense to ease up and spare the team. He's always got to beat the clock on his route."

"Well this time he didn't!" John Jay said. "And he won't be driving for us again. Can you fix it?"

"Yep, I'll have it good as new, but it's gonna take a while. Y'all just enjoy a bite of breakfast and I'll get to work."

John Jay followed Jared into the small adobe station. It was only one room with a table, a fireplace for cooking and two pallets in the corner for sleeping. It was very much like other stations they'd seen along the way. The floor was hard packed dirt and smelled dusty in spite of the overwhelming aroma of coffee bubbling over the fire.

A gaunt older man didn't speak as he poured coffee for them. The two men settled into roughhewn chairs at the table, and soon the old man set tin plates in front of them with a type of shortcake baked in the coals and some dried beef. Surprisingly there was butter, something they'd seen little of on the trip. Not all the stations had received their supplies in time for the inaugural run.

Ormsby took his meal outdoors to study the layout of the station. John Jay had noticed his insatiable curiosity about everything. The man would stand looking off into the vast distance of the plains, his mind no doubt forming the words the people in New York would be eagerly waiting to read. His tales from the first mail run were history in the making.

Wiley seemed to have vanished into the brush behind the station, which was just as well. John Jay's temper hadn't been improved by the food. The delay to fix the tongue would far exceed any time

Wiley might have made on his break neck scramble to beat the clock. They couldn't afford a driver like him.

To give himself something to think about other than the delay, he walked over to Ormsby, who was leaning over to peer under the coach at the undercarriage.

"She's a beauty, isn't she?" John Jay asked with pride.

Ormsby's head came up with a snap of surprise. "I've seen a lot of hotel coaches in New York," he said. "They don't need to be as rugged as these cross-country ones. This looks more intricate in design."

"It is," John Jay said with pride, dropping down on his haunches, knowing he had an interested audience. "Abbot and Downing make one of the strongest coaches in the business. They're used all over the world, especially in South Africa, South America and Australia. Mexico even buys some."

"Why are they stronger?" Ormsby asked. "What can they do to compensate for this?" His hand moved to indicate the vast country they were in.

"Just by using the best materials, and employing the most skilled men they can find." He pointed to the way the coach was curved along the bottom, not sitting square and rigid. "The curve makes the ride easier for the passengers. Those layers of thick leather straps you see are called through braces. They run the entire length of the coach so it rides on them. Without 'em you wouldn't be able to stand the journey, you'd be begging us to let you out so you could walk back to New York."

Ormsby grinned. "There are days when I think I'm ready to do just that, but I'm getting used to it." He studied the through braces. "And those help?"

"They have a double purpose. They also help absorb the shocks for the team so there aren't any heavy jerks on the traces due to rocks or ruts in the road. As fast as this coach travels, we'd ruin the horses without it, and we couldn't pull the weight we do."

"Just that little strap?" Ormsby joked, for it was obviously more than that.

"Yep, that little strap consists of fifteen layers of cowhide."

"A Concord must be terribly expensive."

"The best always is. Fifteen hundred dollars is a lot of money, especially when we had to buy so many of them. Just look at these wheels," John Jay couldn't resist the urge to brag about the amazing conveyances. "Each spoke is handmade and fitted and balanced to the rim and hub. The wood is dried in such a way that it can stand extremes of temperature without shrinking or warping,"

"I can hardly see where the wood is joined." Ormsby ran his hand over the joints they were discussing, finding them smooth as glass.

"That's their trademark," John Jay said standing up. "Want to hear an interesting story about a Concord?" He could see by the eager gleam in Ormsby's eyes that he was. The two of them walked to the head of the coach to watch the progress of the repairs on the tongue.

"Lots of these coaches are shipped around Cape Horn to California. We even shipped a few of ours that way recently. On one trip, a storm hit just as the ship was rounding the horn. It sank. Three months later a salvage crew began bringing up the cargo. They brought the Concord out of the salt water. The leather wasn't worth much by that time but the coach itself wasn't damaged. They fixed her up, put her to work, and she's been in service ever since."

"That's amazing!" Ormsby said, his mind already at work on how to incorporate that into his dispatches. "How about the mud wagons we use sometimes?"

"Abbot and Downing makes them too, but they're cheaper. Only five hundred dollars. They have the through braces, but you've no doubt noticed the ride isn't nearly as smooth."

Talking helped pass the time. John Jay would have been nervous as a cat otherwise. As it was, the moment the station master pronounced the job completed, and the team hitched, John Jay sprang to the box. Jared and Ormsby scrambled aboard to keep from being left behind.

Of Wiley there was still no trace, but John Jay hadn't expected him to show his face. He'd no doubt catch a ride back on the east bound stage when it came through.

The following day, Monday the twentieth of September, they pulled into Colbert's Ferry on the Red River at ten in the morning. John Jay was pleased that even with the delay at Blackburn they were thirty-four hours ahead of schedule. That is, he was pleased until he learned there was no fresh team waiting. They were a day and a half early.

John Jay was fuming but helpless. For once they had a leisurely dinner. The station master was a half-breed Indian named Ben Colbert, a young man, not yet thirty. John Jay learned that his white wife was his third one, and that he'd owned the ferry for five years.

Several children roamed in and out, barefoot, but looking happy and well fed.

What John Jay found most amazing was the fact that Colbert owned a large gang of slaves who were at work on the banks of the river, cutting away the sand to make the ascent easier for the coach. He listened idly as Ormsby skillfully engaged the man in conversation, no doubt to report to his readers.

Colbert admitted to owning twenty-five slaves and spoke of wanting a length of cable to manage the ferry crossing. Ormsby suggested he purchase some of the Atlantic Cable. John Jay remembered reading Ormsby's reports from the decks of the ship that laid the first cable under the ocean. For two weeks there had been faint but serviceable telegraph communication with Ireland. Then, inexplicably, the cable ceased working.

Colbert considered the cable too expensive. He considered his slaves the best stock there was with his increase of about four a year. He also told how he was able to grow corn on his farm and many other crops. It was one of the few stops along the way where they had sugar, butter and pastries.

Their host was eager to hear the news from St. Louis and Washington. John Jay and Ormsby obliged while Jared sat silently, a man of few words in the company of people he didn't know.

They lingered long enough to give the horses a rest, but there was no choice except to keep going. There was no telling how long it would take for the fresh horses to arrive. The coach was loaded, they were just about to head down to the ferry crossing when Colbert gave a shout. The horses were coming.

They wasted no time in unhitching the spent horses and exchanging them for the fresher ones. The fare for the ferry crossing was a dollar and a quarter, and once on the other side they were in Texas.

Again John Jay pressed the pace. They stopped only to change teams and eat. Most of the stations in this section weren't built. At times, the distances between them was as short as twelve miles, other times it could be as much as thirty-five or even seventy-five.

Having to travel such long distances without fresh teams slowed them even more. Often times everyone walked to spare the exhausted animals on the steep hills.

20

This was Indian country. John Jay was aware of Ormsby's nervousness, but he was game. He wore a gun on his hip and swore he knew how to use it. From inside the coach he kept constant watch. Next to him on the box, Jared's eyes were constantly on the move.

From Choctaw country they passed into the land of the Comanche. These were fierce, unpredictable people. One minute they would greet the whites peaceably, the next they would attack with a ferocity that left no survivors. There were grisly tales of mutilated bodies.

Some of the stage stations in Texas were also military posts. The presence of soldiers, it was hoped, would keep the Indians from becoming too aggressive. It didn't always work. Texas was vast, the soldiers few.

Up until now, the only Comanche John Jay and the Concord met was a woman riding a pony, watching over a herd of cattle. She only stared at the strange wagon as it passed.

One of the more unique characters who took over the lines for a section of western Texas was a man with a sandy head of hair and an unkempt beard, an old frontier man by the name of Captain Skillman. He was forty-five, dressed in buckskin, and wore several pistols and bowie knives. He told the fascinated Ormsby, who rode on the box with him, about the days of the first mail runs from San Antonio to Santa Fe. A fight with the Indians on each trip was considered part of the contract.

Skillman's job now was to guide them across the desolate Staked Plain, a stretch of eighty miles with no water. There were no stations as yet. They started out with four mules pulling a mud wagon and eighteen being driven along behind.

John Jay studied the mules with apprehension. There would be no more stock for a hundred and thirteen miles, only the ones with them. It would not be a pleasant undertaking but he was glad to have a man who knew the trail as well as Skillman. In places the road was poorly marked, nearly invisible.

On Monday, the twenty-seventh, they reached the muddy waters of the Pecos River. There were still no fresh mules available. The ones they had were rapidly playing out, and were the last of their stock.

They traveled up the Pecos on a jolting, dusty road, moving at a snail's pace, stopping often to rest the exhausted animals. Finally they were able to ford the high waters of the Pecos about three miles above a place called Pope's Camp. Even there the water was flowing rapidly and nearly covered the hubs of the wagon. After thirty miles of flat prairie they camped at sunrise near the head of Delaware Creek, not far from the New Mexico border.

Captain Skillman gathered buffalo chips to fuel their fire. The coffee was gone, they had to be satisfied with jerked beef, raw onions, crackers that were slightly wormy, but which no one complained about. There was also a bit of bacon.

Conversation was minimal. Everyone was aware of the exhausted condition of their six remaining mules. Whether or not they would make it as far as Pinery, where the fresh stock was supposed to be waiting, was a matter of conjecture. There were miles of foothills in between, and a climb up Guadalupe Peak.

In spite of the beauty of the scenery no one was in a mood to appreciate it. They each were trying to imagine what they would do if the mules gave out. Who would walk to Pinery to bring back help and how much more time they would lose.

Once the team was refreshed they took to the road again, Captain Skillman on the box. John Jay tried to sleep but was aware of every movement of the Celerity wagon, attuned to each bit of stress on the mules.

"We don't seem to be getting any closer," Ormsby commented, watching the tall peak taunting them with its pine covered slopes.

John Jay gave a sigh, admitting to himself he wasn't going to be able to sleep. The wagons motion was more jarring than that of a Concord. "It always gives that feeling. I've been through here on horseback and it's the same illusion."

"Do you think our team will make it?"

John Jay didn't rise up from his prone position on the opposite seat. "If we had horses I'd say there was no way. Mules are a lot tougher, but even they have their limits. This is going to be the slowest time we've made so far. It's going to put us even further behind."

"We should be able to make it up, shouldn't we?"

John Jay had to admire the young man for the stoic way he'd accepted the hardships of the trip. He hadn't even complained about some of the food they'd had to eat, such as the wormy crackers. When it came to hunger the stomach didn't remain delicate for long.

"With luck, Mr. Ormsby, with a lot of luck," With that, John Jay pulled his hat over his face to end the conversation. He knew he couldn't sleep but he wanted to be alone with his thoughts. His mind was ranging far ahead to the California desert, to one particular oasis. What was Abby doing now? Was she standing on the hill in front of the station, peering to the east, waiting for her first sight of the coach?

He could picture the fiery hair she kept tamed into a bun at the back of her neck. Occasionally she'd wear it in braids but John Jay felt Cassidy wouldn't like being reminded of her life with the Indians. He wished he could see her with her hair flowing down her back in all its raging glory, those strange wings of white almost glowing in the sun. Closing his eyes he could picture her head against his chest, her hands exploring his body.

Ruthlessly he banished such notions from his mind. How stupid could he be having such thoughts about another man's wife? Why couldn't he have been the one to find Abby in the Indian camp? Why couldn't he have carried her off to become his wife? No, that couldn't have worked out. She didn't know the ways of the white man any more. She was very much a savage herself.

If that's true, how could a man like Cassidy hold her? Why would she stay with him? His thoughts tortured him. Again he thought of taking her away, but Cassidy was his friend. It was hopeless. He'd have to face it. Abby could never be his woman, could never live in a civilized manner without embarrassing them both.

They were still five miles from the peak when they camped at Independence Springs.

John Jay took Ormsby to show him the natural curiosity of the spring that boiled up the sand. They had to dig a little to bring sweet, cool water to the surface to slake their thirst and that of their failing animals.

John Jay stroked the mules, feeling their fatigue in every bone of his own body. He shared his father's love of animals, his father's desire to keep the stock strong and healthy. It was contrary to his nature to force such a burden on dumb animals. It was also contrary to his nature to fail his father. The mail would go through.

The next five miles would be the toughest. It would be mostly uphill. If there had been any way to lighten the load, John Jay would have done it. There was no need of talking it over, once the trip resumed and the trail became steeper, everyone walked. Everyone except Skillman, who seemed able to command the best effort of the exhausted animals. John Jay walked along side, urging them on with soft words of encouragement, then with harsher commands when they began to falter.

On the downhill stretches John Jay and Ormsby jumped onto the side of the wagon, clinging there until the next slope slowed them again. Skillman expertly rode the brake on the downhill portions, easing the burden on the team.

It took hurling rocks to force the mules to cover the final distance to Pinery. It hurt John Jay as much as it did the mules to fling rocks at their flanks to drive them on. He was never so relieved to see the corral come into view with its heavy pine timbers. Guadalupe Peak reared its head above them, the air here was cool on their heated bodies. With tears in his eyes John Jay was at last able to free the six exhausted mules from their traces.

"They look plumb spent," Riley, the station master said as he came forward to take over.

"See they get an extra measure of oats for a few days, Riley," John Jay said. "They deserve a long rest and the best care you can give them."

"They'll get it, don't you worry none. Now you go in and see to yourself," Riley said, indicating the log station. "There's a pot of venison stew and some baked beans."

"Sounds good to me," John Jay said, but even then was reluctant to relinquish the team he'd been forced to use so harshly. One of the mules staggered as Riley and his son led the animals toward the corral.

The next day, in Guadalupe Canyon, a stretch of steep, stone covered hills, they came upon the first stagecoach out of San Francisco which had left one day earlier then the St. Louis mail. It was carrying five passengers and was eight hours ahead of schedule.

The two parties exchanged congratulations and bits of news, and Ormsby added his dispatch to the New York Herald to the east bound mail. When they pressed on, John Jay was on the box of the Concord they'd switched to, with a fresh team of four horses, Skillman inside regaling the fascinated Ormsby with tales of his travels.

After camping at Crow Springs to eat and rest the team, they were thirty miles from the next station of Cornudos, and still within sight of the jutting peak of Guadalupe behind them. There were massive boulders of red sandstone with natural basins in them which collected rain water. Often the water stood in these tanks year round.

They were moving across a high plain covered with grass and mesquite when John Jay had the first inkling of serious trouble. Directly in their path sat a large band of well mounted Indians. His heart sank as he recognized the fancy head dress of the warriors of the Comanche nation.

Before he could even give a thought to turning the coach and hightailing it back the way they'd come, he heard whoops from behind them. He sensed rather than saw Ormsby and Skillman reach for their guns.

"No use," he warned them. "There's too many. Let's see what they want."

John Jay pulled the team to a stop and set the brake. "No shooting," he warned again. Skillman already had the door open and was stepping down. He, too, had seen the futility of resistance.

With a sinking feeling John Jay watched warriors come from every direction, moving slowly, yet purposefully toward them. He recognized from the elaborate war bonnets that several powerful chiefs were among them. The shields, with their many feathers and intricate designs indicated this was a gathering of many camps. It didn't help to note there were no women or children among them, only warriors in their prime who could make fast work of their tiny group.

Skillman stepped out to talk to a chief mounted on a white horse, his headdress more elaborate than any of the others. In rapid sign language the two communicated. Finally Skillman turned to a tense John Jay and Ormsby.

"They've never seen anything like this 'swift wagon' before. They saw the other one come through but were too far away." Skillman gave a shrug. "I guess they're just curious. Let's go sit in the shade."

"Sounds like a good idea," John Jay said, knowing they had no choice. "Ormsby?"

Waterman Ormsby was staring in fascination at the warriors who completely encircled them, war ponies pressing forward for a better look at the strange red wagon. The warriors scarcely paid them any mind when they walked to a clump of trees a short distance away and sat in the shade.

It took all of John Jay's will to sit and pretend unconcern as the Comanche braves dismounted and approached the coach. What if they destroyed the mail, or more importantly, the coach itself? He was relieved, but still tense, to hear laughter and comments as the brightly dressed warriors surrounded the coach, touching the shiny red paint, running fingers over the leather through braces and opening doors to peer inside. Several entered to sit on the leather seats. They ran their fingers over the tapestry lining, studied the gas lamps.

John Jay was sorry now that Jared had left them. If there was going to be trouble, he would have made one more gun. Even as the thought occurred to him John Jay shook his head at the futility of it. If the situation turned nasty the three stage men didn't stand a chance. There was no cover, no place to hide. They could only sit in the shade and wait to see what happened.

Already they were far behind schedule. Today would have made up some of it. Time seemed to pass slowly as new warriors swarmed over the coach. As long as they were laughing, John Jay hoped that was a sign they were merely curious, not interested in the horses or prisoners. If the Indians decided to take the team they would be stranded sixteen miles from the next station.

Much later, John Jay slipped his watch from his pocket to glance at the time. Three hours had passed. Captain Skillman nudged him, bringing his attention to the bronze faced chief motioning to them. Slowly the three stood up and made their way through a throng of Comanche warriors to where the man in the elaborate headdress stood.

"You go!" the Chief said, waving his hand at the coach. "Go swift!"

John Jay didn't wait for a second invitation. Everyone climbed aboard and with a crack of the whip John Jay set the Concord lurching down the road. Even the horses seemed relieved to be free of the exuberant Indians. Ormsby was going to have quite a story for his readers.

The mail continued its inexorable way across New Mexico, through land so bleak and bare it supported little life. Arizona Territory was hot and dusty, the stations poorly stocked. At Fort Yuma, on the Colorado River, they were ferried across to the California side where the road dipped down into Mexico in order to avoid vast stretches of sand dunes.

John Jay felt his heart quickening with the nearness of Seven Springs. They'd been making good time, making up most of what they had lost.

They reached Carrizo Creek, a barren looking gorge in the desert. To the south west were lava strewn hills, to the north west lay the valley John Jay longed to see.

From Carrizo they reached a place called Palm Spring, named for the two lone palm trees that grew there. Here they had to dig for water, but soon had ample for the team and for themselves. Not far from the spring they passed another coach from San Francisco, and Ormsby had another dispatch ready for them.

John Jay rode the box. The team seemed to sense his eagerness, or perhaps they just smelled the water at Seven Springs and moved eagerly. His gaze was on the mountains surrounding the valley, tall and timber studded. It was a beautiful spot, a lush place to graze cattle and sheep. His heart gave a funny lurch as jealousy swept over him. He could picture himself in this wilderness with a wife like Abby, a woman who knew the ways of survival in this often harsh land.

He was so intent on his thoughts he almost forgot to sound the bugle. At the first notes, his team of matched bays seemed to pick up speed, eager for water, and oats and rest.

John Jay's gaze scanned the surrounding brush covered hills, searching for the bright bit of color that would tell him where Abby was. If he didn't see her, he didn't know what he would do. For over a thousand miles she was all he thought about.

He could see Cassidy harnessing the fresh team as the coach rambled up the hill and rolled to a stop in front of the station. Hot and hungry John Jay set the brake and jumped down.

Wes was there to unhitch the team.

"Grubs inside," Wes said with a nod of his head toward the station.

A movement at the door caught John Jay's eye. He'd know that brilliant color anywhere. He saw the delight leap into her eyes, felt the leap of his own pulse, and hoped his face wasn't as revealing as hers.

Intent on Abby, John Jay didn't see the frown that touched Wes's brow as he looked from one to the other. He saw Abby's shy smile widen to greet the latest arrivals.

"Come and wash up," she invited, aware that the other men from the coach were staring at her as well. They hadn't expected to see such a young, beautiful woman in this harsh place.

A bowl of water and rough towels were prepared for them to wash away the trail dust. John Jay tried not to stare at Abby, tried not to feast his eyes like a starving man, which was exactly how he felt.

At the previous stations he couldn't wait to get back on the road. This was one stopover where he tried to delay, wanting to see as much of her as possible. He could feel her interest too, knew she was trying not to watch him the way he was trying not to watch her.

On the table she placed some of her best rabbit stew and biscuits. John Jay was hardly aware of what he ate, but heard the others complimenting Abby on the excellent food. Hot meals had been rare of late, making this one especially welcome.

"We've been expecting you for days," Abby said, her voice sounding more breathless than he remembered.

"We've had delays. No fresh teams, no water, Indians, you name it, we've been through it," John Jay said, trying to keep her at the table. "You must have been busy with the stages coming through from San Francisco."

"Yes, we don't have as much spare time around here anymore. Did you say you had trouble with Indians?" Her dark red brows were almost touching together as she frowned. Better than anyone she knew the resentment of the Indians toward the continual encroachment of the whites.

"Comanche's. They wanted a closer look at our 'swift wagon'. They held us up for about three hours while they climbed all over it, then told us to go."

"Go swift!" Waterman Ormsby repeated. "What a relief that was!"

John Jay was the last one to finish eating, the last one to go outside where the coach stood ready. He couldn't delay any longer. It had been so painfully short, so bitter sweet. His gaze told her he wished he could stay. Her answering gaze said she would miss him. "Good luck!" Cassidy called as the coach began to move. "Safe trip!"

21

Abby stood by the door of the station watching the stage move out, John Jay's broad shoulders working to control six eager horses. She tried to school her face not to reveal her thoughts. All these months she'd waited for his return, and now he was gone, taking with him a part of her heart. Even worse was the fact she didn't know when, if ever, she would see him again.

His driving job would be completed with this first run. John Jay was more than a driver. From others passing through she learned that his father had offered him a superintendent's position on any section of the road he wanted.

The superintendent for this section had already been appointed. Westin lived at Oak Grove, further up the mountain where the coach was now headed. That told her John Jay wouldn't be taking it. His life and his family were in the east.

Perhaps it was better this way, though it broke her heart to even think it. What good would it do to see him, to feel her heart leap when he smiled, to savor the sight of his clear blue eyes, to watch the sway of his lean hips when he moved gracefully about the station.

She felt Wes's presence beside her, and though she didn't look at him she knew he understood. Somehow he had seen what was in her heart and didn't condemn her for it. There was nothing either of them could say.

"Got any of that stew left?" he asked when the coach had disappeared into the desert.

"Yes, there's plenty." Her gaze turned to her husband who had also been watching the coach. "Cass?" His name still felt stiff to her lips.

"I'm hungry as a bear. I'll go wash."

Glad to have something to keep her mind occupied, Abby went into the station. She hadn't been able to eat while it was filled with John Jay's presence and now she had little appetite, though she sat down with the men and poked at her stew.

"John Jay's making good time," Cassidy said, unaware of Abby's start at the sound of his name. "If he doesn't run into any more trouble he'll make San Francisco smack on time."

Wes gave a low chuckle. "If I know that boy he won't be satisfied with being on time. He'll drive like the devil himself to prove it can be done in less than twenty-five days." For the first time since she could remember Abby found herself praying; praying John Jay would be safe. She'd been aware the white man's ways were returning to her consciousness. It wasn't an easy process. She learned from the women who passed through, ones who had no inkling where she'd spent the past years.

From the women she learned to darn, to mend clothing. She was given recipes for meals suited to this tough land. In return she'd given them capes made of rabbit fur and treated their ailments.

She grimaced when she remembered Cassidy's reaction when she told him she'd given a woman one of her warm capes. "You don't give them away!" he said angrily. "You sell them. Get money!"

So she had. She made more capes and when one of the wives saw her fine work she had to have it. Abby made the deal but before she could put the money away Cassidy had taken it. Where he hid his money she didn't know. She was beginning to realize there had to be quite a bit of it stashed around the station.

In the white man's world everything was accomplished with money. It became important to Abby to have some of her own. From the women passing through she soon saw the difference between the ones who had money and the ones who didn't. She'd seen the tired, defeated look of the ones whose husbands sold everything they had to make the long trek to California. In the ones who were better off financially, Abby noted the women often had a sparkle in their eyes. They had less reason to fear going hungry or where they would live. Money gave them confidence.

She remembered the conversation with the sparkling emigrant Sarah Barker, middle aged, with four lively youngsters. She'd purchased one of Abby's capes, sensing Abby wanted to conduct the transaction privately.

"That's a smart thing to do," Sarah said, patting Abby's hand after she'd slipped the coins into the pocket of her dress. "A woman has to have some money of her own. If she's smart she protects herself. Men don't realize what can happen to a woman if they die suddenly. Even though the husband has money, a male relative often steps in and takes over. The wife might be lucky to get anything. I know a woman who was turned out of her own home by her brother-in-law."

Abby snorted with anger at the thought. "I'd like to see anyone try to turn me out of my own home!"

Sarah's smile said she admired her spirit. "Most women are brought up to be submissive, not to fight. They do what the menfolk tell them, and you can be certain it's always to the man's advantage." Sarah gave a sigh of regret. "Unfortunately that's the way of the world, honey. The only way a woman can stand up for herself and go her own way is if she has money. If she's penniless she's forced to depend on some man. She has no choice."

Abby absorbed the lesson. She sensed the truth of it, saw how Cassidy expected her obedience, and knew if anything happened to him she would be in big trouble. She needed to know where he hid his money. Barring that, she needed money of her own.

As Abby bent her head over her stew, her mind was deep in her own thoughts. She was aware of Wes and Cassidy talking about the stage. She knew she had to make a plan. Life in the desert was uncertain. Indian's came for their stock. Renegades and outlaws came down the trail. Life sometimes hung by the keenness of your hearing.

On the rocky hillside, not far from the station, a small cave was formed by large boulders. It wasn't big enough for a person, but it was a place to keep her meager horde of money. It was a start. With it she would put food and things she would need if she had to leave this place in a hurry. Just because she lived the white man's way didn't mean she should grow careless. She'd learned to take care of herself, and must continue to do so.

Even before she reached the station with a string of quail slung over her shoulder she sensed something in the air. Perhaps it was some inner sense warning her, for there was nothing unusual about the two strange horses tied out front. Passersby often stopped for supplies. Yet she sensed this was different. Slinging the quail over a mesquite branch, she silently approached the open door of the store, remaining out of sight of those inside.

The booming voice riveted her to the spot. It was a voice she would never forget as long as she lived. Her first instinct was to run and hide in the brush, a sense of total panic. With an effort she calmed herself. She was Mrs. James Cassidy. Jacob Bristol had no power over her. He was nothing more than a visitor.

Straightening her back Abby smoothed down the faded dress, wishing it didn't show the wrinkles where she pulled it up between her legs to tuck into her belt like trousers, or the spots of dirt and blood. Cassidy frowned on her wearing men's pants, even though she sometimes changed into them when she was away from the station. She kept a pair hidden with her stash of goods in the rocks.

Gathering her courage, her green eyes were glinting with fire that spelled trouble. Cassidy's voice sounded too jovial in her ears.

He knew her feelings for her uncle, but he would make the man welcome.

Abby stepped from the bright sunshine into the dark interior of the adobe building, feeling its coolness. The two strangers were faced away from her and hadn't heard her silent approach. It gave her eyes a moment to adjust before Cassidy spotted her. His subtle change of expression told Abby he saw the simmering fire in the eyes.

"Uncle Jacob," she said, with little warmth in her voice. "What a surprise."

The big man spun around, his dark eyes narrowing under his bushy red eyebrows. She felt his gaze sweep her from head to toe, could feel his mind churning.

"Abigail!" His big voice boomed in the small room. "Praise the Lord, it's really you! All these years I've searched and worried. The Lord's mercy has spared your life."

"Did any of the others survive?" Abby couldn't help asking. It was something that had been in her mind ever since that terrible day in the desert.

"Two women and some children were bought back from the Indians a few years later. I'm not sure but what they should have been left with the heathens after all that time." His pious scowl told Abby his feelings. "The children had learned godless ways, the women had been with those savage men, their souls forever damned."

Abby's eyes flashed with green sparks. "Why should they be damned?" She dared question him and saw his brows shoot up in surprise, then furrow into a dark scowl. Abby was no longer afraid of that warning sign. "They were blameless for whatever happened to them," she said firmly. "Surely the Lord is merciful enough to recognize that."

"Fornication is a sin! They deserve no mercy! They must spend their lives in penance."

Abby knew that fanatical gleam, knew he could go on for hours about the fate of sinners. She spoke quickly to forestall him. "How did you find me?"

The question brought a halt to his prepared speech. He sputtered a moment, realizing the young woman was not cowed by him. His deep frown told her he didn't like it. He was used to inspiring fear or feelings of unworthiness in the souls he tried to save from the fires of hell.

"It was surmised by the soldiers who came upon the scene after the massacre that you had survived. The only bodies buried were those of my dear brother and his wife. I warned him no good would come of his selfish desire to leave his home and travel into the wilderness. He should have stayed and honored his brother. His punishment was sent from God…"

"Bull crap!" Abby exploded.

Jacob's mouth dropped open in shock. Cassidy's shoulders heaved with an effort to keep from laughing. The man with Jacob looked warily from one to the other, wondering how this slip of a young woman could stand up to the fiery wrath of a man of God.

"He left the farm because you worked us like slaves. He wanted something better than your constant preaching of doom for us sinners." Abby couldn't stop now that she'd started. All she could think of was the life on Jacob's farm, the endless work followed by hours of preaching. "We had to escape to a place where we could control our own lives."

"Hah! Where was the control once the Indians struck? It was just punishment…"

"Don't talk to me of punishment." Her voice was deadly quiet, her fierce glare a match for his. "We had bad luck along the way. Our original wagon train had to leave us behind. We joined with other stragglers but there were too few of us. We must have been too tempting for the raiders to resist."

"You show disrespect for your elders!" Jacob snarled. "You, too, have been contaminated by the godless ways of the heathens. Your Pa would whip you good for speaking to me in this manner."

Abby's sudden smile took the venom out of his look to one of surprise. "I don't think so, Uncle Jacob. I think he always wished he could stand up to you. The only time he did was when we left the farm even though you tried everything to keep us there."

"I knew it was a terrible mistake! A family must stay together! It is God's way."

"It's your way!" she accused. "You needed the free labor."

"On your knees you wicked woman! Repent your willfulness, your disrespect!" Jacob's finger pointed to the ground in front of him, his eyes a fierce scowl, his red beard bobbing with anger.

Abby glared down at the dirt floor where he was pointing and deliberately spat there, her eyes mirroring her contempt. Jacob reared back as if to hit her. Abby's eyes defied him but when Jacob became aware of Cassidy stepping forward to his wife's side he clenched his fist impotently at his side.

"Mr. Bristol, I'll thank you to remember that Mrs. Cassidy is my wife. Any man who raises a hand to her will answer to me."

"You tolerate such insolence from a woman?" Jacob demanded.

"I never heard her speak that way to me so I figure she knows you better than I do. She had her reasons for not wanting to live with you after her parents were killed."

"What choice did she have captured by savages and forced to do God knows what in their vermin infested village!" Jacob's lips curled in disgust.

Abby's smile remained fixed in place. "I was no captive, Uncle Jacob. I lived with them by my own choice. They were my family."

"I was your family! You belonged with me!"

"Why? How would you have treated me?"

Jacob was sputtering at her audacity to challenge him, something even men didn't dare do. "...Why...like a daughter."

"Like the daughter you beat with a strap?" Abby challenged.

"I do not believe in sparing the rod. I teach obedience and the fear of God."

"No, you teach hate and fear...of you."

Jacob drew himself up to full height, towering over her, his fists clenched at his sides. "God will punish you for your wicked ways. You are no child of God. You have been tainted by heathens and surely you will die in the fires of hell!"

"Somehow that sounds better to me than to have spent these past years with you."

"I searched the wilderness for you. I knew you were somewhere in this area."

"I know. I saw you."

"You saw..." The man's face was mottled with anger. "I came here today to see for myself you are alive and safe, but I pity this good man for taking you for a wife. You have lain down with savages. You are not fit to live with God-fearing white people."

Cassidy's eyes smoldered with sudden fire. "I think you've said enough, Mr. Bristol. My wife's past is my business and no one else's. I'll thank you to keep your dirty thoughts to yourself. You are no longer welcome here."

"I have no wish to stay and have a woman treat me in this manner. If she were my wife I would beat her until there was no stubbornness left in her."

Cassidy shook his head with pity. "I feel sorry for your wife, Bristol, I feel real sorry for her. She must be afraid to open her mouth."

"She speaks only with respect for her husband. Never would she dare to speak as your...wife does."

Cassidy grinned. "It does make things right lively around here," he said, giving his wife an appreciative look. "It takes a real woman to stand off raiding Indians, to prepare meals for all the stagecoach passengers passing through, assist the settlers, and put meat on the table with her hunting. I couldn't ask for a better wife."

Seeing he would find no sympathy from Abby's husband, Jacob glared at the young red-haired woman before him. She had turned into a real beauty. It was a shame she had been ruined by the Indians. She was no longer fit to live in white society. He could take her and erase the heathens touch. He could bring her to redemption, but here, with Cassidy, she was beyond his help. He saw no shame in her bearing. She faced him as if there were no sin upon her.

"God will punish you," he warned, then strode out the door, his friend behind him.

Together Abby and Cassidy followed them outside, watched the two mount and ride out. Jacob's face thunderous with suppressed anger.

Cassidy chuckled. "I have the feeling Brother Jacob isn't used to being talked to that way. Must have been a right shocking experience."

Abby's eyes were troubled. "I couldn't help myself. The moment I knew it was him it was as if everything from the past came boiling out, things my father would have liked to say to him, things I had to say for him. I couldn't play the part of the obedient niece any longer."

"Why should you?" Cassidy said putting his arm around her in an unaccustomed display of affection. "He's got no say about anything you do. What a joyless home he must have with his view of a punishing God. I thought maybe you exaggerated some with your childhood memories of him. Now I see that you didn't. There's no worse enemy than one who sees himself as having God on his side."

Abby gave her husband a smile full of gratitude. "If I hadn't told him what's been festering inside me I think I would have split a gut."

Again Cassidy chuckled, his hand reaching up to touch her hair, noticing the way the sunlight made it catch fire. "You've grown into quite a woman, Abigail Cassidy." He drew her against him, his lips coming down on hers.

For a moment Abby resisted, feeling conspicuous on the front porch. She could feel her husband's arousal, knew he wanted her, and wanted her now. Inside she felt grateful to him, her senses still fired by her encounter with her uncle. They were alone at the station now. Wes had disappeared days ago. No coach was due for several days. When Cassidy drew her inside Abby went willingly. For once she felt a stirring inside her.

In their bedroom she quickly shed her dress and her shift, watching Cassidy strip off his clothes with haste. She admired his hard, strong body even as he paused to drink in the sight of her. Her youthful body was filling out more with each passing month, ripening into the curves of a woman. Her breasts were fuller, her body strong from her hunting and from hard work.

Cassidy drew her hard against him, pressing his lips hotly to hers, but only for a moment. He was too impatient to wait. He bore her down on the bed, his breath rasping loudly in the small room as his hands explored her body. Abby responded by touching him, her own fingers rubbing over ridges of hard sinew and muscle. Eagerly she met his fierce kiss, her legs wrapping around him. Something was building inside her, something new and startling.

Moments later Cassidy's body covered hers. She wanted to ask him to wait, to go slower and let her enjoy this feeling, but his hardness drove into her. She knew then it would be over much too soon. His passion was a feverish burst of thrusts followed by a loud groan and a stiffening of his entire body. She wanted to hold him closer, to urge him not to stop but knew it would be useless. He moved to lay beside her, leaving Abby on the brink of a precipice with no way down. She tried to tell herself it was her fault she had been left behind. Yet she couldn't deny Cassidy had been very abrupt. They'd come into this room only minutes ago.

She couldn't talk to him about it. His satisfaction was obvious in the way he lay sprawled. Hiding her disappointment she sat up Indian fashion, letting his seed drain out of her. She felt guilty doing it, knowing he wanted a child, that he watched for signs. He didn't realize she was careful not to let it happen. A baby would be nice but she didn't feel secure enough yet to want that responsibility.

Minutes later Cassidy reached for his clothes and went out to check on the horses. Abby heaved a sigh of frustration and went outside to clean the quail. Instead of feeling loved, Cassidy's love-making left her restless, somehow sad. Her gaze strayed to the surrounding hills with a momentary longing for the freedom they offered. Sighing again she retrieved the quail and bent to the task of plucking them.

22

With the arrival of autumn came gentle days and cool nights. Abby didn't have as much time to hunt as before, but fortunately her traps around the garden yielded a seemingly unending supply of rabbits. The best pelts she cleaned and hid until she could offer them to settlers passing through.

The frequent arrival of the stagecoaches made her think of John Jay. She wondered where he was, what he was doing now. Did he ever think of her the way she thought of him.

Would she ever see him again?

Christmas came. Wes spent the holidays with them, making holiday ornaments and carving angels and wise men out of wood or cactus. He was clever and inventive, trying to coax Abby out of her blue mood, one Cassidy hadn't seemed to notice.

She baked pies and fresh bread. For their Christmas dinner she baked stuffed quail with sage dressing. Cassidy sent to Warner's Ranch for apples that grew in the nearby mountains.

Her pies disappeared almost as fast as she baked them.

If a coach came through the station would ring with the sound of Christmas carols, Abby's soft voice blending in with Wes's more powerful one and Cassidy's slightly off key bass. They surprised each other with silly gifts. Abby carved a roadrunner out of mesquite wood and pasted real quail feathers on it. She made Wes a vest of rabbit fur for the cold nights ahead and her husband a buckskin vest from deer hide. For herself she made moccasins.

Cassidy bought several dresses for her, plain, unadorned ones for working around the station. Sometimes the women passing through offered Abby a glimpse of the latest fashion in their trunks. She saw silks, satins, laces and frills. Though she would love to see what she looked like in such dresses they were of no practical use at Seven Springs.

With the New Year the nights grew colder still. Abby snuggled close to her husband at night, listening to him snore. She longed to visit some of the places the immigrants talked about; Los Angeles, San Diego, San Bernardino. Exotic names for which she had no image. She hadn't seen a town since she came west.

Twice her Kumeyaay family came to visit, making brief camp in the hills behind the springs, away from the areas frequented by the white settlers. She learned Moyla had married Little Otter and now lived with the Yuma people near the Colorado River. Hahro looked fit as ever, and her young brother Weatuk, was growing into a sturdy, handsome young man. He was very shy around her, seldom speaking, but she talked to her mother, Opachuk, learning the gossip of the People. She also learned Night Wolf had been very angry when he learned she had gone away with a white man. He had stalked away and hadn't returned since.

Abby felt a twinge of guilt. She wouldn't allow herself to think what might have been had she stayed to accept him as her husband, wouldn't allow herself to wonder if she might have been happier. Not that she was unhappy, she scolded herself, it was just a nagging feeling that something was missing in her life.

There were days when she could escape her duties briefly and ran for the sheer joy of being free under the open sky. She ran to keep her wind strong. Cassidy thought she was hunting or gathering wild grasses to make baskets or clay to make pots. He was proud of the skills she'd learned with the Indians especially since it cost him nothing and made their lives more comfortable…though he would never speak of it to those who passed through.

Her keen hearing warned them of the approach of riders or stagecoaches, even before the horn sounded. At times she melted into the thick tangle of mesquite with a rifle when strangers approached. They were all alone here, easy prey for outlaws or Indians who wanted their stock.

If she heard the riders, it meant they weren't Indians, who Cass would never hear. So Abby needed to always be alert.

During the winter Abby continued her studies with Wes, learning history from his books, reading poems, and learning about philosophy. Her mind was quick to absorb the lessons and was always thirsty for more. She practiced her writing until she saw the change from a childish scrawl to the flowing style of an adult.

Summer came again, bringing with it oppressive heat. The blazing sun seemed to sear the hills and the desert floor, yet the hardy plants withstood the assault, adapted by millions of years of just such fury. Whenever possible Abby slipped away into the hills, bathing in a spring to keep cool.

Above her a golden eagle circled with deceptively lazy movements, looking relaxed, not showing its relentless scanning of the ground below for the slightest movement.

Gliding from the cool water, Abby sat naked on a rock at the edge of the pool, her body glowing golden brown as she began braiding her long copper hair into one long plait. She knew the immigrant women tried to avoid the sun with their long dresses and bonnets. To them, sun browned skin was not considered attractive.

Their former way of life seemed a hundred years removed from this barren desert. There were things about her appearance that would give the good ladies back home the vapors, from her all over tan to the unladylike muscles that came from surviving off the land, as well as the hard work of caring for her garden, cooking sometimes large meals for the stagecoach passengers…even helping with the stock, feeding exhausted stage horses extra oats and sometimes washing and grooming them.

Even though the presidential election was still a year away, things were already heating up in Washington. Candidates were making themselves known. The issue of slavery was dividing the country. Talk of succession from the Southern States grew stronger. If a Northerner was elected, there would be a mass withdrawal of the slave states. No one seemed to take the middle ground, you were either pro-slavery or anti-slavery, and passions ran fierce.

One afternoon when the station was quiet, Cassidy found Abby working in her garden. He brought her a cup of cool water from the well pump. She drank it down, grateful for the excuse to stop. Something was obviously on his mind.

"I'm thinking of taking a trip to San Diego," he said. "I want to see a friend about investing in some property in the mountains near the place called Cuyamuca, a place where I can grow hay and invest in cattle. I don't intend to live out here forever," he said, his gaze fixed off in the distance to where that property lay. "How'd you like to come along and have me buy you a proper dress, like a real lady wears?"

Abby's eyes lit up with excitement. "You mean it? You want me to come along?"

"Sure. You been working hard and so have I. It will be cool by the ocean. There'll be parties to attend, maybe a play or a concert. I've got friends there who will be happy to put us up for a while."

"But….the station?"

"I've already talked to Wes, plus Warner is sending one of his men down to help out while we're gone. I'll be bringing back supplies so we'll take the wagon.

"When can we leave?" She was so excited she wanted to drop everything and leave right this minute.

Cassidy chuckled at her excitement. "In two days' time. Think you can stand the wait?"

Abby threw her arms around him, hugging him fiercely. "No, I can't wait. I want to go now."

He laughed and hugged her back. "Me, too, but we got a few things to get under control first. You just keep working that garden. I've got fences to check."

Abby went back to work with renewed vigor, her fatigue of minutes ago completely gone as she began to hum softly to herself.

Before they left, Abby again saw Cassidy talking to the two Mexicans with the wagon. It was right after another wagon train had passed through. This time one of the Mexican's saw her watching them. His gaze changed from mild disinterest in what her husband was saying to a malignant sneer. Cassidy's attention was directed to the other man and missed it. The man's cruel gaze seemed to hold a promise for the future.

Minutes later the two boarded the wagon and headed east along the trail into the desert. Abby knew they were going out to retrieve furniture or stock left behind, that was how Cassidy made some of his money. She knew he often sold horses, mules, cattle or sheep to anyone who would pay the price. She had the feeling he wanted to take most of his money to San Diego, someplace safe.

When Cassidy realized she had been watching he offered no explanation. She wanted to tell him those men had almost raped her sister but had the feeling he wouldn't care. There were times when she sensed his love of money took precedence over all else. It was a feeling which served to keep her emotions reserved where her husband was concerned. In many ways he was a good man but there was a side of him she didn't quite trust.

As long as the two Mexicans kept their distance she said nothing. When they were in the area she was doubly careful, moving like a shadow through the brush and hills she had come to know so well. With the preparation for the trip to San Diego she had no time to think about them, but threw herself into finishing the hoeing of her garden, to washing their clothes and pressing them with an iron heated in the fireplace.

The next day was her last hunting trip to leave fresh meat for Wes and his helper. She noticed several emaciated cows had been added to Cassidy's herd, as well as two mules which could barely stand. On one of them open sores oozed pus from where harnesses had cut into the animal's flesh. Abby felt so sorry she made a salve for the wounds and brought both mules' oats and some choice cuts of grass. The animals were too exhausted to wander far from the springs, but the grass there had little chance to grow tall due to the settlers who camped there frequently.

The trip to San Diego also meant a chance for Abby to renew acquaintance with Ramon and Vicenta Carrillo. She felt the stirring of excitement as she climbed into the wagon beside her husband. With a wave to Wes they headed toward the distant mountains.

The trip was slower than when she had arrived on horseback, but there were bedrolls in the wagon and plenty of supplies. For the Carrillo's Abby had gathered honey from a tree hive the way Pion had showed her, and baked several loaves of fresh bread. When they arrived at the rancho, Vicenta enveloped Abby in a warm hug while Cassidy and Ramon shook hands.

"It is wonderful to see you," Vicenta said with dark eyes dancing with pleasure. "We have thought of you often, and had word from the settlers and the stage drivers that things were going well at Seven Springs." She tried to reach around Cassidy's large body and hug him too. "How long can you stay? We want to keep you for a long time."

Cassidy chuckled as he held Vicenta by the shoulders and looked at her widening middle then at Ramon's. "Not too long," he teased. "Or we might get fat and sassy like the two of you."

Vicenta slapped his shoulder in mock anger. "When you get to be our age one of the few pleasures you have left is eating. As you will find one day."

"Yeah, you are getting pretty ancient. How old are you now? Fifty some?"

Vicenta laughed heartily. "Fifty some is close enough. Now come inside. I have prepared a special dinner in your honor. Enchiladas, refried beans, that salsa you like so well, and a big steak, rare and juicy."

"Oh my, Vicenta, you sure know how to tempt a man." Cassidy threw his arm around Ramon's shoulders. "Any time you get tired of this woman I'd be glad to take her on as my cook."

Ramon cast his wife a teasing glance. "I will give that some serious thought." Ramon had to jump fast to escape the kick aimed for his backside. They were all laughing as they went into the ranch house where Maria, the Indian girl brought them fresh lemonade. Abby smiled at the young girl, happy to be back with friends. She was aware that both Maria and Vicenta had dropped their gazes to her middle, looking for signs of a child.

"How are things going with you, Ramon?" Cassidy asked when the first greetings were over and they were seated in the sala. It was a serious question not meant to just pass the time.

Ramon gave a brief shrug. "The cattle are fat and healthy. We lose a few now and then to either the Indians or the rustlers, I'm not sure which, but the price of wool is good."

"Has the government ever come through for the Indians?"

Sadly Ramon shook his head. "It is criminal what they have done to those people. They force them to stay in designated areas, but they have never been given an actual reservation. Any white man who decides he wants their land can petition the governor and get it. The Indians have always taken their living from the hills, the desert. If it weren't for the gardens they now grow the corn and beans, they would long since have starved. Whenever I can, I give them work here on the ranch and pay them with beef and supplies. A few other ranchers do the same, but the sad fact is every time something is missing it's the Indians who get the blame. They almost strung up one brave for horse stealing, only to find the horse and the guilty cowboy over in Temecula."

Abby listened with interest and with sadness. She knew how the white man looked down on any race other than their own. Through ignorance they closed their eyes and their minds to the truth.

Cassidy frowned at Ramon's statement. "We have some men who are too quick with a rope. Vigilantes accomplish little in the way of justice if they hang the wrong man."

"It happens wherever the law is too far away," Ramon said with a sigh. "We have soldiers nearby in Camp Wright, but there aren't enough of them to be everywhere. I'm surprised we haven't had any attempts at holding up a stagecoach."

"Joe Smith has been doing a damn good job of keeping the stage route in San Diego County clear. He's not someone the bandits want to mess with," Cassidy said.

Ramon nodded. "Not to mention the fact that tampering with the U. S. Mail is a federal offense, and ever since Juan Flores was hanged last year for killing that store keeper in San Juan Capistrano, the banditos have been less active."

Vicenta excused herself to supervise the preparations of supper, but Abby was interested in the men's discussion. "What about this bandit we've been hearing so much about lately?" Abby asked. "This Vasquez?"

Ramon's look turned grim. "Tiburcio Vasquez. He's a bad one. He's been seen recently in the Palomar Mountain area. That's too close for comfort. Some say he's responsible for the disappearing cattle."

"I thought he was up north," Cassidy said, accepting the cigar Ramon was offering him.

The two men were silent for a moment as they lit up and puffed.

"Things grew too hot," Ramon said. "Too many posses with ropes on his trail."

"Let's hope the soldiers soon make it too hot for him here," Abby said.

"Joe Largo, the one you call Joe Smith was through here last week," Ramon went on. "He says he's not going to be working for Butterfield much longer."

Cassidy's frown deepened. "I'm sorry to hear that. Did he say why?"

"Seems he has his eye on a bit of property near Pala. This stretch of the line is in need of hay to feed the stock as well as fresh meat."

Cassidy gave a nod, his expression showing his appreciation of the cigar. "He'll make more money doing that, I expect, but tough men like him are hard to find."

Ramon nodded his agreement. "He's done his bit for California. He and Cave Couts helped survey the California Mexico border. He also helped Jim Birch plan the route for the so called Jackass Mail from San Antonio to San Diego, then acted as the San Diego county supervisor for the line. He's fought his share of Indians and bandits."

"Yeah, I guess he's earned a rest, but we're sure gonna' miss him."

The conversation turned to a discussion of the politics. Representing California were two U. S. Senators, D.C. Broderick and William H. Gwin, with Gwin being the senior senator of the two. Broderick was elected in 1857. From his first days in Washington, Broderick hadn't been well received by the other senators, where Gwin was well known and well liked.

Already Gwin had served six years in office. Stories of Broderick's political games in California had preceded him. He was vehemently opposed to slavery in California, where Gwin was for it. Broderick had even spoken out against slavery before the assembled thirty fourth Congress. Of the 31 states, only nine or ten were actively striving to maintain slavery. With twenty six million people in the country, only about six million were intensely interested in the extension of slavery.

During the same month that the first Butterfield Overland Mail had made its first run, John B. Weller had been elected Governor of California. He was a former U. S. Senator, a man well acquainted with the ins and outs of government. Slavery had officially been abolished in California in 1858, though it was a fact that Indian slaves could still be purchased in Los Angeles, a fact the state legislature was rapidly moving to halt.

Abby listened to the conversation of the two men as it led from politics to railroads.

"What will happen to the Butterfield Mail when the rails meet?" Ramon asked. "Now, carrying the mail from St. Louis to San Francisco in twenty three or twenty four days is the fastest way, but the rails will be faster yet, without the necessity of so many stations and men."

"The way I figure it," Cassidy said. "The Overland mail can't last more than four or five years, so I'm making plans based on that assumption. Right now, the immigrants find the Southern route attractive cause it's open year round. There's too many stories about whole wagon trains trapped by snow storms in the Rockies or the Sierras. A lot of 'um died. But, like you say, once the rails stretch across country the Southern Route will dry up, I'm looking at a place called Cuyamaca. There's a piece of land there I'd like to have. I'd like being closer to San Diego, which is why Abby and I are headed there for a spell. Possibly I'll buy a piece of land close to town as well where we can build a house."

Ramon's smile was genuine. "Sounds as if you are making plans for the future. That is good, amigo. Vicenta and I are most fortunate. We will stay here with or without the stagecoach. We do not need it to survive. My friend, John Rains, was most generous to grant us a loan to pay the taxes." He shook his head. "For years we have lived here without having to pay for the privilege. Now we must pay taxes or we lose the land. It has happened to many of the Spanish families already. The gringos have taken full advantage of the fact we often speak no English, and are defrauding us out of our land. When a Spaniard or Mexican takes such a matter to the courts, the court always sides with the gringos."

Cassidy nodded in agreement. "It's been happening too often."

"Take Pio Pico," Ramon said, waving his hands at the surrounding land. "Once he owned all of this. Twice he was governor before California became a state. His land holdings were immense. Now he has only his Ranchito, as he calls it, which is only nine thousand acres. His fortune is gone."

"The sad thing is that the Spanish are too trusting," Cassidy said. "When someone offers to lend them money, or someone asks for their signature to guarantee a loan, they are too eager to take the money or help out. They have little concept of what the interest rates were doing to them in a very short time. Then, when they can't repay the loan, or make good when the other fellow defaulted, they lose their land for a fraction of what it's worth."

"It is true," Ramon said sadly. "We are too trusting. We are fortunate to have a friend like John Rains. He is always ready to help."

Cassidy had to restrain himself from commenting. He didn't especially trust Rains. The man had a reputation of over-extending himself and had called in loans that resulted in a loss of property in the very way just described. He hoped Ramon was right about Rains and that these good friends wouldn't be added to the ranks of those who had lost their land.

"How will you repay him?" Cassidy couldn't help but ask.

"We have many cattle. When the loan comes due we will sell what we have to."

"What happens if the price of beef goes down?" Abby felt compelled to ask. She had seen the tightening of her husband's mouth that the Carrillo's had borrowed money from Rains, and she had her own feelings about him. "It seems to me there's more and more cattle in these hills. There might be an oversupply."

"Ah!" Ramon waved his hand dismissively. "There will always be a market for beef. I have no fear of that. And, should such a thing happen, I am certain John would merely extend the time of the loan. He would never put us out in the cold."

Abby and Cassidy's eyes met, both thinking the same thing. They hoped Ramon's trust was not misplaced.

Their stay at the rancho passed too quickly. During the day, Cassidy rode out with Ramon to see to the many cattle he owned. Abby passed the time with Vicenta and Maria, exchanging stories of the people who passed through on the stagecoaches or on the immigrant wagons. One afternoon she paid a visit to the Kupa village to see friends there. It made her sad to see how things had changed for the Indians, restricted to smaller and smaller areas for survival.

Early on the morning of the fourth day Abby and Cassidy climbed onto their wagon and headed south toward San Diego. It would be a long trip. A group of soldiers came up behind them on the trail and warned them about the presence in the area of Tiburcio Vasquez. The man was a cold-blooded killer, and the mountains around Warner and Carrillo ranches covered a large area with many hiding places, as Abby well knew from the time she had spent with the Kumeyaay. It would not be easy to find the bandits.

After the oppressive heat of the desert the mountains felt deliciously cool. Abby's sharp gaze kept watch as they traveled. Both she and Cassidy had rifles close at hand. Though Cassidy didn't speak of it, Abby knew he had a lot of money with him. She could feel it in his nervousness as he pressed to keep close behind the soldiers.

They both breathed easier once they left the mountains behind and began to cross the ranges of foothills between them and the coast. The first night they camped well away from the trail, not lighting a fire, eating only cold food. On the second day, they caught up with several families traveling to San Diego and formed a train for mutual safety. Abby enjoyed the opportunity to get to know the families in the evening when they camped. Her healing skills were quickly put to use to treat one of the children with a chronic cough. Abby didn't tell them the herbal tea remedy she used was given to her by a medicine woman. That she, herself, was considered a medicine woman. She knew that would have drastically changed the way her abilities were viewed.

The next morning the mother told her it was the first time in a week her son had slept through the night. At camp the following night another of the women came to her with a female problem that Abby was able to ease as well. The women were so pleased they couldn't stop talking about her wonderful ability to heal.

Once they reached San Diego the families went their separate ways. Cassidy drove to a new home near the center of town, a large, two story brick building. Along the front of the second floor was a long veranda and large bay windows. Abby was overwhelmed, never having seen such a beautiful home.

She was introduced to their hosts, Charles and Violet Champion. Charles was a slight, dapper man with a quick smile and even quicker wit. Violet resembled her name with her sweet face, soft smile and a warm gentleness. The couple was in their mid-forties, with three children living at home and two married. Mary Louise, eighteen worked for one of the hotels in town. Jeffery, fourteen, was a shy, gangly teen ager who seemed in awe of Abby and her violently red hair. The youngest was Susan, a dark eyed charmer of seven who looked very much like her mother.

Charles owned a mercantile in the center of San Diego and was part owner of the hotel where his daughter worked. The Champions welcomed them warmly. Abby was rendered speechless when she saw the room she and her husband would be sharing. It was situated on the second floor overlooking the sprawling city, and, in the distance, San Diego Bay. It was her first glimpse of the ocean. Her excitement was difficult to contain when Cassidy promised to take her there.

"Harriet will draw your bath," Violet said, introducing them to the housekeeper. "You'll want to wash off the trail dust. Supper will be ready in an hour. I hope that will give you enough time."

"More than enough," Cassidy assured her, ever the genial guest. "Abby and I will be down directly."

Violet gave Abby a shy smile then left them to bathe and change. Abby was so excited with the room she plopped down on the bed, bouncing on the feather mattress.

"It's so soft. How can you sleep on this?"

"Just wait," Cassidy promised her. "You'll find out its sheer heaven."

While Cassidy bathed Abby unpacked their clothing, hanging it in the armoire or placing it in drawers. The one room was larger by far than any of the rooms at Seven Springs. Its wood paneling gleamed with a rich luster, there were gas lights on the walls, the first she'd ever seen. All the furniture was European with exquisite hand carved detail. Some was mahogany, some oak, and some cherry wood. The curtains were sheer and soft to her fingers as Abby explored every inch of the lovely room. The floor was covered with a large Persian rug in a colorful blend of greens, whites and yellows.

No one had to tell her it took money to have a home like this. She knew it with every fiber of her body. She also knew one day she wanted to own a home just like this one.

At that thought her smile faltered. She would be welcome, that is, if no one knew about her past. Living with Indians was almost worse than being a woman of easy virtue.

One of the women they traveled with told Abby about the houses in San Diego where women accepted pay for taking care of the physical needs of men. It was a further shock to learn even married men were known to frequent such establishments. She wondered if Cassidy ever had.

23

Abby was curious about everything. She was eager to see the city, eager to see the ocean and to meet the people Cassidy had come to do business with. Along with the eagerness was also the fear that she might do something to embarrass her husband. She vowed to think before she spoke and to watch her manners. Violet would be an excellent model for her to observe.

Abby wore one of her new dresses to dinner, a cotton dress of mist green decorated with inserts of ecru lace and ribbon. The bodice fit her snugly, revealing the ripeness of her figure, the skirt accentuating the curve of her hips, and the smallness of her waist. But she was quick to see the dress was hopelessly different from what the other women wore, especially Violet, who wore a dress of whisper soft material Abby didn't know the name of, with froths of lace at the sleeves and around the neckline. A cameo broach decorated the snug fitting bodice while a gold chain with a heart shaped diamond pendant lay against her throat.

Even the high button shoes Violet wore were the finest leather, white as snow and supple. Abby was learning just by observing, and saw just how much she didn't know.

Most days Cassidy disappeared to conduct his business while Abby remained with Violet. She was curious about the running of such a large house and found her hostess more than willing to instruct her. Abby was amazed by the water faucets in the kitchen rather than having to carry it in by bucket or by vigorous pumping. There were many things she had never seen before, an ice box for keeping milk and other foods cold, exquisite European made furniture that was a far cry from the hand-hewn chairs she'd always known.

The cupboards and pantry in the large, airy kitchen made Abby realize how dark and dingy her home was with its thick adobe walls and dirt floors. The woven grass mats on her floors were not as warm and cheery as Persian rugs on hardwood floors. Even the braided rugs in some of the rooms lent an air of cheerfulness to Violet's house, as did the paintings on the walls.

Abby studied everything, absorbing color schemes and decorations. The house with its lawn and beautiful trees and flowers almost brought tears to her eyes with its loveliness.

In the evenings she and Cassidy were invited to the homes of his business acquaintances. Abby would have felt hopelessly out of place if her husband hadn't allowed her to purchase a new dress and if Violet hadn't given her another. Though Violet was thinner than Abby they were able to alter the dress so it fit nearly perfect.

Abby was readily accepted by the women but was aware of the sometimes lustful gazes of the men. Cassidy was envied for having a wife who was so beautiful and shapely. He didn't bother to tell them about her past. He figured it wasn't any of their business, and he liked being envied by important men. There was a definite advantage to having an attractive wife. It made him noticed. Cassidy had his own plans for the future, and being accepted by the cream of San Diego society was definitely a high priority.

One evening the dinner party was at the home of a prominent San Diego judge, Horace Hartnell. In the elegant formal dining room, wall gas lamps lit the assembly of many of San Diego's first families. Along with Cassidy's hosts the Champions, there were lawyers, merchants and large land holders. Dinner was just about over, the men anxious to retire to the library and their cigars when

Hartnell's man servant came into the room and spoke quietly to him.

"There are two gentlemen to see you, sir, a Doctor Gwin and a Congressman Scott."

Before Horace could react, faces of those close by, who heard the exchange, recognized the names and looked up expectantly. A murmur went around the table, and even before Horace could rise, the two visitors came into the room, their expressions mirroring their sense of mission.

"Sorry to barge in this way," Dr. Gwin said, a tall, imposing figure with a mane of thick, silver-grey hair. Beside him was the smaller, but equally imposing young congressman. "I have important news."

Most of the people in the room knew Dr. Gwin, as he preferred to be called, even though he was a United States Senator. At fund raising affairs the senator had met most of them before.

Horace took a moment to introduce the two visitors around. For once, the ladies were not eager to escape the talk of politics. The presence of two such distinguished men interrupting their dinner surely meant something of importance had taken place.

Abby was in awe of the dynamic senator with the intense blue eyes. Even without being told she knew he was a man of immense power. Cassidy was leaning forward, eager to hear what the man had to say.

"I'm sorry to bear the news that Senator Broderick is dead," Gwin said, waving away the chairs the manservant brought for him and Congressman Scott. "We're on our way back to Washington and decided we'd stop in San Diego and bring you the news in person."

Horace Hartnell was on his feet, consternation in his face. "What happened? How did he die?" Broderick was perhaps not well liked but his influence reached every corner of the state.

Gwin gave an eloquent shrug. "It was a duel. Judge Terry called him out on the field of honor. Senator Broderick died three days later of his wound."

"And Terry?"

"Not a scratch. Broderick's shot hit the ground in front of him. From what I understand, Terry took careful aim. He was shooting to kill."

A murmur of angry voices went around the room. News of duels was nothing new. Though illegal they still were an accepted way to settle matters of honor. It was not the first duel Broderick had fought. It was also no secret to anyone in the room that Broderick and Gwin had been arch enemies, politically, for many years. During the recent elections they had both campaigned with fiery tongues which vilified the other.

"What will happen now?" Charles Champion asked. "Who's going to take his place?"

"That is yet to be decided," Scott put in. "Someone will be appointed at a later date I would imagine. We're carrying the news to Washington. The decision will be made there."

"If I have my say," Gwin said grimly. "He will be a Lecompton man. Broderick was tearing the state apart with his anti-slavery views. He wouldn't recognize the will of the people. The pro-slavery majority should be allowed to make the decision for California. Economically, this state needs slavery in order to develop its vast resources to the fullest."

Hartnell, who was a Southerner, nodded. "We'll show them the will of the people in the upcoming presidential election. The South will have its say."

Abby was shocked to see so much Southern sentiment. To her the issue of slavery was a moral one, very clear cut. She had seen a little of slavery on the wagon trip through the Southern states and territories. It shocked her even at the tender age of ten. From what she heard at Seven Springs the issue was a volatile one. Even here in this room she could see sympathies were divided. The land owners wanted to own slaves to work the land and provide cheap labor for their business enterprises. Yet, how could any rational human being condone it?

Beside her, her husband nodded his agreement. "We'll overwhelm any Northern candidate. The South will be victorious."

Abby had a bad feeling as she listened to the talk. Minutes later everyone left the table, the men going to the library to continue their talk over brandy and cigars. Abby would rather listen to what the men had to say, but knew she wouldn't like it even if they would allow it.

She'd heard much about Senator Gwin from the people passing through Seven Springs. He had been in the senate for five terms and was a well-known power in Washington. In addition, he was a top advisor to President Buchanan, whom he privately called a 'weak ninny' saying he refused to take a stand on the large issues facing the nation. Gwin was doing his best to guide the president's thinking on the issue of slavery. With Kansas Territory applying for statehood, whether they would vote to become a slave state or not was a hot issue. The Southerners were urging them to join the ranks of the slave states in order to broaden their power base in Washington.

In the parlor Abby sat with the ladies sipping tea while Judge Hartnell's sixteen year old daughter played a hand carved rosewood piano. The instrument had a delicate tone which Abby listened to, transfixed. She had seldom heard such music and could easily ignore the obvious mistakes made by the nervous girl. She remembered the organ one of the women on the wagon train had played one evening. She remembered the lively music at the Carrillo's rancho, and that of the Kumeyaay, the drums and flutes. Music gave pleasure, yet her Uncle Jacob had been violently against music in any form. It was sent by the devil he frequently declared in his strident tones, to tempt men and women into the ways of wickedness.

Abby's mind drifted to her uncle's frequent tirades. When she was younger she hadn't thought to question his pious views. He was an adult, therefore he must be right. Now she knew his views were not those of most men. Jacob saw evil in everything. She wondered why.

The Kumeyaay saw joy and peace. It was obvious to her which ones were happiest. Jacob seemed to have no capacity whatever for joy and thanksgiving, he was too busy searching out evil, real or imagined.

One of the kitchen helpers came into the room to Mrs. Hartnell who was seated near Abby. The whispered conversation included the words labor and baby, and from the worried expression on the girl's face Abby knew there was a problem.

"Excuse me," Mrs. Hartnell whispered to those around her and left the room. Abby hesitated a moment then followed.

Behind the big house were several smaller buildings where the staff lived. Abby followed Mrs. Hartnell to one of them where she could hear cries of agony coming from the dark interior. At the door she paused to listen, allowing her eyes to adjust.

Mrs. Hartnell was smoothing back the hair of a young Indian woman whose face and body were contorted with pain. Her hostess looked helplessly to the old Indian woman sitting on the floor nearby, chanting. It was the only way the old one knew to assist with a difficult birth.

Abby looked quickly around the room. There was no water, no light. She knew what she had to do. "Mrs. Hartnell," she said, coming forward, her confidence bringing a look of hope into the woman's eyes. "May I be of assistance? I've helped deliver a number of babies."

Relief flooded the woman's eyes. "Oh, thank you. We can't get any of the doctor's to come because she's Indian. She's been in labor for two days now. The baby won't come."

"I need hot water, soap, and some clean towels," Abby said taking command. "And please light the lamp."

Mrs. Hartnell didn't argue, doing exactly as her young guest asked. She lit the lamp, setting it on the table beside the laboring woman, and quickly went out to see to the water.

Abby sat beside the young Indian woman, speaking softly to her in the Kumeyaay tongue. Black eyes opened to look at the white woman who had come to help her. The young woman's body was bathed in sweat, her coarse, black hair saturated with it. Abby could see her strength was rapidly ebbing. She was also aware of the old woman staring at her suspiciously, startled by her use of the Indian tongue, but she didn't cease her chanting. The songs were to urge the spirits to allow the birth of the child.

Stripping away the thin blanket covering the young woman Abby began to feel of her distended belly. Under her fingers she could feel the strength of the contractions which tried to expel the child, and located the infants head. It came as no surprise to find it high in the womb rather than pointing downward toward the birth canal.

Enyaa had shown her a few methods of delivering difficult babies. She hoped those skills would be useful now or this woman would surely die, and her unborn child with her.

When she turned toward the door, impatient for the water she needed to scrub her hands, she saw a tall young Indian man standing outside, worry etched in every line of his face.

He knew his young wife was in serious trouble, that the birth was not a normal one.

He stared at Abby through the open doorway, the questions he wanted to ask showing clearly in his eyes. With nothing more to do until the water was delivered Abby covered the young woman again and stepped outside to talk to him. He understood the Kumeyaay tongue and seemed relieved to find she spoke it so fluently. It made her seem less threatening.

"The baby is turned the wrong way," she told him. "It happens sometimes. I have seen it before. I will try to turn it so that it will come naturally."

"This is her first one," he said in a voice filled with worry. "I want her and my child to be healthy."

"So do I," Abby assured him. "I will do all I can. A few words with the spirits might be helpful too."

The young man nodded to show he understood. It was unusual to have a white woman speak of the spirits as if she believed in them. Always the whites told him the only true god was their god, the one who lived in a place called heaven, and knew everything you did, good or bad. Those who believed in the old ways never spoke of them in front of whites. He moved to the back of the small house, to a place under a tree where he sat Indian fashion and began chanting a prayer to Amaayahaa.

When the water was delivered Abby quickly washed her hands with soap, all the way to her elbows. Next she washed the young woman.

"What is her name?" she asked Mrs. Hartnell.

"Til-pu," was the answer.

"Ah, Roadrunner," Abby translated. "Now we will see what we can do to help our little roadrunner."

The girl's scream of agony tore at Abby's heart as she began a slow internal examination. Mrs. Hartnell looked pale as she watched, but she didn't turn away.

Til-pu screamed her agony as contractions wracked her body. She was long past the point of trying to be brave, there was only a sea of pain that engulfed her beyond her ability to endure.

Mrs. Hartnell took one of the towels and dabbed at Abby's forehead as the sweat threatened to run down into her eyes. Time seemed to pass in slow motion as Abby worked the babe into position. She knew she wouldn't be able to turn it completely, she would have to bring it feet first.

Her sensitive touch felt the child was weakening. The strain was too much for his tiny heart, and if the ordeal wasn't ended soon it would not survive. She could feel sweat soaking her beautiful new gown but she ignored it. Her fingers worked carefully until she had both feet in the birth canal. Slowly she began to pull with a steady pressure, assisted by sudden hard contractions. Abby felt rather than saw the old Indian woman's eyes hardening at the young girl's anguished screams. She seemed about to interfere in what she must consider an unnatural way of assisting a birth.

"It's coming," Abby said to forestall her. "I've got it."

Mrs. Hartnell and the old woman watched as tiny feet emerged, then slowly a red, squirming infant. There was an audible sigh of relief as Abby lay the babe on a clean towel. She sterilized the scissors over the lamp flame before she cut the cord and began to bathe the tiny infant.

"You have a son, Til-pu," Abby told her. "We will guard him well." She turned to Mrs. Hartnell. "The father is outside. He will be happy to know the news."

Mrs. Hartnell was smiling broadly as she went out. Abby tended to mother and child until she knew the danger had passed for them both. The father came to stare in awe at his tiny, naked son. He saw his wife sleeping peacefully after her ordeal and reached out with shaking hands to hold the babe. He cradled him carefully, his expression one Abby would never forget, reverence and love.

As Abby made ready to leave he looked at her, speaking in the language of the Kumeyaay. "I know you are the one called Eagle Woman. We have heard of you. My wife and my child owe their lives to you. We will not forget."

Abby smiled, glad Mrs. Hartnell didn't understand his words. "And I will not forget you," Abby said, trying to sound casual. Then she turned to Mrs. Hartnell. "With so many settlers passing through Seven Springs, we see many things. A little healing knowledge is a tremendous help. It's just something I've picked up over the years."

Mrs. Hartnell nodded. If she had any more questions she didn't ask them. Inside the house Abby tried to regain some semblance of her former elegance. Her hair was damp from sweat, her gown now wilted. She cleaned up as best she could. When she returned to the parlor the men had joined the ladies and some of the guests were taking their leave.

Abby was the center of attention when it was learned of the miracle she had just performed. It made the good-byes warmer, more heartfelt. Cassidy stood at her side, eager to bask in the reflection of his wife's popularity. Abby could almost feel him rubbing his hands together with glee. More than anything he wanted to be accepted by these people.

Dr. Gwin and Congressman Scott were already gone, their ship would not be in port long. They were bound for Panama for the overland trek to the Gulf and a waiting ship bound for New York.

When they were the only guests remaining, Judge Hartnell clasped both of Abby's hands in is. "We are most grateful to you, my dear, for saving Til-pu and her baby. She and her husband have been with us for several years, since before they were married. She's been so excited about the arrival of a child."

"She'll need to be watched for a few days. She's very weak and so is the babe. He almost didn't make it into this world and he arrived tired. With rest they should both be fine."

"Don't you worry, we'll keep a close eye on them," he assured her. "You are welcome back here any time to check on them."

"Thank you, Judge Hartnell," Abby said. "I'll want to do that."

The ride home with the Champion's in the pale moonlight was a pleasant one. Abby and Cassidy sat in the rear seat of the covered surrey, a lap robe over their knees to keep them warm. The only sound was the clop clop of the horse's hooves, the jingle of the harness, and the occasional barking of a dog.

As they traveled along the hill top from the judge's house, the bay of San Diego lay before them, silver and glowing in the moonlight. A steamship lay in the bay, white smoke billowing from its stacks. No doubt the one carrying Dr. Gwin and Congressman Scott to Panama.

"Do you think they'll ever build the canal they're talking about?" Abby asked, her imagination fired by the proposed feat.

Cassidy shrugged. "It makes sense. The trip around the Horn takes too long, not to mention the danger of sudden storms. That's where James Birch, the man who started the Jackass Mail, was lost. He was still a young man when he went down with a ship."

"But I've heard the isthmus crossing is dangerous too," Abby said.

"It is, partly because of malaria and other jungle fevers. But there's also danger of an uprising among the natives. Still, it seems somewhat safer to cross Panama than to use the other proposed route through Nicaragua."

"They seem to change leaders so often there."

"That's the whole problem," Cassidy said. "Just when we negotiate what looks like an agreement for the canal, their president gets tossed out of office or killed and we have to start all over."

"Then why do some people think Nicaragua is still the best route?" Abby asked.

"Because of the lake that covers a good portion of the distance. It would make the job of building a canal a lot simpler."

Charles was no longer listening quietly to their conversation. "What do you think the chances are for Nicaragua?" he asked.

"Non-existent," Cassidy said. "Too much political unrest. And even though they agree they want the canal they can't agree on anything else. I'm afraid any money paid out by our government wouldn't be used for the project."

"That could happen in Panama as well," Charles said.

"I'm sure a lot of pockets will have to be lined," Cassidy said. "But the work would still get done, especially if the United States can buy out the French interest."

"France seems determined to be the one to build it," Charles said. "It seems to me the final decision will rest with them."

Cassidy gave a disgusted snort. "I don't know why they want to stick their noses into something so far away from home. This is our hemisphere. We're the logical ones to run the canal and see that the work gets done."

"What do you think about Broderick getting himself killed?" Charles asked.

"Good riddance, if you ask me. I'll bet he was responsible for most of the corruption in San Francisco. I hear you could buy a political office by paying him half of your first years' salary. He greased plenty of palms, and half the state officials were in his pocket." Cassidy had never been a fan of the late senator.

"Not to mention his anti-slavery views," Charles said, flicking the reins across the gray's back gently. "Dr. Gwin wants California to join the Southern states."

Abby closed her eyes and tuned out the talk of politics. The issue of slavery came up more and more often lately. She could see it was dividing the country into two factions, neither one ready to change their stand.

At first she'd dismissed the talk of war, but from what she'd been hearing lately she was changing her mind. California was sharply divided, that much was glaringly obvious.

24

The following morning, Cassidy took Abby with him when he started for the wharf. From their room at the Champion's, Abby had watched the ocean in its many moods. Today the sky was clear blue, as was the ocean, with fog hovering out near the horizon.

At different times of day, the great body of water might glisten like polished turquoise, or turn dark under gunmetal skies, or when enveloped in a soft mist that left the water nearly invisible from the hilltop home.

The thought of finally being able to see it close up had Abby's face flushed with excitement. In the back of the buggy was a picnic basket Harriet, the housekeeper, prepared for them.

It was a warm, sunny summer day. Abby knew well the heat of the desert. This coolness was more like the mountains where the Kumeyaay spent their summers.

Her heart gave a little lurch when she thought of the mountain village. She missed her Indian family, missed Enyaa, her medicine teacher, and especially her sister Moyla. By now, her baby would be born, but Abby didn't know how she would ever see it. She couldn't travel to Yuma, but eventually Moyla would bring her baby to show her family, and would pass by Seven Springs.

On the way to town, Cassidy stopped by Judge Hartnell's home so she could check on Til-pu and the baby. Both were much stronger and Abby could detect no signs of infection in either one. The tiny boy suckled contentedly at his mother's breast. Again Til-pu and her husband gave their thanks to Abby, leaving unsaid between them the knowledge that without it, neither mother nor child would be enjoying this moment.

Abby sang softly to herself as they approached the beach. She was feeling at peace. Cassidy listened to her song with a lopsided grin. It wasn't often he heard her sing. It made him think Abby was happy with him and didn't regret her choice to be his wife.

The crash of the surf silenced Abby's song when Cassidy drew the carriage to a halt in a grove of trees south of the wharf. Across the bay Abby could see the gleaming white sand of Coronado Island, and see the restless surge of the waves. She leaped from the buggy and ran toward the water, her excited laughter rippling in the cool breeze.

Seagulls wheeled about overhead, seeking out the air currents in their never ending quest for food. The sand here was different from that of the desert. This was finer, softer, and paler in color. It sucked at her shoes as she tried to run, eventually slowing her mad rush. At the edge of the water she stopped, her rapt expression taking in the roll of the waves, the foam that accompanied each fresh surge, and the sound each crash made. She was barely aware of Cassidy following her, his eyes only for her and her childlike delight.

"It's so beautiful!" She sounded breathless. "So....endless."

Wanting to touch the water she plopped down in the soft sand and removed her high button shoes. She wanted to experience the texture of the sand with her bare feet, feel the coolness of the water.

Cassidy chuckled but couldn't imagine himself acting so young and carefree. A moment later she sped back to him, grabbed him around the neck and playfully wrestled him down onto the sand. Like a streak of lightning she pushed him down onto his back and began to tug at his boots. Cassidy grinned at her enthusiasm and didn't have the heart to say no. He allowed her to remove his boots and socks, then he helped her roll up his pant legs so they wouldn't get wet. A moment later she was gone again, splashing in the edge of the waves.

"Slow poke!" she taunted. "See if you can catch me!"

Cassidy jumped to the challenge and raced after her. He loved the sound of her laughter as she sped along the wet sand, her bare feet making no sound, her long skirt pulled high so he could see the flash of her shapely legs....an enchanting sight.

Abby's mane of red silk had slipped from its pins and flowed behind her as she ran. Cassidy gave chase, loving her, wanting to capture her lush body against his. She was fast, too fast for his lumbering size. He was breathing hard when he gave up the chase, knowing she would come to him. The water was so inviting he waded out to his ankles, feeling the cool foam swirl about him.

He could imagine what Charles Champion or Judge Hartnell would say if they could see him now, but a quick look told him they were alone on this long stretch of beach.

When Abby realized he'd given up the chase and was wading along the shore, she turned back, kicking up foam as she ran.

"You're too fast!" he admitted as she came closer. He could see the green sparkle in her eyes, the flush of her cheeks. "This is more my speed."

Abby laughed. "Perhaps I should make you chase me more often," she teased. "It is good to know how to run fast. You never know when you might need to."

Cassidy grunted in agreement but knew he wouldn't do anything about it. As long as he had a fast horse he would let the animal do the running. When Abby ventured close enough, he grabbed her by one wrist and pulled her against his hard body.

"Now I've got you," he said with a soft laugh. "Your speed won't help you now."

His lips sought the hollow of her throat. Abby let her arms go around his shoulders, reluctant to break his good mood by pulling away. She felt wonderfully alive, her breath quickening as his lips moved over her heated skin, trailing along her throat to one small ear. A shiver went through her at the sensation of his warm breath in her ear, his gentle nibbling.

She had released her skirts and felt the tug of them as the surf wet them even more. A moment later, Cassidy swept her up into his arms and carried her across the sand to the trees. She was startled by his great strength, was aware of the glaze of passion in his eyes. She had wanted to play, he wanted to make love. A soft sigh escaped her lips as she looked around, hoping to see other people about. Unfortunately there was no one.

Cassidy set her down beside the wagon and reached for the blanket he'd brought for their picnic. He spread it on the soft grass in a clump of brush nearby, then came for Abby and carried her, depositing her on the blanket on her back.

Stretching out beside her, Cassidy began to kiss her moist red lips, his hand cupping the swell of her breast. Abby tried to empty her mind of all thought and just enjoy the moment, but too often these moments left her disappointed. She never seemed to achieve the release her husband found, leaving her to wonder if there wasn't something wrong with her that left her unable to feel deeply enough.

His lips grew fierce and demanding, his hands pulling her skirt up, and her long petticoats. He touched her soft mound possessively, sending waves of sensation through Abby.

A moment later he stripped her of her pantalets and pushed her skirts up about her waist.

Opening the front of his pants he quickly mounted her, driving his hardness into her unprepared body. Abby gave a gasp of pain which he seemed not to hear. The thrusts began, sharp and quick. With a feeling of resignation Abby knew it wouldn't last long. It never did.

His groans of passion built to a feverish peak, he grunted a few times then rolled off her, sated. Abby lay without moving, her carefree mood completely shattered.

After a moment she pushed down her petticoats and her gown and sat up. Her husband's eyes were closed, his smile almost a smirk. A moment later he was snoring. Just once she wished she could share that feeling with him. Restlessly she stood up, embarrassed by the way her gown was wrinkled from his weight. Retrieving her pantalets she pulled them on and smoothed her clothes as best she could as she walked barefoot toward the water where her shoes and his boots lay. She might as well be alone now. Cassidy would not awaken for a while.

A sadness crept over her as she walked along the deserted beach. Her thoughts began to drift idly, and as happened quite often, she pictured the tall, slim figure of John Jay Butterfield. She could see the merry light in his blue eyes, the wide smile that curved his generous mouth. Why couldn't he arrive on a stagecoach one day and demand that she come away with him.

Even as she thought it she knew it was no use. Even if he asked she wouldn't go. She had made a vow to her husband, one she would not break. Cassidy came along at a time when she needed him. He hadn't tricked her or taken advantage. They had an agreement. In return for his name and respectability, she helped him run the Seven Springs station.

This trip to San Diego convinced her they wouldn't always live in the desert. Cassidy was ambitious. He liked the city life. And, at some point in the future, he planned to move here, but only when he would financially be able to enter the society of people like the Champions and the Hartnell's.

Abby wasn't certain how she would like living here, or if she could run a fancy house such as the ones she'd visited. Part of her yearned to live like a white woman. Part of her would be happy living forever in a Rancheria in the mountains.

What made her saddest was that the Kumeyaay way of life could rapidly be coming to an end. Already there were too many whites crowding in on them. Men who wanted more and more land for their cattle. Only the isolation of the Kumeyaay lands had kept them from feeling the encroachment the Kupa and others had experienced. There was neither gold nor good grazing. Since the Kumeyaay kept no horses and only a few cattle, the little grass they had was adequate for their needs.

But, increasingly, the young men wanted to leave the Rancherias to learn the ways of the white man. There were jobs at the ranchos for laborers and cowboys, but there was also the white man's whiskey. Once an Indian tasted the fire, had felt his brain burn with its corrupting pleasure, he no longer retained the ways of the People. He followed only the seductive promise of whiskey and degradation.

Abby stopped, staring out at the vastness of the open water, watching the circling seagulls. How could she have been so happy just a short while ago when the ways of her people were in jeopardy? It was a revelation that she still thought of the Kumeyaay as her people. She would always belong to two worlds. A part of her had become as savage as the land. The city held no lure for her, the parties, the constant talk of war and politics, the women's chatter of babies, houses and fashions.

The Kumeyaay were gentle, uncomplicated. She always knew where she stood with them. With the whites she was never sure. Though many of the women of San Diego seemed to accept her, she couldn't know what they said behind her back. Did they suspect her past? How would they react if they knew?

Her thoughts gave her no peace. She was suddenly feeling she had turned her back on the Kumeyaay even though she had vowed to do everything she could to protect them and their way of life. It was time to make a plan.

When she realized Cassidy was awake she turned back, suddenly aware how hungry she was. Picking up their shoes she hoped he wouldn't get any more ideas about making love. She wasn't certain she would meekly submit.

Cassidy, too, was hungry and dug into the basket to lay out the food on the blanket where they had so recently made love. He made no mention of the interlude, as if it had never happened, and that, too, left a sadness inside her.

"Til-pu's boy sure is a cute one," Cassidy said, his gaze sliding to her middle. "I keep hoping one of these days you're going to have something to tell me. We been married for over a year now. Seems like it should be happening."

Abby lowered her eyes, glad he wasn't watching her face. How could she tell him she was doing everything she could to make certain it didn't happen, that she wasn't ready for motherhood. A part of her wondered if she ever would be.

He seemed to sense her hesitation. "There isn't any reason why you can't, is there? You do want a family?"

"Yes," Abby said truthfully. "I'd like to have a big family." What she didn't tell him was that she wasn't certain she wanted his child.

He grinned. "Maybe we got us one today." He seemed so pleased with the idea that Abby couldn't tell him she'd taken the same precautions she always did, still feeling his seed wet and sticky on her thighs. And, as always, she drank the special tea Enyaa had helped her gather.

She was relieved when Cassidy loaded their basket and blanket onto the buggy and helped her up to the seat. Behind her she could hear the surge of the surf, hear its roar when the waves broke. She would carry the sound in her heart. Perhaps, one day she could return here to view it again.

Abby was ready to leave San Diego two days later when Cassidy loaded up the wagon. She was restless and lonesome for the open wilderness, tired of always having to be properly dressed and careful of her behavior lest she embarrass her husband.

Their wagon was loaded with supplies, a few new clothes for Abby along with bolts of material and sewing things, some for her use, some to sell at the station. Mostly there was coffee, sugar, flour, beans, and barrels of salt pork. There was even tinned food, and other items the immigrants would be out of by the time they had crossed the Desert of Death.

Cassidy whistled to himself as they traveled so Abby could tell he was well satisfied with the outcome of the trip. He'd made important contacts, and was able to purchase the land he wanted at Cuyamaca where he could graze cattle and plant grasses for them.

There was much talk about his beautiful wife and how she'd saved the life of the Hartnell's Indian servant and her infant. The men had been taken by her, the women found her warm and friendly, and most important, no threat to those husbands with a wandering eye.

Cassidy thought himself fortunate to have a wife like Abby who didn't ask for anything. She accepted what he gave with gratitude but was able to provide her own clothing and food if necessary. He wanted to be certain she would be accepted by those friends in San Diego. For their station, Abby wove mats and baskets, and didn't ask for any of the things wives seemed to find essential; the fancy curtains, wall hangings and furniture. Abby was the perfect mate for him, and could only be more perfect if she would conceive a child.

25

The state elections of 1859 ushered Milton S. Latham into the office of governor of California. John Warner, of the Warner Ranch, won a seat in the state assembly. John Rains, the man whom Abby had met at the Carrillo Rancho, ran for state senator, losing out to a former general in the Mexican army, Andres Pico. Pico's brother, Pio, had twice been governor of California prior to statehood.

Governor Latham remained in office only five days. When the federal elections were held, he was elected to the United States Senate to take the place of the late Senator Broderick.

John G. Downey stepped from the lieutenant governor's office into that of governor.

Andres Pico belonged to Dr. Gwin's Chivalry branch of the Democratic Party. Soon after the first of the year Pico introduced a joint resolution to divide the state of California into two separate states. One of the new states would be pro-slavery, the other anti-slavery.

In Washington, the new session of Congress was more turbulent than any of its predecessors. Lines were being drawn. Knives were sometimes brandished on the floor of the House as members went armed. Debates became more heated. Northerners and Southerners alike were against the incumbent President Buchanan.

John Rains attended the National Convention in Charleston, South Carolina, but the delegates were not able to agree on a candidate. In June, the Southern Democrats met in Richmond, without Rains, and nominated vice president John C. Breckenridge. The Democratic Party was split on the issue of slavery. Breckenridge was part of the pro-slavery faction. The Northern states convened in Baltimore and put forth their own nominees.

Before returning home, John Rains journeyed to Washington. He wanted to propose the possibility of bringing water from the Colorado River to the desert.

In the year 1860, a number of important events were taking place simultaneously. The nation was gearing up for a bitter presidential election. The Transcontinental Railroad out of St. Louis and San Francisco was stretching across the wilderness plagued by labor problems and the rivalry between work gangs. Plus, there was more money to be found in California in the gold fields and men frequently deserted their railroad jobs, lured by exaggerated stories of gold nuggets laying upon the ground. There were problems with hostile Indians, and with the transporting of supplies to where they were needed to continue the laying of the track.

In addition to the Transcontinental Railroad, a transcontinental telegraph was being strung, pole by pole toward the west coast, but at that time, the fastest route for mail was still the Butterfield Overland Mail. That is, until the formation of the Pony Express in 1860. The culmination of a dream by the freighting company of Russell, Majors and Waddell. It could carry only mail, and whereas the stagecoach could average 100 to 125 miles every twenty-four hours, the Pony Express rider could cover 250 miles. Relays of riders crossed the wilderness from St. Joseph, Missouri to Sacramento in ten days.

For the average traveler in that year, especially those looking for a new home, it took one hundred and fifty days to travel from ocean to ocean. Telegraphs were in constant use in the east and parts of the south, but the wires had yet to reach California. Once that happened, and once the railroad was completed, the course of the U.S. Mail would change. There would be faster means of travel than stagecoach.

John Butterfield Senior found the running of the overland mail an unprofitable business. Each year it seemed to dip further into the red and he was forced to pour more of his own money into the venture to keep it operating efficiently. The government contract, which at first seemed so lucrative didn't come near paying the expense of the gigantic payroll and the amount of stock and supplies that had to be replaced due to Indian depredations and natural disasters.

At the Republican presidential nominating convention, with the knowledge that the Democrats were divided between North and South, their victory seemed assured. Stephen Douglas was a popular candidate with William H. Seward and Salmon P. Chase as contenders. Unfortunately for the latter two, they both managed to offend too many voters. The convention managers sought a different type of candidate. He must be anti-slavery, yet not an extremist. Preferably he would come from a large state.

Only one man fit the specifications; Abraham Lincoln of Illinois. On the third ballot it was evident that Lincoln it would be, with Hannibal Hamlin of Maine as his vice presidential running mate.

The Republicans took little notice of the voices from the Deep South claiming they would secede if Lincoln was voted into office. Stephen Douglas was one of those who did take notice. As he campaigned in the South, perhaps he sensed defeat was possible and began urging Southerners to accept the outcome of the election. He warned that the North would never permit the Union to be destroyed.

Speaking at Raleigh he told a frigid audience, "I would hang every man higher than Haman who would attempt to resist by force the execution of any provision of the Constitution which our fathers made and bequeathed to us."

It was a valiant attempt which was doomed to failure. Though Douglas drove himself to the point of exhaustion to spread his message, it was not well received. In fact, the arduous speechmaking no doubt contributed to his untimely death within a year.

At Seven Springs, Cassidy eagerly watched the unfolding drama in the newspapers delivered by the Butterfield stagecoaches. Abby listened to the debates that raged between her husband and anyone who would engage him.

Wes dropped in from time to time, continuing to teach Abby about history, poetry, and nature. She was an eager pupil, improving her reading ability month by month, learning to do figures fast enough to keep books for Cassidy at the station.

Cassidy tolerated Wes's anti-slavery views because the man refused to debate it. What he believed was not subject to question. Abby held her tongue, not letting her husband know her views differed from his. He assumed she felt as he did, knowing Indian tribes sometimes took their enemies as slaves, but he wasn't aware this was not a practice of the Kumeyaay.

Late in the spring, just before the desert temperatures began to soar, Abby looked up from her garden where she was weeding, to see three riders coming up the trail from the south. A soft breeze stirred the dust from the hooves of the horses and the two pack mules behind.

Abby felt a catch in her throat. One of the men...there was something about the way he sat his horse, the way he wore his hat pushed back on his head. A cry of joy was torn from her throat as she dropped her hoe, jumped the garden fence and ran down the trail toward him.

She gave no thought to what her husband might think, though it was fortunate he was out checking his stock.

One rider moved out ahead of the others toward Abby. With a whoop he swooped her up into his arms, holding her high off the ground. Abby gloried in her first embrace by John Jay Butterfield, her heart singing with joy.

He swung her up behind him, their words of greeting stumbling over each other's.

"I thought you'd never come back," Abby said, hugging him hard enough to bring a grunt.

"Silly girl," John Jay said, trying to still the tripping beat of his heart. He hadn't known he would be so affected by seeing her again, hadn't let himself admit how much he'd missed her.

"Of course I had to come back. I have to keep an eye on this stage line, don't I?"

"We heard you were superintendent in Arkansas," she said excitedly, breathing in his musky, dusty scent. To her it was the sweetest smell in the world.

"I was. I managed to stay with it for a year," John Jay said. "But my feet got to itching, and fortunately dad asked me to take a run along the line and look for problems."

Abby detected a note of worry in his voice. They stopped at the well and Abby slid down with the grace of an expert rider. She glanced at the other two men who were watching them with amused smiles.

"This is Jared," John Jay said to introduce her. "He was my shot gunner part of the way on that first trip."

Jared nodded and touched his hand to his hat. "And this here's Dusty, the best wrangler and best cook this side of the Mississippi. Gents, this is Abby Cassidy, as you can tell, an old friend."

"Shucks," Dusty drawled. "She don't look old to me."

Jared nodded again, his gaze missing little of the looks that flashed between John Jay and the beautiful young woman.

"My husband is out with the stock," she told them. "Why don't you see to your horses while I fix you some venison stew."

"Sounds good," John Jay said with a wide grin. "The past few days have been hard tack and jerked beef. I sure could use a fresh meal. Got any of them big tortillas? I haven't tasted any that good since the last time I was here."

"I made some yesterday," Abby said. She ran for the station while the men washed the trail dust from their faces and hands. They turned their horses into the corral before leading the mules down to the springs where they would set up camp.

At the moment no one else was camped there so they were able to pick the best spot under the willows. By the time their camp was set up and their bedrolls airing out, the aroma of venison stew filled the air. The men washed up again and headed for the station.

They had barely sat down when Abby heard Cassidy ride in. He entered warily until he saw who the visitors were. There were handshakes and greeting all around. Abby set a place for her husband. He'd been gone since early morning so he would be ravenous too.

"Good to see you, John Jay," Cassidy said as Abby set a steaming bowl of stew on the table near him. He served himself first then passed the bowl to John Jay. Abby brought warm tortillas and some of her homemade butter. Eager hands reached for them as she took her place at the end of the table opposite her husband. "I wondered when you'd show up again."

"My father asked me to check the line," John Jay explained. "We've had problems."

"Oh? What kind of problems?" Cassidy asked.

John Jay's grin was rueful. "All kinds. Stations abandoned, stock run off by bandits or Indians, roads in need of serious repair, wells caved in. You name it, we've had it." He spooned the thick stew with wild onions and chunks of venison onto his plate before he went on. "We expected to make money from the subsidy the government gives us, but it hasn't worked out that way. In fact, we're losing so much money they're calling for my father to resign."

Cassidy halted his spoon in midair. "Damn fools! If anyone can hold this thing together it's your pa. Them other fellows don't know what they're up against out here."

John Jay nodded in agreement. The other two men ate with single-minded concentration on their food. "I happen to agree, but I think it would be a good thing if dad got out now. There's no way the overland can keep going much longer anyway. I think he's about convinced to cut his losses."

"What will happen then?" Abby asked, unable to bridle her curiosity.

John Jay looked at her, noticing the way the sunlight through the open window struck her hair, turning the white wings on each side glowing. The effect was to make her seem ethereal, unearthly. He half expected to find a baby had arrived during his absence, curiously pleased there wasn't.

"I've come to look for a piece of land. Possibly in the San Bernardino area. I hear there's some rich land there, good for cattle now that the Indian's have settled down a bit."

"You thinking of becoming a rancher?" Cassidy asked.

"Thought I'd give it a try. I like the climate in California." John Jay's grin was lopsided. "I'm tired of New York winters and shoveling snow. I'd like to see green grass year around and mountains with snow, close enough to look at but not close enough to work in it."

Cassidy chuckled. He'd only experienced deep snow a few times. "I can see why you'd feel that way. I nearly froze my toes off one time and I don't want no more of that. I'll take the desert any day." There was a moment of silence while everyone ate, then Cassidy turned the conversation to the inevitable topic. "What's the news from Washington?"

"You probably know more about that then I do. We've been on the trail for almost a month, trying to settle problems as we find them. We get the news same way you do, by newspaper when we see a coach, and word of mouth."

Abby listened to the talk change to politics, seemingly a favorite topic of the men these days. Cassidy brought John Jay up to date on happenings in California. John Jay talked of the sentiment in the South he'd noted as he traveled west, particularly in Texas.

It was difficult for Abby to keep her eyes off John Jay. She wanted to feast her eyes on his handsome face, on the tiny lines that appeared in the corners of his blue eyes when he smiled, on the way his eyes danced with humor. Her husband, in comparison, was more taciturn, smiling rarely, laughing seldom, and then only in the company of men when they passed the jug around.

She was glad Cassidy wouldn't sell whiskey at the store. Indians sometimes stopped by to ask for it, and Cassidy could make more money if he did. It was one of the things Abby admired about him. He didn't provide something that made them go out of their heads. There was trouble enough with some of the mountain tribes as the white man encroached farther and farther into their hunting grounds. Cassidy foresaw bad times to come. The local Indian agents made treaties with all due pomp and ceremony, promising food and supplies, then Washington refused to honor them. It was always the Indians who were the losers.

John Jay and his companions remained at Seven Springs for three days, resting their tired animals. At least that was what John Jay said. He knew, and Abby sensed, it was for another reason. These were their only moments to be together. They had to savor each word, each meeting. It would have to last them for the months ahead.

One ray of hope was the fact John Jay wanted to settle in California. San Bernardino was closer than Arkansas. Surely they would see each other more often.

A deep sadness came over Abby as she walked toward the hills, her bow slung across her shoulders. Normally her eyes and ears were alert for game. Today she was suffering the tortures of being close to John Jay and pretending to see him only as a friend.

Her arms longed to hold him tightly against her, to allow her fingers to stroke his face, to explore his long, lean body. Guilt flooded through her when she realized she had no such feelings for her husband. She endured Cassidy's touch but found no joy. No longer did she permit herself to hope it would ever be different. The touch of his hands stirred nothing inside her, only numbness.

The hunt yielded nearly a dozen quail, taken by her bow and arrows so she wouldn't flush every bird in the area with a gunshot. She was returning to the station to clean them when she heard the sound of a male voice singing a rousing ditty. She recognized the voice.

Unable to help herself Abby moved silently through the brush. The sound was coming from the furthest spring from the station. Most likely John Jay was washing his clothes, she told herself, yet hoping to see more of his powerful body. And she wasn't disappointed. His naked flanks were toward her as she crept closer, spying him standing knee deep in the water, splashing himself.

His upper body was darkened from exposure to the sun. Some men never removed their shirts when working so the skin of their chests and backs remained a pasty white. John Jay's skin looked smooth and tan, rippling with muscles that made her mouth go dry. She had often tried to imagine what he'd look like, now she could carry that picture vividly in her mind.

Crouching in the shadows of a mesquite she couldn't stop herself from watching him. He was magnificent. She wanted desperately to join him in the water, to splash him, to play, then make sweet love. She felt a tightening at the pit of her stomach at the thought of his hands on her. It would be different with him, she knew that with every fiber in her body. Yet she could not go to him. Would not go to him. There could be no pleasure in breaking her vows to her husband.

Abby caught her breath when John Jay turned toward her and she was able to see all of him. A shudder of longing went through her. Tears came to her eyes. He was so beautiful she closed her eyes against the sight of his nakedness. It had been difficult before, now she would forever carry his image in her mind. This was far different from the time she and Moyla had spied on the young men frolicking naked in the river. This was a man she cared about and desired.

She waited until John Jay's back was again turned to her before she slipped away, wiping her tears. What if he took a wife and settled in San Bernardino? What would she do then? I'll die, her heart whispered.

John Jay felt a trembling in his body, only partly from the chill of the water. There was no mistaking the glint of the sun on red hair. He didn't want to stare, didn't want her to know he was aware of her hiding place. He was curiously pleased she'd wanted to see him, but was forced to turn away before a certain part of his anatomy could betray him. Even then he could feel her gaze caress him, felt his body quicken with desire. She was so beautiful, even more so now as she matured. Why had he come back to be tortured? He wanted her, and for the first time was certain she wanted him as well.

He found himself wishing she would come to him, strip off her clothes and join him in the water. He wanted to see all of her the way she could see him. Why was he planning to add the pain of living closer to her? He could kid himself all he wanted about the reasonable price of land, the climate, but in his heart he knew there was only one reason he had chosen California. He must be a glutton for punishment.

Abby headed for the station, her heart hammering with frustration. She wanted him near, yet now that he was, she suffered more than when he was far away; a bitter-sweet suffering. The sound of a far off bugle alerted her to the approach of the westbound stage. She ran the rest of the way and began to lay out food for the passengers. There were still some tortillas, a fresh pot of beans with salt pork added and within a few minutes she had enchiladas heated.

The six hungry passengers and driver gave Abby no time to think of John Jay. There were two children. Abby found herself watching the little boy who was about four years old, thinking how she would love to have a son, a son who resembled his father, with laughing blue eyes and a mouth which was quick to smile. That image was never banished from her mind for long no matter how hard she tried.

The driver was the last one to eat. When John Jay came in it was evident the two were well acquainted. Abby served John Jay then slipped from the room. She couldn't bear to be around him, afraid she would let her hands stroke him as she walked by.

From his pocket the driver pulled a letter that had obviously been handed from driver to driver all along the route. "It's from your pa," the driver said. "We was to find you even if we had to go out of our way to do it."

John Jay accepted the letter hesitantly, sensing it was bad news. Feeling the curious eyes of the driver and shot gunner, he was reluctant to open it, wanting to be alone.

Leaving his food untouched, John Jay went out into the waning light, to the ancient mesquite which grew behind the station. The limbs curved along the ground as if the weight of the years had worn it down. With his back to the twilight sky, he sat on the thick trunk and tore open the battered envelope. He recognized his father's thick scrawl at once.

Jay Jay,

Hope this finds you in good health. By the time you read this I'll be back home in Utica. My good friends Bill Wells and Henry Fargo decided they could no longer loan me money to keep the stage line afloat. The $600,000 a year from the government might have seemed like more than enough in the beginning, but with all the problems we've had, near as I can figure, it's costing more than $60 for each piece of mail we carry.

As of this date, I am no longer associated with the Butterfield Overland Mail though it will continue to bear my name. You can stop your check of the line as soon as you receive this.

Bill and Henry have assured me they will honor any debts you have contracted on our behalf up until the time this letter reaches you.

I'm hoping you will be joining me in Utica. It's been a long time since all the family has been home together. Can't say as I'm sorry to be out from under the constant worry about the mail. The distance is just too great to control.

Come home soon.

Dad

John Jay scanned the letter several times, absorbing the message. It was over! The Butterfield Overland Mail was no longer his concern. He was cut free sooner than he expected. It wouldn't be necessary for him to return to St. Louis now.

For a moment he considered responding to his father's summons to the family home. He missed his mother, his brothers and sisters. But it no longer felt like home. He was free now to look for a place to build a home of his own.

A look of pain flickered across his face when he pictured his new home with Abby. He could visualize a flock of red haired children running about a yard. He could picture love and laughter. His hand curled around the letter, crushing it, not even aware what he was doing.

Turning away from the station he stalked away, blindly.

Abby saw him walk away in stony silence, saw the letter flutter to the ground. Wanting to save it for him, she reached down and began to smooth out the wrinkles. She couldn't stop herself from reading. The news was bad and had obviously upset him. Though her heart ached for him she sensed his need to be alone. Tucking the letter into her pocket she went inside.

She didn't see John Jay until breakfast the next morning. During the morning meal he told Cassidy and Abby about the letter. To Cassidy it held little importance. The mail would continue as before.

"What will you do now?" Cassidy asked.

John Jay shrugged. "Guess I'll head over to San Bernardino and take a look at some land."

Cassidy nodded. "Why don't you go by the Rancho Cucamonga and talk to John Rains. He knows the area. He can tell you who to see."

"Sounds like a good idea. We'll be heading out tomorrow, but before I leave I want to write a letter to Wells and Fargo to let them know what I've found on this trip. And let them know I won't be communicating further."

"Why don't you just let them find it out for themselves? Seems like they could have helped out a friend one more time."

John Jay shook his head. "No, I'm glad Dad is out of it. Another loan wouldn't have helped. It would only put him further in debt."

"What do you think he'll do now?" Abby asked, wishing she'd had a chance to meet his father.

"He still has business interests in Utica. It isn't as if this thing broke him by any means, but it might if he tried to hang on." He gave a half-hearted smile. "It'll take a lot more than this to get him down. He has one of the sharpest business minds I've ever seen. I don't see how he remembers all the things he does."

"He sounds like a wonderful man," Abby said with a wistful smile, thinking how lucky he was to have a father at all. She was trying not to dwell on the fact he would be leaving tomorrow.

After dark, Cassidy went down to John Jay's camp to play poker with Jared, Dusty and John Jay. An orange moon slipped upward from the distant mountains, to hang like a giant ball, shedding its pale light across the darkened desert. The brush, the nearby hills Abby knew so well, took on a different look, half shadow, half pale light.

At the spring, Abby could see the flicker of the campfire and the dark silhouettes of the men. Walking past her garden into the open, she stood staring at the gilded moon. It was a moon to be shared.

From the distance came a plaintive, lonely wail of a coyote which soon brought an answering cry, then an entire chorus. Abby listened to their eerie song, unafraid of the creatures of the night. Across the sky in front of her she watched the silent flight of an owl on its nightly hunt. In the brush she could hear the scurrying of tiny creatures.

Her heart was aching with the knowledge John Jay was leaving and she could do or say nothing. She could not acknowledge her feelings.

She walked farther, past the corral and along the trail that had been carved into the desert floor by countless wagons, animals and people; people who seemed to come in unending waves.

Before them they pushed the Indians out of their homes and took the best places for themselves. In her lifetime she would no doubt see it happen to her own people, the Kumeyaay.

For a time she wandered about in the darkness, feeling the moon's golden rays bathing her in unearthly light, watching it change color as it climbed. From rosy orange, to silver, so bright it hurt her eyes. It seemed to pick up the silver hue of the wings of her hair making it glow just as brightly.

26

Abby was unable to move, the brilliant glow of the moon held her, whispering something. The vision came unexpectedly, filling her mind with images of a city bustling with people and carriages. Some of the people she felt she recognized, yet knew she had never met them before. All around her she sensed danger, an evil force she couldn't identify. Cassidy wasn't there, she had no feeling of him anywhere. Jacob's florid face flashed in front of her eyes, then faces of the two Mexican men with lust-filled eyes. Their images quickly gave way to that of a number of Indian warriors, their gazes too filled with lust.

Abby remained frozen as images flashed through her mind, disjointed, too rapid to capture. She shivered as they finally faded, knowing what had just happened. In the bright moonlight she had opened her mind and been touched by a vision. Most of it didn't make sense, had flashed by her too fast, too many things she didn't recognize. One thing she knew, it was a warning of change to come. She needed to be ready.

"Abby?" The voice startled her. In her intense concentration she hadn't heard him approach. She turned to see the concern on John Jay's face as he saw her shivering, which she hadn't even been aware of. "Are you cold?"

It was a mild night for early spring, with no touch of cool. She shook her head. "No...I..." she couldn't have told Cassidy but she felt John Jay would understand. "I was having a...vision, of the future, I think. It happens sometimes..." She didn't know how else to explain.

"I've heard Indians seek out visions," he said with no show of skepticism. "But I didn't know they could come on like this."

"I guess I was open to it somehow."

"What was it about?"

"I can't make much sense of it," she said. "I just know something is going to happen. I wasn't at Seven Springs any more. I was in a city, some place I've never seen. There were a lot of people. Some weren't what they seemed and I was in danger."

"Have you had these...visions before?" he asked, coming closer.

She nodded. "Sometimes. They always leave me disturbed." She shook off thoughts of her vision, feeling they were too personal to share. "How is your game going?"

John Jay glanced back to where the glow of the camp fire was barely visible. "I couldn't concentrate. I decided I'd better get out before I lost my shirt. I saw you walking...I didn't want to come, but I couldn't stay away."

It was the closest either of them had come to admitting their feelings. Abby was too shaken by her experience to have control of her emotions. "I...I'll miss you when you're gone." Her voice sounded choked.

"I won't be far away..." He sounded as miserable as she felt. "If you ever have need of anything..."

She nodded, feeling tears gathering at the back of her throat. "I'm glad you're going to be close," she whispered. Just as she thought she might step closer to him and lay her head against his broad chest she drew in a sudden shuddering breath. "We shouldn't be here like this."

"I know. I'd...never do anything to hurt you, Abby," he said softly. "I wouldn't dare lay a hand on you because if I did, nothing on earth could make me leave you." He gave a sharp grunt. "Your husband is my friend. I'll ride out of here tomorrow and I'll do my best not to come back." He sounded as if he didn't have much hope of that.

Abby nodded miserably. "But that don't stop the thinking."

"Yeah, I haven't learned to do that yet," he admitted. "Someday, maybe, but not yet."

"May the spirits keep you safe," she whispered. "And may you ride with God."

John Jay gave a twisted smile. "With that much help I'll be fine. You take care of yourself. And remember, if anything happens, if you ever need me..." He reached out as if to touch her flowing hair, his eyes tortured. Then he turned abruptly and strode away. Abby watched him go until tears blurred her sight.

A cloud moved across the moon, leaving her standing in shadow. She was filled with darkness as tears streamed down her cheeks. Good bye, my love, her heart whispered.

27

The discovery of gold in Colorado in the previous year had stemmed the flow of emigrants into California. Some of the men who hadn't done well in the California gold fields followed the lure of new riches, traveling across country to try their luck in Colorado.

Stagecoaches continued to pass through Seven Springs regularly. The fact that John Butterfield Senior was no longer at the helm was barely noticeable. Abby listened to hair raising tales of Indian attacks, stations found deserted with all stock and personnel gone.

In April came the news that the Pony Express was now carrying mail from St. Joseph, Missouri to Sacramento. St. Joseph was selected because it was the western most terminal of the telegraph. The feat of the Pony Express riders was astounding. Some of them little more than boys.

The ads for riders which appeared in the San Francisco paper prior to its inauguration read: "Wanted – young, skinny, wiry fellows, not over eighteen. Must be expert riders, willing to risk death daily. Orphans preferred. Wages $25 a week…"

Each pony was to carry no more than 165 pounds, including mail and rider. Every eye in the country was focused on St. Joseph the morning of April 3, on Russell, Majors and Waddell's first rider.

Abby eagerly read the account of how the train out of Hannibal, Missouri traveled 206 miles in four hours and fifty one minutes, a feat that had been regarded as impossible. In spite of that, the train was still late. It was a quarter past seven in the evening before the mail was wrapped in oil slick and placed in a mochila, a sort of saddle bag which was built right into the special-made saddle. The locks were put in place to safeguard the mail, the keys to which were only at two locations; St. Joseph and Sacramento.

The first rider was ready and eager, dressed in the costume of the Pony Express riders, the red blouse and blue trousers. John W. "Billy" Richardson made a splendid sight in his gloves and black boots. His saddle and bridle were bespangled with silver and embroidery. A brass band blared. With a loud cheer the rider was off, into history.

Billy changed horses four times before he dismounted at Granada, Kansas and handed over the mail to his replacement, Don Rising. Don followed an old military trail through the reservation of the Kickapoo Indians who were peaceful, friendly farmers.

The first run reached Sacramento in nine days and twenty-three hours, one hour ahead of schedule, a distance of nineteen hundred miles. The first eastbound mail took exactly ten days. Abby compared that to the twenty-two to twenty-five days of the Butterfield Overland Mail. It was obvious the Pony Express cut the delivery time by more than half.

The transcontinental telegraph out of San Francisco had reached as far as Carson City, Nevada. Important messages could now be sent quite rapidly from coast to coast.

At that time no one had yet to realize the importance of the shortening of the time gap. It only became apparent after the events which followed the Presidential election later that year, and in the opening months of 1861.

In the months that followed, Abby and Cassidy watched the newspaper accounts and listened to drivers and passengers discussing the fearlessness of the Pony Express riders who faced their greatest danger crossing Paiute territory in Utah and Nevada.

From their first encounter with the white man the Paiutes had resisted their encroachment. When the Mormons came to settle the Great Salt Lake, the Indians tried to drive them away, only to find their arrows were no match for bullets. Instead they resorted to lone travelers, stealing horses and cattle.

The lone traveler was often the swift Pony Express rider. Here again, as with the powerful stage line horses, the splendid condition of the animals made a difference. The grass fed muscles of Indian ponies were no match for the long, grain fed muscles of the Express ponies.

But if the Express ponies had the advantage, the way stations were at a disadvantage. With their horses and supplies they were too tempting a target. Only one Express rider was reported killed, and even then his riderless horse galloped in with the mail.

Life at Seven Springs went on as before. The recent drought was killing off cattle in many areas of Southern California. The price of beef was rock bottom as ranchers frantically sold stock before they all perished. Unable to repay his loan, Ramon Carrillo had been forced to give John Rains half interest in the rancho. Cassidy told Abby there would eventually be trouble over that.

In May came the news that the Paiutes were on the warpath, nearly eight thousand strong. By this time, many of them had rifles. No part of Nevada was safe.

On May 31, Alexander Majors temporarily suspended the Pony Express due to the danger. The Paiutes were taking a deadly toll of stations and stock. Newspapers clamored for the governor to send troops. The governor acted, but in doing so he greatly underestimated the enemy. A force of one hundred and five men left Carson City under Major Ormsby. Neither the major nor any of his men had any experience in Indian fighting. They took no precautions against sudden attack and were ambushed so effectively that the major and nearly half his men were butchered.

It was finally the government who stepped in to dispatch a force of regular troops. In the midst of a snowstorm in the month of June, the troops drove the Indians into the mountains and put down the rebellion.

The Pony Express was suspended for only a period of three weeks. On June 26. They resumed operations, but the Indian depredations had cost the firm of Russell, Majors and Waddell a whopping $75,000. Many of their riders quit because of the deprivation and danger.

The newspapers picked up an account of what some of the idle riders, stage drivers, stock tenders and ranch men had accomplished during the three week hiatus of the mail. Forty of them, well-armed and well mounted, led by Wild Bill Cody, who had been driving stage, rode into Indian territory to look for stolen horses.

At the head of Horse Creek, twenty miles out of Sweetwater Bridge, the riders found an Indian trail running north toward the Powder River. From the tracks they could discern some of the horses were shod, no doubt stolen.

The trail was easy to follow and they moved rapidly after their quarry. At the Powder River they followed the tracks down stream until it eventually turned west along the foot of the mountains. At the tributary of Crazy Woman's Fork, it became obvious that the Indians they were pursuing had been joined by another band. The tracks weren't more than twenty-four hours old.

The riders were now in the heart of Indian country. They advanced with caution. At Clear Creek, another tributary of the Powder River, they at last spotted horses grazing some three miles away. It was a sure sign the Indians were nearby.

Never before had the Indians been tracked so far into their own country so they neglected to post scouts. Wild Bill and his men held a council. They were outnumbered by about three to one. Their plan was simple, to wait until dark and creep up on the camp on horseback. At Wild Bill's signal that night, they made a wild dash into the midst of the Indian camp, firing in every direction to stampede the horses. It worked. The Indians were so astounded they put up little resistance.

Four days later, when the group arrived at Sweetwater Bridge, they had retrieved all of their own stock plus a hundred Indian ponies.

Wes recounted the tale with relish as he and the Cassidy's sat around the dinner table. He had a way of spinning out the news to where it sounded like a great adventure. Abby was mending one of her husband's shirts, smiling at Wes's expression as he read.

If Wes noticed the sad, wistfulness of her smile these days he didn't comment. Abby missed John Jay with a constant ache. She longed for him to return, yet knew he would not.

With June came the return of hot summer days. Each day spent under an unrelenting sun. Abby knew it would grow even worse in the months to come. Relief seldom came until well into September, sometimes even October. The bright blue of the sky showed no hint of clouds. No storms to cool the air. Abby shed some of the undergarments she wore during the winter.

The stagecoaches came with their usual regularity. She watched for the annual trek of the Kumeyaay and spent time with them at their nearby camp. Cassidy knew she was with her Indian family and said nothing about the hours she spent with them, accepting the additional work without complaint.

Abby learned that Moyla and her baby were thriving, and that her sister was happy with her Yuma husband. That bit of news brought a tiny ache to Abby's heart which her mother didn't miss. Opachuk reached out to grip Abby's hand.

"We are not all so fortunate," she said with dark eyes full of knowing. "For you it did not happen. Is this man good to you?"

Abby nodded. She couldn't fault her husband.

"The ways of the white man are different from ours," Opachuk went on. "In our village if a marriage does not work it is easy to go separate ways. There is no shame. I understand that with the whites it is different. A woman is expected to remain with her husband all her life, no matter what. That is foolishness. When a woman is young she needs an older man to teach her about life and give her children. Later, she can be her own woman and look for a man she can love. If a husband turns out to be a bad man, or he leaves her for another woman, she can always try again. She is not made to feel she is unworthy."

Abby nodded, knowing well the easy ways of Indian marriages though many did endure for a lifetime, such as Opachuk and Hahro. She knew what her mother was trying to tell her but also knew she could never leave Cassidy. He needed her. There was no place for her to go.

"You have chosen not to have a child by this man," Opachuk said with an accuracy that startled Abby. "Does he know?"

Abby shook her head, suddenly ashamed she was cheating her husband out of something he wanted very much.

"Do not feel shame, my daughter," the older woman counseled. "You are destined for other things. Enyaa has spoken of them. For Eagle Woman there will be sadness and joy. It was foretold. Your time for love will come."

Abby thought of John Jay but she could not make herself hope for such a miracle.

The stage from St Louis was late that night. When Abby returned to the station after dark it still hadn't arrived. Cassidy had food ready and prowled outside, listening for the horn, his rifle cradled across his chest. In the infinite stillness of the desert often they could hear the coach coming long before the horn was sounded.

Abby could tell her husband was uneasy. Normally he didn't worry about the coaches. Their arrival could vary greatly depending on problems encountered along the way. It had to be something more bothering him. She joined him outside on the small rise by the pump where he was looking across the desert. He heard her approach, and even without words he could feel her concern.

"Earlier today, when you were gone, a couple of men came through on their way to San Diego. They said there's a small band of renegade Indians operating between here and Yuma Crossing. They've hit a couple of stations and driven off stock. I think it best we stay armed when we go about our business."

Abby understood his concern. Before she could give voice to it she picked out a faint sound in the distance. Cassidy saw her listening, already aware his wife's hearing was much keener than his.

"It's the coach," she said finally. "It's moving very slow, as if they have exhausted horses or trouble."

"They'll be tired and hungry," he said. "I'll get the horses ready, you see to the food. Keep a close eye out, and keep your rifle handy."

It seemed to take forever for the coach to reach the station. Abby had the table set, the food was hot. Light from the windows spilled out into the darkness.

When the coach did come in sight, all the passengers were walking along side, doing their share to spare the exhausted horses, who obviously were at the end of their strength.

Foam dripped from their mouths and lay in layers across their flanks and shoulders.

Cassidy began to unharness them at once, knowing he would have to spend a lot of time with the exhausted animals if he was to save them. They wouldn't be able to work again for quite a time. The harnesses would also require work to keep the leather from rotting from salt and sweat. The passengers went right to the well to wash up and drink cool, fresh water.

"Trouble, Gus?" Cassidy asked the driver as he climbed down from the box, his movements slow from fatigue.

"No horses at Carrizo or Palm Spring. We had to rest the horses a lot or we wouldn't have made it this far. Be sure they get an extra measure of oats. It hurts me to work animals that hard."

The passengers looked weary too as they headed for the station. "There's hot food," Cassidy told them.

There were four passengers, two older ladies who looked enough alike to be sisters, a well-dressed man and a shorter, thin man who appeared to be traveling with him.

Abby barely glanced at the four when they straggled in. She felt the intense gaze of the larger of the two men but she was used to that. He was of medium build. When he removed his hat and dropped it over a peg by the door she saw thick, wavy brown hair. Even to her inexperienced eye she knew his clothes were the latest fashion and expensive. His boots, even under layers of dust spoke of money.

As she served them venison stew with warm tortillas and beans she could feel the way the man's gaze followed her every move. With some men she knew they would like to catch her alone, knew lust when she saw it. This man's look was something different, more like speculation, curiosity. When the four were served she escaped outside to help her husband with the horses.

Both the driver and his shotgunner were helping, but she sent them in to eat, they both looked as tired as the horses. Wanting to keep the team separate from the other horses, Abby led them to the corral behind the station while Cassidy hitched the fresh team. She began to rub them down, wiping away the layers of foam and salt. She could feel the heat emanating from their overworked bodies, knew they had to be handled carefully until they cooled down or they would be ruined as work animals.

Cassidy soon joined her and together they worked, rubbing down the horses before they could even let them drink. After a time, Abby was aware someone was watching her. She wasn't surprised to see the dark-haired man standing at the edge of the corral, one boot propped on a lower rail.

"You're good with horses," he said conversationally. "And you're also a good cook. Best we've had in a long way."

Abby glanced at her husband. His back was to her as he talked to Gus and his partner on the far side of the corral. She knew the man was well aware of where her husband was. She didn't answer him.

"My names Everett Drayton. I own a couple of hotels in Los Angeles." He paused as if expecting comment from her. When it didn't come he went on. "You're a mighty pretty young woman to be stuck out here in this wilderness. I can always use someone like you in my hotels. We serve the best food and provide the best accommodations in all of Southern California. I need good people."

"What makes you think I'd be good enough?" Abby asked, not sure how to take the man's offer. He wasn't offering anything indecent, just a job.

The stranger grinned, showing straight, white teeth gleaming under a dark moustache. "It's obvious you have to work hard out here to keep food on the table for the passengers, help your husband care for the animals, and keep an eye out for…scavengers like the ones who're hitting the outlying stations. This can't be an easy life or a safe one. I can offer you a job, a place to live in the city."

"Why would you offer all that to someone you've never seen before?" she asked, barely glancing at him as she worked.

"I consider myself a pretty good judge of people. A woman needs to own pretty things, be around other women. Out here you're isolated. You're too pretty for the men to leave alone." His gaze shifted to the bulky figure of her husband. "You've got a good man to look after you but I'm sure there've been times when he wasn't close by, and some hombre passing through, who hasn't seen a woman in months, let alone one as pretty as you, well… He just might not ask permission."

For a moment Abby considered what he was saying. It was true, she had to be wary of strangers. At first she thought this man was going to be another one trying to sweet talk her, but the way he looked at her had never been with the naked lust she'd seen on the faces of other men.

From his pocket he took a card and handed it to her. "This is where you'll find me in Los Angeles. If you need help getting there just send word."

Abby barely glanced at the card before slipping it into the pocket of her dress. It couldn't hurt to have a place to go if she ever needed it.

"I'll keep your offer in mind, Mr. Drayton."

He smiled again, showing off his teeth. She had no doubt most women found that smile charming, and thought him handsome. Throw in the lure of money and he must have his pick of the ladies.

"I hope you do that, Mrs. Cassidy. Out here, one never knows what tomorrow will bring."

As he turned away Abby shivered with the knowledge his parting words were true. She didn't want to think about them. It had been a long time since any of their stock had been bothered. They couldn't allow that fact to make them careless.

Gus called for the passengers to board. Abby stopped her work with the horses long enough to watch Everett Drayton join the others. Even in the faint moonlight she could see confidence in the way he walked, the easy way he carried himself. Under the gray coat she'd seen the outline of a pistol. He was no dandy. He appeared to be a man who could take care of himself. She had a feeling he was on the level about offering her a job. As to why, she wasn't quite sure.

Minutes later the coach rolled out with a crack of the whip and a cry from Gus. Abby listened to the sounds as they disappeared into the night. Part of her was wishing one day she could board a coach and let it carry her away from Seven Springs. Part of her wanted just what Drayton said, pretty things and the company of other women.

Within minutes all thoughts of Everett Drayton and his strange offer were driven from her mind. More pressing was the need to save the six spent horses. Then she'd have the supper dishes to clean, and by the time she got to them, the food would be dried and difficult to remove. She and Cassidy wouldn't get to bed any time soon.

28

Wes drifted in the next day. He said little about where he'd been but Abby suspected he'd been sick. He looked unusually thin, the lines in his long face deeper, more pronounced. When she placed food in front of him he didn't eat with his usual gusto, just picked at it and selected some of the more tender parts. She could tell her husband noticed as well but said nothing. He wouldn't pry into Wes's business.

When she found time to get away to hunt, Abby placed Drayton's card with her supplies in the rock cave. In the brush she was doubly careful, moving like a shadow the way Pion had taught her. She was filled with a sense of foreboding that wasn't caused entirely by the stranger's words. She sensed the presence of others in the area, others who meant trouble.

Cassidy seemed to sense it too. She noticed he was never far from his rifle, his gaze frequently on the trail or sweeping the surrounding hills. Wes, too, had taken to wearing a gun belt, something he'd never done before. Abby carried her rifle into the brush when she hunted but only for self-protection. She didn't want to call attention to herself. Her bow was silent and equally deadly.

A wagon train came through a few days later. Abby saw Cassidy seek out the leader to ask about trouble along the trail. Though they hadn't been bothered the man confirmed the fact there were renegade Indians in the area. Their party was too large for the small bunch, but they were hitting the unprotected stage stations and running off stock.

The wagons stayed for two nights. Everyone felt safer with the extra eyes to watch for trouble. For those two nights Abby and Cassidy slept soundly. Abby hadn't realized just how alert she'd been before, how afraid to sleep deeply.

On the third morning the wagons pulled out before dawn. Their desert trek was almost at an end, their stock was rested, and soon they would be in the cooler air of the mountains. Since she was awakened by all the activity, Abby took her rifle and her bow and headed for the hills, hoping to bag a deer. She debated taking one of the horses but decided if the deer was too big to carry she'd come back for one.

At mid-day she paused to eat some of the jerked beef she'd brought, sitting in the shadow of rocks, blending in. There were a lot of deer tracks but so far she hadn't been close enough to use her bow. Even though it would have been an easy shot with a rifle she resisted the urge.

In the noonday heat the deer would bed down in the shade. Her chances would be better if she too rested and waited for them to come to the spring which lay just over the ridge.

It would mean remaining here all afternoon, but it was the only chance she had of succeeding. The settlers had taken a lot of their fresh meat, which she needed to replenish.

A loud cry from above drew her gaze up. High overhead, a golden eagle circled, making sharp, tight movements. She could have sworn it was watching her. Again its harsh cry seemed like a warning as it slowly glided off toward the mountains.

It was time to go on the hunt. Abby slipped through the rocks like a ghost, crossing the ridge at a crouch so she couldn't be spotted against the sky. She found a shady place where she could watch the spring and get a clear shot with her bow. Testing the direction of the wind she was satisfied the deer wouldn't catch her scent and settled down to wait, letting her mind wander freely, puzzled by the appearance of the eagle. Closing her eyes she drifted off to sleep.

She came awake with a start, disoriented. Something had awakened her. Instinct kept her from moving except to turn her head. The spring was deserted except for two ravens that had come to drink. By the position of the sun she could tell it was late afternoon.

From the distance came the sound of gunshots, her head turning quickly to pinpoint the direction. It came from over the ridge, the way she had come. Scrambling to her feet, she slung the bow around her body and grabbed her rifle. Another time she would be angry with herself as she flushed a covey of quail, the loud whirr of their wings startling her. But she was intent on one thing.

She crossed the ridge, again keeping low. Her heart was hammering with dread as the shooting continued without let up. It was exactly as she feared. The shots were coming from the station.

Abby began to run, choosing her way carefully through the brush, flushing more quail as she went. She was too far away for that to be a danger. She'd have to be more careful though once she got closer. Quail liked to stay around the springs. Flushing a covey there would betray her approach.

Brush scratched at her arms and legs as she pulled her skirts up so she could run faster. She wanted to shed the rifle and bow which were impeding her but knew she might need them both. She prayed she wouldn't be too late.

Even as that thought crossed her mind the shooting ceased. Straining her ears she listened but the harshness of her breathing covered any other sounds.

The brush was too tall to see over, and she swore at herself for being so far away. Her usual light tred was discarded in her haste. The pounding of her moccasins, the sound of air being forced in and out of her lungs blocked most sounds from beyond. But she thought she heard the sound of horses, many horses.

It wasn't until she was almost at the station that she forced herself to halt and listen, breathing heavily. She heard no other sound.

Off in the brush came the call of a quail attempting to locate the rest of the covey, and an answering call. A bird began to sing somewhere in the brush.

Abby's heart was pounding with fear and exertion as she crept closer, staying under cover, making no sound. She knew exactly the spot she wanted, dropping to all fours then wriggling on her belly into the protective cover of mesquite. From there she could see the station. Nothing moved. The silence was unnatural. Though she couldn't see the corral she knew it was empty. The absence of the normal stamping and snorting of nervous horses told her that.

It seemed a long time but actually was only minutes that Abby surveyed the scene. What finally made her leave her hiding place was spotting the tracks of many horses leading off into the desert toward Carrizo. The marauders must have waited until the wagons were gone before they came in. They must have been watching from the cover of the rocks, perhaps for days.

Abby had no intention of being careless even though she felt the danger had passed. She gave the loud trill of a bird call that Cassidy and Wes would recognize. Only silence answered. As anxious as she was about her husband and Wes, she moved silently to the back of the station. Through the brush she could see the corrals were both empty, but she spared no thought for the stock.

With her rifle ready, she reached the north end of the station, moving to where she could see without being seen. A hot breeze tugged at her hat, cooling the sweat as it formed on her forehead. She felt nothing. Every sense alert. Pressing herself against the coarse adobe wall she peered around the corner, her gaze rapidly scanning the yard, the well, the other corral, swiftly, not stopping at any point even though she recognized Wes's blue plaid shirt on the still form by the corral.

There was no sign of her husband. Her steps were measured as she slipped around the corner, inching her way with her back against the building. She ducked her head as she passed the open window of their bedroom, hearing no sounds inside. On the front porch both doors were standing open, shell casings were scattered everywhere, bullet holes evident in the adobe bricks.

Abby moved toward the door of their bedroom, squeezing inside, past the partly open door. Her moccasins made no sound on the dirt floor as she peered into the kitchen. Seeing no one she moved on, crossing the room quickly so she wouldn't be spotted from the other rooms. The second bedroom was also empty but in her quick stride across the kitchen Abby's gaze had registered a boot clad leg on the floor of the store.

Growing more certain she was alone, Abby moved through the office into the main room. Cassidy lay on the floor in a pool of blood, his rifle nowhere in sight. Store supplies had been scattered, no doubt as the renegades took what they wanted.

Abby felt her heart hammering in her chest as she let her gaze rest on the still form of her husband. There was no sign of breathing. One last look outside the open front door convinced her no one else was there. Only then did she lower her rifle and go to her husband.

She touched his neck for a pulse, willing it to be there.

A deep sigh racked her body when she was finally forced to admit the truth. Cassidy was dead. The back of his shirt showed two bullet holes. He had no doubt been shot in the back through the window across the room while he was firing out the front door.

Abby wouldn't let herself react, suppressing her emotions ruthlessly as she picked up her rifle and went out the front door, crossing the yard to the corral where Wes lay sprawled in the hot sand. Her gaze swept the area again and again as she moved. All was quiet. As she neared her friend she could hear the sound of his ragged breathing.

Finally satisfied there was no danger, Abby lay her rifle down as she knelt beside him, looking for wounds. She turned him over on his back, surprised at how light he felt. He coughed rackingly, then his eyes fluttered open. He gave a half smile when he saw Abby's concerned face.

"Renegades," he whispered, the words coming with great effort. "Six...Yuma's, I think." He struggled to focus his eyes on her face. Her taut expression told him the answer even as the question formed on his lips. "Cass?"

"Dead," she said softly.

He nodded, his eyes closing as if he wanted very much to sleep. "Go...to Carrillo's," Wes urged. "They looked....for...you. Go!" Great spasms of coughing racked his fragile body bringing a froth of red foam to his lips. He gasped a few times, struggling for breath. His eyes began to glaze. "Sarah," he sighed, then his body went limp, his eyes glassy and staring.

"No, Wes," she pleaded. "Not you too. I couldn't bear to lose both of you."

She drew him close to her body, hugging him, willing life to come back to his body. It took her long minutes to realize it was useless. Wes was finally with his beloved Sarah. She had the feeling he had not found death unwelcome. He had been lost without the woman he loved.

For a time she rocked him, crooning the death chant. Then, as the sun began to dip to the horizon she knew it was time to act, and dragged his body into the shade of a mesquite. Going back to the house, she knelt beside her husband, wanting to feel sorrow, wanting to give vent to her grief. All that came to her mind were the mourning songs of the Kumeyaay.

Rolling Cassidy onto his back she let her fingers caress his stiff, cool cheek. Somehow she had to find the strength to bury two men she cared about. It made her think of another hot day on the desert when she had dug a grave for the two people she loved most in the world.

As darkness fell, there was only the sound of chanting and that of a shovel, digging into the soft dirt beyond the corral, under the willow trees.

Abby searched the brush for any stock that might have scattered at the sound of gunfire, finding one strong mule. She used him to drag the bodies to their final resting place, wrapping them in blankets. Long into the night she searched out rocks, carrying them in packs on the mule's back to place on the graves. She had to keep them safe from scavengers.

When it was finally done Abby sank down in exhaustion, kneeling at her husband's grave. She touched one of the stones, wishing it was his warm body. Her chanting gave way to silent tears.

All through the remainder of the night she knelt beside the two mounds of stone, talking to them, shedding tears and singing songs of mourning.

As the rosy spikes of light touched the desert Abby became aware of thirst and hunger. She hadn't eaten since the previous afternoon. She rose stiffly from the cool sand and walked back to the station, leading the mule with her, rifle in hand. She would ride him to search for more stock that might have been missed. A stagecoach was due later in the day. They would need a fresh team.

She ate cold tortillas and beans, not wanting to take time to light a fire. Bareback she rode the mule into the brush. She gave no thought to Wes's warning that she should leave. Her duty was to the station, to the mail. If she had to, she would run the place alone.

In the brush she located one of the exhausted team horses they'd taken in only days ago. He was in no condition to be put back in harness, but Abby could find no more horses. She hoped Carrizo and Palm Spring had been restocked.

She returned to the station in time to prepare a hot meal for the coach passengers. She worked automatically, knowing what had to be done. There was a curious numbness that kept her from thinking, from feeling.

It was mid-afternoon when the sound of horses penetrated her consciousness. She went outside to see a herd of horses being driven from the direction of the Warner Ranch. The vaqueros drove the animals to the springs to drink, their gazes taking in the broken empty corral. The leader dismounted and walked to the station where Abby stood, her rifle held loosely at her side.

The Mexican tipped his hat, his dark eyes troubled. "Senora, the renegades have been here too?"

"Yes, yesterday."

"El Senor?" He seemed to know the answer even as he asked.

She motioned toward the graves. His gaze followed her motion and he winced.

"Senor Cassidy was a good man. I have known him for many years. You are alone here?"

Abby nodded. "I'll stay as long as they'll let me."

The man shook his head. "You cannot stay here alone, Senora, it is not safe, and I have no men to spare. I have barely enough to get these horses to Carrizo. We will leave horses for you and repair your corral, then we must hurry to deliver the rest. On our way back we will take you with us to Senor Carrillo. One of my men can stay to run the station until a new station master can be sent."

Abby had no choice but to agree. Somewhere in the back of her mind a question formed; where will I go? But she didn't allow it to surface, didn't look for an answer. Her duty was to the station. Later she would think about herself.

Before nightfall the corral was repaired. She served a hot meal to the vaqueros and when they drove the horses off into the approaching darkness she felt very much alone. An hour later a coach rolled in. Abby didn't need to harness a fresh team for them. They met the horses on the way and replaced their exhausted team on the trail. There was only one passenger so they didn't spend much time at Seven Springs. They were already hours behind schedule. The driver promised to carry word of Cassidy's death to the line superintendent at Oak Grove. He urged Abby to come with him but she refused. She would stay until someone relieved her.

It was a strange feeling when Abby closed up the station that night, locking the doors and windows, listening to the night sounds which suddenly seemed louder and more threatening. The bed felt empty without the solid presence of her husband. At this moment she would even welcome his lovemaking. Exhaustion claimed her.

Abby woke as usual as the first light of day filtered into the room through the shutter. For a moment she was disoriented, wondering why she didn't feel Cassidy beside her or hear him stirring in the kitchen. Often times he would be the first one up to light the fire. Instead the station felt cold and empty. With a shudder of anguish, memories flooded back.

She dressed quickly and started a fire in the kitchen. No coach was due today. She could feed her stock, then perhaps take another ride through the brush to see if there were other animals she'd missed the day before. The renegades seemed interested only in horses. She could also use some fresh meat for supper.

The vaqueros wouldn't be back for another day at least. She should start thinking about what she would be taking with her when she left. Her first destination would be the Carrillo's ranch. She dreaded telling them what had happened, but knew they would welcome her into their home as if she were a member of the family. Once there, she would decide where to go next.

For her supper she had fresh rabbit, setting it in the oven to bake. There were dishes from the previous day to clean. That kept her busy inside the station. The first hint of trouble was the sound of footsteps behind her. It took an effort not to freeze but to keep on with what she was doing as if she hadn't heard. Her knife was concealed in the pocket of her dress and one hand slid slowly toward it as she kept on with dinner preparations. Her hand closed around the knife hilt when suddenly rough hands seized her, one clamping around her wrist to keep her from drawing the knife, the other wrapping around her chest, imprisoning her against a strong masculine frame.

"Oh no, senora," a voice hissed in her ear. "I know you are swift with a knife."

Abby went cold. She'd know that voice anywhere. She struggled against the vise-like arms that held her, finding no leverage to fight. Another man came around in front of her and snatched the knife from its hiding place. His grin was full of triumph.

"So, puta," the Mexican's lips curled into a sneer. "I knew one day Cassidy would not be around to protect you, and Miguel and I would take our revenge. It has been a longtime coming, and will be all the sweeter for it." His black gaze shifted to his partner. "Tie her to the chair. The Indios have taught her too many of their ways. I do not trust her."

The man behind her moved swiftly, yanking Abby's arm up behind her back so sharply she cried out. She didn't dare struggle or the bone would snap. Rope was lashed around her wrists before she was yanked back to a chair and tied. Even her ankles were bound, leaving her with nothing to fight her captors with but her furious glare.

"First we fill our bellies," the leader said, sniffing the rabbit she was cooking. "We have been many weeks without warm food cooked by a woman." His black eyes glinted with cruelty, the lust written clearly for her to see. "And many weeks without the feel of a woman under me. I am looking forward to showing you what you missed that day in the mountains. You and the other puta."

He reached out and touched a strand of fiery hair which had come loose from her bun. Abby turned her head away but it did no good, she couldn't escape his touch. The man laughed, a sound full of triumph. He had her where she couldn't escape and was in no hurry to take his revenge. He would make her wait and taunt her with what they would do to her when their bellies were full.

The other man found Cassidy's private stock of whiskey in the bedroom and poured two liberal portions. They grinned as they studied their helpless captive. Abby knew they wouldn't be gentle with her, and doubted they would let her live when they were done. She had humiliated them. Their male egos would not forgive that.

She was forced to watch while they took the rabbit from the oven then helped themselves to beans and tortillas. Both men watched her while they ate, taunting her with their eyes, slopping down food, making a mess of the table in the process. The way they downed the whiskey told her they were building themselves up for what came later. She was trussed up, helpless, unable to move even her hands which were becoming numb. It made her furious to think she had become so careless, that she hadn't foreseen what these two jackals would do when they heard she no longer had Cassidy to protect her.

"It is good we ran into those vaqueros," Miguel said, his gaze sliding over Abby's full breasts. "Otherwise we would not have known the senora was here all alone, eh, Crispin?"

The leader chuckled, juice from the rabbit running down his chin. "We said we would come to keep an eye on you in case the renegades came back. It is a shame you were gone when we got here."

His words confirmed Abby's suspicions that they couldn't let her live. Witnesses knew they were coming here. She fought the panic that threatened to overwhelm her, fought to stay calm and remember the things Pion had taught her. Surely she was a match for two drunken men.

She couldn't let them guess what she was thinking, didn't want them to be on their guard. She pretended to be frightened, letting tears come to her eyes.

"See," Crispin motioned toward her with his rolled up tortilla, his look contemptuous. "She is a woman like any other. She tries to sway us with her tears. Next, I want to hear her beg for mercy."

It'll be a cold day in hell before I do that, Abby wanted to say, but she cowered in her chair to the delight of the men. They drank more of the whiskey, and when their bellies were full they swept the remaining food and dishes onto the floor, leaving only the whiskey bottle and two glasses.

"Now we have a little fun," Crispin said, his dark eyes glinting with cruel intent. "Untie her from the chair, but do not untie her hands. I do not trust this she-dog."

Abby didn't struggle as Miguel untied her from the chair, she tried to keep her wrists from being retied too tightly but the man was taking no chances, he yanked the rope so tight it bit into her skin. Crispin shoved her into the bedroom she had shared with her husband, her hopes dissolving as Miguel pulled the bed away from the wall. She'd hoped they'd grow careless. They hadn't.

Crispin grabbed her arm and flung her onto the bed on her back. Abby's hair tumbled loosely about her shoulders, her skirts settling far above her knees, revealing her shapely legs. She was helpless to do anything when Crispin slid a bold hand along a bare leg, pushing her skirt higher. Abby was glad she was wearing smalls, there were hot days when she didn't bother with them.

The only sound in the room was the harsh breathing of the two men. Abby was less certain of her ability to fight them. She had only her feet, and one chance was all she would get.

She was contemplating her move when Miguel suddenly grabbed one of her ankles and slipped a thong over it, yanking her leg wide so he could tie it to the bed post. Desperately Abby lashed out at Crispin, her foot catching him across the chest, knocking the breath from him. He gave a sharp grunt of surprise, then his black eyes glittered with fury as he smashed the back of his hand across her face. Stars whirled before her eyes as weakness invaded her limbs. For a moment she was stunned, but that moment was all it took for Miguel to secure her other ankle into a slip knot and tie her to the other post.

Desperately Abby struggled to free herself, but yanking on the thongs only cut off circulation to her feet. Crispin drew a long, razor sharp dagger and held it up for Abby to see.

"You see, puta, you are no match for us. You were lucky last time. You took us by surprise. This time you will not escape. You will pay for what you did."

Trying not to let them see her fear Abby glared past the blade into Crispin's black eyes. It had no effect. She was helpless and they knew it. The leader climbed onto the bed between her legs. As he knelt there, he bent forward over Abby, grabbing the neck of her dress with one hand, the other bringing the knife close to her face.

To taunt her he touched the pointed tip against Abby's throat, but she knew he wasn't ready to kill her. He wanted to see fear in her eyes, a satisfaction she refused to give him. Her eyes were cold and hard as she glared up into his.

With a harsh chuckle Crispin dipped the knife down to her dress and slashed, separating the material all the way to her waist. Both men leaned closer to stare at her exposed breasts, the heat of their gazes scorching her, making her want to shrink away from their lustful gazes.

Miguel dropped to his knees to see better as Crispin fumbled to open his pants, clumsy from the effects of the whiskey and from eagerness. The knife dipped lower to her bunched up skirt as Abby tried not to look at the rigid thing thrusting out of his trousers. Perspiration stood out on Crispin's forehead as he stared at what he was about to bare.

Abby struggled to sit up, trying to butt him with her head. Crispin laughed cruelly and back handed her again, knocking her flat. Suddenly his grip on the handle of the knife tightened and a look of surprise came into his face. His eyes grew larger. Abby watched helplessly, as did Miguel, as Crispin raised up from his haunches, his fingers opening around the knife as it slipped from his grip. He pitched forward on top her, eyes rolling back in his head.

A movement at the door took Abby's attention. A painted warrior filled the doorway with menace. It was then she saw the knife protruding from Crispin's back. Realizing the danger, Miguel went for his gun. Before his fingers could close around it a spear came hurtling across the room, embedding itself deep in his chest.

Miguel gave a startled grunt, tried to draw the gun only to find his fingers wouldn't obey the command of his brain. His eyes began to glaze even before he fell back on the dirt floor.

Abby was aware of Crispin's dead weight on top her, but a moment later the warrior dumped him on top of his companion. He stared down at Abby, who was half exposed and totally helpless, her face already swelling from the force of the two blows. Behind the red and black paint and expressionless eyes Abby couldn't fathom what he was thinking. She might have been rescued from one dead-ly situation only to be trapped into another.

The tall Indian reached for the knife stuck deep in Crispin's back and used it to cut the thongs binding her legs. Next he rolled Abby roughly onto her side and cut the thongs on her wrists. If she had any thought of fighting it disappeared with the prickling feel-ing of blood returning to her numb hands. She wouldn't have the strength to hurt him. It would be better to wait.

She grasped the front of her dress trying to hold it together to cover herself from his interested gaze. The warrior's glance quickly swept the room, taking in the clothing on hooks.

"You dress," he ordered in the Kumeyaay language. "For ride."

He motioned toward her shirt and trousers which Abby was more than thankful to reach for. It meant he didn't intend to rape her. At least not here. She wondered if he was one of those who had stolen the stock. He seemed to be in a hurry. From outside came the yip of a coyote, yet Abby knew it wasn't a coyote at all. The war-rior motioned for her to hurry.

"At least look the other way," she told him in Kumeyaay.

"Quickly!" he ordered. "Or I take you like that."

Abby had no intention of going with him with her dress gaping open, so she had no choice but to struggle out of her slashed ruin of a dress and pull on the brown plaid shirt she favored. She pulled trousers on over her smalls, cinching them with a buckskin belt she had made. Then she put on her sturdy boots. She didn't know where this man was taking her but she wanted to be dressed for the wilderness.

He snatched a heavy mackinaw jacket from the hook and tossed it to her, followed by her hat. He stepped over the two dead men to the outside door, then motioned Abby out. For a brief moment she toyed with the idea of resisting but knew he would take her by force, might even tie her. It was better to obey now and hope for a chance to escape later.

She barely looked at the bodies as she stepped over them, past the tall warrior, inhaling the scent of his musk. Beyond him another warrior waited, mounted, holding two horses ready for riding and two more he'd taken from the Mexican's wagon.

The warrior behind Abby didn't wait for her to mount but lifted her with surprising ease, depositing her on a horse, then vaulting onto another. They didn't take time for the stock in the corral, it would slow them down. Her captor grabbed the reins of her horse, leading the way into the thick brush around the springs, to the Indian trail.

A number of plans flashed through Abby's mind as she looked from one Indian to the other. It was difficult to see their faces under all that paint. The second man was shorter, stockier then her captor. She debated slipping off her horse and running into the surrounding brush to hide. They were moving fast enough that if she jumped from her horse she would no doubt stumble and fall. They would have her before she could scramble to her feet.

One by one she rejected plans that occurred to her. For the moment, while they were on the move, she was safe from their attentions. She wondered why they had come back for her. She had the feeling these were the same renegades who had killed her husband and Wes. They had come back for her, but not to kill her. The alternative frightened her even more.

She wasn't at all surprised when they headed south in the direction of the Mexican border. Mexico was the obvious place to dispose of stolen horses. The Butterfield brand was too well known elsewhere.

All through the night they traveled through the hills, following trails Abby could barely see. The men seemed to know exactly where they were going. Often times she thought she saw other fresh tracks but it was too dark to tell for certain.

She was hungry and thirsty. The two Mexican's had eaten her dinner. Fear left her mouth dry as the desert but she knew better than to complain, she merely snatched at mesquite pods as they rode. It helped to ease her thirst.

It was nearly daylight when they came to a water hole. The two men drank first, only then was she allowed her turn. She drank greedily, ignoring the brackish taste. Next the animals were watered. On the ground Abby could see signs of many other horses, most of them shod.

More than likely it was the stock from the station.

The men conversed rapidly in a language she didn't understand though some of the words were familiar. Only then did it dawn on her the warrior had first spoken to her in the tongue of the Kumeyaay. He knew who she was.

At the remote water hole she gave no thought to escape. She didn't know this area and feared heat and thirst more than she did the two men. They, at least, made no move to bother her, ignoring her for the most part. Gingerly Abby touched her face, finding it puffy and swollen. One eye was swollen so badly she could barely see. Perhaps it was something to be grateful for. She must look a rare sight. Soon the puffiness would turn black and blue. It would be some time before any man found her pretty, a fact that right now gave her a measure of comfort. She could only hope it was enough to protect her from these two men.

The horses were given a brief rest and a chance to graze on the sparse grass that had escaped the earlier herd. The tall warrior took some dried meat from a pack on his horse to the other man and to Abby. Before she could do more than take a bite he was motioning her to mount. Before she could protest, or mount herself, he swung her up onto her horse. They ate as they traveled.

The two warriors carried water with them which they used for the horses the next two times they stopped to rest. Abby was allowed no more than a sip, and noticed they, too, used the mesquite peas.

Even before the sun was very high in the sky, Abby knew the day would be a scorcher. She'd long since shed the mackinaw, tying it Indian fashion to the blanket in front of her. With the shirt she could roll up the sleeves and open the top two buttons to allow air to circulate next to her skin.

At times she was aware of the tall warrior's gaze, studying her, but he didn't speak except to give orders. Other than to put her on her horse he didn't touch her. She was thankful for that, but when they reached their destination it might be another matter. No doubt they were trying to catch up with the ones driving the stolen horses.

29

In the early afternoon they halted in a rocky canyon with only open desert spread out before them. Heat waves danced across the sand, creating the image of a large lake. Abby had seen many such illusions, knowing it was a false one. To trust the eyes in this case was to be lured to an agonizing death on the blazing sand.

Here in the canyon was a spring large enough to provide grass for the horses, and several cottonwood trees for shade. The tall warrior took the blanket saddle from her horse and spread it on the sand in the shade, motioning Abby to sit. Too weary to argue, she obeyed.

The horses were hobbled and left to graze.

When the two men ignored her, Abby felt the tension in her slowly unwind. She wanted to keep an eye on them but was so tired she leaned back against the trunk of the tree to rest her eyes.

The next thing she knew she awakened to find the tall warrior resting on his haunches beside her, watching her. She couldn't stop the alarm that filled her eyes as she recoiled from his nearness. It was only then she realized he was holding food. He waited patiently while she gathered her courage enough to reach out to take the offering, another piece of dried meat and a hard biscuit made of baked acorn mush. It wasn't very tasty but it was filling and nourishing.

She was surprised to realize she had slept for several hours. The sun was dropping toward the horizon, and though it was still hot it would be cooler soon. The horses were ready to travel, and as soon as they had eaten they set out across the hot sand.

Abby had been able to drink her fill at the tiny oasis, and now their water sacks were again full. She gave no thought to where they were going or why, feeling curiously detached, uncaring. The life she had known at Seven Springs was gone forever. She didn't care what happened to her now. No doubt she would end up as a slave to one of the Indians, most likely the tall one who had killed for her. He seemed so remote, so cold, she doubted he would take the time to get to know her. She would no doubt be his slave and his sex partner, and knew it wasn't at all unusual among some tribes for a man to share his slave with other men.

Her main fear was the sharing. She was aware that the shorter man looked at her with contempt. But, with the other, she couldn't fathom the way he looked at her so intently, sometimes as if he liked what he saw, other times with a look of anger.

Her captor continued to lead her horse, even though she would not have tried to escape in this barren land. In the maze of canyons she had long since lost her bearings, knowing only that they were headed south.

It was evening of the second day when the call of a quail sounded from the rocks ahead. They'd crossed a tract of burning sand and were again in low foothills. The tall warrior answered with a quail call of his own. Abby knew they had caught up with the slower moving herd. There were times when she'd seen their tracks. Where there were horses, there would be forage.

The tall warrior dropped back closer to her, his gaze sweeping her with a quick assessing look. He motioned for her to roll her sleeves down and button her shirt. She was only too glad to comply, even if it did make the heat unbearable. He also motioned for her to hide more of her hair under her hat. Abby quickly repined her long hair on top of her head then pulled her hat down over it, tucking any loose strands out of sight as best she could.

A small gourd appeared in the man's hands and before she could protest he dipped his fingers into it and stroked them down one of her cheeks then the other. Several more dabs created a pattern. He was marking her as his property. That both heartened and frightened her. Soon they would be in the camp of the renegades. Their leader might challenge his right to have her to himself.

As they rode into the small camp, Abby forced her chin up, knowing she must make a strange sight with her ill-fitting men's clothes, a hat pulled low over a face that was battered and marked by black and red paint.

A warrior she guessed to be the leader stood up and came over to them. Looking at Abby curiously as he talked to the tall warrior. Her captor dismounted then pulled Abby down beside him, his tone making it clear she was his. She could feel the intense stare of the leader, a heavy set man, wide through the shoulders and middle, but all muscle.

The warriors all wore buckskin leggings over their loin cloths, each painted in an individual way. Abby did no more than let her gaze sweep the camp then stare into the distance. She didn't want to meet the gaze of any of the men. The sight of them didn't do much to reassure her. It was obvious they were renegades. There was no friendliness in their faces, and once they were certain there was no threat to their camp they settled back into preparing their evening meal.

The leader grunted in disgust, as if not understanding why any warrior would go to so much trouble for such an ugly woman and turned away. Abby thought she detected a lessening of tension in the tall warrior beside her. He was different from the others, though she suspected they were all from the Yuma tribe. This one was tall, well-muscled. His waist narrow, widening into shoulders that hinted at great physical strength. He carried himself with a confidence that spoke of great skill as a warrior.

None of the others showed any interest in her as her captor shoved her toward the shade of a large rock. The boulders here formed a sort of cove that was deeper than Abby first thought. The boulders were too tall to scale and formed a perfect holding place for her. She'd have to pass through the warrior's camp to escape.

At the moment all she wanted was rest. She hadn't slept at all the previous night, afraid the warrior meant to have her. But the two men had taken turns sleeping for the few hours they stopped. The food she'd been given that day had been barely adequate, yet the men had eaten no more than she. The sight of three rabbits roasting over an open flame made her mouth water. She refused to look at it though, didn't let them see how hungry she was. She knew only too well the ways of some Indians. They despised cowardice and displays of emotion. In any event, there was no guarantee they would share their food with her.

Instead of thinking about her hunger she checked out the camp by studying the lay of it in case an opportunity for escape should present itself. She could see five men, but guessed there were at least two more in the rocks standing guard. That made a party of nine counting the two who brought her here. The odds were not at all in her favor. Any escape attempt would have to be well thought out. If she made a try and failed, the tall warrior might not be able to protect her from the others. She caught her captor's gaze as if he knew what she was thinking.

Abby sank down into the shade. At this moment she wasn't capable of thinking straight enough to try anything. She would bide her time

The tall warrior brought his bed roll and dropped it in the shade next to her. Abby tried not to cringe away from the thought of the coming night. She didn't know what she would do if he tried to force her into his bed. The other men pretended to ignore her but from time to time she could feel their curious gazes, their attempts to see through the white man's clothing to what might lie underneath.

Once, before they ate, the tall warrior took Abby into the rocks away from the eyes of the men so she could take care of her bodily functions. He turned away, allowing her privacy. For that she was grateful. The man spoke little to her, only in grunted commands, which at this point she did not disobey.

She was grateful, too, when he brought her a portion of meat and a hard biscuit for dinner. Slaves were often treated like dogs, fed only scraps and beaten for the slightest infraction. Her captor hadn't mistreated her. At least, not yet. But she couldn't help wondering what the days ahead would bring. One thing he had accomplished, he had given her no time to think about her husband and what she had left behind at Seven Springs.

If only she could get to her little cave for the money and weapons which were hidden there. If only she could get to the Carrillo Rancho where she would be safe. A picture of the flashy Everett Drayton popped into her mind. If she could find her way to Los Angeles she could accept his offer of a job. But first, she had the slight obstacle to overcome of nine painted, fighting-fit warriors.

She had tried to pay attention to the landmarks as they traveled in case she has an opportunity to escape. From the direction they were headed she guessed they were in Mexico,

As darkness fell the tall warrior vanished into the rocks. When another man came into camp to eat she knew he had gone to relieve the man on guard duty. He would be away for several hours, which left her alone with the others. Abby huddled into the shadows of the rock, hoping none of the others would grow curious enough to take a closer look at her.

She listened to the sounds of conversation by the fire. Her eyelids began to droop but she was reluctant to move and call attention to herself. Next to her was the tall warriors sleeping robes. She wanted more than anything to crawl into them, but when he returned he would take that as acceptance.

The rocks cooled against her back, causing her to shiver. In the faint firelight she could see her mackinaw under the bed roll and moved silently to retrieve it, retreating again into the shadows. The jacket brought enough warmth that she slipped into an uneasy sleep.

Sometime later she came awake with a start, aware she was not alone. It was very dark. The fire had died into glowing coals. The tall warrior had returned and was spreading out his robes for sleep.

"Come," he said in the Kumeyaay tongue. "You will be warmer with me."

Abby shook her head, suddenly wondering how he knew she understood him. At her refusal the man came to her, dropping to one knee. Her heart began to pound loudly in her ears but there was no threat in his gaze.

"It is only warmth I offer," he said softly. "This is not the time for more, though the others must think it is so if you are to be safe among them."

Abby's eyes widened at his words. It almost sounded as if he knew her. He read the questions in her eyes.

"I know your heart yearns for freedom, but there is nothing left for you at the place from which I took you. It was unfortunate your man died. I did not wish that. It was not by my hand." A tremor went through Abby's body at the thought of her husband dead; cold in the ground. Yet she felt reassured that this was not the man who shot him in the back. "These warriors must think you are content to be my woman. We will stay with them long enough to collect my share of the money for the horses, then go our own way." He paused for a moment to let her digest that.

Once the two of them were alone Abby knew her chances of escape were greater, yet he had to know that too. He was asking her to be patient for now. She frowned, suddenly aware of a sense of familiarity about him. Behind the paint she couldn't see his features, but in the darkness, with only the shadow of the moon on his face she recognized him.

"Night Wolf!" she gasped.

He nodded. "Yes, Firehair, it is Night Wolf." He said it in such a definite way that Abby felt it was almost a threat. She had spurned him by leaving the Kumeyaay village before he could ask her to be his wife. She saw the anger in him, the tightening of his mouth. This was not the boy she had known. This was a man, a warrior, and she was now his captive.

"Come, we will sleep before we wake the others."

Abby was too numb with cold and shock to do more than resist feebly as he pulled her down onto his fur robes. He quickly removed her boots then opened the bed for her. Too exhausted to argue Abby let him push her back and cover her. A moment later he joined her, making her aware he wore nothing at all. A riot of emotions churned within her, until exhaustion forced them away. The man drew her closer. For a moment she was afraid he wanted to make love to her, but he had said he would not. Night Wolf would keep his word. She burrowed into his warmth and was instantly asleep.

The morning was crisp, clear and bitterly cold. With only cold venison and one of the hard biscuits Abby soon found herself mounted and riding beside Night Wolf. Again she had hidden her hair, her bulky mackinaw bundled about her. She tried not to think how comfortably she had passed the night, how it felt to be held in a man's arms all night long without him trying to make love to her.

They drove the stolen horses south, deeper into Mexico. She couldn't help but notice the way the Indians kept a close watch on the seemingly empty desert around them, sometimes sending out a scout when they could spare a man from the drive. This was dangerous country. Often times the fierce Apache ranged into Mexico, and the Yaqui, once a peaceful tribe who tried to live the way of the Spanish, had turned on their exploiters. They, too, were known to steal horses, and these might prove too tempting.

Abby also noticed the Indians knew where to find water in this barren land. She guessed it was not the first time stolen horses had been brought here by these men. She wondered how long Night Wolf had been one of them. Today he was remote, silent.

At first, she resented having him lead her horse, but as the day warmed, and she shed her jacket, she was aware of the interest of the others. She realized she was safer with Night Wolf. He was making it known she belonged to him, and though she railed silently against it, she dared not express it in front of the others. She kept her hat pulled low, sitting her horse with all the dignity she could muster, thankful for the bruises and swelling on her face.

For two days they moved deeper into Mexico, traveling through land which seemed devoid of life. There was little game, the plants were not ones Abby was familiar with. She wouldn't know how to find food in this place.

When the Indians made camp that night there was only hot sage tea. No fresh meat. Night Wolf left her to go hunting. While he was away she sat quietly, afraid to move, afraid to call attention to herself, aware the men surreptitiously watched her. The leader especially was showing more interest. He detached himself from the others and came to where Abby was sitting on a rock away from the fire, her mackinaw again pulled snugly around her.

She wanted to look for Night Wolf but knowing it was too soon for him to return. She also knew she could not cower in front of this man. When he dropped to his haunches in front of her she made her gaze frigid.

The heavy set warrior stared back, his gaze attempting to see past the bruises, past her hat and the layers of clothing. He reached toward her hat but Abby slapped his hand away. Startled by her daring the man hesitated a moment as if deciding what to do. A crafty look came into his dark eyes which Abby knew spelled trouble.

Her hand surreptitiously moved toward the knife at his waist, then with a suddenness learned from her years of living with Indians, his knife was in her hand, the sharp point held just under his chin.

The man froze, seeing deadly intent in her eyes, his own widening with shock that a woman would dare to take his knife. For a moment they both stared, neither giving way. Abby was unsure what to do next. An angry Indian could be worse than an angry rattlesnake, and far more deadly.

She was aware the others had stopped what they were doing to watch. The leader would not want to lose face by being bested by a woman. Then a voice interrupted the standoff, deadly calm and equally dangerous.

"Black Horse, the woman is telling you she belongs only to me. It is the agreement you made." Night Wolf stepped closer, the tension in his body showing he was ready to fight.

Black Horse turned to look at Night Wolf, a tall powerful figure in the deepening night. At his feet were two freshly killed rabbits. Black Horse could see that if he pressed his interest in the woman he would have to fight. On the other hand, there was the promise of fresh meat.

A tense smile formed his hard mouth into a grin.

"I was curious why Night Wolf would want such a white woman. One who looks like a man."

"She will do for now," Night Wolf said.

Abby felt anger at his words, as if she were merely some toy to be thrown away when he tired of her. Yet, in the night he had not touched her.

Black Horse shrugged and stood up. Abby handed him his knife before she could be ordered to do so. Returning it to his belt in one swift movement, Black Horse cast Abby a contemptuous glance then stalked away.

Abby breathed a sigh of relief, wanting to tell Night Wolf how glad she was to see him, but he picked up the rabbits and walked away.

The men all shared the meat Night Wolf provided. No more was said about Abby. The incident seemed forgotten, yet Abby was not fooled. She felt the smoldering resentment in Black Horse. There was hatred in the gaze he directed her way when Night Wolf wasn't looking.

Later, as Abby lay beside Night Wolf, her heart beating with an erratic rhythm from his nearness, she felt for the first time how difficult it was for him not to touch her. His hand moved caressingly along her arm, the long slow breaths he took telling her he wanted her, his body tense next to hers.

He didn't turn to look at her when he spoke, very softly, but not the words she was expecting. She hadn't wanted to feel anything for this man. She had thought the Indian part of her life had been left behind forever. Now, she realized how easy it had been for her to slip back into the old ways. How easy it would be to stay with Night Wolf now that she no longer had a place where she belonged.

"Tomorrow, Firehair, we will reach the rancho where the horses will be sold. You must stay close to me. These are not nice men. I will give you control of your horse but you must be very careful. I feel Black Horse's eyes. He will plan his revenge on both of us, but only after he no longer needs my help. Once the horses are delivered it will be different. We must not let him know we suspect. We must be clever like the fox. Black Horse will not let us ride away."

30

Abby felt a chill go through her. She knew Night Wolf spoke the truth. He had noticed the way Black Horse glared at her and realized they would both be in extreme danger once the horses were sold. Tomorrow would be a day fraught with tension. Abby knew she would obey him and stay close. He spoke also of the danger of the men they would be meeting at the Mexican Rancho, which was all too easy for her to visualize after the incident with the Mexicans at Seven Springs.

All that stood between her and a cruel fate was a tall, bronzed warrior. This time it would be one against many. If she had anything to say, it would be two against many.

In the morning, when the first touch of rosy dawn painted the sky, Night Wolf turned to Abby in the warmth of their robes. He drew her against him, his lips moving over hers gently, without passion. Abby felt her heart begin to pound even though she knew he wasn't wanting to make love to her. She wasn't ready to feel things for another man. It was too soon. In the camp she could hear the others stirring.

Night Wolf was aware of her lack of response. His gaze was tender when he looked down at her. "We were meant to be together, Firehair. You denied it by returning to your white world, which holds no place for you now. I will always take care of you and protect you." From his bedroll he drew a knife and gave it to her. "Today, until we are free of these men, it may be necessary for you to protect yourself. And, you must obey me if we are to live." Abby nodded, her eyes telling him she understood.

"The others will use some of their money to buy more guns. We used all our ammunition, and the Mexicans are always eager to sell us guns. I must have one too or we will be outmatched." When his lips touched hers again Abby felt a fierce surge of longing. She didn't want to feel anything for this warrior, didn't want to return to the Indian way. She couldn't forget the man who had so recently been laid to rest at Seven Springs. A man she had tried to love. A man who had never started a fire in her blood.

For a moment another face appeared in her mind, a sun-browned face with a wide mouth made for easy laughter, of startling blue eyes with their hint of mischief. John Jay was far away, a world away from this savage desert and the savage men who formed their secret plans for her and Night Wolf.

Abby banished her wayward thoughts and accepted the hat Night Wolf handed her, using it to hide the fiery nature of her hair. She put on her boots as Night Wolf readied their horses.

There was little to eat, only a crumbling biscuit. Abby didn't complain, she knew there would be food once they reached the rancho where they were to sell the horses, food to buy with the money they received.

As they herded the horses Abby now had control of her horse, yet she stayed close to Night Wolf. Though he looked straight ahead she sensed he knew exactly where the others were. Several times she saw Black Horse in conversation with the others, no doubt hatching a plan. Night Wolf would have noticed too.

They began to see more vegetation in the desert, hills turning green from recent rain.

They began to see scattered cattle among the scrub. When they topped a rise there were buildings in the distance, and a river with lush grass crowning its banks. Here the cattle were plentiful, a hardy, half wild breed that ran away at their approach, tails in the air.

Several vaqueros rode out to join the drive, herding the horses into a large corral. On a rise, above the river, surrounded by cottonwood trees, Abby saw the main ranch house, a sprawling old adobe with a porch in need of repair and chickens strolling around the yard. A number of children were playing at the river bank, one was fishing.

For a time Night Wolf was able to stay with Abby by the corral, both of them aware of the curious looks of the vaqueros. Night Wolf's glare was enough to keep them at bay, but Abby could see the covert glances thrown her way by their Yuma companions. She knew the real danger would come once they left the ranch to return to California.

She had a bad feeling about this place and wondered if Night Wolf felt it too. Black Horse was haggling price with the owner of the rancho, a short, bandy-legged man with a wide sombrero. He wore two pistols about his hips and had the hard-bitten look of a man who had carved out his place in the wilderness and kept it by force of arms.

A pipe was lit and tobacco smoked by Black Horse and the Mexican ranchero under the shade of a giant cottonwood. Abby stood by her horse, using it as a shield. She knew Indians didn't do anything in a hurry. Night Wolf casually handed her the reins of his horse, motioning her to stay alert in case they had to leave in a hurry. He knew there was no danger of her fleeing in this foreign place. She would only be fleeing one danger into another. At least with him she had an ally and a protector.

Night Wolf moved near enough to hear the bargaining when it resumed following the passing of the pipe. He could see the Mexican ranchero was used to dealing with Indians, and knowing their ways, displayed no impatience. The condition of the horses was discussed, Black Horse extolling the fine condition they were in, the ranchero saying they were too skinny to be much good. Soon the conversation turned to price and the haggling went on.

Eventually it was settled. The two bargainers stood up and shook hands. The ranchero barked orders to his men who rode off immediately, then he pulled a pouch from inside his shirt and began to count gold pieces into Black Horses hand.

Night Wolf made certain he received one of the rifles which were brought back by two vaqueros, and two boxes of cartridges. The guns were old and much used, and Night Wolf checked to be certain it was loaded, grunting his satisfaction.

The other Yuma's were clearly excited to have fresh rifles, having discarded the ones used at Seven Springs for lack of ammunition.

A wagon load of supplies was brought to be divided among them. Night Wolf took his share, tying it securely to his horse as well as Abby's. He didn't want anything bulky to flop around if they had to ride hard.

During the haggling Abby had edged their two horses to some hay which had been spilled near the fence, letting them eat. It might give them an edge.

When the others mounted, Night Wolf boosted Abby onto her horse. He swung up gracefully, his strong legs clamping around the belly of his horse. Abby was glad the stallion looked so powerful, with the large chest of a runner. Her own mare had a quick step, carrying her head proudly with ears pricked forward, eyes alert. Though the mare's long legs looked dainty, Abby had the feeling she would do her best to keep up with the stallion if they had to flee.

The other Yuma's seemed careless about their horses, not caring for them properly. If something happened to their mount there was always another one to buy or steal. Two of the Butterfield horses were traded for Mexican ones, ones without the distinctive brand, to carry supplies.

Without the herd of horses the return trip to California would be much faster. The Yuma's were in a hurry to put as much distance as possible between them and the Mexican ranchero. The day was almost gone and they needed a safe place to camp.

Black Horse followed the river, moving at a brisk gallop until the horses began to tire. Abby could tell Night Wolf didn't like the pace, wanting to save their horses. If there was trouble, it would come once they were camped.

On a rise, at the edge of some low hills, Black Horse picked a grove of cottonwoods and poplars, where boulders formed a half circle five hundred yards from the river. A grassy depression formed a natural corral for the horses. Abby made certain she knew every bit of the terrain around them. Night Wolf would be doing the same.

Black Horse had selected a place that would be easy to defend. One grumbling guard was posted high on the rocks where he could see in all directions. A fire was soon lit, food unpacked for the evening meal. Abby went cold when she saw the jugs of liquor. With a whoop of delight Black Horse opened one and began to drink. It passed from one to the other. She saw Night Wolf lift the jug to his mouth, taking a long swallow before he passed it to the impatient man beside him. She wanted to tell him how dangerous the liquor was, but was helpless to do more than listen to his laughter mingled with that of the others. She began to fear for both their lives. How could he be so foolish?

Then she began to see. Night Wolf didn't heft the jug as often as the others, and when he did, she had the feeling he was not drinking. As the others began to swagger and laugh for no reason, Night Wolf did the same, sometimes staggering.

Abby stayed close to the rocks where she could see their horses. She wanted to be able to ride out at a moment's notice, if necessary. Beside her was the bedroll and supplies. When no food was put on to cook, Abby searched for something to eat. Her only food all day had been the biscuit at dawn. She found jerked beef, spicy and delicious.

Hidden in the shadows she slipped some of the dried meat and other small items inside her shirt. They might be forced to ride out with just their lives. She put on her mackinaw and filled the pockets with rifle cartridges and food.

The warrior who was supposed to be on guard left his post to share the liquor, which meant soon all would be drunk, and either very dangerous or very sleepy. Abby hoped it would be the latter. Night Wolf let one of the others bring up the subject of dividing the money.

Reluctantly Black Horse began to pass it out.

Abby stayed alert to everything in the camp and around it. Her gaze, hidden by the brim of her hat, explored ways to leave unobserved. Night Wolf seemed to be doing the same, she knew him well enough by now to know he was not careless, especially not with these treacherous men. Their lives hung in the balance.

Black Horse took another long swig from the jug, liquor dribbling down his chin and shirt. His gaze slid sideways to the shadows where Abby was half hidden from the firelight which had been allowed to die down. Noticing his interest the others also turned their attention to her. Abby could see the tension that came into Night Wolf's body, watched him stagger along behind, carrying the jug, urging one of them to drink, hoping to get their minds off her.

Abby desperately wished she could disappear into a crack in the rocks. She dare not run. Her hand tightened around the knife hidden in her jacket.

Below them one of the horses let out a loud whinny, its head turned to the south. An answering call came from somewhere in the distance, which was quickly silenced. Black Horse and the others turned toward the sound. Night Wolf slipped into the shadows not far from Abby.

With a quick motion, Black Horse sent his warriors into the rocks to investigate. They had been gone only minutes when Abby heard the first shots.

Quickly she slipped down the hill to the horses, taking the bridle for hers and Night Wolf's. The gun fire was far enough away that she could lead the two horses into the rocks away from the camp. She tied them then went back for the bedroll and supplies.

She heard shouts, both in Yuma and Spanish. As she grabbed up the bedroll Night Wolf materialized out of the shadows, causing her to jump in alarm.

"The vaqueros," he spat. "They've come to take back the gold. Our bullets are no good. They don't shoot."

Grabbing the bedroll away from her Night Wolf started for the horses. "No," Abby told him. "This way."

She led him to where the horses were tied. He quickly secured the bedrolls and supplies on the two horses and almost threw Abby onto her mount. He vaulted onto his stallion and headed into the rocks without looking back, knowing Abby would follow.

The night was dark. Abby would have all she could do to follow the shadowy figure in front of her, but knew her mare would follow the stallion. She turned to look back. The shots were more scattered now, and before long the rocks cut off any sounds.

Night Wolf kept a fast pace, running the horses when they came to open desert. It was dangerous but they had little choice. As of this moment, the Yuma as well as the vaqueros were their enemies, and in the sand, there was no way to hide their tracks.

By dawn they reached a long range of mountains that paralleled the desert. Abby had seen them in the distance when they drove the horses south, now Night Wolf would use them to hide. From a high hill he stopped to look back. Abby wasn't certain but she thought she saw something dark on their back trail.

Night Wolf made no comment, choosing the rocky hillsides rather than the faint game trails. Often times he brought up the rear on foot to hide any sign of their passing. He pointed out where he wanted her to go then followed. It was time consuming and that was one thing they didn't have to waste.

Soon Night Wolf again took the lead, seeking out long canyons which led deeper into the mountains. They allowed the horses to lead them to the tanks where rain water had been trapped, and let them drink and rest. Abby brought out dried beef, biscuits and water. The standing water was too brackish for them. Night Wolf restlessly scouted the rocks to seek the best way.

When they moved on again, he changed direction, turning more east than north, angling back toward the desert. In one ravine he urged the horses into an easy lope, eating up distance, having no choice but to leave tracks in the sand. The tracks wouldn't be distinct, and it was impossible to tell how long they had been there, but Abby knew their pursuers would read the signs, though they would be slowed considerably whenever Night Wolf concealed their path.

In late afternoon they came upon a grassy shelf on the side of a rock strewn hill. It took Night Wolf's stallion only a moment to locate a spring hidden in the rocks. Here it was safe enough to hobble the horses and remove their packs.

Though she was tired and sleepy Abby set about gathering only very dry wood. They would risk a small fire for hot tea, salt pork and beans. While Abby saw to the preparations, carefully tending the fire to show no smoke, Night Wolf went to scout the area. She knew he would be selecting the direction they would travel when they left, as well as possible escape routes.

It seemed unlikely their pursuers would be very close. Perhaps they had given up the chase, but Abby held little hope for that. If it was Black Horse, he would want his revenge. If it was the vaqueros, they would want their gold back.

With warm food in her stomach Abby couldn't stay awake any longer. Night Wolf covered her with his robes, doused the fire, then again slipped off into the rocks.

She didn't know how long she'd been sleeping when Night Wolf woke her. He showed her where to keep watch on their back trail before he slid into the robes warmed by her body and was instantly asleep.

For a moment she watched him, glad they were finally on their own, even if they weren't safe yet. Then, remembering the danger she turned to watch below. It was still light enough to see anyone following. She suspected Night Wolf would sleep only a short while then they would travel in the darkness. His night vision was like that of an owl. Their pursuers couldn't read their signs in the dark and would have to wait for daylight.

The sun warmed rocks turned cool as the sun sank below the horizon. Abby rubbed a hand across her eyes to ease the strain of staring into the distance. Only rarely did she close her eyes to rest them, careful not to fall asleep. Night Wolf had entrusted her with their safety.

A movement in their camp caught the corner of her eye and she saw Night Wolf was preparing the horses. He filled their water jugs from the springs then motioned for Abby to join him. She took one last look down the hill, her gaze searching the deepening shadows. She thought she saw a movement but couldn't be sure. Seeing her intent stare Night Wolf joined her. After a moment he nodded. "They come."

"Who?" Abby asked.

"It is too dark to see. Come, I know the way."

Before they left the camp Night Wolf scattered the remains of their fire and erased all sign of their being there. An Indian wouldn't be fooled, the vaqueros might.

The trail was rougher as they climbed a rocky hillside, winding across sheer granite slopes sprinkled with low scrub. The horses had to pick their way carefully as Night Wolf avoided dirt areas which would leave tracks. They climbed upward into shadows as darkness descended around them. Abby trusted his judgment. Thoughts of escape never entered her mind. Though they didn't speak, Abby could feel a comfortable silence between them. Twice they stopped to rest the horses while Night Wolf scouted ahead on foot. Sometimes they were forced to dismount on the steepest inclines, but Abby refused to complain even when she felt too exhausted to take another step.

They halted under an overhang of rock while Night Wolf scouted ahead. Abby sank down gratefully, falling asleep at once. The horses stood patiently, resting also. Night Wolf returned sometime later, his moccasins making no sound to betray his presence. Finding Abby asleep a tender smile curved his lips.

He removed the blankets from the horses then gave them water from their precious supply. He fed them acorn cakes because there was nothing else. Then he spread his robes beside Abby and drew her next to him. She didn't even awaken, just burrowed closer to his warmth and sighed softly.

They slept soundly until dawn then moved on without taking time to eat. Night Wolf led the way on foot. The rocks were treacherous. A misstep might send them tumbling down the slippery granite mountainside to certain death.

At the top of the ridge Night Wolf paused to choose their path. Soon the going was easier, allowing them to move faster. Within a few hours they were on a faint game trail leading toward the desert. They found a water hole with enough grass for the horses, and rested there.

There was no sign of pursuit. Abby was beginning to hope they had lost them. In the sandy bottom of a ravine Abby moved the mare alongside the stallion.

"How long did you ride with Black Horse?" she asked, curious about his reasons for choosing to steal horses.

He gave a shrug. "It was one way to get back at the white man," he said, not looking at her.

"Have you had trouble?"

He nodded, his eyes turning hard. "They have pushed my people onto land that is no good. Our hunting range is filled with the white man's cattle and his buildings. He invades our mountains searching for the yellow metal he worships. They have killed many of our people, including women and children."

Abby's brow creased with concern, knowing he spoke the truth. She'd heard enough talk from the soldiers and settlers passing through Seven Springs to know the same thing was happening over and over wherever the white man found Indians on land he coveted.

"Why do you want the white man's gold?"

"I want it for the things it can buy our people. The white man comes with treaties, promising food when he takes away our hunting ground, but the food never comes, or else it is such a small amount it does not fill our bellies for more than a few days."

"Where will you go now?"

"To the village of the Kumeyaay," he said, glancing at Abby. "It is land that I know. The Yuma will not search for me there if they are the ones who track us. The vaqueros would not follow for long. They are afraid to cross the border, or to venture into the land of the Apache."

"I would like to see my village again," Abby said wistfully. "It's been a long time."

"We will go there," Night Wolf said.

Contented with that, Abby dropped back to follow along behind, letting her mind drift aimlessly. It was good to be free again, not to be tied to a place. She had seen the white man's world, she'd been to San Diego, but she loved the wilderness, the open spaces. Though she felt she was defying the fates by being with Night Wolf, she had no intention of returning to Seven Springs. There was nothing to return to.

Across the scorching sands of the desert they kept the fastest pace the horses were capable of, and even though there was no sign of pursuit, both she and Night Wolf felt it just the same. Both continually looked back expecting to see that same black dot just at the limits of their vision.

They crossed the border into California. This was an area they were both familiar with. Night Wolf knew exactly where he was going, turning into a westerly direction, leaving clear tracks in the sand. Though Abby saw places where they might have concealed their passing, Night Wolf seemed unconcerned.

31

Low hills began to rise around them, barren, black with volcanic rock. Night Wolf turned into one of the long ravines which cut a path into the heart of the hills. Beyond lay the mountains which were the home of the Kumeyaay. With the heat of summer they would be living in the coolness of the oak and pine forest.

In the bleak hills Night Wolf had chosen, there was no water. They hoarded what they had, giving it to the horses, taking little for themselves. Mesquite grew in clumps along the edge of the ravine, its mature peas easing their thirst. The pace didn't slow.

The side of the ravine closed in around them, narrowing sharply. Uneasy, Abby could only hope he knew where he was going. The sides became too sheer to climb, towering above them. If there was no way out when they reached the end, they would be trapped.

Night Wolf followed the dry stream bed deeper into the canyon, which curved toward the west. Here the sides were so close the horses had to walk single file. Piles of rock and dirt collapsed from previous storms and floods sometimes partially blocked their way, forcing them to scramble over on foot, leading the horses

Abby became worried, afraid that around any bend they would find their way solidly blocked by a cave in. If they were forced to turn back there would be no place to go except into their pursuers blazing guns.

Again the canyon forked, both arms which would become swollen with water during a storm. Night Wolf didn't hesitate, choosing the arm to the left. Here again he could easily have covered their tracks enough to at least delay those following, but he didn't pause.

Ahead of them Abby could see solid rock walls reaching up a thousand feet. It looked to be a box canyon. Worried she looked at Night Wolf. He seemed unconcerned. Then she noticed the green vegetation at the base of the cliff that the horses snatched up as they rode by.

The horses picked up their pace, ears focused forward, which told Abby there must be a spring. But the sheer walls showed no way to leave this deep canyon. When they came to some damp sand, Night Wolf dismounted and began to scoop out a wide bowl to allow water to seep to the surface. He tasted it before he would allow Abby or the horses to drink. It was sweet and cool. Abby had to stretch out on her stomach to drink while Night Wolf held the horses back. Abby splashed her face when her thirst was slaked, wishing she could take off her clothes and wash, but she was too conscious of their pursuers.

When she turned to ask Night Wolf what came next, he was gone, leaving her to water the horses, who eagerly drank, and used their hooves to dig deeper, snorting their approval.

More water bubbled up.

Abby looked with longing as cool water filled the depression. Her clothes were sweaty from long hours of riding. She longed to wash them, at least her shirt. It would be many hours before those following could catch up.

Except for the horses she felt totally alone. There was some grass around the alcove that the horses could feed on, so she pulled off their blankets and packs. Both of them dropped to their knees then began to roll in the sand with seeming great enjoyment. When they got to their feet they shook themselves vigorously then set to grazing.

Night Wolf might not be back for a long time, and, unable to resist the need to feel clean Abby began to strip off her clothes. Her first step into the shallow pool brought a gasp of pure pleasure at the sensation of cool water against her heated skin. She sat in the middle of the pool, closing her eyes in delight as she began to splash herself.

It felt wonderful to finally be free of her hat and all the clothes she'd had to stay bundled up in against the prying eyes of the Yuma, and she had suffered from the heat. Her long mane of auburn hair tumbled freely about her shoulders. It, too, she dipped into the water, wishing she had soap to wash with. She had to be content with scrubbing her head as best she could.

When her body felt clean, she took her shirt and began to wash it, draping it over one rock and scrubbing with a smaller one. If Night Wolf wanted to ride out she could always wear the shirt wet, it would soon dry on her body in the searing heat of the desert sun.

There was no sound to tell her Night Wolf had returned but she felt his presence behind her. She was aware of how she must look to him, kneeling to wash her shirt, her naked back to him. Though she considered slipping into the wet shirt she knew it would hide little as it clung to her body.

A moment later he sank down into the pool beside her. A quick glance told her he had stripped off his loin cloth and leggings, displaying all of his body in all its muscled magnificence. Her mouth went dry as she quickly averted her gaze. She heard his laughter as he splashed water over himself. Then he splashed her playfully. She was afraid to allow herself to respond to his teasing. The next moment he grabbed her arm and fell back into the pool, pulling her on top of him.

Startled she struggled, much too aware of his strong muscled chest against hers, his partially aroused manhood pressing against her stomach. His eyes were full of mischief, yet underneath burned the fire of his desire.

"Too many nights I have lain awake with you beside me and not been able to touch you as my heart cried out to do. I have felt your body against mine when I kept you warm. I could not take you knowing the others were close by, listening. You were afraid of me then. Do you fear me now?" His dark eyes were flaring with passion.

Abby's mouth moved as if to speak but those compelling eyes drew her into them. She was no longer aware of the cool water swirling around them, saw only his full lips as they moved toward hers. Her mouth opened for him as he took possession.

She knew she should deny him, knew he was asking for what she couldn't give. But just for a moment she would savor the strength of his desire, delight in his magnificent body pressed tightly against hers.

He must have sensed her uncertainty and drew back. "It is too soon, I know," he murmured, his hands brushing her long fiery hair back from her face, fingers stroking her cheek tenderly. "Many times in the night I have longed to hold you to me, to show you what is in my heart." His eyes darkened with suppressed passion as they roamed over her still bruised face, as if to see beyond the marks. "You are beautiful with your fiery hair spilled about you. I have dreamed of it often." His gaze smoldered. "When you went away with the white man I thought it would be forever just a dream. I had returned to your village to ask for you as my wife only to find you had gone away. I couldn't believe it was true. I thought you knew I would ask for you."

It almost broke her heart to see the look of despair in his eyes. She reached out to stroke his shoulder, watching his eyes brighten at her touch.

"I would have gone after you, I was furious enough to, but Hahro talked me out of it. He said you were never meant to be wife to an Indian, that you were where you belonged."

Night Wolf stared into the distance, his eyes unseeing. "It took me a long time to accept that. Even after I knew where you were I dared not go close to the place or I would try to see you. There are those of us who grew to hate the white man as the years went by. We all suffered in some way at their hands and banded together to take what we wanted of his food and horses. Riding with Black Horse I felt like a warrior again. When I knew we would steal horses from the place where you lived I made up my mind to take you away. I did not want anyone killed, but Black Horse could not understand why I felt that way and seemed to go out of his way to make certain..." he broke off. "I was glad you weren't there. I'm not sure what he would have done if you were. He seemed half crazy that day, wanting to kill."

Night Wolf straightened and strode from the water, gathering his loin cloth and leggings and putting them on. Abby followed, letting her long hair shield her body from his gaze until she could wrap a blanket around her. He hadn't finished his story and she was eager to hear the rest.

"If we only stole horses we might be tolerated as a nuisance and the army would not come after us. But to kill men of the overland mail, this would not do. I knew I could not ride with Black Horse again or surely we would all be hunted down and killed. When we rode away with the horses I knew I had to go back after you. I could not leave you in that place alone. It turned out I was right, the jackals had come." His eyes smoldered with remembered anger at how he found Abby with the two Mexicans. "It was the first time I have enjoyed taking a life. I would have killed them over and over if I could that they would dare to place their filthy hands on you."

He leaned down to press his lips warmly against hers. "You are mine now. You will be my wife, my woman, when you are ready. You will not regret leaving the white man's way."

Abby couldn't respond. In the back of her mind a protest was raised which she didn't give voice to. There wasn't time to explain her feelings.

Night Wolf took his bow and his spear and with a last tender smile vanished into the rocks.

Though she was tired after days of little sleep, she forced her muscles to move. Her shirt had dried quickly in the sun. She wished she had other clothes to wear, something cooler now that it was no longer necessary to hide within the bagginess of the pants and shirt. She longed for the light material of a cotton dress, but that would come later. When she was again dressed, she gathered sticks for the fire.

Here, deep in the canyon, she didn't have to be careful of smoke. It dissipated quickly in the constant breeze that moved through. She took tortillas and some dried cactus blossoms they'd gotten from the Mexican ranchero. When Night Wolf returned with four fat quail, she prepared them for cooking while he brought more wood.

She was thinking how quickly she had slipped into domesticity with him. It felt comfortable. He provided, she cooked. It hadn't been that way at Seven Springs where she had been the better hunter.

"What about those behind us?" Abby asked later, tearing at the juicy quail meat with her teeth. "We have spent a lot of time here."

He nodded. "We control the only water for many miles. It is why I chose this spot."

"You've been here before?" she asked, relieved they weren't trapped.

Again he nodded. "The way is difficult from here on, but the trail is open. I have already checked and cleared it of rocks. We will not leave until we know who follows. We can defend this place, and we will have water. They will not."

Abby saw his plan. Rather than continue never knowing if they were still being pursued, Night Wolf had chosen to make a stand here. In the desert he had fired some of the boxed cartridges for the rifle. They were good. It was only the ones the Mexicans loaded into the rifles that were duds.

"When do you think they will come?" she asked.

Night Wolf looked up at the darkening sky. "Soon it will be dark. Their horses will smell the water and be hard to control. If they think we are trapped in a dead end they will wait until dark to come in."

As soon as they had eaten, Night Wolf slipped away into the rocks to watch the trail for signs of their pursuers. Abby hoped he wouldn't try to get too close to them. She doused the fire and returned the uneaten food to the packs. They might have to leave in a hurry. She led the horses away from the water and hobbled them where there was sparse grass.

She moved everything away from the spring, taking the bed robes to a sandy cove behind some rocks so the wild animals could come in to drink. Hidden in the shadows she settled back to watch.

The first visitor was a small screech owl. It made several low passes over the spring before it landed. With a last careful look around it walked into the shallow side of the pool, and dipped its beak into the water. Tilting its head back the small owl let the water run down its throat, then drank again. A moment later it lifted into the air on silent wings.

Several rabbits came, and small rodents. Still later four coyotes came. They seemed to sense the presence of the horses, and even her in the shadows, but took their drink none-the less. Then vanished like shadows into the rocks.

Abby sensed Night Wolf's return when a rabbit which had started for the pool dashed for cover. Night Wolf made no sound, moving like a ghost. He skirted the spring, staying in the shadows and came to where she was sitting. He seemed to know exactly where to find her.

"They're camped down the canyon, Black Horse and two others."

Abby nodded. She suspected it would be them. It would take another Indian to track Night Wolf.

"I know Black Horse," Night Wolf said. "He will make his move in the night. He has little choice in this narrow canyon. You will remain here with the rifle for protection."

"No," she protested. "You will need it."

"I need only my bow or my knife. They will have to split up. I need silence as my weapon, not the cursed weapon of the whites." He seemed remote, his face showing no expression, preparing himself for the night to come. "If they come," he said grimly. "Do not stay with the horses. Hide in the rocks. Perhaps they will be satisfied with the gold."

Abby didn't want to think about Night Wolf not returning. She fought back emotions churning close to the surface. He would not want to hear her pleas or cautions. She nodded to show her understanding.

"Try to rest," he told her. "They will not make their move until late. I will be watching them."

Without a word he slipped away into the rocks before she could utter any of the words she wanted to say. She was more frightened for him than for herself. For a moment she debated what to do next. He was right about her not staying close to the horses. She would be too easy to find if she did.

Hiding some of their supplies in the rocks, but leaving the gold where it could be easily found, Abby moved silently among the rocks, climbing until she found a shadowed spot where she could look down on the canyon floor. She wished it was narrower here, but the canyon had opened into this small oasis where the spring appeared.

In spite of Night Wolf's urging to rest, she knew she could not, not when he was in danger. Cradling the rifle in her arms she settled down to watch the shadows below for any sign of movement, to listen for sounds.

Abby strained her ears, anxious to know how Night Wolf was faring. What if he failed? What if he didn't come back? After all, he was one man against three. For a moment she considered taking one of the horses and going on alone, but dismissed it. She had to see this through just as he did. He was risking his life, could she do any less?

A faint sound somewhere in the rocks made her strain her ears again, listening for some clue as to its location. All was again silent. She realized she was barely breathing, but even that tiny sound seemed too loud for the silence.

Sensing a movement rather than hearing it, Abby froze, blending in with the shadows.

She dared not move even her head to look yet all her senses were screaming of danger. Gripping the rifle tighter she let her finger close around the trigger, not knowing from which direction the danger would emerge.

Suddenly powerful arms came around her from behind. Her sudden intake of breath was cut off ruthlessly as she was dragged backward, her rifle clattering noisily against the rocks as she threw it down. Close to her ear she heard an angry hiss of breath at the noise. Instinctively her hand closed around her knife.

Her lungs felt as if they would burst as the giant hand covered both her nose and mouth, closing off her air. Already her head was starting to swim as she stabbed upward into the beefy arm that was suffocating her.

With a yelp of surprise Abby was flung away from her captor, landing in a heap in the sand. Her hat was skimmed off by a rock she brushed against, allowing her auburn hair to tumble about her shoulders. Gasping frantically for breath, Abby turned onto her back to face her enemy, her knife poised for the attack she knew would come.

Drawing up her legs, Abby assumed a low crouch as the man came closer. She didn't have to see his face to know it was the most dangerous of the renegades, Black Horse. She could feel his fury in the hiss of his breath as she braced for the attack.

Without a sound a pair of leather leggings appeared at her side. She looked up to see Night Wolf, a knife poised in his hand even as she saw moonlight glinting off Black Horse's wicked looking blade.

"You were foolish to follow," Night Wolf told his enemy. "You will not take my woman or my gold."

Black Horses laugh was full of confidence, yet Abby could see him glancing around for his companions. "I shall have both, Yuma coward. You were lucky to get away when the treacherous Mexican dogs attacked. It will not happen again."

The heavy set Yuma warrior crouched for the fight, his glance raking over Abby, taking in her fiery hair which framed her face. His chuckle was full of menace. "I see why you kept her hidden from us. Red scalps are very rare."

Night Wolf's eyes never left Black Horses as he motioned Abby away. "Do not look for the others," he told Black Horse in a deadly voice. "Twice my blade has tasted blood this night."

"Then I shall have all the gold," Black Horse taunted. "And enjoy the rest of the night with the white woman before I leave her, along with you, for the buzzards."

The two warriors circled each other warily, knives poised. Abby drew back, outside the arena formed by a circle of rocks. She could do nothing but watch, her breath painfully tight in her chest. Black Horse had the advantage in the length of his arms and in weight. He was a bull of a man. Night Wolf was more compact, his muscles trained for combat and hunting, his chest large from hours spent running.

The first clash came with all the fury of two rams bashing horns. Night Wolf seized Black Horse's wrist to control his knife hand even as Black Horse grabbed his. With powerful legs and the strength of their arms and backs, they strained for advantage. Black Horse ducked, stepping in close to Night Wolf and yanking him off balance. As he fell, Night Wolf dragged his opponent with him.

They writhed in the sand, each striving to straddle the other, knives flashing in the faint light but drawing no blood. Night Wolf lashed out with a powerful kick catching Black Horse in the kidney area. It was enough to wrest the Yuma leader free. Both men jumped to their feet, Black Horse snarling his anger at the painful blow. He lunged blindly, slashing at his enemy who was suddenly not there. Instinct made the maddened leader whirl to block the attack from the rear as Night Wolf ducked under the knife to get behind his opponent.

Again they locked wrists, bodies straining to break the other's hold. Night Wolf's strength held Black Horse away, refusing to allow him to trip him again. Black Horse feinted backward then drove suddenly closer to Night Wolf, trying to drive his knee up into his groin. Night Wolf twisted his body, taking the brunt of the blow on the thigh, then tripped his off-balance enemy and dropped him into the sand. As Black Horse fell, he jabbed with his blade, raking it across Night Wolf's ribs. A thin line of blood began to well up immediately.

Night Wolf seemed not to feel any pain, nor did he hesitate even a moment before he followed his enemy to the ground. His blade snaked out so silently Abby couldn't follow it as Night Wolf slashed downward. A gurgling cry of outrage and surprise came from the downed Yuma leader.

Black Horse remained seated on the ground, gasping for breath. His murderous gaze focused on Night Wolf, a snarl of fury died away into a fit of coughing. Clumsily his hand reached for the knife he had dropped, trying to close his fingers around it.

Abby stared at the blood welling out of the man's chest, watching in horrified fascination as it flowed down his chest to puddle in the sand. The Yuma leader made one last effort to seize his knife then fell backward. His chest gave one final shudder.

For several moments neither Abby nor Night Wolf moved, staring at the fallen warrior as if to be certain he was dead. Finally Night Wolf went to him and felt for breath.

"He is dead," he pronounced. "We will leave him and the others for the buzzards and the coyotes."

Abby suddenly found the strength to move, rushing to him, only to come to a sudden stop at the sight of blood running down his stomach.

"You're bleeding!" she gasped.

Night Wolf put a hand to the wound. His attempt at a smile didn't entirely come off. "I am fortunate to have a medicine woman to tend me."

Abby led the way back to camp, knowing by his awkward shuffle that he was in more pain then he was willing to admit. Gingerly he sat on a rock as Abby started a fire. The first order of business was to clean the wound and see how bad it was.

From the bottom of her shirt she cut a wide strip, then ripped off both sleeves to use as dressing. In the morning she would find herbs she needed to prevent infection.

"They were foolish men," Night Wolf grunted as she bound him tightly. "We will take their horses and their gold. It would be a waste to leave it behind."

But later, when they located the horses, they found no gold. It appeared they had fled from the vaqueros with only their horses. No food, no gold. It was no wonder they had followed Night Wolf and Abby knowing they had both.

32

When they reached the mountains, Night Wolf headed for the village of the Kumeyaay, leading the three horses of the Yuma warriors. Her people would be happy to have them.

Both he and Abby were looking forward to resting after their long, hot trek, to bathing in the mineral pools. The coolness of the mountains was a relief, the scent of pine revived their spirits. The relief lasted only until they reached the valley of the oaks. Abby stared in confusion. Where were the ewas? Where were her people? There was only a scattering of grazing cattle.

She looked at Night Wolf seeing no confusion in his look, only tight-lipped anger. "The white man has come," was all he said, his anger giving way to sadness.

Without a word they rode across the valley, Abby searching for some sign of the happy village which once existed here. It might never have existed at all so completely had it been obliterated.

The respite they had been looking forward to was delayed. Abby glanced anxiously at Night Wolf, knowing his wound was paining him by the deepening lines around his mouth. It seemed an effort for him to sit erect on his horse. Crossing the valley they headed into the high mountains, to the second camp of the Kumeyaay. It was normally reserved for later in the summer. Abby knew if they were forced to live there now, the area would not support them for the rest of the summer.

As they climbed the rugged mountain trail, the sound of gunshots echoed from the rocks. It was not close enough to be a danger, but came from below them. Night Wolf motioned Abby to a place of concealment in the rocks, telling her to stay hidden while he investigated on foot.

He wasn't gone long. "White men," he said, confirming Abby's suspicions. "They have shot two deer." He swung up on his horse and they continued on their way in silence, leading the three horses. They were both aware of the significance of the white man's invasion of the Kumeyaay's valley. It meant less hunting ground for the Kumeyaay whose method of stalking deer could not compete with the deadly accuracy of rifles. As a result, the deer would become more wary and fewer in number.

It had happened to the Kupa, whose Rancheria was on land claimed by the Warner Ranch, their hunting greatly restricted. The proud Kupa were forced to accept gifts of beef from Jonathan Warner to keep their children from going hungry.

Abby felt anger and a sadness all mixed together. She'd hoped it would never happen to the Kumeyaay. A shudder went through her at the realization the tribes were now fighting for their very existence. She'd been away. She hadn't seen it happening. Hahro and Opachuk hadn't spoken of it when she last visited them.

At the high camp Abby was relieved to find everything as it was before. The children were playing, dogs barking at them as they rode in, and the adults calling out greetings.

Opachuk came out of her ewa as Abby and Night Wolf stopped in front of it.

"Daughter, it is good to see you," Opachuk said, her wide grin showing several missing teeth.

Abby slid from her horse, wanting to embrace her Indian mother but knowing it was not her way. "Mother, we are happy to see you. Night Wolf and I have come a long way."

Opachuk's look was full of curiosity as she watched Night Wolf slide wearily from his horse to stand beside Abby. The gesture told of the bond between them, something Opachuk was surprised to see.

"You are welcome in my house," Opachuk said with typical Kumeyaay hospitality.

"Hahro hunts for our dinner. Come, I will make tea."

"I will see to the horses," Night Wolf said. "We have brought these animals to help with your hunting."

Abby wanted to urge him to rest but knew his pride would be offended. She would secure herbs from Enyaa and tend to his wound later.

While Abby and Opachuk went inside, Night Wolf placed the packs and supplies by the side of the ewa, then led the horses to a grassy slope, hobbling them so they could graze. Curious children followed, watching everything he did. They seldom saw horses in the village.

Night Wolf returned to Opachuk's ewa, seating himself on the men's side of the fire, across from Abby. His gaze was warm when it touched her, causing her spirits to lift.

"We went to the low village," Abby said. "There were only cattle."

Opachuk paused in her preparation of the gourd cups of tea, her face showing the depth of her sadness. "We returned from the desert early in the summer to find our village had been destroyed. Men with rifles told us it was now grazing land for their cattle that we could no longer live there."

"How could that happen?" Abby asked. "It has belonged to the Kumeyaay since the beginning."

"It is so," Opachuk said with a nod of her head. "But the white man does not recognize our right. Wahss went to see the Indian agent at Temecula. He was told the land had been given to a white rancher. We can no longer use it. Wahss asked how we will hunt, how we will survive. The man said he will find a place where we can live, a place that will be ours according to white man's laws, but we must remain there and not go to our winter camps in the desert."

Abby saw the darkening of Night Wolf's expression as he listened. "What will my Indian brothers do?" he asked.

Opachuk shook her head, lines of frustration and worry etched into her aged face. "We do not know. There are only a few who want to accept the white man's reservation. The rest want to live as we always have. A few of the young men even speak of fighting for what is ours."

"Fighting has never been the way of the Kumeyaay," Abby said, surprised.

"It is so," Opachuk said. "Some of our young men have worked on white man's ranches. They have seen the ways of the white man and know what has happened to our brothers. Most must live in certain areas. They cannot hunt and they go hungry. Food promised by the white father does not come. Sometimes they must steal a cow to feed their children, but when they do, the white man threatens to shoot any Indian he sees off the reservation."

Night Wolf clenched his fist in impotent anger. "It has happened so to the Yuma. Once we hunted all the land along the big river. We defended our land against the Apache, against the Mojave. Our men have always been warriors, but the white soldiers have killed many, forced the rest to live where the land is barren, where there are no deer. I and some of the young men refused to stay there. It is why I rode with Black Horse, to steal white man's horses, to kill if I must to remain free as my people have always been."

Abby knew the futility of his stand even as she understood it. He was not a man to be confined to a reservation. He needed the freedom of the desert and the mountains, the freedom to go where he would in the wilderness which was rapidly dwindling in size under the encroachment of settlers from the East.

"I will talk to the Indian agent," Abby said, knowing she had to do something to help. "I will ask their plans for the Kumeyaay, tell him this land is yours."

Opachuk nodded but there was no hope in her expression, as if she knew it was already too late.

For a long moment Night Wolf's expression was brooding, then he, too, nodded? "You are white," he said. "They might listen to you."

It was the first time Abby wished she were a man. She knew how white men felt about women. Their place was in the home, as mother and helper to her husband. Women who spoke out on important issues were about as welcome as the plague.

Abby and Night Wolf spent the night in the dwelling of her Indian family, after he finally allowed Abby to change the dressing on his wound and apply steeped herbs. The cut was ragged but fortunately, not deep, and there were no signs of infection.

Hahro and Opachuk's children were now grown with homes of their own, but the next day, Night Wolf began to build an ewa to share with Abby, in spite of her protests that he give his wound a chance to heal. In a warrior's way, he ignored her. Or perhaps he felt if he didn't marry her as soon as possible she would slip away from him again.

Some of the villagers came to help, heartened by the addition of a warrior to their ranks.

The young men began to seek out Night Wolf, asking to learn his fighting skills. After a discussion with Wahss and some of the elders, permission was given. It told Abby the sad state of affairs if the Kumeyaay were preparing to fight. It had never been their way. Now they were pushed, and knew it could only get worse. If they were forced out of this high village there would be only the rugged rocks and canyons of the mountains.

As Abby stood on a hill at one end of the valley, she tried to see it through the eyes of a white man. There was grass for cattle, a narrow stream. She tried to tell herself it wouldn't happen here, yet she knew how fast settlers were coming to California. Every week at Seven Springs she had seen them, wagons of them, an unending stream.

They came for land. They came to raise crops and cattle. And here it was good for cattle. One day the hooves of cattle would grind the dwellings of the Kumeyaay into the dust as they had done at the low village site.

That evening the village held a celebration for their newest members. Abby was given gifts for her soon to be completed ewa, and rushes for making baskets. There was feasting on venison, patties of acorn mush, water cress, peaches, and gallons of hot tea.

In the dancing around the fire, the men as well as the women were showing off their skills. Abby, too, danced with the women, her gaze meeting that of Night Wolf who danced with the men across the fire. In his dark gaze she saw a happiness to be here among her people, a happiness to be with her. She was anxious about the coming night, not knowing what she would do if he tried to take her alone into the darkness. She was drawn to the handsome warrior, just as she always had been, yet she couldn't help but feel this was wrong....that it was not meant to be.

Something had gone badly awry. Her vision had not foretold of this life for her, but one far different.

The dancing and singing went on far into the night. At times Night Wolf came to her and they danced together, moving in a circle around the fire along with other couples. Abby didn't realize the picture she made with her flaming hair catching the glow of the fire, her emerald eyes dancing with the joy of being with her people again. Night Wolf was clearly entranced by her.

Both of them were suffering from fatigue after their long flight across the desert. Until their ewa was completed, they would sleep at the hearth of her Indian family. Abby was thankful for that, and in a way thankful for Night Wolf's injury, which made her feel guilty. She wasn't ready to think about taking a husband so soon after Cassidy's death. She needed time to grieve.

Alone she stole away from the festivities to her blankets, too exhausted to stay awake any longer. She didn't even hear the others come in later.

It was nearly dawn when Abby was awakened by a keening chant somewhere outside. She recognized it as one she had sung herself, the Kumeyaay song of mourning.

For a time Abby lay, drowsing, the chanting a part of her awareness. Another's sadness had the power to touch her when she felt her own sadness, her own need to mourn.

But reality waited for Abby when she got up and was asked to look at the young girl who had died. She knew at once from the sores on her face, the cause. It turned her heart to ice, knowing what small pox could do to a village. Had seen what it did to a wagon train of emigrants who at least had some natural resistance to the disease.

"I must speak with the elders at once," she told Enyaa. "The white man's disease is here. We must take immediate steps or more will die."

Wahss, Hahro and all the older men of the village came at Abby's summoning. They sat outside near last night's fire, seeming impassive, yet they could not disguise the worry in their eyes. They had heard of this dread white man's disease, knew it had struck other villages, with few survivors.

"We must move swiftly if we are to stop this disease from spreading," Abby told them, the determined light in her eyes telling them how dangerous the situation was. "No one must leave this village until the danger is passed, and no one allowed to visit."

The father of the dead girl watched her with eyes dulled by grief. Her heart went out to him because she must add to his misery. "In the home of Mara the disease lives on. It must be burned with everything in it, clothing, cooking pots, baskets, and especially blankets," she stressed. "Even the clothing her parents and the other children wore. We must all reach into our hearts to help any family this disease strikes." Her gaze moved to each man, seeing their doubt at the rashness of her words.

"Her family must build a new home at the edge of the village and stay to themselves. The disease can be passed on to others even before you know you have it." She looked at Mara's father. "You must refrain from touching others, even your own family. Mara's mother especially must be careful too, since she has no doubt touched the sores. The greatest danger is to her and her other children."

Night Wolf stood behind the seated council members, watching Abby, feeling proud that the men listened to her. He saw their respect and knew it would be done as she asked. There was great danger in this place, but not for a moment did he consider leaving. He sensed the Kumeyaay needed Abby if they were to survive.

Once the council made the decision to follow Abby's directions, the entire village was called in and the danger explained. Even in their grief, Mara's parents sadly agreed to do what was best for the village. Even as their ewa was burned, with Mara's body inside, others were building them a new ewa at the edge of the trees.

Abby stressed the importance of not having physical contact with anyone, not even each other. An uneasiness settled over the village. Any sickness was treated as if it were small pox. Abby was called immediately and the sick person was not to be touched. Within a week she had two more cases of the dread disease. One was a brother of the dead girl, the other, the mother.

Abby cooked for them, nursed them. She bound the boy's hands so he couldn't scratch the oozing sores. She gave no thought to the danger to herself. She gave orders for the herbs she needed and the women gathered them for her. But in this case she knew her skills were inadequate. The husband was immediately moved out of the house where sickness had struck again, isolated in another ewa, unable to help his family except by hunting and avoiding others.

All laughter was gone from the village, even the play of the children subdued. Everyone watched to see where the disease would strike next. There was constant activity as Abby ordered more ewas built. They were going to need them. Night Wolf donated the one he was building, others needed it more.

Within another week these ewas had become hospitals for the sick, with only Abby allowed to tend them. She wore a cloth over her nose and mouth when she was with them and was careful not to touch the open sores. Other than that, she hoped her natural resistance to the disease would protect her.

She refused to stay with Night Wolf and her family, afraid of infecting them. There was unhappiness in Night Wolf's eyes but no argument. He understood the danger, would gladly have faced it with her, but respected her wishes. She was the medicine woman. He did what he could to help, going out with the men and women to gather material for more dwellings, using the horses to carry it. Other days he hunted, once bringing in a large ram taken from the rocks of a steep canyon. It was cooked whole, in a deep pit in the ground, providing enough meat to feed the entire village for several days.

Some of the children died first, then adults developed the signs. Most died. Only a few survived, though they were weak for a long time. Abby ruthlessly burned bodies and ewas. At times there was grumbling about the strictness of her orders, yet no one could doubt she was the only one who could help them. They saw her tireless tending of the sick, saw the days she went without sleep because she wouldn't endanger anyone else.

It was over a month before Abby realized there had been no new cases in almost two weeks. The worst was passed. She had lost weight during the long siege, not eating properly, devoting all her energy to the sick. Once, when one of the recovered women began to help her, she fell into an exhausted sleep, not awakening for twelve hours.

The quarantine of the village kept the disease confined. Word spread quickly through the neighboring villages about their plight and no one came to visit anymore. The small pox had been contained.

Abby awoke from her long sleep just as the glow of morning touched the sky with ribbons of gold and scarlet. Wearing a buckskin dress which hung loosely on her thin body, her fiery braids hanging down her back, she looked at what had once been a happy village. There were burned out spots where ewas had stood. The ewas were scattered now rather than set in the usual pattern. She tried not to think about Opachuk, Hahro, and one of their grandsons, gone now, tried to forget the stench of burning flesh.

Her eyes smoldered with anger, wondering how the disease had come into this remote village. What white man had given it to Mara? Had she been caught alone in the forest? There was no way to know. Those who could have answered her questions had been taken by the disease.

She knew the others must feel the same desolation. There was no longer hope and joy, it had been erased by the scourge which had visited them. Something had to be done to restore life to the living.

Walking away from the village Abby stood on a hillside facing the rising sun. Raising her arms, palms upward in welcome, she stood for a long time, opening her mind. When she first came to the village with Night Wolf she had thought to live with him here, become his wife as he wished, but now she sensed it was not to be. In a fleeting burst of images she knew she and Night Wolf would be parted. She would try to help the Kumeyaay from within the white man's world. That was her destiny.

She stood for a long time with open arms, eyes closed, not feeling any fatigue. Once the visions died away she was still reluctant to move, reluctant to face the day.

Wrapped in her own thoughts it took some time for the rumbling noise to penetrate. Opening her eyes she searched the sky, finding no clouds which would bring thunder, yet the rumbling grew louder. Turning to look beyond the camp she saw something in the distance, moving closer. A wide dark mass.

With a cry of alarm she ran for the village, shouting a warning to the sleeping Kumeyaay. Sleepy-eyed people poked their heads outside, heard her warning, grabbed their children and fled into the rocks as the thunder grew into a roar. Abby saw Night Wolf grab up two small children, even as she did the same, and fled before the pounding danger.

From the corners of her eyes Abby could see cowboys whipping the stampeding cattle into a frenzy, driving them straight into the heart of what had been, moments before, a sleeping village.

Helplessly she set down her charges in the protection of the rocks, then watched homes smashed by wave after wave of wild-eyed, bawling cattle. With wild whoops and gunshots the cowboys drove them through the village until nothing was left standing.

"We don't want you here no more!" One of the men yelled at the helpless Kumeyaay. "Get out or we'll come back with the herd to grind you into the dust!" The wild gleam in the rancher's eyes told Abby he meant every word. "This is my range now. The governor gave me legal right!" Several more shots were fired into the air and with wild whoops of laughter the cowboys rode after the vanishing herd.

The thunder died away into silence. From the shelter of the rocks the Kumeyaay stared at their ruined village. Slowly they straggled back to the trampled ground, searching listlessly through the rubble for anything salvageable. It was pitifully little. What the small pox hadn't accomplished, the cattle had.

Abby saw the hopelessness in the faces of the women, the men bewildered by the terrible deed. She saw Night Wolf standing in front of the ruin of what he had hoped would be their home together, his eyes burning with anger and hatred. Many of the younger men looked equally hurt and angry. No one could understand why the white man had done this thing.

Abby joined Night Wolf picking through the rubble for anything that hadn't been destroyed. Her sleeping robes were ground into shreds, her baskets crushed. When she finished her search they had Night Wolf's gold, his knife and his spear. The rifle had been shattered, cartridges ground into the dirt. He didn't even search for them.

As the shock wore off, the elders of the village gathered along the stream with their pitiful belongings. Abby could see there was no fight left in them. Their spirit had been broken along with their village. She sat on a rock a distance away, watching. She didn't have to hear the words to know what was being said. They were deciding where they would go. If they rebuilt here, the village would only be destroyed again. As it was, they were without food or blankets, most of their hunting weapons useless. Many of the materials used to make weapons as well as baskets were gathered in different places during their yearly travels. The sharp arrows and spear points came from obsidian found at the desert lava flows. The wood for arrows and spears came from the desert as well.

Many of the water holes in the desert were dry now. The Kumeyaay would have to stay in the mountains to survive. Abby watched the women moving through the forest and along the stream, gathering water cress and roots to feed their children. For the adults there would be no food this day.

She should be helping, but she too had been infected by the feeling of hopelessness. She felt anger building against those who could do something so cruel. How many Kumeyaay would have been trampled if she hadn't been awake? How many children would have died?

Fury filled her. Somehow she had to help. Somehow!

Their immediate need was to keep from starving. She thought of the supply of food hidden near Seven Springs. The gold would buy food, blankets and weapons. There was food at the Seven Springs station and at the Warner Ranch. Night Wolf's horses had vanished in the confusion.

It dawned on her that Night Wolf was gone along with a number of the young men.

With a sense of dread she knew they were holding their own council. A council of war.

Knowing she had to do something to help, Abby decided to go after the horses. They wouldn't go far. She took a rope and bridles and searched out the tracks. Ignoring the growling of her stomach. Abby refused to eat, refused to be distracted. It was as if her hunger was punishment for being white, for being part of a race who could do such a senselessly cruel thing.

Two hours later she found the horses grazing peacefully in a meadow. They raised their heads at her approach, nostrils flaring with remembered terror. Seeing Abby, they settled back to grazing, allowing her to approach and bridle them. Using a rock to help her mount, Abby headed back for the destroyed village, her heart full of pain. Her Kumeyaay parents were gone. Hahro hadn't lived to see this terrible thing. Perhaps he was more fortunate than she thought. He and Opachuk were together somewhere. It had to be a better place than this.

33

When Abby returned to the site of the village she saw no one. It was deserted. They had gone to seek shelter for the coming night, knowing she would follow. Their choices were few. They needed water nearby, and would no doubt head upstream into the canyons. There were several caves where once their ancestors had lived, their drawings scrawled on the walls in secret places.

Along the way she saw several young men were hunting with weapons they had been able to salvage. She didn't see Night Wolf and could only hope he hadn't done anything foolish.

She caught up with the Kumeyaay just as they reached the caves. Along the way they had gathered pine boughs, tall grass, and anything else they could use to make their beds. Many were practically naked. There had not been time to even gather a dress or a blanket. The pathetic sight stirred Abby's anger anew. She would find a way to help. Her people had done this. She would find a way to make it right.

In the faces of the People she saw the knowledge of what she, herself, feared. They were no longer a free people. Soon they, too, would be living on land given them by the Great White Father, to eat or starve, at the whim of the local Indian agent. She wasn't fool enough not to realize some of the agents lined their own pockets at the expense of their helpless charges.

With one of the young men who knew how to ride, Abby went to bring pine boughs. Many would be needed if they were to sleep warm this night. The horses became beasts of burden as the stacks of branches and reeds on their backs grew larger. Abby no longer rode, she walked. Her face set as if in stone, expressionless in the way of the Kumeyaay, her heart filled with pain and anger.

For two days she waited for Night Wolf to return. Five others were missing as well, hotheaded young men, just coming into manhood, young men eager to prove themselves in the eyes of the elders. In the event they were doing something desperate Abby convinced Wahss to send men back along their trail to erase all sign of their passing. They didn't want the white man to find them again.

The People began to do things which had never been necessary before. They posted guards at night, and built their fires in caves, sleeping there in family groups. They lacked the materials to construct ewas.

After two days Abby knew she could wait no longer. The children were hungry, the adults denying themselves in order to feed them. Early the next morning Abby rode out, taking two horses. If she succeeded she would need them both.

She wished she had a hat to cover her vibrant hair. It was too noticeable. At least on horseback she had more chance of outrunning pursuit, but it would be best to remain out of sight.

Rather than take the stage road, she chose the Indian trail, which would take her down to the desert. It took her most of the day just to locate it, then she dismounted to check it for signs of recent travelers. The only tracks were those of animals, rabbit, quail, and deer. Just before dark she camped in a cluster of rocks just off the trail, not allowing herself the luxury of a fire. She stayed close to the horses while they browsed among the rocks for grass, eating berries and roots herself, then later using pine boughs for warmth as she slept.

Unable to sleep for long, Abby awakened to bright moonlight. Restless, her hunger driving her, she packed her few belongings on her horse, and leading the other, set out again, the trail alight in silver. The water she carried in two large gourds she gave to the horses. She could do without until they reached the springs.

The trail was rough and rocky. By late afternoon Abby reached the hills south of Seven Springs. Strangely she felt this was now enemy territory. She didn't want to be seen until she was ready to show herself.

Leaving the horses far out in the brush, she crept to the spring farthest from the station to fill her gourds with fresh water for them. When they were watered and had settled down to graze, she moved toward her hiding place in the rocks. As she moved through the brush she set her snares as she passed them. Hopefully she would find fresh meat when she returned.

Also in her cache was one of her old dresses, which would be better to wear right now than her buckskin. Unbraiding her two pigtails, she rebraided into one long plait to hang down her back, making herself look more like a white woman than an Indian. She also took some of the gold pieces, but was not so foolish as to enter the station with them, leaving them hidden nearby.

As she approached the station through the brush, she was careful not to flush the quail she could hear clucking in the dense brush.

Hearing voices, she disappeared into the undergrowth, crouching as she moved closer. The sound of a woman's voice startled her. At her garden Abby saw a heavy set, middle aged woman hoeing weeds. Her soft humming seemed strangely out of place. It had been too long since she felt like singing. The small pox had taken too much away from her.

For a long time she watched the station, seeing a thin man come out the front door and walk down to the corral. From the way he kept looking to the east she guessed a stage was due. If that were so, the woman should be inside cooking. Smoke came from the chimney, so no doubt there was food being prepared. Perhaps there were others here as well.

Moving to a place where she could see the corral, she saw four horses with the Butterfield brand and two without, which must belong to the new station master or to others inside.

Glancing up at the position of the sun Abby knew she dare not delay any longer. The food was desperately needed. She gave little thought to the way she looked in a faded, wrinkled dress hanging on her thin frame.

Abby stood, concealed her knife in the pocket of her dress and took a deep breath to steady her nerves. She moved around the station so the woman would be the first to see her. As she stepped out of the brush the woman's eye caught the movement, her head coming up sharply. For a moment it looked as if she would reach for the rifle leaning on the fence nearby, but seeing no harm in this skinny young woman she glanced toward the corral.

"Henry!" she called out. "We got company."

The man came scurrying, following his wife's gaze. His eyes widened at the sight of Abby's bedraggled condition.

"Land sakes, child, where did you come from?" He looked out into the brush, tension coming into his body as he suspected a trap.

"I'm alone," Abby said. "I've come a long way and I'm very tired and hungry." As she spoke the words she realized it was true. It seemed forever since she'd been able to rest.

"Half-starved by the look of you," the woman said, putting down her hoe and stepping over the low fence. "Come inside, miss. There's hot food a plenty. My name's Millie Pierce. This here's my husband Henry." The man nodded, still staring at her with a wary expression.

"I'm Abigail," she said, hoping they wouldn't connect her to James Cassidy. She wasn't certain she wanted to be recognized as she followed Millie into the station, seeing the changes since she'd been gone. It seemed years ago. Was it only months?

The smell of food wiped all thought from her mind. She followed Millie's directions to wash herself in the basin in the kitchen.

Doing the cooking was a young girl who resembled Millie both in her build and in the shape of her eyes.

"This is our daughter Henrietta," Millie said, then to the girl. "Abigail here is half starved, dish her up something hot."

Abby felt guilty as she dug into the stew the moment it was set in front of her. There was warm cornbread and fresh cooked greens from her garden. She tried not to think of the empty stomachs back at the caves. Most of the People would not eat again tonight. Yet she knew it would do no good to drain her own strength further. She needed food if she was to help.

Henry went about his business while Millie watched in fascination as Abby put away a generous helping of stew. Henrietta showed little interest in anything except her cooking. Her expression was placid, devoid of life.

"How long's it been since you last ate?" Millie asked, her curiosity getting the better of her.

"Days, I think," Abby said. "Except for roots and berries." She wondered what story she should tell these people. Before Millie could ask more questions they heard the sound of the stagecoach pulling up outside. Millie got up at once.

"You stay right here," Millie said. "We'll be feeding the passengers in the other room."

Abby was glad for the distraction, glad too the passengers wouldn't be coming into the kitchen. She didn't want to deal with a lot of questions.

The chatter of voices, the sounds of a meal being served made Abby homesick for her life here. It should be her fixing this meal and serving it. It should be Cassidy hitching the new team then taking care of the tired ones. Closing her eyes against the images flooding her mind Abby was too self-absorbed to hear the tread of boots entering the kitchen.

"Abby?...Mrs. Cassidy?" came the startled voice.

Abby's eyes flow open to see Gus, the driver coming in with a coffee cup in his hand. He was staring at her as if she were a ghost. She knew how she must look to him.

"….Hello Gus," she managed to say, blinking back tears.

"We'd about given up hope," Even the grizzled driver seemed moved by the sight of her. "John Jay and every one he could get into a saddle been looking for you."

"John Jay?" She had purposely pushed him out of her mind these past months. "Where is he?"

"Right now, I'm not sure. I know he spent a long time tracking you after two dead Mexicans were found here, and you were gone, along with all the stock. He said the trail led into Mexico. How did you get away?"

"It's a long story Gus," she said, weariness etched in her eyes. "Just tell…John Jay and the others that I'm fine and not to look for me."

"If you'll pardon my saying so, Mrs. Cassidy, you don't look fine. You look like you're ready to drop." Gus's eyes were filled with concern, he clearly didn't believe her.

Abby glanced toward the other room. "I don't want the Pierce's to know who I am. All I told them is that my name is Abigail. I want to buy some supplies and leave, and I don't want anyone coming to look for me. Tell John Jay there's going to be Indian trouble in the mountains and to stay away from there."

Gus obviously didn't like what he was hearing. Abby straightened her back and looked him fully in the eyes. "I mean what I say, Gus. I know what I'm doing and I'm doing it of my own free will. Tell them to leave me be!"

The old man shook his head. "It ain't right, ma'am. It just ain't right. But I'll tell 'em." He would have gone on but Henrietta came into the room for more food. Gus went to the stove to fill his cup with hot coffee, and with a deep, troubled frown left the room.

Abby breathed a sigh of relief. Her stomach was full now. She wanted to buy her supplies and leave. As soon as the stage was gone she would do just that. It took a bit of convincing that she could pay, but she was given everything she asked for, and perhaps a bit more. The Pierce's didn't need to be particularly bright to know the food was desperately needed by people who must be in as bad shape as this young woman.

Henry helped Abby load the horses with food, blankets, cloth, knives and cooking utensils. The load was heavy but Abby had no choice. It was too far to come back for more. She had only a few more coins of her precious gold in her pockets when she left, wearing trousers and a shirt, her faded dress tucked in the packs.

On the way back Abby didn't spare the horses or herself. Stopping only briefly to give them water and let them graze, for herself she ate only what she found along the way. Rechecking her snares she had two plump brush rabbits. She took time only to clean them and wrap them in water soaked cloth to keep them fresh. The snares she took with her.

Her return to the camp was greeted with the most enthusiasm the people had been capable of in a long time. The food was quickly prepared in the large pots she brought. For the first time since the village was destroyed everyone went to bed with a full stomach.

There was still no word from Night Wolf. Abby curled up alone in one of the new blankets in the back of the cave. All around her were families, old people, half the village. The other half were using another cave nearby. The Kumeyaay had been forced to revert to the ways of their ancestors, only without the bounty of abundant game.

The following day Night Wolf and the five young men returned, all of them mounted on horses bearing the brand of a local ranch. Abby's heart was filled with dread. She knew how the white men viewed the stealing of horses. If caught, a horse thief was immediately hanged.

Two of the young men were carrying rifles. Slung across two of the horses were freshly killed deer. There would be food for a few more days. Her gaze met that of Night Wolf as he threw his leg over his horse's withers and slid to the ground. This was a man she almost didn't recognize. There was a hardness in his face she hadn't seen before. He motioned to her and stalked away into the rocks for privacy. She followed.

Night Wolf didn't stop until he reached a high rock where he could see a long way down the canyon. From here the land seemed eternal, empty except for the wild creatures.

When Abby stopped beside him she followed his gaze into the distance, knowing what he must be thinking. Soon this place, too, would be filled with the white man's cattle. There was no place left for the People.

Night Wolf didn't look at her. His face didn't soften. Abby felt an acute pain in her heart, not knowing what to say to this stranger. His heart had gone someplace where she couldn't follow.

It was many long minutes before he spoke, his voice seeming to come from deep inside. "It is time for you to return to the white world. Our lives have changed. The path I have chosen is not for you. I will not be caged like some white man's dog. I was born to live free, to hunt as our ancestors have always hunted."

"My place is with you." Abby said, wanting to believe it, aware of the faster beat of her heart as she felt him slipping away from her. "The people need me."

He shook his head and for the first time she detected the sadness in him. "We will be fighting the white man. I cannot ask you to fight with me. I prefer to die a warrior. If you want to help the People, do it from within the white man's world."

Abby heard the wisdom of his words but her heart was suddenly barren. Their time together had been too brief, she wasn't ready to let it go. The thought of him giving his life so uselessly made her search deep within herself for the right words to sway him.

"Night Wolf, I respect your desire to die a warrior, but the rest of the People do not have that choice. Their spirit has already been broken. If the white man comes and tells them to go to a reservation they will go." His face was impassive, she had not touched him. "Once that happens the way of the Kumeyaay will die, just as it is dying for the Yuma. The white man brings teachers to educate, white man's clothing, white man's ways, until there is nothing left of the People. That must not be allowed to happen. They need a strong leader within the village. Someone who will keep their ways alive. Someone who will see to it that the children learn the stories of their ancestors, know how once the Kumeyaay ranged freely over the land and that life was good."

A look of pain flashed into Night Wolf's eyes but was banished a moment later. "I know what you say is good." His voice sounded heavy with the weight of his decision. "I know our ways must be kept alive or the white man will swallow us. But in honor, I will die a warrior." His decision was a final declaration and Abby knew it would be useless to argue.

"And there is nothing left for us?" she asked in a small voice. Night Wolf turned to look at her, his gaze filled with anguish.

"I almost did not come back to tell you. My heart aches to think we must part. I wanted to grow old with you in the way of our people. Perhaps the spirits allowed me to steal you for a little while but I am not destined to hold you forever." He took her hands in his, squeezing them until she thought her bones would snap. "When I think back on the time when life was good I will always think of you. I have wanted you for my wife since I first saw you, and I waited impatiently for us to grow up. When you went away with the white man, I wanted to follow and steal you. You are a white woman. You must be with your own people. There was nothing I could offer you except a life of hardship."

"One of the reasons I went away with Cassidy was because I knew if you came back to our village and asked me to be your wife I would say yes. My vision told me that was not meant to be. My path lies apart from yours, though it pains me to know it."

"Your spirits will guide you, Firehair. Listen to them. Help our people, for I know that in your heart you will always be part of the People."

Abby nodded, unable to speak for the lump blocking her throat. She wouldn't let him see her cry. "May the spirits guide you, Night Wolf, to do what is right." She turned away from him, walking blindly along the rocky path, her vision blurred by tears.

34

A bby didn't see Night Wolf again. By the time she returned to the caves hours later, he and the five young warriors were gone. Her heart seemed weighted with lead as she prepared for her own departure. She knew now what she must do.

The good-byes were painful, the eyes of many of the People were reproachful. They needed her. They needed her strength to keep them from losing hope, but she knew her strength would aid them more from the white man's world.

One of the young men rode with her as far as the ravine near the Carrillo Rancho. The horses were more valuable to the People, so he would take hers back with him.

Alone, with only what she was wearing, Abby walked out of the brush toward the ranch house. She was spotted at once by one of the vaqueros who remembered her. Within minutes she was welcomed, fussed over, and water was drawn for her bath.

Weeks followed with a slowness that left Abby impatient to be about her work, but there were things to take care of first. She was Cassidy's wife. There were certain monies and property that were now hers. The money she would need to help the People. She sent for the Indian agent, Norbert Simmons, at Temecula, in writing telling him what had happened at the Kumeyaay village.

It was several weeks before he arrived to interview her in person. Though he promised to look into it, the only thing he could tell her was that the land did indeed belong to the rancher, and that he had been threatening to take action if the government didn't do something to move the Kumeyaay from his land. With the problems they'd been having with the local tribes they hadn't found time to inform the Kumeyaay they had to move.

Simmons told her what land was proposed as a reservation for her people. Knowing the region well she wanted to weep. It was not fit land for man or beast and she told him so.

"You take the best and give back the worst!" she told him with the flashing of green fire in her eyes. "Is this how we deal honorably with a people who have never caused problems for you? They have gone hungry since they were driven out of their village. They were left with nothing. Stampeding cattle ground everything into dust. No blankets, no clothing, nothing to cook with, not even a gourd to carry water."

The man had the grace to look chagrined but Abby wasn't certain it was sincere. Too many white men looked on the Indians as little more than animals and therefore not due normal human consideration.

"We don't know anything about that. But we've also been having plenty of problems with some of the local tribes. The ranchers here bouts are demanding we call in the army to get the ones who've been stealing their horses."

Abby's face hardened. "Who were they stolen from?"

"….Why, Abe Overmeyer, who owns the Kumeyaay land now."

"Don't you think that is little enough compensation for people who are now destitute because of him and have no way of replacing what was destroyed?" Abby asked. "They didn't steal from anyone else did they?"

The man shook his head, his eyes clouded with thought. "Come to think of it, no."

"It is not an entire village that is responsible for what happened," Abby told him. "Some of the young men have left the village to live in the hills rather than be pushed onto a reservation. The army isn't needed to deal with the problem. It isn't an uprising, it's only a few men. You wouldn't find them with the Kumeyaay. The villagers don't want a fight. Their spirit has been broken. Those braves have gone their own way."

She hated to tell him that, fearing for Night Wolf's safety, but if she didn't, the rancher's outraged howling might be enough to bring in the army to deal with something that wasn't a problem.

Simmons seemed relieved to hear it, nodding to show he understood. "I didn't want to call in the army no how. I got enough problems without them stirring things up. I'll have a talk with Overmeyer. Once he realizes I know he took the law into his own hands he'll change his tune."

Abby gave him a dazzling smile, seeing the way he blinked in surprise and how his chest suddenly swelled. She began to see the power she could have over men if she wanted to use it, something she had been vaguely aware of before. With some of her weight back, with new clothes made for her by Vicenta's maid Maria, Abby looked totally different from the bedraggled waif who had arrived weeks earlier.

"Thank you, Mr. Simmons. I know you'll do all you can."

Not certain he wanted to be dismissed yet, he didn't have much choice when Abby stood up to show him out.

"I'll keep you informed," he told her, but she knew it was only because he wanted an excuse to see her again.

"Yes, please do that," she said, letting him take her hand as a parting gesture. Her gaze hardened the moment the door closed behind him. This was a facet of her personality she saw emerging. The man was a user, she knew that with a certainty. It would do him good to have the tables turned on him for a change.

She also knew she could not continue to live off the generous hospitality of Ramon and Vicenta Carrillo. The money she received from Cassidy's estate she would leave in their safe, taking only a small amount to Los Angeles. She thought of one man willing to help her, Everett Drayton, the man who had offered her a job. She still had his card which she'd taken from her cache in the hills of Seven Springs.

"Must you leave so soon, querida?" Vicenta asked her that night at dinner. "We enjoy having you here, don't we, Ramon?"

Dutifully Ramon answered that they did.

"I'm grateful to you both," Abby said, not to be swayed by their arguments. "I have friends in Los Angeles." It was just a tiny lie. "I will be fine there. I'll take the Thursday coach when it comes through."

Vicenta looked unhappy. "I fear for you all alone in that big town. It is said to be quite lawless there."

Abby's smile was meant to reassure her. "I won't be alone. When I know where I will be staying I'll let you know. Los Angeles isn't that far away." Just enough that they wouldn't be able to keep close tabs on her. Abby was already making plans as to what she would do when she reached town.

If Drayton's job offer was still good, the extra money she earned would pay for her keep without touching Cassidy's money, which she could use for lawyers if necessary, and for food for her people. Someone had to see that justice was done, and she had the feeling it wasn't going to be Indian Agent Norbert Simmons

35

John Jay stared in helpless silence at the distant hills where Henry Pierce said Abby had disappeared with two laden horses. After seeing Gus in Temecula he'd ridden straight to Seven Springs, not stopping except to rest his horse for brief periods. Even at that, he was days too late.

At least he knew she was alive. He'd suffered with all sorts of horrible images when he learned what had happened at Seven Springs. Cassidy was dead. The story could be pieced together about how the two Mexicans came to take advantage of Abby being alone at the station. It was thought she was spared the ordeal of rape only to be carried off by at least two Indians. Their tracks blended with those of the stolen horses.

He had tracked them for days, crossing the border into Mexico. There he'd had a run-in with Apaches and barely escaped with his life, losing his pack horse and all his food. It rankled to have to turn back in defeat.

Somehow she had survived that ordeal too and she was somewhere nearby. Pierce spoke of her sorry condition, how thin and tired she looked. He also knew that somewhere in the mountains she was living with Indians. It would be hopeless to try to track her. She was too wary for that. He would ride to the rancho of his friends the Carrillo's. Perhaps Ramon or some of his men would know the location of the Kumeyaay village.

From what he understood of the life in the mountain villages, there was plenty of food. Why then was Abby in such need? Or was she being forced to buy supplies for the ones who had stolen her. The questions bounced around in his mind. There was only one thing to do and he dare not delay. He felt a sense of urgency.

Though he was tired and long overdue for sleep, he traded his tired horse for a fresh one at the stage station, covering the miles swiftly across the desert and into the San Felipe Valley. Late the following day he reached the Carrillo Rancho, so exhausted he was swaying in his saddle.

Vicenta clucked over him like a mother hen, filling his stomach with hot beans, steak and her delicious salsa and tortillas. After being assured Abby was safe, and they'd explain later he was shown to a bedroom to get some sleep. Ramon would return in a few hours and that would be time enough to talk. John Jay was too tired to argue, falling asleep the moment the door closed behind Vicenta.

Later, at the dinner table John Jay looked far more presentable than when he rode in. He'd shaved the four day stubble of beard, bathed and put on clean clothes. It felt good to be in a home filled with warmth and love but he wouldn't allow himself to be lulled by the comfort.

"You said you know where to find Abby," John Jay said the moment they were seated and began to pass the large platters of food. Any other time he would have savored the chicken with rice, the fresh vegetables, beans and freshly baked bread.

"She was here until five days ago," Vicenta said, surprised by the concern she saw in his eyes. Yet she couldn't help feeling it was a good thing. In spite of Abby's claim she could take care of herself, Vicenta suspected a woman alone, and especially one as beautiful as Abby, could only find trouble.

"Five days!" The dismay on John Jay's face was obvious. If he'd stopped here on his way to Seven Springs he might have seen her and saved himself precious days. "How was she? Where has she been?"

"She was with us for several weeks while she settled the financial affairs of her late husband. As soon as that was done, she met with the local head of Indian Affairs to tell him what had happened to her people, the Kumeyaay. How a local rancher stampeded cattle through their village, destroying it. And this after a siege of the small pox."

"She arrived here looking thin and worn out," Ramon said with a worried frown. "But at least 'Chenta was able to fatten her up a bit and get her some decent clothes before she left."

"Even though she offered us money," Vicenta said. "We couldn't take it. She was a friend in desperate need. As soon as she finished the business with the Indian Agent she caught the stage for Los Angeles."

"Los Angeles! Why?"

Vicenta shrugged and looked to her husband for help. John Jay turned his attention to the ranchero who gave a sad shake of his head.

"There were things troubling her," Ramon said slowly. "I'm certain she didn't tell us the entire story of what happened after she was taken from Seven Springs. She said only that one of the Indians protected her from the others. He was someone she knew from before."

Ramon took his time, accepting the salsa Vicenta handed him, then buttering the warm tortilla. John Jay tried to stem his impatience, too used to the lackadaisical ways of the Spanish to expect anything else. It had never bothered him until now. He couldn't think of eating until he knew everything Ramon knew, ignoring the tantalizing scent curling under his nose from his full patter.

"Evidently the Indian brought her back to her Indian family, the Kumeyaay, only to find that one of the villages was gone, now used by a new rancher to graze his cattle. At their mountain village she arrived at the same time as an outbreak of the small pox. It must have been a terrible time, but with Abby's knowledge of healing they didn't lose as many as they would have without her." Ramon concluded.

Ramon began to eat, cooling the hot fool by blowing on it. John Jay felt tension knotting his stomach, leaning forward with his arms on the table as he willed Ramon to hurry. The Spaniard was oblivious to the young man's impatience.

"She survived the epidemic, nursing the sick ones," Ramon concluded.

"Pobrecita," Vicenta put in. "She was so thin and pale when she arrived. We had to fatten her up before we could let her go on her way."

"What happened after the epidemic?" John Jay asked.

"That was when the rancher, a white man," Ramon said. "Stampeded his cattle through the village, destroying it totally. Fortunately no one was hurt."

Now John Jay knew why she had needed those supplies so desperately.

"The rancher told them if they tried to rebuild the village he would destroy it again, said the land now belonged to him."

"Was that true?"

Ramon nodded, continuing to eat as his story unfolded. "The Indian agent, Senor Simmons was here. He told Abby it was true, that a man named Overmeyer now owns the land, however he was not to take possession until the Indians could be moved. Simmons was looking for a suitable reservation site for them."

John Jay grimaced in distaste. He hated that word, knew what it meant to the Indians who were helpless to fight the endless stream of settlers demanding land, and still more land. Then he began to see the pattern to the story. He could guess why Abby wanted Cassidy's money, why she'd spoken to the Indian Agent. She would try to help her former people, who right now must be utterly destitute.

"Did Abby say where she would be staying in Los Angeles?"

"She said little about her plans," Vicenta said with a worried frown, her gentle brown eyes showing concern. "She said she had friends and would be staying with them."

"Did she mention any names?" John Jay was wondering who she could possibly know since she'd never even been there.

Vicenta shook her head. "No, she didn't mention a name. Eat your food, my friend, it is getting cold. You cannot help her by going hungry. We will tell you all we know."

Realizing he was starving, John Jay tried to restrain his impatience as he began to eat, asking again for every detail of Abby's visit.

When he rode out the next morning for Los Angeles, he still had no idea where to find Abby. His father had an old friend there who owned a mercantile, so that gave John Jay at least one connection. In a town of fifteen hundred people, one red haired beauty shouldn't be too difficult to locate.

Abby looked around her hotel room feeling she was in an alien world. The whale oil lamp had fancy designs etched into the glass. Her furniture was plush, the carpeting thick under her shoes. She'd never seen a bed so wide with a gold colored cover that looked too expensive to touch let alone to think of sleeping under.

The pitcher and bowl that held water for washing was hand painted with elaborate scenes of city life. Her highboy and dresser were of finely varnished wood that glowed like satin. She hadn't wanted to spend this much money for a room, but the man at the stage station advised her that the Bella Union was the only hotel that would accept a woman alone. She couldn't afford to stay more than a night or two. She hadn't thought to ask the man at the desk about Everett Drayton. She was so dusty and tired from the long, jolting stagecoach ride that all she wanted was a bath and a hot meal. Her bones ached from being bounced for hours over rutted roads.

When she went downstairs for the evening meal Abby first stepped outside, watching for a moment the bustle on the busy street, the laden wagons, the cowboys, the carriages. There was money here, but she could also feel greed lurking in the shadows. The scent of money always attracted scavengers.

It didn't take long to find what she wanted, a boy of about nine roaming the streets alone. He looked dirty and unkempt. When he found Abby watching him he approached her warily.

"Would you like to make ten cents?" she asked.

The boy's eyes widened. "Sure!" Then with more caution. "What do I have to do?"

"I'd like you to take this message to Mr. Everett Drayton at the address on the envelope."

The boy stared at it without comprehension. Abby flushed when she realized he couldn't read. She told him the address. "Do you know where that is?"

"Yeah, it's a hotel."

"Yes, that's the place. You take that to Mr. Drayton and return to me with the answer. I'll be in the dining room, and you shall have your ten cents."

The boy looked doubtfully toward the Bella Union. "They won't let me in there."

"Yes, they will," Abby assured him. "What's your name? I'll tell them to expect you."

"Danny, ma'am," he mumbled.

"My name is Abigail Cassidy. You just ask for me. I'll be having dinner."

From the look on his face at the mention of food Abby realized why the boy looked so unkempt, no doubt he didn't have a home. He nodded and darted off in the twilight of the dusty streets.

A woman alone seemed something of an oddity Abby soon realized as she was seated in an obscure corner, out of sight of the many patrons. The fact she was a widow was the only thing which gave her respectability, she was quick to realize, plus the fact she paid in gold coins.

In San Diego she'd seen enough to know how the affluent behaved so she could copy that behavior now. She'd learned how effective an unflinching stare could be when a man was telling her she couldn't do something. He soon began to stammer and soon after gave in.

Intentionally she ordered a large meal, ignoring the startled look of the waiter that such a small woman could eat so much. Many items on the menu she didn't recognize but when it came, the steak was thick and almost rare the way she liked it. There were potatoes and green vegetables, and other items that tasted good even without her knowing their names.

The boy came back sooner than she expected. The alerted maître d' showed him to her table, his nose wrinkled in distaste. Danny watched the man depart with suspicious eyes before he turned his attention to Abby, his gaze not rising above her laden plate. When he finally looked up she couldn't resist mocking the maître d's supercilious attitude. Danny giggled.

"Sit down, my young friend," she said. "It's a good thing they stuck me off in this corner so we won't be disturbed. Did you find Mr. Drayton?"

Suspicion came into his eyes. "I want my dime."

Abby didn't blame him for being suspicious. She drew the dime from her pocket. He withdrew a note written on expensive paper and handed it to her, at the same time snatching the dime with grimy fingers. His gaze was again on her plate or she was certain he would have bolted from the room.

Abby picked up her plate and set it in front of him. "A little bonus for being so quick," she said. Danny didn't have to be urged. His hands were clumsy with the fine silver service but he dug in and ate swiftly, looking around as if someone might snatch it away. Abby was fascinated by his crude manners.

"Do you have folks?" she asked, putting the letter into her pocket to read later. Right now she was more interested in her first acquaintance in the city.

He shook his head. "They died of the small pox just before we got to Los Angeles last year."

She knew just how that must feel. "Don't you have any other family?"

He shook his head. "Not out here. They're back east but they don't want me."

Abby could barely understand him for all the food in his mouth. "Who do you stay with?"

He shrugged but didn't answer. She guessed he wasn't staying with anyone. He must be living by his wits, often times without food.

"Surely there's some place that will take you in," she said quietly, watching the way his alarmed gaze flew to hers. Seeing no threat even though she had guessed the truth, he swallowed a piece of steak.

"Yeah, there is. I stayed two weeks and was whipped five times."

Abby could see the mixture of pain and anger in his eyes as he stabbed a chunk of steak.

"For what?"

"Because I wouldn't pay attention to the teacher, because I didn't make my bed just right, and because I talked to the kid in the bed next to me after they turned out the lights."

Abby felt her heart ache for him. It could easily have happened to her after her parents were killed. Instead she had the freedom of the mountains and the desert. No one had ever raised a hand to her while she was with the People.

"So...you left."

Again he shrugged not wanting to admit it.

"It's not easy being on your own at your age," she said softly.

He gave a sharp snort. "What do you know?" he demanded, his angry gaze taking in her fine dress and hat. "You have money to stay in a big place like this, and eat food like this..." His anger died away abruptly as he realized she could snatch the food away from him. He dug in, faster than before.

"Slow down, Danny," she said gently. "I'm not going to take it away from you." He was reassured, but only a little. His cheeks bulging with food. "And, believe me, my friend, I do know what it's like. My parents were killed in an Indian attack on our wagon train when I was about your age."

He stopped chewing and stared at her, his large brown eyes questioning. "Some of those who weren't killed were taken captive. I ran into the brush so the Indian's couldn't find me. I was the only one left. Believe me, I didn't dress like this then. I ate what food the desert provided when I was taken in by some friendly Indians."

Danny looked about quickly to see if anyone overheard her statement.

"What's the matter?" she asked.

"Don't tell anyone you was with Indians," he urged her, his little face serious. "I hear talk…"

"About women who lived among the Indians?" He nodded, not stopping his chewing.

"I know," Abby said. "I've seen it too. It's as if the woman is suddenly tainted somehow, not fit to be around white folks. It's not true what they say about Indians, Danny. Those people aren't savages just because they don't wear many clothes and because they live in homes made of brush."

"I saw them bring an Indian into town once," Danny said, forgetting his food for a moment. "A whole posse brought him in…like they'd really done something good. He was all beat up, and he was young, maybe twenty. He never said a word, not even when they roughed him up before locking him in jail, and not even when they took him out two days later and hung him." For a moment the boy was deep in his memory. "I thought it would be a good thing to hang an Indian so I wanted to see it." Danny struggled for words that seemed to stick in his throat. "It wasn't right what they did. They didn't even care if he was the one who took the horse or not, he was guilty just because he was an Indian..." Danny's voice died away to a whisper. "I cried when they hung him. He was the bravest man I ever saw, and he didn't even hate the ones who were doing that to him."

Abby's eyes filled with tears at the depth of the boy's pain. The poignancy of the lesson he learned. The boy's voice was still a low whisper.

"When it was over...I was ashamed I was white, ashamed of those men who laughed while a man died...with honor."

"Honor is very important to the Indians," Abby said. "It is almost a way of life."

Danny looked at her with new respect. "So it wasn't the horrible life white men imagine, was it?" he asked.

She shook her head. "I was never abused. I never went cold or hungry."

"In that place where they put me," he said bitterly. "I had all of those. I was beaten, the dormitory was cold, and when we didn't obey the rules, we were sent to bed without supper."

Abby saw the maître d' watching them with a tight, disapproving expression. Danny followed her gaze.

"I...guess I'd better go." He began stuffing his pockets with any remaining food. Knowing they must be dirty Abby tried not to grimace.

"Where can I find you, Danny, if I need your help again?"

He stood up, leaving a clean plate behind him. "I'll find you." He started to leave.

"Wait," she said, picking up a plate with a thick slice of chocolate cake, holding it out to him. "I can't eat this..."

He snatched the cake and bolted out the door. The maître d' looked her way to see if the boy had done something wrong. When Abby left the dining room he didn't speak but his expression spoke volumes. Abby merely smiled at him melting his heart just a wee bit with her beauty as she swept out of the room.

In her room Abby turned up the lantern and held the note from Everett Drayton close to it.

Welcome to Los Angeles, Miss Abigail. I learned of Mr. Cassidy's untimely passing some weeks ago. I was hoping you would remember my offer of employment should you find yourself inadequately provided for. I will call for you at ten o'clock tomorrow morning to take you to your new lodgings. You may start work when you have had a few days to become acquainted with the city, I shall endeavor to be your guide.

Your servant, Everett Drayton

Abby smiled with relief. There was a job for her. She also had the feeling that the less she said about her true reasons for being in Los Angeles, the better. If Drayton wanted to believe she was without means to support herself so much the better. He might be inclined to be more generous, thus enabling her to keep Cassidy's money to help the People.

The next morning Abby had her few belongings packed when Everett Drayton came for her shortly after ten. He was a fine looking man, she noted, when she opened her door for him.

His smile of greeting was wide, his eyes dancing with pleasure.

"Miss Abigail, what a delight to see you again." He captured her hand in his, kissed it and held it a moment longer than necessary. "I've thought about you often since I learned of your poor husband. I'm truly sorry."

"Thank you, Mr. Drayton. Please come in." Abby offered.

Drayton stepped into the room followed by a coarse young man of about sixteen who gave Abby a thorough once over with eyes too old for his age.

"Alex, take the lady's bags down to the carriage," Drayton said, and without a word the boy took the two bags and left.

Drayton looked around the room, noting its plush furnishings. "Very nice," he commented. "I'm afraid my hotel isn't quite as fancy, but we do good business. A lot of important people stay there." That was one of the things Abby was hoping to hear. "I'm surprised you stayed here at the Bella Union."

She knew what he meant, it was quite expensive. She gave him a rueful smile. "When I asked the stage driver, this place was highly recommended as being proper for a lady traveling alone. I didn't know just how expensive until it was too late. I'm afraid it took all the money I had with me." It wasn't really a lie, the rest was hidden in the bottom of one of her bags.

"Don't you worry about that," Drayton said expansively, taking her arm and leading her out of the room. "I'll have both meals and lodging for you, and with your experience at Seven Springs, I'm sure you won't find the work nearly as taxing."

"I'm not afraid of hard work, Mr. Drayton."

"I'm sure you're not, Miss Abigail. But you're a woman who should have pretty things and hands soft enough for a gentleman to hold. Los Angeles has a lot to offer a woman who's both smart and beautiful."

Abby wondered if there was more behind his words than was apparent. Something about Drayton made her cautious. He was taking over her life, arranging everything, and she wasn't certain she liked it.

The room she was taken to, at the rear of the Continental Hotel, wasn't as plush as the Bella Union, but it would suit her just as well. It was small, the furnishings mismatched enough and old enough to look as if it had been taken from guest rooms when they'd become eyesores.

Some had obviously been broken and repaired.

She didn't have to try the bed to see if it was comfortable as the one she'd slept in last night, she knew it wouldn't be. It looked lumpy.

Drayton showed her the hotel dining room, the front desk and the office where she would be working. She'd be helping to greet and register guests and do some of the book work. Drayton assured her she would soon master the accounts since she had done the same for her husband.

He took her to his private office, a room that could easily have fit in with the décor of the Bella Union. His desk was hand rubbed walnut with intricate carving. Everything in the room spoke of money, and good taste. There was a small table set for two.

"We'll be having brunch here," he told her. "This way we won't be bothered by guests. I know a great many people," he explained. "And sometimes they want to chat when I have other things to do. You haven't had breakfast yet have you?"

Abby shook her head. "....I didn't want to go down to the dining room alone again." Thinking of the dining room made her think of Danny. He'd said he'd find her. She doubted she'd seen the last of him.

"Good." Drayton seated her formally in a way Abby wasn't used to, though she'd seen it in San Diego. "The food we serve here is mostly plain fare, but it's well prepared and there's plenty of it. We want our guests to get their money's worth."

A knock came at a side door and without waiting for an answer an older woman came in with a pot of coffee. She kept her eyes downcast except to shoot a sly look at Abby. For the second time Abby felt as if she'd been thoroughly assessed by one of Drayton's employees and the same conclusion reached.

Perhaps they thought there was something more to Drayton's attentions than that of an employer. It was a puzzle Abby didn't have time to pursue. The thin woman was gone as silently as she came, this time leaving the door ajar.

Abby added both cream and sugar to her coffee, a luxury she seldom could afford. One sip of the coffee told her it was totally unlike what she'd prepared at the station. The flavor was smooth and rich. Drayton smiled when he noted her appreciation.

"Good coffee is important to a hotel," he told her. "Give a guest a little more than they expect. That's what brings them back."

Abby listened to everything he said about the hotel. It was information she needed to be a good employee. She also had the feeling he never gave such personal attention to other prospective employees. Perhaps he was making an exception of her because she was an attractive woman.

"Later this afternoon a seamstress will be coming to your room. I want to have some dresses made for you."

Abby was startled. "Mr. Drayton....I can't expect you..."

"Nonsense, my dear," he said with a wave of his hand to dismiss her objections. "I require a certain look in my front offices. Think of it as a uniform I am providing. It's all part of your compensation."

He went on to discuss the terms of her employment. In addition to her room and board, and clothing, it seemed she would receive a small wage, but even that seemed enormous when Abby had to connive and sneak each bit of money she'd earned at Seven Springs.

Breakfast was served by the same thin faced, silent woman. Abby's plate was heaped with potatoes, scrambled eggs and the largest biscuits she'd ever seen. She wished Danny was here to help her eat it.

Drayton told her about Los Angeles while they ate, and she began to look forward to seeing the town with him. He was a pleasant companion, full of knowledge and eager to show her around. Abby was lulled into thinking she was going to like it here after all.

36

After breakfast Drayton handed her into his carriage to show her the town. Abby was surprised at how wide the streets were, how well laid out the town was. On some streets the dirt was packed hard from constant traffic. Horses and wagons bustled about the streets. A number of two story buildings lined the main streets. On side streets she could see homes of all sizes, from quite small to large and sprawling, with trees and flowers in the yards.

She saw stores with fresh vegetables displayed out front, and women with baskets shopping. Abby couldn't imagine anything other than walking out her door to her garden. Here in town there was no need for her to do even that much, her meals would be provided. She wouldn't need to cook at all.

Drayton seemed to know everyone. He was greeted frequently along the way with many speculative glances cast in her direction. When he introduced her as a new employee of the hotel some of the men's eyes would light up until Drayton made it clear she would be office help. The look then died away. It happened with each introduction, leaving Abby puzzled, and with a feeling there were things going on she didn't understand.

All around the small town Abby could see hills, orchards, and signs of cattle and farming. The streets smelled of horse manure, and of exotic foods. She tried not to stare at men dressed in dark tunics, with yellowish skin and long pigtails hanging down their backs, moving with strange mincing steps.

"Ever seen a Chinee before?" Drayton asked. Abby shook her head. "They were brought in as slave labor to work the gold mines and build the railroads. Now a lot of them live in town. They have strange ways, eat strange food. People stay away from them."

Abby heard a couple of young boys hurling taunts at the two Orientals. From Wes's teaching about geography she knew the men were from China, that their civilization was an ancient one. The boys followed the two for a while, calling out names Abby had never heard before but were obviously insults. Finally one boy became bold enough to yank the pigtail of one of the men before they ran off laughing.

Abby had expected some of the adults to run the boys off, but they hadn't, merely laughed and went on their way. It made her angry at the boys and uncaring adults. It was easy for her to see the parallel between the treatment of the foreigners and that of the Indians. The white man it seemed had no tolerance for other races. It was a sobering thought, telling her just what she would be up against trying to help the Kumeyaay.

She glanced at Drayton to see his reaction, but like the others he was grinning. On one of the side streets Abby saw a movement in the shadows. Her vision was used to shadows and distances and quickly picked out Danny watching her drive by. She gave a tiny wave of acknowledgement which he didn't return, just stared after her.

Drayton showed her the Plaza where homes of the first Spanish families to settle Los Angeles could still be seen, homes of the Lugos, the Sepulvedas and many more. The Plaza Church showed its Spanish influence with its high steeple and cross.

It reminded her of the small country church she'd attended as a girl. She longed to go inside, to sit quietly and gather her scattered thoughts. Without even looking at Drayton she knew he wouldn't like it. Perhaps one day she would come here on her own to make peace with the church, to erase the images which had become tarnished by the preaching of her uncle.

Uncle Jacob, who's God was full of anger and vengeance.

Not far from the church Drayton turned into a street narrower and busier than any of the others. Carriages and horses were everywhere. Raucous music came from many of the saloons, creating a discordant cacophony of sounds. Men staggered drunkenly along the wooden sidewalk, there were shouting voices and arguments, women wearing garish dresses with more makeup on their grinning faces than Abby had ever seen, and on some, red hair she knew couldn't be natural.

"The Mexicans call this Calle de los Negros," Drayton said, making Abby wince at his pronunciation. "We just call it Nigger Alley. It's the wide open part of town, with gambling in every saloon and ladies to provide any service a man could want."

A man came flying out of one of the saloons, landing on his stomach directly in their path. A burley man wearing a white shirt with sleeves rolled up to show massive forearms followed him out, tossed him his hat, and told him not to come back.

Drayton chuckled as he guided his horse around the man who was slowly sitting up, bobbing drunkenly. He glanced up at the carriage, then took a second look at Abby, grinning.

"Hiya sweetheart!" he called to her. "I shore could do with the company of a pretty gal like you." His gaze shifted to Drayton, suddenly widened with alarm as he mumbled a quick apology. "Didn't mean no harm…" was all Abby heard before his voice faded away.

Abby looked to Drayton for an explanation but found none. He gestured to the busy street. "If you think this is something, you should see it at night. It's even wilder then."

A couple of brightly clad ladies on the wooden walkway waved to Drayton and men called greetings. It seemed her new boss was well known in this unsavory quarter as well.

Abby sighed in relief when Drayton turned the corner and the saloons and noise were left behind. It had only been a block long but Abby knew it was not a part of town a lady would visit. At night there must be knifings and shootings aplenty. A part of her mind couldn't help but wonder why Drayton had taken her there.

Her gaze shifted to the hills surrounding the town on three sides. A cool breeze stirred the air, bringing with it the feel of the ocean twenty-five miles away. This town had a different feel to it than San Diego. It wasn't as civilized, as if violence lay smoldering just under the surface.

Back at the hotel Abby was relieved to be on her own for a while. The seamstress came to take her measurements but said little. She'd received her instructions from Drayton. Later, he introduced her to the hotel staff, informing them she would start work the next morning. Abby felt, rather than saw the smirks which followed them as they walked away. She knew they thought they were lovers. His attitude was so proprietary, as if it was only a matter of time before it became a fact.

That evening Drayton arranged dinner for them in his private office. He was an amusing companion with his stories of the town, about hotel guests and even some of his employees. Abby found she wasn't required to say much, just listen. She was happy to do just that since he was filling her with information about her new home.

In the days that followed, Abby didn't see much of Drayton, she was busy learning the running of the hotel. At first the middle aged man who was to teach her the books, treated her like an imbecile, but that only lasted until he found she really did understand what he was saying and was quick with her sums. He seemed surprised she was serious about learning, but he then began to teach her in earnest.

There was much to learn. There were the guest room revenues to account for as well as from liquor, meals and other special services Abby hadn't yet learned the nature of.

What Abby found strange was the fact her help wasn't really needed. Drayton had two good men. Robert to handle registration of the guests, and her mentor, Edgar, to balance the books and work back up for registration.

Finding there was no one to supervise the maids Abby took on that duty as well. Some of the help was lazy, their sloppy work had resulted in complaints from guests. Once Abby began to check on their work it quickly improved.

There was one room at the end of the hall Abby wasn't given a key to. She was told she didn't have to worry about it. It was under the personal supervision of Mr. Drayton. She wouldn't have thought another thing about it if she hadn't seen different men coming and going from the room, each with his own key.

The dresses Drayton provided were of excellent quality and so beautiful Abby hardly recognized herself in the mirror. Some were cut so low in front she refused to wear them around the hotel without first adding a lace handkerchief. It came as something of a surprise to see what a difference clothes made in peoples attitude toward her. Some of the gentlemen even requested her company for the evening but Abby was quick to tell them she didn't socialize with guests. The men seemed surprised by her answer and a bit puzzled until they saw her with Everett Drayton on the evenings he came by to have dinner with her.

Though he kept his own private room at the hotel, he didn't spend much time there. It was obvious he had other business interests though he never discussed them with her. What made her uneasy was his attention to her, as if he were telling everyone she was his and not to get too friendly. Yet he never made an improper move. She dreaded it happening because she was not in the least attracted to him and was uncomfortable with his show of interest.

Finding time to call on government officials wasn't as easy as Abby anticipated. She worked long hours at the hotel, and by the time she was through for the day, it was too late to find officials in their offices. Not only that, she was often too tired to think straight.

The guests quickly learned they could find a sympathetic ear and would being their problems to her, whether it concerned the hotel or Los Angeles in general.

Several times she saw Danny hanging around the hotel but any attempt to talk to him was futile. He seemed angry, but if he wouldn't talk she couldn't find out why. Once she saw him behind the hotel going through the trash, no doubt looking for food scraps. Within his hearing she told the cook to fix him something to eat and put it on her tab. Danny didn't refuse.

He looked hungry and desperate.

Weeks passed quickly. Once, when Abby learned one of Governor Downey's assistants was in the hotel she was on her way to his room when she saw him disappear into the room at the end of the hall. Undaunted she followed and knocked. There was no response. Putting her ear to the door Abby listened. No sound came from within, yet she knew a number of men had gone in there in the past hour. She tried the knob only to find it securely locked. It was a puzzle, one it suddenly seemed important that she solve. She had been told not to bother about that particular room, and if any of the maids cleaned it she had no knowledge of it.

On her fourth week in Los Angeles Abby went out on an autumn afternoon to run an errand for the hotel. She dropped off papers at an attorney's office, purchased some office supplies at the mercantile and was on her way back to the hotel when she heard the sound of several horses pacing her.

At first Abby thought it must be her imagination but when she stopped to look into the window of one of the stores, she could see the reflection of two riders in the glass, who also stopped and were looking directly at her. Her mind whirled with a sudden feeling of danger. It was late afternoon and there weren't many people on the street. Before she could consider what to do she realized one of those wide figures looked familiar. She turned to look into the fierce gaze of her uncle.

"So it is you, niece," he said in his powerful voice. Even those words managed to sound like a condemnation. "I heard your husband was dead and that you were here in the town. I might have known you'd fall into evil ways."

"Evil ways?" she asked, her eyebrows going up as she forced a smile to her lips. "What is evil about working to support myself?"

"It is the way of it, woman!" he boomed. "You are steeped in wickedness, living amongst devils."

Abby didn't want to lose her temper. "I work in a hotel doing bookkeeping, surely that is proper work for a woman."

"For how long will that devil's spawn let you do that? He has you right where he wants you. I've come to take you out of this wicked Babylon. You must be cleansed of your sins."

"I have no sins, Uncle Jacob, except for the ones in your mind," she said firmly. "I have no intention of going with you. I am happy here."

"Jezebel!" he hissed. "Have you no shame! You must be saved from this life of sin!"

Jacob urged his horse toward her, his burley friend doing the same. Abby suddenly realized he was planning to take her here and now. If the store behind her had been open she could have slipped inside, but it was after business hours.

Before the horses could crowd close enough to cut off her escape Abby ducked past them and ran into the middle of the street looking for help. She could feel them coming after her. At the sound of a carriage rounding the corner she ran toward the sound, seeing to her relief Everett Drayton bearing down on them.

"What do you think you're doing?" Drayton demanded, his hand moving close to his gun. "Leave that woman alone. She works for me."

Jacob's fierce gaze focused on Drayton as he stopped his carriage beside Abby.

"So you are the devil who corrupts the people of this town." A long finger stabbed toward Abby. "This is my niece. I have come to take her from this evil place."

Drayton looked to Abby for confirmation. She nodded but lifted her hand for him to help her up beside him. "I have no wish to go with him."

"Sir, the lady wishes to stay. I would suggest you be on your way and not bother her again." Drayton flicked the reins and the carriage moved away from the two men on horseback. Behind them the silence was palpable.

"Thank goodness you came along," Abby said, knowing she wouldn't have been a match for her uncle and his friend. "I was afraid he would take me by force."

"I wasn't aware you had any relatives," Drayton said, his brow narrowed in a frown.

"Uncle Jacob isn't someone I'd like to claim as family."

"I can understand why. A most unpleasant fellow." He turned the carriage down a side street to the livery stable behind a hotel. Expensive drapes were closed, but from the main lobby came the sound of a piano and intermittent laughter. Windows were open on the second floor with sheer curtains billowing in the breeze. It was the first time Abby had been down this street. What little she could see of the buildings and furnishings looked rich and elegant.

"What place is that?" she asked, there were no signs.

Drayton hesitated a moment. "It's a private men's club. Very exclusive. Some of the richest men in the country belong to it."

Abby distinctly heard the sound of women's voices and raucous feminine laughter, but before she could ask more questions, Drayton turned the corner into the stable and a man came out to take the horses. Everett lifted her down and escorted her toward the back door of the hotel, a proprietary hand on her arm. She sensed something different in his mood, but before she could pursue that thought a shadow flitted by them.

"Here! What are you doing?" Everett demanded of the fleeing figure.

Abby turned to see Danny running down the alley with scraps of food in his hands.

"You stay away from here, damn you!" Drayton yelled after the boy. "I've told you not to come around here. Next time I'll take a whip to you!"

Abby was so startled by his vehemence she drew away from him. "But...he's only a boy. A hungry boy."

"I don't care," Drayton said, his lips pursed with annoyance. "I don't want him around my place and giving it a bad name."

Before Abby could argue further he opened the back door for her, successfully diverting her attention.

"I've been meaning to talk to you for several days now, my dear," Drayton said. "I'd like you to have dinner with me in my office. Why don't you run up to your room and put on your prettiest gown, I think you'll like my ideas for your future." His smile was full of charm as he took a cigar from his pocket and lit it in a manner Abby had become familiar with. His squinting gaze seemed to study her through a haze of smoke. "Yes, I think you'll be very pleased with my plans. Be back here at seven."

"Yes, Mr. Drayton," she said, curious to know what he had in mind. She was more than satisfied with her position.

"Everett," he corrected her. "From now on you're to call me Everett."

She wanted to tell him that wouldn't be proper but decided she could do that later. He obviously had a different job in mind for her. In these past weeks she'd shown him what she could do and perhaps he was going to offer her something with more responsibility. Eagerly she went to her room to prepare for their dinner together.

She knew which dress he wanted her to wear, the green satin with black lace at the neckline and sleeves, the one that made her gasp when she first tried it on. Since then she'd seen other women in their finest dresses in the hotel and knew it was not as improper as it seemed. The waist was so snug, the bodice so form fitting Abby couldn't help fanning herself with the black lace fan that was an accessory.

Black lace lay gracefully about the open neckline and fell in scallops over the full skirt. She didn't want to think what a dress like this must cost. With it was a matching hat with a hint of a veil falling just to her eyes. As she surveyed herself in the tarnished mirror Abby saw a woman she barely recognized, an elegant, beautiful woman.

A sound from outside attracted her to her window. Drawing back the curtain she saw a flash of reddish gold streak by just above roof top level, wheel about and come back. People in the street stopped, pointing at the unusual sight.

Abby drew in a sharp breath as a golden eagle came back, and hovered outside her window, its bright eyes connecting with hers. For a moment they were locked together, eye to eye. Then with a loud cry the eagle wheeled about and was gone.

Shaken by the encounter Abby instinctively knew it was a warning. For the first time since she came to Los Angeles she dug her father's knife from the bottom of her satchel and slid it under her garter. Still not satisfied, she found her medicine bag and slid it into a pocket. Only then did she leave the room, suddenly wary of the coming supper with Drayton.

On her way to his private office, a number of male guests tipped their hats to her and she was aware of their admiring, even flirtatious looks. As she turned toward the hallway to Drayton's office she saw the smirk on the desk clerk's face as he watched her. It seemed he was saying to himself, "I knew it. She sleeps with him." It annoyed her enough that she stared at him until he flushed and looked away.

The door to Drayton's office was open in anticipation of her arrival. A table had been set up, complete with a white tablecloth, the hotel's best china, silver plate and crystal, which was reserved for special guests. Two white candles in ornate silver holders added to the elegant setting.

"Ah, my dear, you are right on time," Everett said, coming to her and ushering her into the room, closing the door behind her. Abby felt an involuntary shudder at the sound. He led her to his private bar to pour her a glass of sherry. Even the wine glass was fine crystal, feeling so delicate in her hand Abby was afraid she would crush it.

He stood back to admire the picture she made. His nod was full of satisfaction. "You are the most beautiful woman in all Los Angeles," he pronounced. "When you dress like that you could be a princess, a queen. In fact, I can make you the queen of this entire town. Every man will know your name."

Abby blushed at his words. She didn't for a moment believe them, but it was flattering none-the-less. She sipped the sherry, finding it smooth and mellow.

"Tonight you shall have only the best. Wait until you see what our chef has prepared. He has outdone himself because I told him tonight was special."

With a flourish he seated Abby, lingering to kiss her hand gallantly before taking his own chair across from her. It was an intimate setting, a romantic one. Abby sipped nervously at her wine. The appearance of the eagle had her doubly on her guard.

Everett, too, was drinking sherry, though she knew he often indulged in stronger spirits. She was eager to hear about his plans for her. The same thin-faced woman came into the room at the summons of a small bell at Everett's elbow. Abby noticed the woman kept her eyes downcast, didn't try to look at her or Everett, just silently served the soup and left.

Everett raised his glass to propose a toast. "To a long and profitable partnership."

Abby's eyebrows went up sharply. "Partnership?"

"In a manner of speaking," Everett said smoothly and sipped his sherry. Abby did the same though she was puzzled. There was no way she was qualified to go into partnership with him.

While they ate, Everett kept up a running commentary on what was happening in town, who the important men were whose names Abby should get to know. She felt flattered Everett would have so much confidence in her ability. She had come to know the operation of the hotel quite well, but surely not well enough be considered anything more than an employee. Though she tried not to show it, she was impatient to hear just what his plan entailed.

There were times during dinner when she noticed his gaze lingering on the swell of her breasts. He seemed to enjoy the low cut of her gown more than she liked, making her wish she'd placed one of her lace handkerchiefs there.

He didn't give her much opportunity to talk, doing most of it himself. She noticed he rarely asked her opinion. The only views which were important were his own. There were things she wanted to talk about. The presidential election would be held in four more days. She wanted to know who he planned to vote for, what he thought would happen if Lincoln was elected. Would the Southern states make good their threat to secede from the Union?

She wondered what the prevailing attitude was in Los Angeles. Were the people for the North or the South? In recent weeks the election was a frequent topic of conversation in the hotel. Of course, no one asked what she thought. Women had no vote.

The roast beef on Abby's plate was cut into fine strips and covered in a sauce tasting of wine and mushrooms. There was rice as well as tiny carrots and a baked apple tasting of cinnamon and sugar. Dessert was custard with raspberry sauce and a sweet wine.

Everett seemed to savor each course, watching her reaction, beaming at her compliments. "For you, my dear, only the very best will do." The gleam in his eyes was a bit unsettling, but the wine made Abby feel mellow. The food delicious and not too heavy.

Taking her hand Everett led her to the leather sofa across the room while the silent woman came in to clear the table. When she had removed the last of the glasses and left, only the lighted candles remained behind. Everett locked the door behind her and poured them each a dessert wine. He set his down on the lamp table at his elbow.

"I want you to taste this special wine," he told her. "Some of my most exclusive guests ask for it.

Abby sipped. It was slightly sweet and yet had a tart aftertaste. It wasn't something she would ask for, but then, she didn't care much for wine. Everett was the expert.

37

"You don't know how eagerly I've waited for this opportunity to be alone with you, to tell you my plans for us. It will be profitable beyond your wildest dreams," Everett said expansively, pacing the room in front of her. "Your name will be known in every corner of California and even beyond. Men will come just to look at you." He gave a satisfied chuckle. "Already the men who have seen you want to meet you. You have no idea how many times I've been approached for an introduction."

Abby smiled to herself, getting caught up in Everett's enthusiasm.

"The Queen of California," he said, sitting beside her on the sofa, urging her to take another sip of her wine before he took it from her and set it on the table beside his still full glass. Taking both her small hands in his, he turned her toward him, their knees touching. "...My queen."

He drew her closer, his lips brushing her cheek lightly, then fleetingly, her lips. It wasn't threatening so Abby didn't try to resist. She was feeling as if she were about to embark on some great adventure.

His hand slid around her waist, pulling her closer, his lips settling firmly on hers. It was a pleasant feeling and though she regretted not having deeper feelings for her employer she willed her body to relax and accept his kiss.

She knew Everett was pleased with her reaction, as he drew her closer until she was pressed half on top of him, his lips devouring hers. Realizing things were getting out of hand Abby made an attempt to pull away, but when Everett felt her stiffen, his arms tightened around her. His mouth forced hers open so his tongue could make a quick foray.

Startled by the intimacy of his tongue, she stiffened even more. There was nothing pleasant about the crude invasion. Yet, if Everett was going to do such wonderful things for her, the least she could do is show some appreciation. That thought was the only thing that kept her from struggling.

Breathing faster now Everett drew back to see the confusion in her eyes. He nodded to himself. "I knew you'd be a special woman," he said softly, his fingertips caressing her cheek.

"You know how to please a man, and what you don't know I will teach you."

His words were puzzling but Abby found herself strangely unable to think straight. Her body began to tingle as she shook her head to clear it. It didn't help.

"I will take you to all the best parties and events in the city, let the men see you. Let them know you are a woman of class. They will see that you are my woman, only mine, and that will make them want you all the more."

Abby closed her eyes, aware of the feather light strokes of his hand on her cheek, mesmerized by its deftness as it drifted slowly down her throat. She felt no alarm as he brushed the swell of her breasts, enjoying the tantalizing of her senses. The wine, the soft words, her excitement for the world he was offering, all conspired to make her strangely unresisting.

Everett drew her closer, his lips insistent on hers. Her moist mouth opened for his possession, her body swaying toward him. One hand closed over a breast, kneading urgently. She gave no thought to resisting, as if all her will had suddenly melted away. Was that her heart hammering so?

A sudden sharp, rapid sound continued to penetrate her dreamy state. Everett drew back cursing violently. With a growl of anger he strode to the door, his face flushed with passion which was quickly translated into anger as he flung the door open.

Alex stood outside, twisting his hat, knowing Drayton was going to be furious at the interruption. The two men spoke in urgent whispers that Abby couldn't hear, but which ended in Everett's growl of resignation.

"Alex, escort Miss Abby up to my room," he said allowing the young male to enter the room. Drayton's eyes were filled with regret as they surveyed her passion drugged state, his reluctance to leave her was obvious. "I'm very sorry, my dear, there's trouble at one of my places near the Plaza. If I don't get down there the place will be wrecked. I'll be back early enough to join you for…dessert." He kissed her hand warmly, his eyes sending a promise of passion yet to come. Then he strapped on his gun belt, grabbed his hat and strode from the room.

Abby tried to stand, feeling unsteady. She hadn't had enough to drink for that to be the cause, and though she didn't like Alex and didn't want him touching her, she couldn't have walked on her own. She could feel the young man's smirk as he assisted her from the room. It seemed as if he'd done this before and wasn't the least bit surprised by her state. It took all her concentration to walk steady and not embarrass herself. She was glad they didn't meet anyone on the stairs.

"It's too darn bad he had to leave," Alex sniggered. "You's really ripe. I kin see that."

Abby tried to puzzle out his words but it took too much effort. He led her to a room at the end of the hall, taking her inside and closing the door.

"Now when I leave, you lock that door. Don't you leave this room for any reason, you got that?"

Abby nodded, wondering why he was giving her orders.

"You lay down and sleep it off. I'll be out in the hall keeping watch until the boss gets back to take care of that needin' you got. Now lock the door behind me."

He went out and it took a great effort for Abby to lock the door, hearing his boots move only a short way from the door. It was too early for bed but she was too drowsy to stay awake.

She'd just take a little nap while she waited.

The room seemed awfully stuffy, maybe a little fresh air would help. She opened the window, inhaling deeply. Pushing the curtains back to allow the breeze she looked down at the street seeing Drayton and four of his men mount horses and ride off.

The bed seemed so far away, with its bright red brocade bedspread as she went to it and lay down. Dimly she realized she shouldn't be here in Drayton's room, but yawned sleepily. When she closed her eyes the room spun crazily making her reach out to touch the wall to stop it. Within minutes she was sound asleep.

Abby groaned in protest, wanting only to be left alone, yet someone kept shaking her, urging her to wake up. Why couldn't they just leave her in peace? Something cold splashed her face, pouring over her eyes and mouth, a voice coming from far away telling her to be quiet.

The shock of cold water and the knowledge of who the voice belonged to brought Abby awake. Something was terribly wrong. There was something unnatural about her drowsiness.

In the darkness of the plush room she could make out the small form of Danny, his eyes wide with fear, his hand covering her mouth to keep her quiet. Seeing she was awake and at least partly alert Danny took his hand away and motioned for her not to speak. She remembered Alex saying he would stand guard in the hall until Everett came back.

Her face flamed with embarrassment as she remembered how close she'd come to succumbing to his charm. Danny whispered close to her ear. "That lunkhead Alex is out in the hall. Drayton left him to guard you until he got back. I heard him talking to his men downstairs before he left."

Abby sat up carefully, feeling her head throb in protest. "What's wrong with me?" she whispered, sensing danger.

"Drayton gave you something," Danny said, his embarrassed gaze sliding away from hers. "Something he uses on women to…"

Realization made her eyes widen. No wonder she felt as if she had no will. She had been given something to rob her of her resistance. He wasn't taking any chance of her saying no.

"But…why?"

Danny gave her a disgusted look. "I didn't think you were that stupid!" His voice was still a low whisper. "Don't you know what goes on next door?"

Abby didn't know what he meant. He saw her confusion and gave another snort of disgust. "Somewhere in this hotel is a door that leads to the place behind here. It's a secret door so all kinds of politicians and important people won't be seen going in and out of the…house where the women are."

The truth hit Abby like a bolt of lightning. No wonder she couldn't hear noise behind that door, the men merely passed thru the room and into the other building to be with the women. That meant Drayton owned both businesses, that he had prostitutes catering to his guests while maintaining the façade of a fashionable hotel.

"He has other houses too," Danny whispered. "Down in Nigger Alley. That's where the trouble is tonight. He had to go down to keep some guys from shooting up one of his places.

"Why didn't he just call in the law?" Abby asked.

"The law don't go in there at night, Miss Abby, it's too dangerous. If Drayton wanted to save his place he has to take some of his gunmen and do it his self." Again his gaze slid away from hers. "I thought you knew what he was…thought you knew why he wanted you to work for him."

Abby's hand flew to her throat as she recalled Everett's words following supper. His offer of a partnership of sorts was not for her bookkeeping ability.

"Oh, Danny," she breathed in mortification. "I was such a fool. I honestly thought he just wanted to help me."

"He's a snake, Miss Abby. He lures young women here, drugs them if he has to, and then puts them to work in one of his houses. You, being so pretty and all, he had bigger plans."

Abby closed her eyes with the realization of just how close Drayton had come to succeeding. "Get me some water," she said, fumbling for her medicine bag.

Danny did as she said, bringing her a glass of water. She dumped some of her herbs into the water, stirred with her finger then drank deeply.

"I've got to get out of here before he comes back." Suddenly she knew exactly what she had to do, her head clearing from the effects of the drug. Trying not to make a sound she went to his closet, looking for something to fit her. She selected black trousers and a dark flannel shirt, changing swiftly while Danny kept watch out the window. She had the satisfaction of leaving behind the fancy dress Drayton had bought her in a crumpled heap. She was so angry at how close she had come to being enslaved by the man she wanted to rip it to pieces, but dare not make any noise. Instead she took the pitcher of water and dumped it over the dress.

Danny gave her a thumbs up in appreciation. She wished she had a man's hat to cover her distinctive hair, but Drayton's were too fancy and too large.

"Let's go," she whispered, wishing she had boots or moccasins instead of high button shoes. She wished she'd never left the wilderness, wished she never tried to use the white man's system to fight for the Indians. She's accomplished exactly nothing, and wasted precious time.

She followed Danny out onto the narrow veranda. It was meant only as ornamentation, not for use. They had to walk carefully to keep the timbers from creaking. Danny led the way to one end, into shadows, showing her how to climb over the railing and up onto the roof of the building next door. Abby followed, feeling the protest of her already out of condition muscles.

Her anger at herself and her stupidity increased.

They crossed the roof silently to a back corner. Here a tree grew close enough to provide an escape route. Abby put herself completely into Danny's hands. He knew every inch of this town. He had to in order to survive.

Once on the ground they stayed to the alleys, to the deep shadows. Each time they heard a sound or a rider they froze. They were only a few blocks from the hotel when Danny grabbed at her arm and pointed to the riders on the main street. Abby's heart dropped to her shoes when she saw it was Drayton and his men. The stillness of the night air carried Drayton's wicked laugh.

"Thanks for the help boys, those galoots won't trouble us again, not with their bodies full of holes. Now, if you'll excuse me, I have a lady who's eagerly awaiting my return."

Abby's face flamed in the darkness as she listened to Drayton's snide laughter and the snickers of his men.

"With all that red hair, bet she'll be a hot one," one commented. "Men will be lining up from here to the Plaza to get next to that one."

"That's what I'm counting on. That bitch is gonna make me a fortune."

Her shame was fed by the men's crude comments. The tugging of Danny's hand reminded her they had to hurry, sparing her from hearing more. They ran down the alley away from the men. Before they could cross the next dark street two forms stepped out of the shadows and grabbed them both.

Abby turned on the man, kicking and biting with all the tricks she'd learned from the Indians. She could hear Danny struggling with the other man but there was nothing she could do to help him. The one whose massive arms circled her waist was a bear of a man, too heavy for her to hurt. He had her from behind, lifting her off her feet, letting her kick and flail uselessly. With a sinking feeling she knew it was a losing battle, she was tiring fast. Drayton's drug had left her weak.

The arm about her was crushing the breath out of her lungs, leaving her gasping for air, strength rapidly draining out of her body. She was suddenly aware that a rope was being lashed about her hands and arms pinning them to her sides. Unceremoniously she was dumped into the back of a wagon she hadn't seen in the shadows.

"Didn't realize you was such a she-cat," came the voice of the man who had subdued her. Abby went suddenly still. She'd know that voice anywhere. "But you saved us the trouble of having to drag you out of that place Drayton calls a hotel."

"Jacob!" she gasped.

"Did you think I'd leave you in that den of iniquity? To sell your soul along with your body? No niece of mine will be allowed to live in sin and degradation. The Lord has delivered you."

Danny bit the arm of the man who was trying to subdue him. With a startled yelp the man loosened his hold enough for Danny to squirm out of his grasp.

"Run, Danny!" Abby urged. "Run!'

The boy cast her a helpless look before he fled down the alley, the lumbering man too slow to stop him.

"Let him go," Jacob told him. "We got what we came for."

Jacob threw a blanket over Abby then climbed onto the wagon. Abby could feel the dipping of the wagon as the other man jumped up to join him. As the wagon began to move she lay helpless, panting for breath. To raise a fuss might bring Drayton and his men. She certainly didn't want to be rescued by him.

The wood of the wagon was hard and uncomfortable beneath her, not to mention cold. She wasn't wearing enough clothes for warmth, but at least she had the blanket which would help, if it didn't suffocate her, that is. Her arms ached from where the rope cut off her circulation. She hoped Jacob didn't intend to leave her tied up all the way to his ranch.

Time passed slowly. Abby felt every jolt of the rough road. She wanted to sleep but her arms were going numb and she felt as if she couldn't breathe under the blanket that smelled of horses and sweat. By twisting her body and kicking her feet she was able to pull it away from her face, drawing clean night air into her lungs.

Jacob glanced back but made no move to cover her again. "I knew you'd come to no good in that place," he said. "You'll come to the farm where you belong. A little hard work will soon take the wickedness out of you."

Abby was too weak to argue. He couldn't keep her locked up forever.

After a time Jacob turned off the road into the shadows of some trees. The other man went to hold the team quiet while Jacob walked to the back of the wagon and reached for Abby, lifting her to a sitting position. She was so grateful he was going to untie her that she didn't struggle. He loosened the ropes then retied them with her hands in front of her, tying the rope to the side of the wagon. She had a bit more freedom but she was still his prisoner.

"Why are you doing this?" she asked wearily.

"For your own good, niece, for your own good. Your folly will not taint the good name of Bristol. I'm returning you to the fold of the Lord so you can be cleansed of your wicked ways."

Abby had heard it too many times to pay much attention. When he climbed back onto the seat and took up the reins she sat for a moment, arguments chasing madly through her mind but knowing it would be useless to voice them. She knew the folly of trying to make Jacob see reason, her father had tried often enough. He knew no reason but his own.

With a sigh of resignation she lay back on the hard boards, pulling the blanket higher to keep warm. It didn't take long for her to cease feeling the jolting, letting it lull her to sleep.

Later she'd worry about what she was going to do about Uncle Jacob.

38

John Jay stood on the steps of the Bella Union, looking up and down the street. Where could she have gone? It was his third trip back to the hotel in hopes someone would remember something else about Abby and who she left the hotel with. All they could tell him was that she stayed one night, and that she left the next morning. No one had seen her go.

He frequented the main streets of town, had asked at other hotels, at stores. No one recalled seeing her. From the maître d' he learned Abby had spoken to a young boy, a street urchin, the man called him, his tight lipped expression disapproving. He had seen the boy give Abby a note, so she had been in touch with someone in town, and had no doubt left the hotel with them. But to where? If she had gone to one of the ranches in the area he might never find her.

Mounting his horse John Jay turned toward the Plaza. There was only one place in town he hadn't checked; Nigger Alley. He hoped to God she wasn't there. The place was notorious for its lawlessness. A woman there would be accosted by half the men on the street. It wasn't the sort of place Abby would go to…at least not willingly. Still, he'd looked just about every other place in town.

He'd noticed them before, men who rode the streets, searching the shadows and hiding places, looking for someone. He'd even seen them go into private homes to search, not asking permission. He wondered if they were lawmen. One of them didn't look to be more than sixteen or seventeen, but from the look of him he was wise beyond his years. He was grim-faced about his task.

"There he is!" a shout went up from the youth. "Grab him!"

John Jay turned to watch the four men urge their mounts into a gallop into an alley, hooves flying in their haste. There were shouts and commotion and finally the unmistakable voice of a young boy.

"Let me go, you bastards! Turn me loose!"

Curious, John Jay followed the sounds into the alley, finding all four men surrounding one small boy which two of them were holding by his scrawny arms.

"Where is she?" the tall young man demanded, his stance in front of the boy threatening. "You were seen that night near the hotel!"

"I don't know nothin'" the boy yelled, then yelped in pain when one of the men twisted his arm.

"I think you do, and you're going to tell me or I'll let Jake here break your arm."

"I don't know!" the boy insisted, yelping again when his arm was twisted behind him.

John Jay drew his gun, the deadly click of the hammer being cocked registering louder than any command.

"Let the boy go," his voice was deadly calm.

The boy went still and so did the four men, all of them looking up the barrel of his pistol.

"You heard me, let him go."

They didn't comply, the youth's face was contorted with anger. "Mister, you don't know what you're messin' in. This little beggar helped a woman escape…a woman who stole from my boss."

"That's a lie!" the boy shouted. "Drayton wanted to turn her into a…" His words were cut off by a sharp blow from the tall youth.

"You shut your mouth, boy!"

"I said let him go," John Jay ordered. "You lay a hand on him again and so help me I'll drop you where you stand. Now git!"

Unable to argue with the gun the young man nodded for the others to release the boy. The four quickly mounted and rode out of the alley, their eyes blazing with fury at his interference.

"You're gonna be mighty sorry, mister," Alex promised. "Mighty sorry."

The moment they were gone John Jay holstered his gun and dismounted. The boy was watching him warily, holding the arm the men had twisted, blinking back tears of pain.

"You okay?" he asked gently.

Danny nodded but John Jay could see his arm was hurting, he could also see the boy was dirty, his clothes tattered, his face gaunt from his struggle to survive on the streets. He also knew the boy wouldn't trust easily. He was too wary for that.

"I was about to find a place for lunch. If you know of a good one I'd appreciate you telling me, and joining me."

Danny's eyes were filled with suspicion. "Why?"

"Number one, I'm hungry." It wasn't true. "Number two, I'm looking for a friend. Maybe you can help. It would be worth me buying your lunch to find out."

Danny wanted to resist the temptation the tall man presented but was too hungry. He'd been dodging Drayton's men for days, only venturing out of hiding because he was getting weak from lack of food. The prospect of a meal, seated at a table with this man to protect him was one he couldn't resist. He nodded, grateful to the stranger. He doubted there was another man in the whole town who would have interfered with Drayton's men, and Alex wouldn't have taken no for an answer, not with Drayton turning the town upside down to find Abby.

"There's a good place up the street," Danny said. He knew because he often picked through their garbage.

"Lead the way," John Jay said, taking the reins of his horse and leading it up the street behind him. At the horse trough he stopped to let his horse drink and to wash up, knowing the boy would take the hint and wash too.

The woman at the restaurant gave John Jay a welcoming smile which faltered at the sight of the ragged boy with him, but only for a moment. She had children of her own and there were nights when she'd set out leftovers in the alley for the boy she knew would come after she had gone home. She also felt a warmth for the stranger who would feed a homeless boy.

"What'll you gentlemen have?" she asked, hands on her ample hips.

"What's the special today?" John Jay asked.

"Beef stew and corn bread," she answered readily. "And apple pie fresh from the oven."

John Jay didn't have to ask the boy if that sounded good, he could see him struggling not to show just how weak and hungry he was. He nodded at the woman. "We'll both have that."

Without being asked the woman came back with coffee for John Jay and milk for Danny before she disappeared into the kitchen.

"My name's John Jay," he told the boy. "What's yours?"

Danny frowned at the unusual name. "Danny," he mumbled, then his curiosity got the best of him. "Why do they call you that?"

John Jay gave a soft laugh. "Because John is my father's name too. To tell us apart, because my middle name is Jason, they called me John Jay. It just stuck. It's better than being called Junior like my older brother Charlie suggested."

Danny made a face at the name Junior and had to agree the alternative was better. He reached for his milk drinking most of it down before he set the glass back on the table, licking at the white moustache it left. He eyed John Jay warily.

John Jay saw the distrust and didn't try to rush into the conversation he wanted to have with the boy.

"You ever see one of the Butterfield stage coaches?" he asked instead.

Danny nodded. "I love watching them roll into town with four horses, to see people get out...wishing I could get on and just ride...

somewhere." His sentence fizzled out, his gaze dropping away from John Jay's, feeling silly now that he had voiced his fantasy. He didn't want the tall man to think he was a sissy.

John Jay's smile was full of understanding. "I know just how you feel, only my dream was to be the driver, the jahou. Even though I've driven many a coach, I still get that feeling every time I see one. I want to climb up on that box and head out into open country, feeling me and those four horses working like a team."

Danny's gaze flew back to his. "You've driven a stagecoach?"

"Many," he responded, leaning back in his chair. "I couldn't wait until I grew up enough to handle the big teams. Sometimes we needed six horses in rugged country. But I started out with smaller hacks and wagons from the time I was old enough to climb up on a seat. Maybe I should tell you the rest of my name. It's Butterfield."

Danny's mouth dropped open. "You own those coaches?"

John Jay laughed and shook his head, his dark hair tumbling across his forehead. "No, my father and his company does, or rather he did."

To Danny that seemed like the most incredible adventure in the world. "Do you still drive 'em?"

"No, not for a while now. I helped my father lay out the road and build the stations here in California. When the first coach left Tipton, Missouri three years ago I was driving. I was driving when it finally pulled into San Francisco twenty three days later."

"Gosh, I bet that was an exciting trip!"

John Jay held his young audience by telling him about that first trip, about the Indians who stopped them for three hours just to look at the coach, scaring the liver out of him and the passengers before they were allowed to go on their way.

"Were you really scared?" Danny asked, still thinking grownups invincible.

"Course I was. What good was a pistol with six bullets against three hundred Indians? I'd have to be awfully lucky...say fifty of 'em with each bullet."

Danny laughed at the ridiculous picture that presented.

"But they were just curious," John Jay said. "Not dangerous. It just delayed us is all."

John Jay went on telling Danny about his adventures as a driver, hoping by the time the meal ended the boy would have enough confidence in him to tell him what he needed to know. From what the men who accosted Danny said, they were looking for a woman. They wanted her badly enough they had been scouring the town for days. He'd seen them, never once connecting them to the woman he was searching for. Now he suspected it was Abby they wanted, and that the boy might know something about her.

Danny was content to let the man do the talking, concentrating on the large bowl of stew the woman placed in front of him. Even she stopped for a moment to watch as he began to wolf it down.

"No use hurrying, young man," she said with a friendly smile. "There's more where that came from."

As the front door opened she called out a greeting to the couple who entered and turned away with her waddling walk.

Danny did manage to slow down. This was one time he could relax with his food. No one was going to take it from him, no one was going to yell at him and chase him away. He decided he liked the stranger with the unusual name, but he wasn't sure he trusted him. He knew the man wanted something from him, and soon, he'd have to decide whether or not he wanted to help.

"You ever hear of a stage station called Seven Springs?" John Jay asked after the apple pie and ice cream had been placed in front of Danny. The boy shook his head, too busy digging into the pie to answer. It was a rare treat, the first he'd had since his new friend Abby let him take the chocolate cake at the hotel.

"I'm not surprised," John Jay said, barely touching his own pie. "It's quite a ways south of here, just at the edge of the desert. There's a stage station there that was run by a man named James Cassidy, an old friend of mine. He took him a wife here a few years ago. A pretty little thing with fiery red hair. Just about the prettiest woman I've ever seen."

John Jay saw the stillness that settled over the boy for an instant before he made a big show of enjoying the pie.

"A few months back, some Indians hit the station to steal the stagecoach horses. In the process they killed Cassidy and a friend who tried to help him defend the stock. Cassidy's wife must have been out hunting, she did that a lot. She once lived with the Indians and knows a lot about their ways."

He could see Danny was now only picking at his pie, his eyes downcast, trying not to act interested.

"The way we figure it, she came back to find the two of them dead, and buried them, by herself. That couldn't have been easy. Cassidy was a giant of a man. A coach came through with a friend of mine named Gus on the box. She was there alone. He said he'd send help and more horses since there weren't any left to spell his team." John Jay let out a long sigh. "We're not quite sure what happened next, only that two Mexicans must have found her there alone. When the Butterfield people got there, they found the two Mexicans dead. From the signs they think they were killed by Indians. Mrs. Cassidy was gone."

John Jay was no longer seeing Danny or the table in front of him, he was seeing the tracks in the sand, the endless desert stretching out in front of him, and his own horrible mental images of what must be happening to Abby.

"When I got to Seven Springs I tracked them into Mexico. Tracked them until the Apaches cut me off and darn near killed me." His voice dropped so low Danny could barely hear him. "I had to turn back. I thought we'd lost her for sure."

Danny stopped toying with his food and looked at John Jay, reading the misery in his face, the look of defeat. He frowned, fascinated now by the story.

"Then I learned she was back, that she was buying up supplies to take to the mountains for the Indians. Next thing I found out she was on her way to Los Angeles, that she supposedly had friends here." John Jay gave a weary shake of his head. "I've been here for weeks and haven't been able to find a trace of her other than the fact she spent one night at the Bella Union. After that her trail vanishes."

John Jay's head dropped toward his chest showing how helpless he felt, how frustrated.

For a moment Danny studied him, debating how far he could trust him.

"Why do you want to find her?" Danny asked.

".....To see if she needs anything...to help her if she needs it. I have this feeling she's in a lot of trouble and she needs my help."

Danny read the need in John Jay's expression, saw the desperate worry, the caring. He wished someone would feel that way about him.

The silence lingered for several minutes before John Jay gave a long sigh and looked at the boy. "Is she the one those men were looking for? Were they after Abby?"

The moment of decision had come. Someone had to help her and Danny knew he couldn't do it by himself. He gave a slow nod.

"Why did they want her?"

Danny hesitated, then knew for Abby's sake he had to take a chance on this man. "She was working for a man named Everett Drayton. Slick as a snake. He charms ladies into thinking he's helping them...he gave Abby a job at his hotel...then he puts them to work in one of his houses."

John Jay's chin shot up, his gaze intent until he saw Danny's slow grin.

"He got outfoxed this time," he said with a feeling of satisfaction. "I was making my nightly rounds looking for food when I heard Drayton telling his men that the big kid Alex was guarding Abby until he got back...that he'd given her some kind of drug. There was trouble down at Nigger Alley and Drayton and his men rode out to take care of it. He was really mad to be interrupted with his plans for Abby." Danny voice trailed off seeing the furious expression on John Jay's face.

John Jay could tell there was more to the story but seeing Danny's pink cheeks he didn't press for details.

"Drayton said he'd be back later to finish what he started." Danny dropped back in his chair, his hands fidgeting restlessly with the tablecloth. "I knew where his room was, so I climbed up on the roof of a nearby building, then in the window. She was sleeping so sound I could hardly wake her. Once she was, she drank some leaves she had that helped her wake up, then we went out the window, and across the roof...I was gonna take her to my hiding place..."

"What happened?" John Jay pressed. "Did Drayton find her?"

Danny shook his head. "Not Drayton. It was a man I'd never seen before. A huge man with a bushy beard that grew just around his chin. She called him Jacob."

"Jacob! Oh, Lord!" John Jay sighed, having heard all about the religious uncle.

"Who is he?" Danny asked, relieved John Jay knew the name.

"Her uncle."

"Uncle! Then why would he tie her up and throw her in his wagon?"

"I know this sounds funny, but to save her."

"Yeah, he said something like that, about her wicked ways. Shucks, she was a nice lady, she didn't want nothin' to do with Drayton. He had to use his drug or she'd have fought him off. He'd have turned her into one of his fancy ladies."

John Jay gave a reluctant grin. "I think he'd have had his hands full trying." Danny's answering grin told John Jay he agreed. "So what else did Jacob do?"

"They tied her up because she was fighting like a she-cat, then tossed her in the back of a wagon, like a farm wagon, and she told me to run when the other one let go of me, so I did. I wanted to get help...but no one would listen. They just told me to go away."

"What did Drayton do once he found out she was gone?" John Jay already knew but wanted to hear what Danny would say.

"He was madder than a hornet! You could hear him yelling half a mile away. He told his men to get out on the streets and not come back without her. I hid out then. I didn't dare let them see me. Drayton's always trying to run me off. He hits me any time he finds me around his place. I don't think he wants people to know what all he's mixed up in. He's got gambling halls and fancy women all over town." He looked at John Jay who was taking money out of his pocket to pay for the meal. "You going after her?"

"I sure am."

"You know where the uncle lives?"

"Not exactly, just that he has a ranch near Temecula. He shouldn't be hard to find once I start asking around down there."

John Jay was in a hurry now that he knew exactly where he had to go and what he had to do. He wasn't certain how safe Abby was with her bible thumping uncle. He saw the tension in the boy, saw the need in his sad eyes. Danny knew he was leaving and in all probability would never see him again.

"You got any folks?" John Jay asked. Danny shook his head, his gaze on the floor. It almost broke John Jay's heart to see his lost expression, the loneliness, the grubbing just to survive with no one to talk to or be with. "I have a feeling I'm going to need a partner on this," he said standing up. "You know how to ride?"

Danny's gaze shot up to meet his, he seemed to be holding his breath. "I could ride as soon as I could walk."

"Then you're my man. You want in?"

Danny came out of his chair with a whoop that turned every eye in their direction. The woman came over to take John Jay's money, her smile telling him she'd overheard part of the conversation and admired him for what he was doing. She patted Danny's shoulder as he went out, and gave John Jay a knowing nod of approval. She wouldn't have to leave scraps of food any more.

39

Abby squirmed uncomfortably on her bed of straw. Her wrists raw from the rawhide ropes that bound her hands. The scents of the barn were familiar; hay, cows, horses, and manure. Jacob had hidden her away in the back of the barn, giving her two blankets for warmth during the cold nights, bringing her bread and water twice a day. She knew he hadn't told his family she was here and that made her uneasy.

The soreness of her back was easing after the switching he'd given her when they first arrived at the ranch. Each time he brought food he prayed over her, entreating the Lord to turn her heart from wickedness. He gagged her when her cousins came to help with the milking, then freed her to do the work of shoveling dung the milk cows left behind.

With each passing day Abby's fury mounted. She knew better than to let him see, it would only bring another switching.

On the fourth day of her confinement Jacob came out after dark to take her to the outhouse. She resented having to depend on him for everything. She felt dirty from not being allowed to wash more than her hands. Her hair had become matted and dull.

Afraid to let him see the knife concealed in her garter, she stashed it on a board near the top of the outhouse. She couldn't get to it when she was tied up but couldn't let him take it from her.

When she came out of the outhouse he led her to the horse trough. Here he had a wash tub full of water and a large towel.

"Take off your clothes," he said.

"...What?" she stalled.

"You are unclean and must bathe. Take off your clothes."

"Not with you here!"

"I am the instrument of the Lord. There is no sin on me. I know you would run away if I gave you the chance. You have not accepted my will. I see it in the wildness of your eyes. You are not obedient. The rod will change your ways."

She wished she could see his eyes in the darkness, yet she could feel the tension in his large body. The last thing she wanted to do was take off her clothes with him watching.

"You will undress woman, or I'll be doing it for you. That is your choice." He picked up the switch that lay on top of the fence. Abby wanted to run but the days without proper food and exercise had robbed her of strength.

She wasn't afraid of Jacob's switch even though the willow hurt like fire when he wielded it. It was the threat of him touching her to undress her that made her do as he said.

After all, it was dark. How much could he see?

Slowly she began to unfasten her shirt buttons. Impatiently he grabbed her shirt as the last button released and yanked it from her, tossing it into the dirt. Abby flushed with embarrassment as she felt his gaze on her breasts, heard the faster tempo of his breathing. She unfastened her trousers but before she let them drop she sat down to remove her shoes. When she did let her trousers fall she stepped quickly into the cold water of the tub, clamping her teeth together to keep them from chattering. She found the soap and a wash rag and began to scrub herself as fast as she could, wanting only to get this over with.

All the while she was aware of the tall man watching her, feeling his gaze devouring her. The pious Jacob's thoughts were far from pure, she was certain of that. How long did he intend to keep her prisoner in the barn without his family knowing? How would he explain it to them later? There was something about this entire situation that didn't make much sense.

In the cramped tub she dipped her hair into the water, raking her fingers through it to remove some of the tangles, then washing it with the harsh lye soap. When she finished she looked for the towel, seeing it too far away to reach.

"Will you hand me the towel?" she asked, aware that Jacob was standing too close to her for comfort. He reached for the towel so Abby stood up, thinking to wrap it swiftly about her. Jacob started to hand her the towel but didn't, staring at her naked body in the faint light of the stars. For a long moment neither of them moved, then she snatched the towel from his hand and wrapped it about her.

"There is wickedness in you woman, and disrespect. I will have to give you further lessons in obedience."

"How can I respect a man who keeps me tied up like a dog?" she demanded, her eyes blazing at him. "Who doesn't even tell my aunt and my cousins that I am here? Why are you keeping it a secret Uncle Jacob? What good will that do? Or do you intend to keep me tied forever?"

"Only until you are cleansed enough to join my family. I will not have a tainted woman in my house." His voice began to raise in his loud, preaching tone. "Your wickedness has been great. You must be cleansed. The Lord will make you whole."

"My so-called sins, Uncle Jacob, are only in your mind." She was trying to dry her cold, shivering body without revealing too much flesh to him, aware of the wet, dripping tendrils of hair on her back.

"You will confess your sins to me, niece, and I will give you absolution. This night we will pray together. I will hear your confession and you will be made whole again."

Abby shivered with the touch of madness she heard in his voice. It was as if he were being driven by something he couldn't control and it frightened her.

He handed her a plain black dress she hadn't noticed lying over the fence. "Clothe your nakedness," he ordered. She hated the dress on sight. She'd seen her aunt and her cousin Annie wear them all their lives, yet she was glad to pull the shapeless thing over her head, thankful for its high neck, long sleeves and loose fit. She wrapped the towel around her hair to keep it from wetting the dress.

Jacob bent to pick up her shoes, leaving her clothes lying in the dirt when he motioned for her to return to the barn.

Abby shivered with cold and with the knowledge Jacob wasn't through with her this night. She could feel his determination to make her confess her supposed sins. All he had done so far was make her very angry.

He took her to the side of the barn where the tack was kept. On a large leather trunk was a candle. He lit that as Abby began to dry her hair. With nothing better to use she took a curry comb used for the horses and began to rake it through her hair. Jacob watched in obvious fascination at the play of the candlelight on her fiery hair.

"The devil has marked you," Jacob's voice was so soft it was almost a whisper. "So that everyone will know what you are. I will change that. I will shear away the sign of your evil."

As his words sank in Abby froze, staring at him. "What are you talking about?" But she knew when she saw the sheep shears laying on the trunk, saw it in the way his avid gaze devoured the blazing glory of her hair.

"Kneel, niece, kneel before me and accept my absolution."

"It's not absolution that's on your mind, Uncle Jacob," she said with all the scorn she could put into her voice. "It's something much baser. You should know it well, I've heard you preach against it all my life."

Jacob was momentarily taken aback by her vehement tone. "Why else have you kept me out here in the barn without Aunt Louise and my cousins knowing I'm here?" Her blazing eyes demanded an answer, but Jacob drew himself up, clutching the willow branch threateningly. Her scornful gaze dropped to it before glaring at him again. "That's the only way you know how to gain obedience! You can't inspire it with your version of God so you have to beat it into your wife and children with that! You aren't teaching them love and obedience, you're teaching them hate."

Jacob lashed the switch across Abby's shoulders but she didn't flinch, too angry to feel it. She saw the fiendish gleam come into his eyes and knew she'd driven him to the edge of his control. If she wasn't careful he would give vent to the violence hidden in his heart, the violence he didn't see or admit to. Drawing in a deep breath to calm herself she faced him without cringing when his arm drew back for another blow.

"I know why I'm here in the barn," she said in a more reasonable tone that stayed Jacob's hand. "I'm here because when you look at me, I see not the love of God in your eyes, but lust. Plain godless lust. You want to become an adulterer, Jacob. You want to do all the things to me that you tell everyone else is a sin. You want to fornicate."

Jacob let out a bellow of rage and lashed the switch across Abby's shoulder and neck. He would have struck her face if she hadn't turned away in time. Her hand came up to ward off the next blow but she laughed softly, knowing it would infuriate him more but unable to stop taunting him.

"Beating me won't drive away the lust you feel. You're the evil one. Not me."

"I found you in that godless city, living in sin!"

"That's what you wanted to believe so you'd have an excuse to come after me. When you found me I was running away from the hotel because I learned what my employer had in mind for me. I was running from evil, and what happened? I ran into more evil, disguised under the cloak of religion."

The switch lashed out again and again as Abby threw up her arms to absorb the worst of the blows. Then she knew what she had to do. She grabbed the switch yanking it from Jacob's hand. Her eyes full of blazing fury, her chest rising and falling rapidly with her anger.

Their gazes locked, Jacob's fist doubled with the force of his anger, his dark eyes ablaze with the tattered remnants of his righteousness. His chest, too, was heaving as he drew great breaths of air into his lungs. His gaze drifted down to her slender figure in the shapeless dress and to her bare feet. He knew she wore nothing underneath. In the starlight he'd seen all of her luscious female form and knew he had felt more than pious concern. His body quickened at the memory.

Abby could see he was one step away from throwing her down in the hay. "Adulterer!" she hissed. "Fornicator!"

Unused to have such epithets hurled at him Jacob lashed out with his open hand, striking Abby across the face, knocking her back into the hay. Her skirt flew up past her knees giving Jacob a clear view of long golden legs. He knew then the words she hurled at him were true. He wanted to throw himself down on top of her and commit sin with her. With a bellow of self-condemnation he whirled and ran into the night.

For a time Abby was too stunned by the blow to move, stars flashing brilliantly before her eyes. Drawing a deep breath she struggled to sit up, one hand going to the side of her face. She was going to have one doozy of a bruise, but at least Jacob was gone, and he hadn't thought to tie her.

For a moment she contemplated escaping. She could get on one of the horses, but at the moment she couldn't summon the strength, feeling dizzy. Jacob wouldn't be back tonight.

Tomorrow she would be stronger, and she would retrieve her knife just in case he came back.

John Jay listened to the crowing of the roosters as he rode into the ranch yard. Reluctantly Danny waited for him by a small stand of cottonwood trees, far enough to be out of harm's way, but at his own insistence, close enough to see what was going on. It was only concern for Danny that had kept John Jay from riding in during the middle of the night and demanding to see Abby. Danny had been exhausted, and though John Jay wasn't ready to admit it, so was he. He'd snatched a few hours' sleep in a grove of trees near the road, but mostly he kept watch over the boy whose life had suddenly become linked to his own.

Smoke drifted out of the chimney telling him the ranch house was astir, his own breath misted in the cold morning air. He didn't dismount. John Jay had the feeling his presence wouldn't be welcome.

"Hello, the house!" he called. "Mr. Bristol, I'd like a word with you."

Within moments the door banged open and a huge man stormed out with a shotgun pointed threateningly at him. "This here's private property!" the man thundered. "You ain't welcome!"

John Jay sized the man up in one glance. Jacob was all he'd been told and more. Right now he was hiding something and that made him dangerous.

"I was told you're a man of God," John Jay said to throw him off balance.

Jacob gave a curt nod but didn't lower the shotgun.

"I'm also told Mrs. Abigail Cassidy is here. I'm a friend. I'd like to see her." He watched the man's eyes narrow dangerously, his grip tightened on the gun.

"I want you off my property!"

"What are you hiding, Mr. Bristol?" John Jay questioned, refusing to be intimidated. "If I leave now I'll be back with the sheriff."

"She ain't here!" Jacob insisted. "...You ask my wife if you don't believe me. Louise! Git out here!"

John Jay looked at the slender woman who timidly stepped out the door. It was obvious she had been listening to their exchange. She didn't try to stand near her husband, keeping a wary distance, a gesture that was telling about their relationship. She was afraid.

"I wish Abby were here, mister," Louise said. "I haven't seen her in so many years I'm not sure I'd know her any more. What makes you think she's here?"

"Cause he's crazy, that's why!" Jacob cut in to forestall John Jay's answer. "And if he ain't out of here by the time I count ten I'm going to blow a hole in him!"

"Jacob!" his wife was aghast. "This man has obviously ridden a long ways. Where is the Christian charity you're always preaching?"

"I don't want no saddle bum comin' in here. There's no telling what he'd do!" he blustered.

John Jay couldn't help but smile at Jacob's ludicrous words. "My names John Jay Butterfield," he said tipping his hat to Mrs. Bristol. "And I'm certainly no bum."

Louise didn't have to be told that. The clothes he wore, his expensive guns, and his horse were all evidence of that. She also knew the name. "I'm right proud to meet you, Mr. Butterfield..." her voice trailed off as her gaze fixed on something behind him. She blinked several times then looked to her husband for an explanation.

John Jay turned in the saddle, his gaze following the line of Mrs. Bristol's toward the barn. A young woman stood just outside of it wearing a shapeless black dress, her feet bare. She looked so thin he might have turned away thinking her only a child if it hadn't been for the violent red of her hair, and the ghostly white wings swept back from her face. His accusing gaze swung back to Jacob Bristol, joining the same look from the man's wife.

"She is here, Jacob Bristol!" Louise accused, her tone one of outrage. "What is she doing in the barn dressed in that old rag?" When Jacob just sputtered Louise drew herself up. "Jacob! I asked you a question. Why have you kept my niece from me?"

"She's not fit to be in the same house with you," Jacob blustered, but he didn't sound so sure of himself now, the barrel of the shotgun wavering. "I was bringing her back to God before I brought her into our home." His gaze shifted away from his wife's accusing one.

John Jay didn't need to watch to know Abby was walking toward them. He could feel her presence in some mysterious way. She stopped just beside his horse, one hand reaching out to touch his saddle.

"Lord a'mercy," Louise gasped when she saw Abby's face. "What happened child?"

John Jay's gaze swung abruptly to Abby, seeing the dark, puffy bruise on her cheek. She appeared pale and weak.

"Your wrists!" Louise gasped again, sickened by the condition her niece was in. Her eyes were ablaze with righteous anger when she turned on her husband. "You've had her tied up like an animal. What kind of monster are you, Jacob Bristol? Your own niece!"

"She had to be shown the way to salvation," he blustered, trying to overcome her scorn and his own guilt.

"Of all the poppy-cock I ever heard out of your mouth that has to be the worst. You kept her out in the cold, and from the looks of her, without much in the way of food….That's why you been wantin' extra bread these past few days. Oh, my sweet Jesus! Abby, you come in with me while I get you something proper to eat." There was cold anger in the look she directed at her husband. "Jacob, you put away that gun and go do your chores. I don't want to see your face for a while."

Jacob's mouth dropped open at his wife's strong words. She had never dared speak so to him before. "He ain't stayin'!" he said, raising his gun again to point at John Jay.

"Aunt Louise," Abby said. "I think it best if I just ride out of here with Mr. Butterfield."

"You know him child?"

"We're betrothed," John Jay said before Abby could speak. "I was aiming to marry her but Mr. Bristol here kidnapped her from Los Angeles."

His statement confused Jacob enough that he was sputtering, "…I don't believe that," he grated.

"I don't care what you believe, Mr. Bristol. Abby is going to be my wife. You've obviously been holding her against her will. The sheriff would be mighty interested to know why." He let that hang in the air, watched Bristol's resolve waver and crumble.

Louise snatched the shotgun out of her husband's hands. "Get on with your chores, Jacob Bristol, the sight of you turns my stomach!"

Jacob hung his head and strode away toward the barn. Louise went to Abby gathering her in her arms. "Mercy, child, I don't know what got into that husband of mine, but this is one time I couldn't keep my mouth shut."

Abby smiled at her. "It's about time, Aunt Louise. I never could stand the way he bullied you and the kids."

Louise gave a snort. "Two of your cousins have already run off because of his strappings. I always thought he must be perfect because he was a man of God. Now I see he's just a man after all." She felt Abby's chilled skin through her thin dress. "Child, you must be freezing. Come on in, you too," her glance included John Jay. "I'll get you breakfast."

"I'm not alone, Mrs. Bristol," John Jay said motioning toward the trees where Danny was raised up in his saddle watching with evident impatience.

Abby turned to follow his gaze, then stared, not believing her eyes. "Danny?" she whispered.

"Bring him in," Louise said. "There's plenty for everyone."

John Jay waved Danny in. He didn't hesitate, urging his horse into a gallop. Abby started toward him, and as the horse slid to a stop Danny tumbled into her waiting arms. They hugged for a long time. Over the boy's head she cast a grateful look at John Jay.

From the door way, the three remaining Bristol children were watching with curiosity, finally venturing out to welcome their cousin, John Jay and Danny.

40

It was many hours before they rode out, their stomachs full. Abby was wearing a dress of Louise's, her shoes retrieved from the barn. Jacob hadn't shown his face during breakfast so it was a family affair, everyone getting acquainted or reacquainted. The Bristol children accepted Danny as part of the family and both Abby and John Jay could see the homeless boy was hungry for their approval.

Jacob was standing by the corral when they rode out, showing no emotion. With Danny riding behind her, hugging her around the waist, Abby felt a flood of relief. She was feeling buffeted by events and emotions. The control of her life had somehow slipped through her fingers, first Everett Drayton had his evil plans for her, then Jacob, and now even John Jay telling everyone they were going to be married without so much as a by-your-leave. Married! Murder might suit her present mood better.

They were barely on the road toward the mountains when Abby pressed her mare alongside his sleek bay stallion. "Why did you tell Uncle Jacob we were going to be married?"

John Jay heard the barely suppressed anger in her voice. He didn't let the sigh escape his lips but he knew what was happening, would have been surprised if it hadn't. She needed an outlet for her anger, and at the moment he was available.

"It seemed the best way to get you out of there without too many explanations." He kept his tone reasonable, calm. Out of the corner of his eye he could see her struggling with her temper.

"Just as long as you realize I don't happen to agree with it. I don't want anyone making plans for my life without askin' me first."

"Don't worry," he said with a slight edge to his voice. "If and when I decide I want to get married, the lady in question will be the first to know."

Abby compressed her lips, puzzling out his answer. Did that mean he lied, that he didn't want to marry her after all? Her emotions were in a jumble. That wasn't what she wanted to hear. He had been in Los Angeles looking for her. Now he was going to think she was ungrateful and probably think himself fortunate she wasn't interested in marrying him.

John Jay had to keep a straight face as he watched her wrestling with her emotions. He wanted to tell her he was teasing but knew it would unleash her temper.

"Where are we going?" she asked finally, seeing they were headed east.

"To the Carrillo's Rancho, I want them to know you're safe."

They were ill prepared for the trip but Abby didn't question him. There were stage stops along the way where they would be more than welcome. They could find both meals and lodging.

"Danny, how come you're with John Jay?" She felt him hug her with happiness.

"Drayton's bullies been tearin' the town apart ever since that night you crawled out his window. I stayed hidden, hoping they'd figure you was long gone. Finally I got so hungry I had to look for food. That's when Alex and his bullies found me." She heard the waver in his voice. She suspected Alex would do anything for Drayton, including murder. "Mr. Butterfield came along and ran them off. He even bought my lunch."

Abby felt a wave of gratitude for the man riding just ahead of them, knowing he was pretending not to hear what Danny was saying. She didn't want to feel gratitude, she wanted to nurse her anger.

"Then you decided to team up?" she asked.

Danny gave a delighted laugh. "After I decided I could tell him what happened that night, he said he needed a partner if he was to get you back."

"I'm glad. It's good to see you."

She and Danny chatted for a while. It was her intent to ignore John Jay. Her feelings for him were uncertain, confused. She wasn't in any condition to make plans for the future. She'd tried to help her Indian family and failed. It was time to regroup and try again. By now the People must be in desperate need of food and other assistance. The thought made her sad. The People were barely able to fend for themselves in an area that provided little. Their way of life all but destroyed by white men who, in their quest for land, recognized no prior claim.

It didn't take long for her strength to run out. She'd been half-starved, sleeping poorly with her hands tied, her wrists chaffed. She began to yearn for her bedroom in Ramon and Vicenta's home, looked forward to long hours of uninterrupted sleep.

Aunt Louise had given them enough food for lunch, which they enjoyed in a grove of oak trees, the horses grazing nearby. The day had taken on the chill of winter, making Abby glad for the extra jacket John Jay had given her to wear. She was aware of his masculine scent clinging to it, stirring her senses with memories.

Danny was wearing cast-offs from one of her cousins, which were in better shape than his tattered rags. There was even a jacket which was a little small but would keep him warm. He didn't complain.

"We'll get another horse at one of the stations," John Jay said as they ate sandwiches of sliced beef on homemade bread. "We ought to reach the rancho sometime tomorrow."

John Jay was aware of Danny fidgeting nervously. By looking steadily at him, the boy finally met his gaze, trying to stop his squirming.

"...Are...you going to send me back to...the pueblo?" He had trouble getting the words out.

"Do you want to go back?" John Jay asked, aware of how still Abby suddenly was.

Danny lowered his head in misery and shook his head.

"Then no, we're partners, remember? We stick together."

A wide grin broke out on Danny's young face, transforming him from a picture of abject misery to one of pure delight. "For always?"

"For always," John Jay repeated solemnly. He looked from Danny to Abby who had resumed eating. It hurt him to see the dark circles under her eyes and knew her endurance had been sorely tested by Jacob Bristol. He wished now he'd given the man the beating he deserved, but he hadn't wanted to do it in front of the Bristol family. Not only that, he had the feeling Bristol had lost his hold of fear over his wife. Louise had finally found her backbone. She would rub the self-styled preacher's nose in the fact he wasn't God so he shouldn't try to act like him.

Abby needed days of rest and good food, and he couldn't think of anyone better to mother her than Vicenta. His heart seemed to swell a little as he watched over his two charges. He didn't dare tell Abby he felt as if they were a family. Now all he had to do was make Abby realize it.

If he had known her thoughts he wouldn't have been concerned. Abby's thoughts, too, were on their little group, a family group. She was glad John Jay was willing to take on the responsibility for Danny. It made her love him all the more for his generous heart, only she wasn't ready to let him know that. Her battered feelings wanted him to suffer a little first, especially after what he said about maybe not wanting to marry her after all.

The night was spent at one of the stage stations. Abby shared a room with the station master's daughter. John Jay spread his bed roll in front of the fire and shared it with Danny. After a warm breakfast in the morning they were on their way, hurrying as clouds began to move in, with undersides growing blacker as the day wore on.

He'd been able to buy a horse and saddle for Danny, so they moved at a fast pace, hoping to beat the storm. There was little conversation. In the distance lightning began to stab fiery forks at the ground, the sound of thunder booming moments later.

The road was easy to follow. Along the way they passed a rancher with his wagon heading for Temecula, a few horsemen who tipped their hats politely to Abby. A trio of Indians on foot stepped off the road to stare as they passed. Abby could almost feel the resentment rolling off them. She suspected they were looking for work and they'd been turned down more than once. Her heart ached for them.

She wished she had enough money to buy up all the mountains and give them to the Indians, but even that would rob them of their self-respect. According to the white man's law it would still be her property, not theirs. She couldn't even deed it over to them for fear someone would find a way to take it away.

Inwardly she shook herself. It was ridiculous to even think such things. Even though she had inherited Cassidy's land near the place called Cuyamaca, she hoped there was some way she could use it to help the People. It was a place she needed to go to, to see what was there.

The horses sensed they were close to shelter, their pace picking up, ears perked forward. They must smell the hay, Abby thought as a gentle rain began to fall. The lightning was closer. Soon it would be dangerous to be outside. They urged the horses into a gallop, covering the final miles to the Carrillo Rancho as the rain began to pound down.

Wet and weary the trio was welcomed into the warmth of the rancho. Hot food was prepared and Abby was soon put to bed for some much needed rest. The Carrillo children took over Danny, drawing him into their world of indoor games to pass the time until the rain was gone.

Ramon smiled at his friend in the warmth of the library over cigars and brandy. "I see you were successful in finding our little butterfly. She has been through much since el Senor Cassidy died."

John Jay nodded. "I guess she thought she could handle just about anything, but how could she fight the deviousness of men like Drayton, and even her own uncle."

"But she is safe now. The three of you are welcome for as long as you wish to stay."

"We appreciate your hospitality, amigo. If Abby wasn't badly in need of a few days rest we wouldn't have barged in on you."

"Nonsense, 'Chenta is much attached to Abby. She'll watch over her like a mother hen."

"I'm still looking for some property, Ramon, is there anything around here that's available?"

Ramon nodded, exhaling a puff of white smoke which swirled about his black hair. "Close to the mountains where the pigeons roost there is a man who lost his wife some years ago. He's struggled to run the place with the help of a few Indian vaqueros, but he's tired, he wants to live with his daughter in San Diego. Ranching is for younger men, he says."

"Tell me about it."

John Jay was familiar with the mountain the Spaniards had named Palomar, pigeon roost, for the wild pigeons which came every year. It was a rugged mountain, wild, studded with pine trees and ponderosa. At first he'd hoped to find a place near San Bernardino. What he'd seen in that area told him prices were high and the land was not prime for raising cattle. Here, in the mountains Abby would be closer to her Indian friends. He sensed her strong feeling of responsibility for them.

"Have you heard anything from the Indian Agent?" John Jay asked, recalling the conversation he had with Abby on the way, about the plight of the Kumeyaay.

Ramon shook his head. "Things move very slowly where the government is concerned. Washington is too far removed from our problems to act with the urgency required. I have hired two young men from her village. I know they use the money to buy food for the others. Their situation is desperate, no thanks to Overmeyer. And, we are seeing raids on some of the outlaying ranchos. Mostly they are losing cattle, and demanding the agent call in the soldiers."

"Do you think its Abby's people?"

Again Ramon shook his head. "These raiders are mounted. The Kumeyaay have no horses to speak of. And the raiders are all warriors in their prime. I think they have broken with their villages and prefer to live on their own, trying to keep to the old ways which have been taken from them."

"I'd like to talk with this agent."

"I will send one of my vaqueros with a message when the worst of the storm is passed."

John Jay spent the next few days with Ramon, riding about the large rancho, helping to check on his cattle. Ramon pointed out the area where the rancho of Juan Noriega lay and John Jay was eager to talk to the man.

Ever since they arrived at the rancho, Abby's mood was one of withdrawal. John Jay sensed she needed time. She both wanted and resented his interference in her life. Until she sorted out her feelings he knew enough to stay away.

That didn't mean he didn't think about her constantly. His mind filled with memories of the graceful way she moved, the intelligence that shone from her sparkling emerald eyes, the spirit with which she faced everything life had thrown at her.

His heart ached to tell her how much she meant to him, to hold her close and feel her pressed eagerly against him. At night the torment became even more acute just knowing she was so close and he was helpless to bridge the gap alone. She wasn't ready, and in spite of the torment it caused him, he was determined to give her the time she needed.

The rain didn't let up for three days. It was a steady rain, one that was very welcome in the hills. The higher mountains were getting their first dusting of snow for the season, evident from the glimpse of white peeking from under the heavy clouds hiding the mountain peaks.

Life at the rancho went on at its normal pace. As soon as patches of blue sky and sunlight penetrated the gray gloom, Ramon and John Jay prepared for the ride to the Noriega Rancho, some twenty miles away.

Abby tried to tell herself she didn't care that John Jay was gone so much. She wouldn't allow herself the satisfaction of asking where he and Ramon were going or if he was coming back. Surely he wouldn't go away without telling her. If he found her company less than pleasant it was her own fault. She felt quarrelsome whenever he was around, her tongue too sharp by far. How long could she expect him to keep coming back for more of her temper?

In truth it wasn't him she was upset with, it was herself. She'd let herself be made a fool of by a man she knew better than to trust. She'd allowed herself to be seduced, figuratively, by his talk of the money she could make, of having everyone admire her for the talents he would teach her. She had no illusions as to how her life would have changed if it hadn't been for Danny.

Seeing him chasing around the rancho, looking carefree and young made her heart leap with gladness for him. For too long he had worried about getting enough to eat, there had been no time for play. The children of the pueblo had been afraid of him, either that, or bullied him unmercifully.

At times she noticed his eyes would seek her out, lighting up when he saw her, reassured she was near before he went back to his play. Words weren't necessary, she felt the bond between them.

On the same day that John Jay and Ramon rode off together, the Indian Agent came to tell her there was no news from Washington. He advised her it would be a long time before a tract of land was granted for a reservation. Congress was notoriously slow to act in such matters.

"Don't they know how desperate the situation is?" she demanded, impatient with the way his eyes never seemed to reach her face, but seemed to hover on her bosom.

"Yes, they're aware of the lack of food and dwellings," he shrugged. "It could take years."

"Years!" Abby was aghast. "In the meantime those people will starve. They can't eat grass and rocks! The government gave Indian land to white men, the least they can do is get off their fat backsides and help those people before it's too late."

Simmons grinned nervously. "Well…maybe there is some way I might be of help." The oily way he said it and the look in his constantly shifting eyes told Abby exactly what he wanted. It took every bit of her self-control not to throw him out the door, bodily. If she gave in to the impulse she knew she'd regret it. For the sake of her people she pretended to misunderstand.

"I'll appreciate any help you can give those unfortunate people," she said, rising to indicate the interview was over. "Perhaps you have friends you can speak with who will help speed things through. Then again," a thought came to her. She wondered why she hadn't thought of it before. "Maybe I know just the person who can get something done. Someone who has the ear of President Buchanan."

That certainly wasn't what Simmons wanted to hear. Abby could see his mind working frantically to absorb that new bit of information. As much as he wanted to do something bold to this woman who looked so highfalutin' but had lived with savages, he wasn't ready to end his career in disgrace if the President found out. He had a good thing going here. For the moment it was best to leave things as they were. There would be other chances to get closer to this not-so-innocent woman. He licked his lips at the thought and reluctantly allowed Abby to show him the door.

41

Abby waited impatiently for John Jay's return. To pass the time she went riding several times with Danny and the Carrillo children. Their lively games kept her from thinking too much. She prepared food and bought a few cows she could take to her people, knowing as she did so how much they would both need it and resent it. Resent the fact they were so dependent on others.

By the second day John Jay and Ramon had been gone, Abby's frustration was building. Vicenta bustled around preparing for visitors, not having time to spend with Abby. Maria's help in the kitchen was all she required.

Late that afternoon the expected guests arrived. John and Merced Rains of the Rancho Cucamonga. That distracted Abby who was eager to hear about what was happening in California now that Abraham Lincoln had been elected. The coaches still came through and from the passing visitors they heard there was tension building all across the country between Northern and Southern sympathizers.

Abby was eager to visit with Merced, to hear about her children, too, who had joined the Carrillo children and Danny in noisy play outside.

Shortly before dinner John Jay and Ramon rode in, with barely time to wash up and change clothes. They looked as if they'd ridden quite a distance. No one asked the nature of their mission which Abby had been hoping for. She tried not to let John Jay know how happy she was to see him, tried to act indifferent. But it didn't quite come off. She found herself watching him, absorbing little details such as the way he cut his steak or how he used his tortilla like the Mexicans to mop up the juices.

"Things are really heating up in Los Angeles," John Rains said when asked about the political situation there. "Already there's dissention among the Northern sympathizers and the Southerners. Fist fights are just about the order of the day." He dished his plate with refried beans, salsa, steak, and a vegetable casserole as they were passed around. "There's still talk of splitting California in two, forming two states, as well as some other ridiculous ideas that don't even bear repeating."

"How about our new governor? Stanford is the first Republican governor California's ever had." John Jay asked.

John Rains gave a quick snort of disgust. "Well, he's pro-Northern, so there won't be any more talk of splitting the state."

"At least we won't have to put up with an Emperor Downey," Ramon added with a chuckle.

John Jay let out a whoop of laughter which was quickly joined by Ramon's. "Emperor!" John Jay repeated, trying to control his reaction in deference to the ladies.

"Yep," Rains said with a nod. "Shore would have changed things around here."

Abby chuckled as she listened to their exchange. She knew, as well as the men, that such a plan could never have worked even if Downey had been reelected. The new world had been started by men escaping the royal houses of Europe. They would never allow the same system to come into being here.

As the men went on to discuss politics, Abby was very interested in their views. It was rare for a woman to display an interest in politics and John Jay was fascinated by the bright sparkle in her eyes as she listened. A glance at Vicenta told him her thoughts were elsewhere.

"What effect did Broderick's death have on the election?" Abby asked.

Rains looked at her in surprise, hesitated a moment before he decided the question was worthy of an answer. "Broderick was a powerful, influential man. Even though Senator Gwin didn't have anything to do with his death, there are still some who think he was somehow behind it. If Broderick were still alive I think Gwin's influence would have swung a lot of people to the South. California is committed to the North."

"Don't you agree with that?" Abby asked, well aware of Rain's views on the question of slavery.

"I think we should be able to decide for ourselves whether we want to keep slaves. They're an economic necessity in the South."

"But you don't think it's wrong to force someone to work for you under the threat of a whip...or worse?" Abby asked, unable to hold her tongue though she caught John Jay's warning look.

Rains gave a crooked smile and refused to be baited. "Ma'am, that question has started more fights than you can shake a stick at. We aren't going to settle that issue here at the dinner table any more than men do with their fists."

Abby had the grace to back off and gave Rains a charming smile. "Spoken like a true diplomat," she said tartly.

"How was your wine yield this year?" Ramon put in to change the subject. "With the weather it must have been good."

"Exceptional," Rains agreed. "I've got a hundred and fifty acres planted in wine grapes now, not all bearing of course, some are too young. When the wine is ready it will bring a good price. I've been told its superior to the wines of Los Angeles. I expect a yield something like 20,000 gallons."

John Jay gave a low whistle. "That's a lot of wine."

"Plus we have raisins, and the fruit trees," Merced put in.

"The rancho is developing nicely," Rains said modestly.

Abby happened to glance at Merced as he said it and saw the tightening of her mouth. Her look told Abby things weren't going as well as her husband would have everyone believe. Merced quickly dropped her gaze to hide her thoughts. It made Abby think of Cassidy's distrust of the man. He'd been decidedly uncomfortable about Ramon borrowing money from Rains. Ramon looked upon the man as a friend. What if it wasn't true?

Uncomfortable with her thoughts Abby took advantage of the momentary silence to ask a question that had been bothering her. She looked to Rains who seemed to know so much about politics. "What's going to happen now that Lincoln is in office?"

Her question brought silence all around the table. Even Vicenta looked at Rains. It was a thought on everyone's mind.

Rains let out a long breath, his beard bobbing as he wiped his mouth and cleared his throat. "Trouble," he said quietly, his gaze revealing his concern. "We have a lot of hot heads now who are running around the state spouting off about their sympathies, with more than a few fisticuffs, but so far, nothing serious. But that won't last. The pro-slavery faction is going to explode. Especially if the Southern states make good their promise to secede."

"What about the abolitionists?" Abby asked. "They've been working for years to convince people of the evils of slavery."

Rains gave a sharp snort. "Damn bleeding hearts! They don't know what they're talking about. They want us to believe a slave's life is cruel and terrible. Yet they're taken care of. They don't want for anything."

Abby eyes flashed with emerald fire. She couldn't help but come back at him. "Except for freedom. What about Frederick Douglas, the former slave, who now writes about what he went through. He was half starved, beaten often and hardly had anything to wear even in the coldest weather. As a child he wasn't given a bed or a blanket, had to sleep in a pantry in the kitchen to try to keep warm. All the children had to find their own niches."

Raines shrugged. "I suppose there's some mean slave holders, just as there are mean men anywhere."

"But Douglas says the system encourages the abuse of slaves who have no rights what-so-ever. A master can even kill them if he wants, they aren't recognized as human beings."

"In my view they ain't," Rains said, unconcernedly taking a bite of steak. "They're plumb dumb, like oxen. They were meant to be slaves."

"If they're so dumb, so impossible to educate, why is Douglas able to publish a newspaper and write books? He's been on speaking tours for years, even in Europe."

John Jay tried to hide a grin as the conversation bounced back and forth between the two. If he'd ever thought of Abby as being half-savage, he was quickly changing his mind.

Obviously Wes, at Seven Springs, had done an excellent job of educating her.

No one else wanted to interrupt. Perhaps others had wanted to challenge Rain's views about the inherent superiority of the white race but didn't want to appear rude, especially after the way that the Spanish-Mexican people were being taken advantage of by many of the later arriving white settlers.

Rains shrugged carelessly. "He had a white father," he conceded, "so maybe he was a tad smarter."

"Tad? Yet, even with his white blood he is still considered to be black. Even if a person has only one drop of Negro blood, they're black in the eyes of society."

"They were meant to serve their betters. I'd have a dozen slaves on the ranch right now if it were possible."

Merced's head came up sharply as she swung an accusing look at her husband. "It's almost that bad now," she said, her chin trembling. "You treat your men like you own them."

Rains gave a soft chuckle, clearly not concerned by his wife's show of temper. "Of course I own them. I pay them for what they do."

"A pittance!" Merced replied.

Again Rains shrugged. "If they'll work for that why should I pay more? It would only spoil them. They'd buy more liquor then they do and I'd have to kick them out and start all over."

"Maybe they wouldn't drink so much if you allowed them some pride in being men."

Rains gave a condescending smile and glanced around the table at the others. "You'll have to forgive my wife," he said dismissively. "She thinks she knows how to run a ranch. It takes a man to do that. A show of strength. She would baby the men and make them totally useless in the fields."

"I would allow them to be men," Merced said heatedly, threw down her napkin and stormed out of the room.

For a long moment there was silence at the table, then Abby pushed her chair back. "I'll go talk to her," she said getting up. "Excuse me."

"Don't bother," Rains said waving his fork with no show of concern. "She'll be okay after she's had a good cry."

Abby's eye blazed at his condescending words. She whirled to go after Merced before she said something she'd regret. Merced wasn't crying, only pacing the floor of her bedroom in agitation when Abby knocked softly at the open door.

Merced glanced at her but didn't stop her pacing. "He treats me like a silly child in front of others," she stormed. "I get so angry I want to hit him!"

"I know the feeling," Abby said with sympathy showing in her eyes. "A lot of men are like that. They think women don't have anything worthwhile to say."

Merced stopped her pacing and faced Abby, her dark eyes still flashing with anger. "I envy you you're independence. You go where you please. You have no husband to restrict you."

Abby gave a low laugh as she settled onto an upholstered bench in the sitting area of the room. "My independence, as you call it, almost got me into very serious trouble in Los Angeles. A woman alone is an invitation for trouble unless she's either very old or very ugly."

Merced's anger faded, her face relaxing into a wry smile. "Don't pay any attention to me. I love my husband, it's just that sometimes..." Merced sat across from Abby in one of the hand hewn oak chairs with an embroidered cushion. "And I wish he would give me more say in the running of the ranch. After all, it belonged to my father, and I helped him often. When papa died, and I married Mr. Rains, the rancho became his! Now I have no say. He won't even discuss his plans with me, he just goes ahead. I am afraid for the future of my children."

"I understand your concern," Abby said softly. "But I think your husband is basically a good man. He wouldn't let anything happen to you."

The Spanish woman's black eyebrows raised in silent question. "I hope you are right. I overhear snatches of conversation...enough to know he is overextended. He borrows here and loans there in a tangle I'm not sure even he can figure out."

"I guess to make money you have to be willing to take a gamble," Abby said, repeating something she'd heard Cassidy say. "Sometimes you lose."

"It's all right for my husband to lose," Merced said, her black eyes darkening with her fears. "But I don't want my children to lose too. I've seen women struggling to feed their children while the husband goes off to the gold fields, or lies drunk. If my husband loses the ranch we will have nothing left except the charity of our relatives."

Abby tried not to give a shudder at the very thought. If not for John Jay, she would be in precisely that situation. "I hope you never have to face that problem."

Merced's expression suddenly brightened, making her look once more like the attractive young woman she was. "I'm sorry to be so gloomy, and it was rude of me to leave the table the way I did. I must apologize to our hosts."

42

A bby lay in the darkness of her room listening to the booming of thunder in the distance. It wasn't all that was keeping her awake. She felt restless now that she'd recovered
from her ordeal with her uncle. A breeze blew the white lace curtains at her window, and though it was chilly she didn't want to stir
from her warm covers to close it.

Merced's behavior was quickly forgiven by her hosts, Rains
seemed unconcerned with typical male nonchalance. There'd been
some of Vicenta's delicious rice pudding for dessert, then the men
retired to Ramon's office for cigars and brandy.

Abby helped to clear the table and helped Maria with the dishes. Vicenta and Merced had rounded up the children to put them
to bed. Now, as she listened to the silence of the house after the
pandemonium with the children, she thought of Danny tucked in
safely with one of Vicenta's boys. Even though he had to share a
bed he was still happy. It had been a very long time since he'd had
a bed at all.

That haunted look still came into his eyes at times when food
was set on the table and he feared there wouldn't be enough for everyone. Her heart ached for him as he tried to behave like the others and take his time when he was used to grabbing and gobbling
before it could be snatched away.

The sharp crack of thunder seemed closer. The curtains billowed with a puff of cold air. Abby shivered though her blankets kept her snug, and listened as the storm drew closer. The mountains needed rain, the streams were nearly dry. In the breeze she could smell the fresh scent of rain-washed air.

Her room blazed with light for a brief instant. Thunder rumbled close by. Unable to sleep, Abby threw back the blankets and sat up, pulling on the thick warm robe Vicenta had given her. Its lemon color looked better on her with her coloring than it did against Vicenta's olive skin. Slipping into warm slippers Abby went to her window to look out. Her view was hampered by the large tree outside, its branches dancing in the brisk wind.

Slipping quietly from the room, Abby felt her way in the darkness to the door to the garden. A gust of cold air almost jerked the door from her hand before she could close it silently behind her. Knowing it was dangerous to venture into the open because of the lightning, she stayed under the overhang of the porch looking toward the mountains.

The sky turned into an incandescent fire dance for an instant followed by a solid boom that nearly shook the adobe ranch house. It reminded Abby of storms she'd witnessed when she lived in the mountains and the desert with the People, and at Seven Springs with Cassidy. The summer storms on the desert had been the worst, with clouds roiling in from the Gulf of California carrying tropical moisture which it shed in a deluge. For days the washes would be treacherous with the threat of flash floods.

Closing her eyes and turning her face to the wind, Abby tried not to feel the weight of the years, of the sorrows she had known. She would soon be twenty years old and already she had buried her parents and a husband. There had been no babies by her own choice, but watching Merced with her five month old and being able to cuddle her against her own breast had brought a longing.

Behind her closed eyelids a sharp image rose to haunt her. A man with mahogany hair and laughing blue eyes. A man who had paid her little attention since he brought her to the rancho, and seemed disinclined to tell her what he was doing. She tried not to give this imaginary baby the same features she knew so well, features she longed to explore with her fingertips.

The brilliance of the lightning made her open her eyes as did the mental images she didn't want to see. Jagged forks ripped through the dark. Abby reached out to touch the cool whitewash of the adobe building to steady herself for what she knew would follow. But all the same she gasped at the fury of the thunder. It was all around her, shaking the house, leaving her breathless with the power of it. She gloried in the storm's fury, her eyes wide and alive as she watched the violent spectacle around her.

Time seemed to stand still. She didn't know how long it was before she realized the storm had passed overhead, that the intensity of the lightning and thunder had diminished. The steady patter of rain filled the garden.

She knew she should return to the warmth of her bed, but she felt too awake, too alive. The storm had made her body hum, her heart sing with joy. She wanted to run through the night on the wet grass, let the rain caress her face and her body with rivulets of silver. Stepping from the cover of the veranda she lifted her face to the sky, closing her eyes as the cool drops bathed her. She didn't care if her robe was becoming wet and clinging, outlining her body. Later she would dry off but right now she wanted to feel a part of the spectacle she had just witnessed.

A sound behind her in the garden brought her abruptly back to earth. It was a human sound. She wasn't alone. All her senses were alert, listening. She didn't have her knife, the thing that was almost a part of her. She hadn't expected danger within the folds of the Carrillo Rancho.

She sensed rather than heard the silent tread. Her Indian senses hadn't deserted her after all. Slowly she turned to look into the shadows, making out the faint shape concealed there. It was no one from the ranch, her senses told her that much, yet there was something familiar…The shadow moved, came alive as a man clad in buckskin stepped into the faint light.

Abby gave a soft gasp when she recognized him. "Night Wolf," she breathed, not certain if she was glad to see him or afraid.

He came toward her with a silent tred, his hand raising to keep her from calling out, showing her he meant no harm. When he came close enough for her to see his eyes she saw the tender expression there.

"I heard you were here," he said softly. "I couldn't stay away." His eyes narrowed. "You have lost weight. What has happened?"

It was her turn to raise a hand to calm him. "It's nothing. I'm better now."

"Tell me who did this thing! I will tear out his heart and feed it to the vultures!"

"No, Night Wolf," she protested, seeing the fire glowing in his eyes. "There is no need. The matter is finished."

"Who finished it?" he demanded, having trouble keeping his voice down so as not to awaken the household.

Abby knew he would settle for no less than the truth. "It was John Jay Butterfield. My uncle kidnapped me from the pueblo and took me to his ranch. John Jay came after me and brought me here."

"What reward did he expect for this?"

"He asked for nothing," she said softly, the truth shining in her eyes.

Night Wolf relaxed. "I have heard of this man. It is said he is a friend to the Indian."

"That's right. He's a good man."

He studied her for a moment, seeing the flush that brought color to her face, sensing her deep feelings for the man. His fist doubled in reaction yet he knew he could not forbid her love. It had never belonged to him.

"What are you doing here?" she asked, concerned now for him. "The ranchers are getting trigger happy with all the stock they've been losing. They want the Indian Agent to call in the soldiers."

Night Wolf spat on the ground. "I have told those young fools they will bring trouble down on the heads of all Indians. To the white man we are all the same, renegade or peaceable. They would like to get rid of us and not have to share the land."

Abby couldn't argue with his assessment of the situation. "Some feel that way, yes, but fortunately there are many who recognize the truth, that it is the whites who are being unfair. They're trying to control those who want a more violent solution, but the more cattle they lose, the harder it will be to control the situation."

"It is the cattle of one white man we take, the one who destroyed the village of the Kumeyaay, and even now he has his men searching out their new place so he can run them off again. I keep some braves in the canyons to make it look as if they have a large force. So far, we've kept them away."

"How are they faring?" Abby asked, fearing his answer.

Sadness came into his eyes. "They go hungry much of the time, even though we try to bring them meat. Their clothing is worn. Some have little more than rags and it is winter."

Abby felt her heart lurch at the thought of her proud people reduced to the status of beggars, barely able to feed and clothe themselves. "Tell them I will be coming in a few days with food and clothing. It is almost ready. When the storm goes, I will be there. Tell them."

Night Wolf nodded. "That will give them something to look forward to. If you really care for them, take guns."

"Guns? Why?"

"Because there is not much game to be found. Most of their weapons are gone. The few guns they do have are out of ammunition. They will have to hunt the white man's way, with bullets, if they are to have food." His eyes smoldered. "And if they are to protect themselves."

"I will see what I can do," she promised.

"Abby...what...?"

They both turned at the sound of a man's voice. Abby knew at once who it was, saw John Jay reach for his gun when he realized Abby was with an Indian. "No!" she cried as Night Wolf leaped at John Jay before the gun could clear the holster. They crashed to the ground, smashing flowers. Night Wolf's powerful hand gripped John Jay's throat as he straddled him. For a moment Abby couldn't breathe watching them struggle for leverage, afraid the whole house would be awakened and Night Wolf would be in even worse danger.

"Stop it, both of you!" she hissed, slapping Night Wolf on the side of his head. "John Jay, he's a friend!"

The struggle ground to a halt, each man staring warily at the other. John Jay turned his hands palm up to show it was fine with him if they called the whole thing off. Night Wolf hesitated a moment then scrambled to his feet, staying close enough to act if John Jay went for his gun again.

John Jay was slower in gaining his feet, careful to keep his hands away from his gun. The two men stood staring at each other, measuring, tension clearly etched in their faces.

Abby took a step closer to Night Wolf. "You'd better go before someone else comes out."

He nodded, barely glancing at her before his gaze returned to the white man. For his part, John Jay guessed who the tall, handsome warrior was and it didn't make him feel any better to find him with Abby.

Night Wolf stepped into the shadows and a moment later faded into the sheeting rain. Abby watched him go, searching her heart for her feelings. She found she cared about Night Wolf and what happened to him, but knew she didn't love him. What she'd once felt for him was now only concern and friendship.

John Jay fought the jealousy churning in his stomach. He hadn't realized the man Abby spent time with had been such a striking man. He would be easy to love. He looked at her now, her hair wet and curling into tight curls, her gown so wet it clung to her curves like a second skin, sending his heart thudding with a desire to touch.

"What did he want?" he managed to ask, still feeling the force of the man's fingers on his throat. He was glad Abby had been able to persuade him to stop. "Did he want you to go with him?"

His question surprised her. In his eyes he saw the fear that she would leave. He did care. She shook her head. "No, he sent me away from him in the first place because he knew I could do more for the Indian from the white man's world, and because the trail he followed would be too dangerous."

John Jay swallowed hard. If he had Abby at his side, as his woman, he didn't see how he could ever send her away….except perhaps for her own safety. Grudgingly he felt respect for the tall warrior.

"Then why did he come?"

"He wanted to be certain I was all right, and to tell me what my people need." Tears formed in her eyes. "They're destitute. Overmeyer and his stampede destroyed everything, their clothes, their weapons, their pots, baskets, and all the food that had been stored. Winter is coming on. They need blankets, clothing, and most of all, food."

"Let's get you out of the rain, you're shivering," John Jay said, taking her arm and leading her under the cover of the veranda. Once sheltered it seemed natural he would draw her into his arms, and natural for her to respond. He was almost as wet as she was, his clothes covered with mud, but neither of them was aware of any discomfort. They felt only the searing warmth of their bodies pressed together.

It was a long time before John Jay could speak. He had to get his mind off the lush curves pressed against him or he would take her straight to his bed. That wouldn't feel right in the home of his good friends. "I'll go with you as soon as the rain lets up," he said, his voice sounding husky in her ear. "I know you've been gathering supplies to take. I want to help."

"If you want to help," Abby said, her shivering now produced by other sensations than cold. "Why don't you talk to the man you claim is a friend of your father, the outgoing President Buchanan?"

"I hadn't thought of that. I'll write to my father before we leave and send it with the next east-bound mail coach."

"Do you think he can help?" she couldn't keep the hope out of her voice. "I know he'll be leaving office soon...."

"I don't know if he can with so much happening right now, but his influence with congress should still be strong. We'll just have to wait and see. Hopefully, once he learns the circumstances, what Overmeyer has done, he can force the issue."

"So there's nothing we can do except help them the best we can ourselves." She tried not to think of the strong thighs pressed so boldly against her own. "They must hate being so helpless, unable to support themselves in the old ways."

"We'll do what we can," John Jay assured her. "Now let's get inside before we both catch our death."

Silently they slipped into the house. He saw her to her room, his hand caressing her face with longing before he opened her door and pushed her inside. He didn't trust himself. As the door closed behind her he closed his mind to the image of her in the yellow robe, her hair wild about her shoulders, her breasts outlined vividly, her hips flaring gently below a waist he was certain he could span with his hands. He wanted to touch her everywhere, take her to his bed and keep her there all night long, warming her with his fire. He stifled a groan of hot need as he headed for his own bed, the rigid force of his desire clearly in evidence.

By morning the sky was clear with only scattered fluffy clouds. John Jay took one assessing look at the sky then set about gathering supplies to take to the Kumeyaay village. Ramon readily donated a number of cowhides and seeds for vegetables. If the weather held, he and Abby would leave the next morning.

Even the children helped, bringing toys and old clothing, a generous act that brought tears to Abby's eyes.

If anyone thought it improper for her and John Jay to ride off alone together no one voiced it. At first Danny had been nervous about being left behind, but he was quickly assured they would only be gone for a few days.

Vicenta seemed unusually happy about the fact they were going off together, and Abby suspected she was hoping for some good news when they came back. Vicenta also prepared food for the two of them for the trip, having it packed and ready the next morning.

It was barely dawn when Abby and John Jay rode out. The morning was so crisp and cold that their breath hung white in the air. Bundled in warm clothing, a poncho wrapped about her up to her ears, Abby felt no discomfort, eager to be in the mountains once again. Even the horses seemed eager for the exercise and moved with dancing steps.

Behind them they led two laden pack horses, two milk cows, and two steers. The stubbornness of the cows slowed the trip, they had never been tied and led before. Finally John Jay had to ride behind them, flicking them with the touch of his rope to keep them moving.

Just past midday Abby stopped in a small canyon where a spring bubbled from the rocks, forming a small pond for the animals to drink. John Jay eased the burden of the pack animals as best he could without being able to remove them, then allowed the animals to drink and graze on the sweet grass growing among the rocks.

They surveyed the secluded canyon, listening to the call of quail in the distance, to the raucous cries of ravens that landed on the rocks above them looking for any scraps of food.

"You know this country well, don't you?" John Jay asked, trying not to think of her as he had seen her the other night, and not entirely succeeding.

She nodded as she prepared their lunch. "Yes, this was my home for many years."

"What was it like?" he asked, curious about every facet of her life. "Did you enjoy living that way?"

Abby gave a wistful smile. "Yes, it was a good life. I learned to help my Indian family gather food, how to make baskets, and pots of clay, how to hunt. There was a freedom in that life that the white man doesn't have. We went where the food was. There was no hurry. We had few enemies."

"Could you have left if you wanted to?"

"Of course. My adopted family offered to take me to the closest ranch so I could return to my real family." She snorted. "Uncle Jacob has never been my idea of family."

"And him being your only family that's where you would have ended up." He frowned remembering the way he had found her at Jacob's ranch. "It's easy to understand why you made the choice you did."

Abby laid out their lunch on a blanket near the pond. A dragonfly buzzed past their heads, landing on a reed at the edge of the water, its gossamer wings transparent in the sun. It was warmer now. They'd shed their ponchos, tying them on the back of their saddles.

John Jay sat on one side of the blanket, picking up a burrito bulging with chunks of beef and beans. "I've always wondered why you married Cassidy," he said hesitantly. "I never had the feeling you were in love with him."

Abby hid her reaction to the question by taking a bite of her burrito, even though her appetite suddenly seemed to have deserted her. It was several minutes before she could make a reply. "I... wanted to love him," she said wistfully. "He was a good man, good to me. It...just didn't happen."

"He was a hardworking man," John Jay said. "Maybe he didn't know how to treat a woman...how shall I say it...in the tender moments."

Abby knew what he meant, her face flushing as she bit again into the stuffed tortilla so she wouldn't have to answer. Her ploy didn't fool John Jay.

"A lot of men don't think a woman is capable of experiencing pleasure in the marriage bed, and don't have the knowin' to find out. Besides, it's easier for them if the woman makes no demands. They don't have to worry about her taking a shine to every stranger who comes through."

"I...didn't...feel anything," Abby admitted, finding she wasn't as embarrassed as she thought. Talking to John Jay was easier than trying to talk to her husband. He seemed to understand her feelings where her husband had never even tried.

"Then Cassidy was a fool. It was his failure, not yours."

"I wanted to feel something", she said softly, her eyes haunted by memories. "Then he'd be snoring and sometimes I'd lay awake for a long time, wanting him to just hold me. But, toward the end, before he died, I didn't feel anything anymore, just felt numb when he touched me."

"You'd been disappointed too many times."

Abby knew she shouldn't be discussing such deeply personal feelings with him, yet it seemed so right. She didn't have a mother to talk to. Vicenta, she sensed, would be too embarrassed. Her sister Moyla would talk frankly with her, but she hadn't seen her in a long while. She had a husband now and a family.

"I thought something was wrong with me until..." her voice faded away, horrified by what she'd been about to say.

"...Until Night Wolf," he finished for her.

Her gaze flew to his, afraid she would see derision there, anger. Instead she found only a look of compassion, of understanding, and not a little jealousy. But he didn't let that rule him.

"I wanted to be the first man to make you feel that way," he said huskily. "I've wanted to hold you since the first time I saw you. You seemed half-tamed, someone who would catch fire when my hands stroked you. It hurt me to know I had no right to you."

Abby found she could barely choke her food down. Suddenly her appetite fled. Her own longings at Seven Springs came vividly to life, the way her hungry eyes would follow him when he was there. The thoughts in the night that wouldn't stop tormenting her.

"It wasn't what you think with Night Wolf," she said softly. "He protected me from the others by pretending to sleep with me. When we were forced to run from them, we were pursued for days. Then he was wounded in a fight with the leader of the renegades. It wasn't meant to be. I knew it, and eventually he came to know it too. Our paths are different."

John Jay gave a soft sigh of relief though he quickly tried to hide it. "Even when I was away from you," he went on, his eyes looking back into himself. "My thoughts didn't give me any peace. An attractive woman would walk by and smile...once I would have been after her in a flash. Now I only think to myself that she doesn't look a bit like you." He shook his head ruefully. "Wanting a married woman was killing me, and no one else would do. I thought I would be hungry for you all my life." He looked away from her. "When I heard about Cassidy my first feeling was that of the loss of a friend. It took a moment before it dawned on me...you were free. It was all I could do not to come running, to grab you before someone else did." He gave a self-derisive laugh. "And that's exactly what happened. I found out you were gone, and by the time I got to Seven Springs the trail was already cold. But I had to go after you anyway." Though he could feel Abby's gaze on him he couldn't look at her.

"I'm glad you didn't find us," she said softly. "They weren't all like Night Wolf. They would have killed you."

"You knew him before didn't you?"

She nodded. "Yes, he came every year to our village to visit relatives. I knew if I stayed with the Kumeyaay, when he came back the next time he would ask me to be his wife."

"And if he had, you would never leave."

Her eyes were dark as their gazes locked. "I knew I wasn't meant to stay forever with them. Even the medicine woman, Enyaa knew it was so."

"So when Cassidy came to your village looking for a woman you knew it was your chance."

"Yes, that was my chance. When Night Wolf returned that year and found me gone, already married, he was furious. He was waiting for a chance to make me pay. The day they attacked Seven Springs for the horses, he also meant to carry me off...only I was out hunting. I didn't get back until it was all over. He hadn't meant for anyone to be killed, but the others didn't feel the same. They drove the horses off, and after a while Night Wolf came back for me...just at the right moment." Her voice faltered. "He killed both of the Mexicans before they had a chance to do...what they intended. Later, when we joined the other renegades, he protected me from them. He meant to punish me. I could see it in his eyes."

"But he couldn't. He brought you back to your Indian family."

"And finding the first village gone, and then the second one destroyed by the stampede, he knew he could not let that go unpunished. He could not take me with him."

John Jay was silent for a while, feeling respect for the tall warrior...understanding why he had chosen the path he had. A path that meant giving up the woman he loved.

43

The sun had dropped behind the distant mountains as Abby and John Jay approached the canyon of caves where the People had taken refuge. In the rocks they could see warriors standing in plain sight, holding rifles. Abby knew this was a bluff, to intimidate any ranchers thinking to find an easy gathering of families. It was likely there were no bullets.

She and John Jay had to smile when they realized several partially hidden warriors weren't men at all, but figures stuffed with grass and sticks. From a distance they looked real.

Some of the young boys came out to meet them and help drive the still reluctant cows, taking them to a side canyon where there was grass and water.

People came from the caves, shouting happily to others at the sight of the laden pack animals. Even Wahss had a smile as the elders dug into the packs to distribute the blankets, clothing and food to the most needy.

Two men who had once worked on ranchos, took ollas to collect fresh milk from the two cows with full udders.

Children laughed in delight to find toys, several balls, hoops and sticks, and dolls. The items of clothing sent them into fits of laughter trying to imagine wearing such things, when they were used to wearing nothing at all.

Abby could only smile as she watched their reaction. Along the way, she had shown John Jay how to collect grass for baskets, branches from certain plants to make bows and arrows. She introduced John Jay to Wahss and the elders, and was saddened to learn Enyaa had not awakened one morning, and had gone to join her ancestors. It made her even sadder that her Indian family was gone too, having been taken by the smallpox.

Already the People had replaced many of their weapons, and the women were busy weaving baskets and firing new ollas to hold food and water, and for cooking. They were quick to take the new supplies and put together a feast with fresh beef, rice, tortillas and fresh vegetables.

For once, everyone had a full stomach, and dancing went on far into the night. John Jay was accepted as a friend of the People and he was as surprised as Abby when he found himself dancing around the fire. The steps were simple enough even he could do them. He danced with the men, Abby with the women.

Later, as some were drifting off to their sleeping places, Abby and John Jay walked into the shadows of the canyon.

"It's good to see them happy," she said, the drums fading in the distance. "And they like you."

John Jay grinned. "I've never been accepted into an Indian village before. These are good people, I don't understand why the whites can't accept that."

"Because they want their land. It's easier to believe they are less than human when they drive them off to make room for their cattle," Abby said, her eyes full of sadness.

"Tomorrow I'll show some of the men how to shoot the rifles we brought, but they have to be ones who won't use them against the white man," John Jay said as they sat on some boulders near the grazing animals.

High on the side of the canyon, they could see one of the men standing guard with more confidence now that they had ammunition for their rifles.

"There are several who will make good hunters, Wahss will make the choice."

"I've been waiting to tell you," he said, gathering his courage, taking one of her hands in his. "When Ramon and I left last week, we went to a place called Palomar where there is a rancho for sale. I've decided to buy it. There's good grazing, and already a good sized herd of cattle, some sheep and horses."

Abby's heart began to beat faster as his gaze held hers in the darkness.

"I think you know how I feel about you. I want us to be a family. You, me, and Danny. And, hopefully, someday, children of our own."

Abby's reaction was one of tremendous relief and joy, followed moments later with thoughts of Cassidy, buried at Seven Springs.

"I know," John Jay said, watching her changing expressions. "It's too soon. But I'll wait, however long you want, until you feel it's right."

She threw her arms around him, pressing her cheek to the coarse stubble of his beard. "I want to be a family with you," she said, smiling happily. "I know I haven't been very nice to you lately."

"It's okay," he said gathering her close. "You've been through so much. You had to have time."

"But I do care for you. I have since the first time you set foot at Seven Springs." Slowly she drew back, smiling into his blue eyes, looking almost black in the darkness. "There's something I want to ask you. It has to do with the People," she said quickly to erase the frown that had appeared.

He gripped both her hands in his and waited.

"From Cassidy I've inherited a large tract of land near a place called Cuyamaca. I know I can't deed it to the Kumeyaay, but maybe they can live there until the government can assign them land of their own."

"I know the place," John Jay said thoughtfully. "A few white families have settled there, but if handled carefully, maybe we can make it work. It's good land, they can graze cattle there."

"Why cattle?" she asked, knowing that wasn't the Indian way.

"Because if this war ever breaks out between the North and the South, there'll be a huge demand for beef. Prices will go up."

"But, how would you get them where they're needed? That desert doesn't provide much in the way of grass or water." She was all too familiar with the desert, as was he, from building roads and digging wells for the Butterfield Mail.

"There's a group of ranchers who've sent men out to scout the best trails, where there's water and grass, but we'd also have to send along wagons with hay and additional water."

"So, they're preparing already," Abby said sadly. "Are they that sure war is inevitable?"

John Jay nodded. "Things will move fast now that Lincoln's been elected. States will secede and form their own government."

"I hope they come to their senses and settle things without bloodshed," she said with a shiver of fear that told her it wasn't likely.

Their gazes met in the darkness, and suddenly the prospect of war was the last thing on their mind. Her hand came up to touch his face, eager to know the rough stubble of his beard. "Kinda tough to shave when I'm on the trail," he said with a slightly crooked smile. "But tryin' to grow a beard makes me itch."

"I like you without the beard. Your face is too handsome to hide it behind whiskers."

The air suddenly seemed electric with a fire Abby had never experienced before. She wanted to touch him everywhere, to kiss him everywhere.

John Jay caught the same fire and they came together hard, their lips meeting and parting to explore each other. Their hands began seeking out first their faces, then his hand was on her breast as he held her close.

His hot breath scorched her face as she pressed closer, her hands seeking the width of his shoulders, then the buttons of his shirt.

Suddenly they were frantic to undress, the cold of the night forgotten. John Jay spread their jackets on the sand where they came together, half undressed, too eager to take more time.

Abby relished the hard muscles of his chest, the way her breasts felt in his greedy hands.

She hadn't known she would feel like this, to want him like this.

When he tried to slow things down, her hand reached for his hard manhood and was guiding it to her. She'd waited too long for this.

"Now," she pleaded. "Now!"

And he was lost, surging into her as if coming home at last, the rhythm frantic. Abby was swept to a place she'd never been before. Gasping, crying out, she suddenly shattered into a thousand fragments, aware of his hot groan against her lips.

The rhythm slowed as they came down from the glorious heights. Abby was half laughing, half crying. "I...I never knew..."

"Oh my," he gasped. "I didn't mean it to end so soon..."

She hugged him to her. "There was no other way."

"Yeah," he murmured against her soft cheek, kissing her tears. "We'll have a lot of time to get it right."

Reluctantly they pulled themselves together, stopping every few minutes to kiss and hold each other, laughing at their half-dressed state as they struggled to look normal before returning to the caves where they would each sleep in a different place. He with some of the young men, her with unmarried or widowed women.

The morning dawned crisp and cool, but fires soon erased the chill both inside the caves and outside.

Abby and John Jay met with Wahss and the elders explaining Abby's offer of her property until the government came through with a permanent home. They also suggested leaving this morning to make certain it would be suitable.

When the elders talked it over, it was decided that Wahss and Chico would go with them to Cuyamaca. One of the young men was sent to the Carrillo Rancho with a note to explain their delay in returning. It wasn't far to the mountain property, and on horseback it could be done by nightfall.

Both Wahss and Chico had some experience at riding, and the four of them carried supplies for two days.

As they started out, the horses were alert and eager, traveling at a steady lope, eating up much of the distance. Once they joined the main trail, they were slowed to a fast walk.

Along the way they passed a few wagons with families who looked at the two Indians curiously, but exchanged friendly greetings.

The hills were covered with oak trees and a variety of chaparral. Occasionally they spotted deer in the distance, sometimes grazing cattle. At a small lake, several young boys were fishing and further on they came to a store that was once a stage stop for the San Antonio to San Diego mail, often called the Jackass Mail. The reason for the name, John Jay told them was because they used part of the same trail the Butterfield Mail now followed, except, not far from Seven Springs, a road climbed up a very steep grade of the Laguna Mountains toward San Diego. The trail was so steep a stage coach could not make it, so instead, mail and passengers were switched to mules to where another coach waited for them on the trail above.

At the store, John Jay asked about Cassidy's property, a place designated as Green Valley. The store's owner, Sidney Harkness remembered Cassidy, and knew the land they had come to see. There were a few white families in the area, he explained, raising a few sheep or cattle, but there were no large holdings. Cassidy's property was probably the largest.

John Jay introduced himself and conducted the initial contact here. As they had hoped, the Butterfield name was well known and carried prestige. Abby and the two Kumeyaay remained outside with the horses.

"The two Indians with Mrs. Cassidy and me are Kumeyaay. They had a village not far from Warner Station, but a man named

Overmeyer bought the land, destroyed the ewas the Indians had built there while they were still living in the desert."

"I've heard they're peaceable," Harkness said, studying the two elders outside.

"They are. They move where the food is each season. When they found their village site gone, they moved on to their next site further back in the hills. They couldn't know that was still part of Overmeyer's range, and when he knew the Indians were there, he sent his men to stampede a herd of cattle through the site early one morning."

Harkness scowled. "No call for that."

"I agree. No warning. Just by luck someone heard them coming and the Indians barely escaped with what they were wearing. Everything else was ground into dust by the cattle."

"I've been hearing about this Overmeyer, bad things. Seems he's got no love for Indians or Mexicans." Harkness looked pointedly at John Jay. "So why are they here with you?"

"We've come to look at Cassidy's land, and maybe move the Kumeyaay here temporarily until the government grants them reservation land." John Jay paused to let that sink in. "These are peaceful people, and badly in need of a place where they can grow things and hunt."

Harkness scratched his bearded chin in thought. "We've a few Indians in the area. They come to the store to trade for seed and other supplies. They mind their own business and local families don't object. If you decide to move them here, you let me know. I'll have a talk with the locals. From what I've heard, that was once Indian land anyway."

"We were hoping it wouldn't be a problem," John Jay said, relieved. "Now if you can tell me where Cassidy's land is, we'll go have a look."

On a map of the area, Harkness showed him where the property started, a much larger plot then he expected.

Abby was antsy by the time he came out. It had been all she could do not to go into the store and demand directions. John Jay's way was best, she knew, but she was impatient.

"It isn't far," John Jay said as he mounted. Abby and the two men followed suit. He didn't speak until they were away from the store. "It seems to be quite large, with a spring and a stream. It was once owned by a rancher, but abandoned because of Indian trouble, probably because that was once Indian land."

Abby drew up beside him. "Did you tell him the People might come here?"

"Yes, and he didn't seem concerned. There are other Indian families in the area. I have a feeling he can smooth the way for us."

Wahss and Chico had listened with interest, nodding. They traveled along the old Jackass Mail road until they came to a large oak tree with strips of metal hanging from the branches.

"This is one marker," John Jay said, and a short distance further he turned off on an overgrown wagon trail.

The area was thick with oak trees, chaparral and other plants the Kumeyaay used for food and medicine. Abby could see the spirits of the two Indians lifting as they surveyed the lush landscape. Topping a rise they saw a wide valley with tall grass and a stream running through. A dilapidated cabin sat near the water, with an equally dilapidated barn nearby. It looked so peaceful it brought tears to Abby's eyes.

Wahss and Chico seemed equally speechless. "This land is yours?" Wahss asked as if unable to believe their good fortune.

Abby nodded. "But it is yours until the government finds you permanent land."

Wahss and Chico shared a look and nodded their acceptance. "It is good," Chico said.

In the distance, a family of deer came down to the stream to drink, flicking their ears at the four riders, but seemed undisturbed by their presence.

"I have papers that will show the boundaries," Abby said. "When we come back I will bring them so we will know the extent of the property."

They rode to the stream to let the horses drink, then turned them loose to graze on the lush grass while they set out the food they had brought, jerky, hard tack and apples from Vicenta's cellar.

A soft breeze stirred the trees. It was so peaceful Abby almost envied the people coming to this place. Someday she might feel as if it was hers, but for now, it belonged to the Kumeyaay.

It was too late to return to the caves, so the four of them prepared to spend the night in the old barn. Even though it had a leaky roof, and no door, it would serve as shelter for the People until they could gather materials to build their ewas.

They inspected the dilapidated cabin and saw it too could shelter some of the families temporarily. The People would not want to stay in it for long. Abby assured Wahss they could use the wood for their own structures, or for repairs to the barn which they could use for their livestock.

There were stalls that afforded some privacy, and Wahss and Chico didn't think it strange that Abby and John Jay made their bed together in one of them.

Abby and John Jay snuggled wearily into their robes to sleep, too aware of the two Indians to do more than hold each other. They felt good about the trip and what they had discovered on Cassidy's land. No she had to remind herself, my land. Sleep came quickly.

The next morning, they stopped at the store to inform Harkness of the decision to move the Kumeyaay people here. When he was introduced to the two Indians, he was surprised to learn they spoke fairly good English, which would help with their being accepted by the local settlers.

Later in the day, when they reached the caves, the people swarmed about them to hear the news. Suddenly there was hope that they could once again live as they always had, on land that could not be taken away.

While they made preparations for the move, Abby and John Jay returned to the Carrillo Rancho to request the help of some of the vaqueros and horses. From Ramon's strongbox, Abby took the deed to the property now in her name, and some money to start an account at the store.

44

The trek to Cuyamaca two days later was filled with laughter at the antics of the children racing around the procession. There were mules to carry supplies, even items local ranchers had contributed once word spread about Overmeyer's actions. He quickly became disliked by the areas ranchers.

Vaqueros from Ramon and Vicenta's rancho led the pack animals and the cows. Along the way, the People gathered anything they could use to build new ewas, to make baskets, or use for food. Abby assured them there were lots of oak trees on the land, one of their major food sources, as well as wild game. So the people were looking forward to their new home. Danny rode proudly at Abby's side, happy to be part of this special procession while John Jay helped the vaqueros with the animals.

It was almost dark before the procession reached the place Cassidy called Green Valley. By then the children were exhausted and hungry. Dinner was mostly acorn cakes, wild onion and a few apples.

Some families bedded down in the old barn, others in the dilapidated house. The young men, or those without families chose spots outside, some near the stream, some in the nearby oak grove.

The vaqueros planned to spend the night and return with the Carrillo's animals the next day, bedding down in the oaks.

Danny was fascinated by all things Indian, and there were boys his age to teach him. He was able to help them with their English. That night he slept with the family of one of the boys, happy to be accepted.

Abby and John Jay took their blankets to a sandy place in a pile of boulders, and were content just to hold each other as they fell into an exhausted sleep.

The morning dawned cold but sunny. The women were up early, preparing food while the men built fire rings of rocks. The youngsters were sent to gather wood for their fires, which was in plentiful supply among the oaks.

There were shouts of farewell as the vaqueros rode out soon after sunup, taking the Carrillo's horses and mules.

Aware of the activity in the camp, Abby was reluctant to leave her warm blankets, or John Jay's warm body. Now that the People were safely here at their new home, their part was finished…except to show her deed to the store owner. Harkness also served as a constable of sorts for the area. That would satisfy any questions as to whether the People had a right to be there.

John Jay pulled Abby closer, mumbling for her to stay. It was a pleasure just to snuggle, too aware of others nearby for more than that.

Only too happy to comply, Abby planted little kisses on his bare throat. "Don't you think we should get up?" she asked, but her actions told him she wasn't any more ready than he was.

They'd slept in their clothes, too cold to take off more than their boots.

"Ummm, maybe later. You feel too good, too warm," he murmured. "It's going to be cold when we get up."

They were still drowsing when they became aware of loud voices coming from the camp. Calls of greeting, high pitched shouts of children.

That noise forced Abby and John Jay to get up, pull on their boots and try to straighten their clothes. They pulled on their mackinaws for warmth and started toward the camp, their mouth falling open to see a stream of Indian families arriving from the south with burros laden with building materials for ewas.

Word had spread about the plight of the People, and other Kumeyaay villagers in the area gathered what they could and had come to help.

Over the next few hours, more Kumeyaay families arrived with everything needed to start a new village. There was laughter and singing and work, as the best area for the village was discussed and mapped out, whose ewa went where. What would have taken months of gathering the necessary items was accomplished in a single day.

The women prepared food while the men worked, spirits were high. Fresh deer meat was brought in as well as quail and rabbit. There would be much feasting.

Abby and John Jay were only in the way, so Danny helped them saddle their horses, and they said their goodbyes.

As they were riding toward Harkness's store, Abby, John Jay and Danny passed several wagon loads of area settlers heading for the People's camp. Wagons laden with anything they could spare to help out.

It did Abby's heart good to know her People were being accepted. For that she thanked Mr. Harkness, who had spread the word.

"I had to do something," he said when they entered his store. "Yesterday when I saw how little they had, I told a few people, and somehow word spread far and wide. I also told some of the local Indians who came to the store."

"I'm happy to see them accepted," Abby said. "After the terrible blows they've had recently this will give them new life."

"And them speaking English will be a big help to me with the locals who don't," Harkness said.

"I know they'll be glad to help," Abby said. "These are peaceable people. They won't give you any trouble."

Abby showed Harkness the deed to the land to prove her right to let the People stay there. It would stop any questions that might arise for him to say he had seen the proof.

"This has been a peaceable area so far," Harkness said. "You can tell that by the fact the white folks have gone to welcome the Indians. Even though they don't have much themselves, they're willing to share."

"There's going to be one big party down there today," John Jay said. "Too bad we have to head back to the Carrillo Rancho. Any time you need to get in touch with us, the Carrillo's will know where we are."

"Good to know," Harkness said, handing the deed back to Abby.

"I bought a rancho up by Palomar," John Jay said, "And eventually we'll be moving there."

"Oh, the old Noriega place?"

"Yes, he's finally going to retire."

"I've heard he has a nice spread there."

"Lots of green hills for grazing cattle. The house can stand a little work though," John Jay said.

"We'll be coming to visit our Indian friends from time to time," Abby said. "And I want to set up an account for them. They don't need much at first, maybe some knives and cooking utensils. Everything they had was trampled into dust."

"A crying shame. Too bad there's no legal recourse. The Indians lived in this land for hundreds of years without knowing about such things as deeds or legal rights, and now any white man can take their land." Harkness said.

"At least they're safe for now," Abby said.

"Any idea what you'd do with the land then?" Harkness asked.

Abby shook her head. "Since I have no idea how long it will take, I won't be making any plans."

Harkness saw Danny eyeing the candy and handed him a lollipop. They boy's eyes grew large at the offered treat and looked to Abby to see if it was okay. She nodded and it was all he could do not to snatch it and run.

She and Harkness set up an account so her People could buy some of the things they needed. She'd told Wahss and Chico about it before they left the camp.

"I'll check in with you from time to time," she said. "To see if you need more."

Harkness nodded, and they said their good-byes as the three mounted their horses and turned toward the rancho.

It was evening before they reached there, and though they missed dinner, Vicenta and Maria were more than happy to warm food for the travelers.

Danny was almost falling asleep in his chair, and was soon hustled off to sleep with one of Vicenta's sons.

Ramon drew John Jay off to his study to smoke cigars and sip brandy while they exchanged news.

The word from the South was not good. Lines were being drawn, states deciding whether or not to form their own union. Already they were putting up names for their president. A few Californians originally from the southern states, were quietly leaving to join the coming fray. Though the military was trying to stop them, they couldn't stop them all.

"So Chiquita," Vicenta said when she and Abby were alone in the kitchen. "Tell me about that hombre in there. I see the look in your eyes...the look I never saw for Cassidy."

Abby blushed. "I can't help it. I love him. We've talked about living on this new rancho of his, with Danny. Being a family."

Vicenta patted Abby's arm, a big smile lighting her face. "I think perhaps it is time for another wedding."

Abby's smile faltered at the memories of her first wedding. "It... seems so soon."

"It's been almost a year," Vicenta insisted, "And in this land we can't always abide by the old ways. There are no laws that say you must wait. Even the good Fathers don't insist."

Abby's smile was full of relief. "I don't want to wait. It seems as if I've been waiting for him for years."

By the next day, Abby and John Jay realized they'd lost all control of the situation. Once Vicenta set her mind to something no one dared interfere. After the initial shock that he was about to become a married man, John Jay put up with the ribbing from Ramon and some of the vaqueros. He let Ramon find suitable clothes for him and was swept up in the preparations.

Word of mouth spread the invitations, and the Father was more than ready to perform a second wedding for the beautiful redhaired woman who had been through so much in her young life.

John Jay took Danny for a walk into the apple orchard where they could be alone, and hopefully find the perfect apple that had been missed by the pickers.

"I reckon you've seen all the activity since we got back," John Jay said, biting into the fruit, juice dripping down his chin.

Danny seemed uncertain about what was coming but hid it by pretending to search for just the right apple. "Luis said there's going to be a wedding."

"That's right. Next week Abby and me are getting hitched. I've bought a ranch at the Palomar, the pigeon roost, and we're going to live there, be ranchers. We want you to come with us so we can be a family."

Danny looked up at John Jay as if he couldn't believe his ears. "You want to be a family with me?" Tears glistened in his eyes.

"Yep, unless you've made other plans."

"Gosh, no!" Unable to contain himself Danny threw his arms around John Jay's waist, hugging him hard. "A family!"

"This is going to be new to Abby and me too. So we all have some getting used to," John Jay said, his eyes welling with moisture as he hugged the boy to him.

"I'll be good! I'll do anything..."

"Hey, partner, just be yourself. We'll all be working together to build a nice spread. The week after next we'll be moving out there, the three of us, plus Ramon is going to loan us a few vaqueros to help out. The place needs some work, and some of Senor Noriega's vaqueros will be staying on."

"Can I be a cowboy?" Danny almost shouted.

"Don't see why not. There'll be vaqueros to teach you, and I'll have some learning to do too. I know a lot about horses, but cows and sheep are something different."

The week seemed to fly by. John Jay was able to buy supplies at the Warner Ranch store, things they would take to Palomar. Plus he needed a wagon to transport everything, finding one at the stage station, and two strong stage horses that were ready to retire from the demanding work of pulling a stagecoach. A wagon would be easier work for them.

There was talk that the Butterfield mail would soon be suspended through the South, and a more northern route was being considered.

45

A bby drew the kitchen curtains aside and looked out into the back yard. John Jay and Danny were practicing their roping on a saw horse with the skull of a bull attached.

Normally the sight of the two together would have made her smile, but she'd had a dream last night and she was worried. She'd long ago learned to pay attention to the dreams that came like visions, warning her of events to come. Her hand automatically went to the growing bump at her waist, as if caressing the growing babe nestled there.

Her concern wasn't for the child, but for events that were drawing John Jay away from their ranch near Palomar, a ranch they had named Eagles Rest, for the nesting golden eagles in the hills nearby.

Tomorrow they would be traveling to the Carrillo Rancho, and the two families would then travel together to Los Angeles to an important meeting of many of the ranchers and some sutlers, whose goods would be needed by the Union Army at their forts in Arizona, New Mexico and Texas.

Danny would stay with the Carrillo children, where he was always welcomed and included in either the work or play.

She knew John Jay would be going with the first wave of cattle, along with other ranchers and their stock, and some of the vaqueros. The cattle in the southern part of California were in desperate trouble because of the four year drought. They were dying from lack of grass. Hay crops failed for lack of rain. The cattle drive would save those animals still strong enough to make the long, difficult trek.

In her dream there had been much hardship, much danger.

Indian attacks were frequent as they took advantage of the white man's preoccupation with the war. Word had come that most of the settlers in southern Arizona had fled to Tucson or Phoenix because the army was spread too thin to protect them.

Though she wanted to beg John Jay not to go, she knew it would do no good. He felt he had a duty to the Union, and he would be deemed a coward if he chose to remain behind.

The meeting in Los Angeles was to plan the cattle drive. A large herd crossing a land of little water or graze required careful planning if they expected their animals to survive.

With a clatter of boots in the back porch, John Jay and Danny came in, laughing and shoving as they washed up for breakfast.

"Okay you two," Abby teased. "No fighting. There's enough for all of us."

"I'm hungrier than a one-eyed grizzly bear," Danny announced taking his chair.

"I'm hungrier than a grizzly bear in a snow storm!" John Jay wasn't about to be out done.

Abby smiled as she brought platters of bacon, scrambled eggs, fried potatoes and biscuits to the table. They could hardly contain themselves long enough to mumble a quick grace, before Danny was reaching for the closest platter.

John Jay grinned at his wife, then his gaze lowered to her expanding waist line. "We got to save enough for our mother-to-be," he told Danny, but he too was reaching for the platter Danny passed to him.

Abby's smile was full of satisfaction. "He's already moving," she said as she took her place at the opposite end of the table from John Jay.

"He?" Danny asked, with a mouth full of bacon. "How can you know it's going to be a boy?"

"I just know," she said, dishing her plate when John Jay handed it to her. She didn't tell them about the dream she'd had several months ago. One that told her there was going to be a baby; a son.

"How long will you be in Los Angeles?" Danny asked.

"A couple of days," John Jay said. "The meeting is on Friday, and we'll probably be back on Saturday."

Danny frowned as he remembered his life in the city. "Look out for Drayton," he cautioned. "He looks like a businessman, but he's really a snake."

"I don't think he'll cause any trouble with all the ranchers in town, but I'll keep a close eye on our mother-to-be."

Danny still scowled as he ate, knowing Drayton wasn't to be trusted. But, with Abby beginning to show she was with child, Drayton would lose interest.

Later, when John Jay and Danny had gone off to do their chores, Abby looked out the kitchen window as she did the dishes. It was a sight that never failed to fill her with pride.

In the year she and John Jay had been here, with the help of several Indian ranch hands, the place had thrived. The fruit trees were young yet, but would soon bear fruit. Her garden supplied her with all the fresh vegetables they needed. The chickens were let out to forage during the day, but locked up at night since coyotes were frequent nighttime visitors.

Their small herd of sheep was just large enough and belligerent enough that the coyotes left them alone. Their cattle roamed the hills around the valley, searching out any bit of forage they could find since even their fields of oats and barley had wilted without rain. If the cattle drive didn't begin soon, they would lose most of their herd.

Oak trees filled the valley, and Abby had never lost her taste for acorn mush, and could gather all the plants she needed for her medicines and for making baskets.

Perhaps the only ones to prosper from the drought were the Indians in the surrounding hills. They didn't need to steal a cow. If they asked the rancher, often times they were given one dying of starvation. Few ranchers begrudged the local Indians that boon. Deer had moved to higher ground where there was more grass. So game was scarce.

Where once the local tribes had roamed far and wide, the ranchers and settlers had taken much of their former lands. Though the Indian agents promised much, their treaties had to be ratified by the U. S. Congress, who merely shelved the requests, unable to make a decision.

Not realizing this, the Indians waited for the promised supplies and reservation land that never materialized. They had no voice. No one listened.

Abby knew all this from meeting with the other ranchers in the area, and was looking forward to the trip to Los Angeles. She missed the company of other women.

The next morning, just after sunrise, they left Eagles Rest in a buckboard that held their luggage, some canned goods for the Carrillo's, and joined other ranchers along the road. The Conroys, Zeb and Imelda had two children, a boy and a girl, who would also be staying at the Carrillo Rancho while the adults traveled together to Los Angeles.

Groups were safer in an area that still had occasional raids by renegade Indians, as well as a few Mexican banditos who were known to attack lone travelers.

Overhead, a lone golden eagle circled, as if pacing them. Its lazy circles telling Abby all was well.

Los Angeles was blanketed by a light layer of fog when the dusty caravan of ranchers reached the Bella Union Hotel. Several young men came to help with luggage, while others took the wagons to the stable next door.

As John Jay helped Abby down, she was startled to see Alex watching her with an open mouth. Then he turned and ran for the Continental Hotel and Everett Drayton.

"Well, that didn't take long," Abby said with a rueful grin as they entered the hotel.

"We knew it was inevitable," John Jay said, not really concerned about Drayton. "Though I do wish I could give him a good thumping."

"Me too."

The next morning, all the ranchers ate breakfast in the hotel dining room, then the men gathered in a meeting room for a strategy session. Some of the wives left to do some shopping but Abby begged off, staying to finish her tea. Sometimes she still felt nauseous in the mornings and today wanted to go back to her room to lie down.

She wasn't really surprised when Everett Drayton slid into the chair across from her, placing his hat on the table. He was immaculately dressed in a suit, dark hair slicked back, looking like a prosperous business man.

"Miss Abby," he said with one of his most charming smiles. "You're a sight for sore eyes. Beautiful as ever."

"Drayton," she acknowledged coldly.

"I heard you and John Jay Butterfield got hitched. What brings you to town?"

"The ranchers are having a meeting," she answered, loathe to give him any information.

"I also heard some other stories," he went on, his charming façade slipping a little. "About you and the Indians."

"Oh? That sounds interesting. Tell me about it." She purposely egged him on.

"That you lived with them for years, and that you maybe weren't so innocent when you married Cassidy." His smirk had a cruel edge to it. "Oh, and you know, I still have some back wages for you. You left town so abruptly. Maybe you'd like to come back to the hotel to collect it."

Abby's smile had a dangerous edge. "Go with you, Drayton? I made that mistake once."

"I could still make you a queen. Men would flock to Los Angeles to see the woman raised by Indians."

"My life with the Indians taught me many things," her voice was deadly quiet. "I was a very good hunter with a bow and arrow. And used a sharp knife to skin a deer. I knew how to handle men who thought Indian women were fair game. I am also a medicine woman who knows about medicines and poisons." She calmly sipped her tea, pleased to see Drayton's look change to a frown.

She turned slightly in her chair and raised her skirt just enough to show the knife strapped to her leg, just above her high button shoes.

Drayton's eyes widened and she quickly dropped her skirt again.

"If you had succeeded with your plan that evening," she told him. "I would have slit your throat the next day."

Drayton's mouth fell open, and as Abby stood up his gaze dropped to her rounded stomach.

"In fact, Mr. Drayton, if you ever bother me again, I will be very tempted to use my knife…where it will do the most good." Her gaze lowered meaningfully to the front of his trousers.

Drayton snatched his hat off the table and stormed out of the room. Abby looked up to see John Jay watching from the doorway as Drayton brushed past him, he was laughing.

"I thought you wanted to thump him," she said laughing.

"Not after the verbal thumping you gave him," he said as they started up the stairs to their room.

Once inside, John Jay cupped her face gently and pressed his lips to hers. "I'm very proud of my warrior wife."

Abby met his kiss, her heart welling with love for this man. "You're missing your meeting."

"They won't get down to making plans until after they talk politics. I'm not missing much. You plan to rest for a while?" She nodded. "Okay." He kissed her again, with more feeling, as if he wanted to stay. Then slowly he drew back, knowing this was not the time. "I'll see you at lunch time."

Abby smiled happily, enjoying his kisses, but knowing he had other obligations.

Reluctantly he left to rejoin his meeting, grinning as he remembered Abby's encounter with Drayton. He'd only heard the last part, but it was enough to know the man wouldn't be bothering his wife again.

He was still grinning when he reached the hallway at the rear of the first floor, but was surprised when the back door to the alley opened and two soldiers in Union uniforms came in.

He immediately recognized Colonel James Carlton, leader of the Union forces in California. They'd met once before in St Joseph, Missouri, in the early days of the Butterfield Mail.

John Jay was surprised to see him here as the Colonel greeted him with a handshake. "Butterfield, I heard you'd settled out here. I'm glad you're going to be part of this."

"Colonel, good to see you." He opened the door for the two men.

All talk in the room fell silent when the two soldiers entered, followed by John Jay. It was obvious they hadn't been expected.

"Judge Hayes," John Jay said to the man who had been guiding the meeting. "This is Colonel Carlton, in charge of the California Regiment of Southwest Operations."

The two shook hands.

"And this is Lt. Johnson," the Colonel said. "I hope you'll excuse our barging into your meeting, but when I heard about it I knew it was an opportunity for me to ask for your help."

Judge Hayes nodded. "We welcome your presence, and any news you bring. I yield the floor to you."

Both Judge Hayes and John Jay took seats, as did the lieutenant. Colonel Carlton stood tall and straight, a man with piercing blue eyes and a no nonsense air.

"Gentlemen, your help is sorely needed. Your plans to aid the Union cause couldn't come at a better time." He paused as his gaze swept over his silent audience. "The latest news is that a group of Rebel Texans are marching toward California. They've attacked two of our forts, taken prisoners, destroyed crops and supplies so that any Union army chasing them won't find food for themselves or their animals."

Not a sound could be heard in the room as the Colonel went on. "Their plan is to take Arizona, then march all the way to the Pacific Ocean. Once they control shipping in California, they expect the Southern sympathizers here will rally to join them. Already, at the Yuma Crossing we've stopped a number of them heading east to join the Rebels."

Again he paused, finding his audience hanging on his words. "We desperately need the beef and the supplies you'll be sending. I'll be sending 1500 troops to Arizona to engage the enemy, hopefully before they reach Tucson. We have our own supplies for the march, so you have only to worry about your own men and your cattle."

"The plan is to leave Warner's in one week. My force will be split in half over a two day period so we won't deplete the meager water and graze along the way. Thanks to the Butterfield Overland Mail, there are wells in the desert for your stock."

His hard gaze swept the room as there was a brief flow of conversation among the men. Then Judge Hayes stood up.

"I think I can speak for all of us when I say we will welcome the company of the army as we drive our herds across the desert. We understand the Indians have become especially troublesome of late."

"That's true," the Colonel said. "With our forces engaged in our own war, they've become fiercer in their raids. A number of settlers in the area have been killed and their women and children taken as captives. The rest are abandoning their holdings because we can't protect them."

John Jay stood up. "The first herd will be at Warner on the 15th," he said, "And we welcome the help of any soldiers who can herd cattle. The second wave will come the following day."

There were agreeing comments all around the room.

"Thank you, gentlemen, I'll leave you to your plans. Our supply wagons will move out a day early with a small detachment. But the first group of soldiers will leave on the 15th. The rest, the next day to help protect your herd and your supplies."

The Colonel and his aide left, and immediately the ranchers and hostlers began making plans for who would arrive on which days. Those with the greatest distance to travel with their herds would form the second wave.

As the men filed from the room, John Jay saw John Rains in conversation with Overmeyer. Both were known Southern sympathizers, but they were also businessmen who first and foremost wanted to make money on the war.

He was surprised to see Jacob Bristol at the back of the room, watching him, and nervously clutching his hat. As the room emptied, Jacob approached John Jay, no longer looking like Abby's blustering uncle. "Butterfield," he greeted nervously. "I have to do my part. I have lots of hay, and a small herd of cows to offer."

"We'll take all the help we can get," John Jay said to put him at ease. 'Do you need help moving them?"

"No, I have neighbors who will have cattle too, we have enough help…but thanks for the offer…Uh, my niece?" he asked awkwardly.

"She's upstairs resting. Do you want to see her?"

"No, no, I just want to know she's okay." His hands were nervously clutching his hat, almost crushing it.

"Abby is fine. She's going to be a mother, you know. You'll be a Great Uncle."

Jacob smiled, the first genuine emotion John Jay had seen. "I'll be danged! A little one. Just tell her I said hello, and...and..." he couldn't go on.

"I'll tell her."

"Then maybe I'll see you on the drive, though I'll be on the second wave." Jacob was looking relieved as he strode from the room.

John Jay headed toward the lobby of the hotel surprised to see Abby waiting for him.

"Was that Uncle Jacob?" she asked, sounding surprised.

"Yes, he's going to be joining the drive."

Abby frowned. "With his fire and brimstone act?"

"No, I didn't see any of that. I think he's changed since that scene at his ranch."

"That I'd have to see to believe," she said as they started toward the dining room. "And I see Overmeyer is here too."

"Yep, where did you see him?"

"From our window upstairs. He and John Rains were in deep conversation out front. The boy from the stable brought his horse and he was saying something about warning someone."

"Oh, Lordy. Wait for me. I'll be right back."

He left Abby open mouthed as he ran for the back door, looking frantically for Colonel Carlton. He saw him mounted on his horse talking to Judge Hayes.

Carlton saw John Jay's urgency. "What's happened?"

"A couple of men at the meeting are known Southern sympathizers. My wife saw one of them riding off, saying he was going to 'warn them'. I'm assuming warn the Rebels of your coming."

"Think he'll head straight for Arizona?" the Colonel asked.

"I doubt it. He's not strong enough for that. I expect he'll go to his ranch and send a couple of his men."

"What's his name?" John Jay told him. "Hopefully we'll be able to head them off at Warner's. Thanks for the warning." The two soldiers turned their horses and headed out of town at a gallop.

"Good work, Butterfield," the Judge said as they went their separate ways.

When John Jay got to the dining room, Abby was sitting with Vicenta and Ramon, with an extra chair for him. Across the room was John and Merced Rains who sat with other families who'd come for the meeting. He noticed Rains couldn't meet his eyes, and knew he was right about the plan to warn the Texas Rebels.

46

John Jay had never been part of a cattle drive, but quickly got the hang of keeping the herd moving. He and his neighbors were fortunate to find enough experienced hands to teach them the ropes. But nothing prepared him for the dust kicked up by the herd, and the noise of cattle bawling, protesting the march.

The wagons had moved out first with barrels of water, hay and supplies, following the first wave of soldiers. Other soldiers stayed with the herd, and others followed behind.

Both Ramon Carrillo and John Rains had contributed most of their herds and they too were helping with the drive, though, they like John Jay had little experience as drovers.

John Jay's horse, a large roan gelding named Ranger, was cow-smart and quick to spot any potential stray which taught him as much as the experienced drovers.

As the herd made its way down the San Felipe Valley, the cows could smell the water ahead. Though the San Felipe creek flowed along with them, its water level was very low. Further along, the creek flowed into a marshy area with heavy growth of cattails and shaded by numerous cottonwood trees. This was the scent that drew the thirsty cattle.

Though there was still quite a bit of daylight left by the time they reached the marsh, their trail boss, Dusty Riggens, said they'd make camp here.

Already the cows had waded into the marsh, drinking and eating any water plants. Getting them moving again would have been impossible. Besides, the animals would need all the graze they could find, there'd be little enough for them on the desert.

The supply wagons had anticipated this location for their first camp and were already set up when the herd arrived. The scent of coffee and roasting beef and beans had the drovers eagerly turning their horses into the ramada.

The soldiers made their own camp nearby, and set up guards around the herd. Though the likelihood of Indians this close to the ranches wasn't expected, they couldn't let down their guard.

John Jay pulled off his boots and stockings, rolled up his pant legs and stripped off his shirt, eager to wade into a sandy area upstream from the cattle. With a towel, he tried to remove the sweat and trail dust, relishing the cool water. He hadn't realized how much dust the herd would raise and was glad for the bandana he used to cover his nose and mouth.

His eyes felt gritty as he splashed his face and chest. Around him, other drovers were doing the same. Fort Yuma was a long way from here, and they would only see water like this one more time at Seven Springs, and, if they were fortunate, at the Carrizo Gorge.

After San Felipe, the days blended into one another. Up at Dawn, a quick breakfast, then trying to start the reluctant herd moving again.

"I never wanted to be a cowboy," Ramon Carrillo groused as he and John Jay rode side by side on the left side of the herd. The breeze was blowing the dust to the other side.

"Ranchero, yes. Cowboy, no. Too dirty."

"I'll have to agree with you there," John Jay said. "I don't think I'll ever get all this dust off me."

"When we get to Fort Yuma, I will find their biggest bath tub and soak for a week."

John Jay laughed. "Sounds like a good plan, but for me, the Colorado River just might be big enough to get me clean."

As the herd moved eastward, sometimes they passed families of Indians who stood out of the way, watching. They appeared healthy and carried their food with them. Sometimes a few of the young boys would run along beside the cows, pretending to be cowboys, drawing laughs from the drovers.

So far, they hadn't lost any cows. At Seven Springs the cattle quickly spread out over the various springs, and were able to find a lot of browse in the surrounding mesquite and other brush.

The former stage station, that had once been Abby's home, had a small store set up so they could replenish any supplies that were getting low. John Jay joined Ramon at the cross that marked James Cassidy's resting place.

With their hats off, they stood in silence. A lot of memories stirred by thoughts of a friend gone too soon. But John Jay could only think that if Cassidy hadn't been killed, he wouldn't be married to the wonderful woman he'd loved from the first time he saw her...here at the stage station.

All of the springs had been muddied by the cattle, but fortunately there was a pump next to the store that the drovers used to clean up before sitting down to a meal of beef stew, biscuits and strong coffee.

Though they would have liked to give the herd an extra day at the springs and the lush growth surrounding them, they were all too aware of the herd following a day behind.

Again, at night, the soldiers posted sentries to keep an eye out for marauding Indians, and trail boss Riggens also posted guards on the cattle that were roaming out of sight in the tall brush. John Jay took a shift from midnight to four in the morning.

A full moon turned the desert a dusty silver. Some of the cows rested, others moved restlessly, often spooked by sudden movements of small nocturnal animals. He saw several coyotes wander through, looking for smaller prey, cows were too strong and healthy for them.

A plaintive song drifted on the night breeze as one of the drovers soothed the herd. The peacefulness of the night made John Jay smile. This might not be such a bad life, if one had no family ties. As it was, he wished he had Abby's warm body to snuggle up to when he was ready for sleep. Wishing he hadn't had to leave her with their child growing in her belly, wondering how she and Danny were managing at the Carrillo Rancho, and if he'd be home in time for the birth of his son.

In the morning, it took a long time to round up the cattle that had roamed all through the heavy growth around the springs. As they moved out, many of the steers objected with loud bellows, and it took drovers lashing them on their flanks with ropes to get them moving.

With only a few hours' sleep, John Jay sometimes dozed in his saddle as they moved across a barren stretch of desert.

About mid-day they passed a party of wagons with settlers seeking a less dangerous area to farm, driven out by hostile Indians. Also with them was a small group of Union soldiers, many of them with wounds from encounters with both Indians and Southern sympathizers.

They were glad to hear there was water ahead, and a store for supplies which were exhausted. The nearest doctor would be at Warner's Ranch.

Riggens questioned them about their own party with the wagons of supplies, water and hay, and learned they were waiting for them at Bow Willow, which would be their resting place for the night. They also learned there would not be enough water available to satisfy a thirsty herd, so troughs were set up in anticipation of their arrival, with barrels of water emptied into them.

At one point along the trail John Jay spotted a small group of mounted warriors watching them. Riggens noticed them too.

"Keep your eyes open tonight," Riggens told the drovers as he made his way around the herd. "We'll no doubt have visitors."

Once the herd was watered and fed at Bow Willow, and bedded down for the night, they weren't allowed to roam. The same plaintive voice drifted in the night air, soothing the restless animals.

The drovers ate in shifts and extra guards were posted by the soldiers as well. All horses were kept close and under heavy guard. The nearly full moon helped light the desert, and the warriors weren't seen again. But everyone felt their presence.

Early the next morning, as they moved out, John Jay felt a prickling at the back of his neck, and knew the warriors were still with them. It kept everyone alert.

This time the supply and water wagons moved ahead of the herd, the smell of hay keeping them moving.

Union soldiers rode both in front of the herd and behind.

Later that evening, as the herd was bedded down at Dos Cabezas Spring, the soldiers and drovers were still on high alert. Though there'd been no further sign of Indians, John Jay could feel eyes, watching.

The Dos Cabezas Spring had many arroyos in the area, many places to hide. In one such arroyo, hidden in the shadows as the sun lowered to the horizon, a lone Indian watched the drover's camp.

Night Wolf was certain now that one of the drovers was the man he'd encountered at the Carrillo Rancho. The man he'd learned from the Kumeyaay was now married to the one he called Firehair.

He knew it was dangerous to follow the herd. With all the soldiers present, their only hope was maybe a stray or injured animal left behind. His food consisted of what the desert provided. His companions were urging him to leave. There were too many soldiers. It was too dangerous.

A bird call further up the arroyo caught his attention. It was a signal from Running Deer to come, a sign of urgency.

Silently Night Wolf slipped thru the shadows, following the repeated call. They all gathered around where his companions had discovered faint signs of a camp. "Maybe three, four days old," Running Deer said. "Yaqui."

"How many?" Night Wolf asked in their Yuman language.

"Five, six. Hunting party," Running Deer answered.

They all knew the most difficult part of the cattle drive lay ahead. Little water, little graze. A long stretch of sand dunes made for tough travel. It would take its toll on man and beast.

All Night Wolf knew was that he wanted to stay close to the herd to pick off any strays. There were hungry Indian villages near the big river that could use the meat. But Yaquis were their enemies, and a danger to them as were the soldiers.

47

Abby stepped out of the tent wiping her face with her bloody apron. It was hot inside, and sometimes the stench of blood, gangrene and urine could be overwhelming.

One tent at the Warner Ranch California Regiment Camp was set up as a hospital. The most serious injuries were treated at Fort Yuma, but any soldiers capable of travel were loaded onto wagons, crossing the desert to the camp.

East of Fort Yuma, were the Texas Rebels, so the injured couldn't be sent that way to other Union forts. Some injuries were from engaging Rebels east of Tucson, where a Union fort had been abandoned in the face of the overwhelming enemy forces. And, with their supplies depleted, the Union soldiers had no choice but to flee.

They then had to compete with the local Indians for the meager game and native foods available, which brought clashes between them. Many injuries to the Union soldiers were from arrows, a few from bullets.

The Indians were quick to take advantage of the disarray of the soldiers, and quick to take guns whenever they could, though fortunately they had few sources of ammunition.

Abby had come to Warner's when the officer in charge learned she was a medicine woman. They needed all the help they could get, and experienced nurses were in short supply.

She quickly learned what was expected of her, and had some of the local Indians gathering the plants she needed to make poultices for the wounded. The Union doctor, Thomas Ordway, was skeptical at first, but saw the herbs worked as well or better than the medicines he was in short supply of. Sporadically medical supplies came from Los Angeles, especially needed was morphine for only the most seriously injured.

Abby stood in the shade of the tent unable to escape the moaning and cries of the wounded. Her hand went to her stomach. The baby was especially active today, and the smells stemming from the tent were making her nauseous.

Drawing in a deep breath of fresh air, she was about to go back inside when Isabel Warner appeared and handed her a cup of hot tea. "Come. Sit," she said leading Abby to some chairs in the shade of a large oak tree. "You work too hard. Your baby objects."

"I know," Abby said wearily, sipping the tea. "But it's so difficult to watch the men suffering. They had to travel a long ways just to get here."

"There's only so much you can do," Isabel cautioned with a motherly pat of her hand. "Much is in God's hands." Her gaze shifted from Abby, looking toward the desert where the cattle drive had gone weeks before. "What do you hear from your husband?"

"Only that he is well, as are Ramon and John Rains. Tired. Dirty. And concerned about a party of Indians dogging them. I spoke to one of the soldiers who was escorting the wounded. They passed the herd below Seven Springs, in the heart of the desert. It was going well. They'd only lost a few head to injuries, and some were lost in the tangle of brush around Seven Springs." She gave a sad smile at her memories of the Springs. "The Indians can use the meat, and I'm certain the drovers don't begrudge them."

"Ah, there's too many soldiers with the herd for the Indians to attack," Isabel tried to reassure her. "They are no doubt waiting for strays or injuries."

Abby enjoyed the warmth of the tea, and the quiet of the after-noon siesta time when the ranch became quiet. Most of the military camp here at Warner was far enough away that its hustle and bustle didn't disturb the ranch. Only the hospital was close to the hot springs. Its hot water badly needed by the wounded.

Weeks passed. Word of the cattle drive was sporadic. Abby felt the life moving in her womb, and doubted John Jay would be back in time for the birth. He wanted to be with her, that much she knew, but she had no word, and the nursing was difficult for her with young soldiers so badly injured. Still, she needed to be here where she might get word of her husband.

Sometimes, Vicenta brought Danny, and some of her children to help at Warner's ranch. Though, these days, hardly any wagons crossed the desert. It was too dangerous. Plus, the natural resources had been mostly depleted by the cattle.

Then came the terrible news of an Indian attack that scat-tered the first herd. Wounded soldiers brought back news of the tragic loss of life, both from the stampeding animals and from the Indians. Especially horrifying to the families at Warner's was the loss of both Ramon Carrillo and John Rains. Of John Jay, there was no news. The last anyone had seen of him he was in the middle of the terrified herd trying to stop them.

Further news from the Union army was that a scouting party of five men, sent ahead of the main troops and the herd, was captured by the Texas Rebels near Fort Tucson. They had stopped at a supply store only to find it full of Texans. A stupid move for scouts.

The Texans, however, let most of them go, keeping only the leader for a time, but then releasing him too. Because once they learned of the large force of the California Regiment cutting them off from their intended goal in California, they knew their plan had failed. They had little choice but to retreat the way they had come. But their retreat was over land they had devastated, to prevent Union troops from the East from following them. They hadn't reckoned on facing troops from California. Now, as they turned tail, they were left with little sustenance for them or their animals.

The families at Warner's anxiously awaited further news, hoping against hope the news they heard had been wrong. Other returning troops told them it was Yaqui Indians who wreaked the damage on the first herd, scattering the animals, killing many of the drovers, and confirming the deaths of Ramon and John. Once the cattle and supplies were recovered from the attack by the survivors, they were distributed to any remaining settlers in the area and to the soldiers at Fort Yuma, and when the second wave arrived, they were driven on to New Mexico. Their trail now lay to the north of the devastation caused by the Rebels. There was still no news of John Jay.

The California Regiment, with the second wave of cattle, drove the marauding Yaqui back to Mexico.

Vicenta Carrillo took the news of her husband's death especially hard. This was the second husband she had lost. Her first, Tomas Yorba was older, and had fathered her first four children. They had news from Judge Hayes who traveled from Los Angeles to visit Merced Rains and Vicenta, to help them put their husband's affairs in order. Merced had remained at her Rancho Cucamonga with her children, trying to make sense of the terrible financial tangle her husband had left. And almost immediately John's creditors began demanding payment.

Abby tried to comfort Vicenta and her children, but her own heart was aching. She didn't know if John Jay had survived or not. Her babe was more active now, and she knew it would only be a matter of weeks before it came into the world.

As the weeks dragged by, she clung to her hope that he had somehow survived. But soon, with no more wounded arriving she was losing hope. Most of the injured soldiers had been moved to San Diego. With no more need of her assistance at Warner, she returned to the Carrillo Rancho to help Vicenta try to cope with the large property without Ramon.

Danny tried to help, but seemed confused by the drastic changes in his world, and the absence of John Jay. He didn't know how to comfort Abby, when he could find no comfort for himself. Instead, he trailed after Jose, who tried to fill his step-father's shoes running the ranch.

It was on an early, cold October morning that Abby had been trying to sleep. The babe unusually active. Dozing fitfully she dreamed of John Jay, dreaming he was back, that he needed her. Throwing back her blankets she grabbed up her warm robe and ran out into the early morning air. Dawn was barely touching the horizon with streaks of red and gold as she ran for the spring at the edge of the yard as fast as the burden of her belly would allow. Her heart was pounding frantically as she tried to peer through the mist.

And, suddenly he was there, stepping forward, slightly bent from his wound, his arms opening to welcome her. Crying, laughing, she clutched him as tightly as her swollen stomach would permit. Then she began to examine him to see how badly he was hurt.

A movement in the mist took her attention. Night Wolf stood with the horses, watching the reunion with a sad expression. She knew then that he had rescued her injured husband to return him to her. As she started toward him to thank him, he leapt on his horse and went thundering into the mist.

"Thank you!" she called, not knowing if he heard. Then she was clutching John Jay, again crying and laughing that he was safe.

"I'm okay," he whispered. "But Ramon...and John..."

"We heard," she said. "Vicenta is devastated. The children feel lost but are trying to keep the rancho running...young as they are... and Danny is helping."

"As we came across the desert, Night Wolf heard you were here now after helping with the wounded at Warner's. He saved my life when the Yaqui attacked the herd." He clutched her tightly to him, as tightly as her large stomach would allow. "The cattle were stampeded. I was shot and would have died under the hooves, but Night Wolf fought his way through the herd and pulled me up onto his horse. It was total chaos."

John Jay's eyes were closed against the bitter memories. "He took me into the hills, found a loose horse for me, and saw to my wound. Then he brought me back across the desert. We were cut off from everyone, hiding, using the Indian trails."

"Why did he go?" she asked. "He has to be tired and hungry."

"I think you know why. He loves you, even though he knows you can never be together. He wants you to be happy."

Tears rolled down her cheeks as she clutched her husband to her. "I...need to thank him!"

"It's not necessary," John Jay said, grimacing as his strength began to fail. "He knows."

Unable to let him go, Abby was suddenly doubled over by a contraction so strong she cried out in pain and clutched her stomach.

Confused, John Jay held her, as with a sudden gush her water broke.

"The baby!" she gasped. "He's coming."

A sudden movement from the house brought Jose, Vicenta's oldest with a rifle, and behind him one of the younger boys. He sized up the situation with a glance.

"Paco, wake mama, tell her Senor Butterfield is back and the baby is coming," Jose ordered.

With Abby doubled in pain the two men helped her inside to her bedroom. Already Vicenta was there, placing birthing sheets and towels on the bed where Abby gratefully sank down.

"He waited for you," Abby said, clutching John Jay's hand. "But... you're hurt. Vicenta..."

"Don't worry, piquena, we will see to him too."

"Come, Senor," Jose said as he supported John Jay who was weakening fast. "This is a time for the women. I will see to your wound. What happened?"

"I was shot…in the side…glanced off a couple of ribs, I think." He let the younger man support him to his room across the hall.

"I learned much from your medicine woman, I will see to your wound. Paco, bring me the medicine box." The boy had been trailing behind, eager to help, and ran for the medical supplies.

Awakened by the noise, Danny sat next to John Jay's bed gripping his hand, so happy to have him back he chattered on about the news as Jose cleaned and dressed the wound.

Dawn found John Jay sleeping fitfully in Jose's bed, too worried about Abby to let go completely. Danny asleep beside him. The muffled cries of Abby in her labor made him want to rush to her side, but knew the women would only run him off.

Vicenta and Maria stayed with Abby. After birthing so many children herself, Vicenta knew what to do. And, not long after sunrise, the cries of a new life filled the hacienda. John Daniel Butterfield had arrived.

Nothing could have kept John Jay from Abby's side as he rushed across the hall, followed by Danny. Vicenta handed him his red-faced infant son, and once he was assured Abby had finally drifted off to sleep, he began walking the hall, Danny at his side. The boy seemed awed by this tiny being who was his brother.

With the help of one of Abby's medicine potions which Jose had prepared for him, the pain of his wound was dulled. It was already weeks old and slowly healing from Night Wolf's tending.

The birth seemed to lift the spirits of the Carrillo family who were still mourning the loss of Ramon. A second visit from Judge Hayes brought news of Merced Rains, who had hastily married a man she hardly knew but whom the Judge assured her was a good man to help her save her rancho. It was the only way she could hold the creditors away.

Vicenta however was able to have property of her own, some from her first husband, and with the help of Jose, her oldest son, she was able to handle the rancho. She and her children were spared the plight of so many widows.

John Jay was vastly relieved to hear that the Texas Rebels had fled back the way they had come when they learned the California Regiment was cutting them off from their goal.

They would not secure California for the Southern cause.

But, in other parts of the country, fierce battles cost both sides a staggering number of casualties. The South had elected their own president and were determined to maintain their right to hold slaves.

Secretly, Abby was thankful for John Jay's wound. Otherwise she knew he would feel honor bound to join the Union cause as his brother Daniel had.

As soon as Abby was able to travel, she was eager to get back to her own home. With John Jay holding the reins, little Jay in her arms, and Danny sprawled in the back on top of their supplies, they headed for their Eagle's Nest Rancho.

Overhead, a pair of golden eagles seemed to keep pace, wheeling gracefully on the air currents, letting them know all was well.

EPILOGUE

As the Butterfield family settled into life at the Eagles Nest Ranch, the climate of California was changing. Due to the prolonged drought, the great cattle herds had mostly disappeared. In their place vast orchards were planted with citrus, peaches, plums, cherries, as well as vineyards of grapes for table and for wine. Wells were dug to tap into the underground aquifers.

The Eagles Nest changed with the times, the valley was filled with orchards and vineyards, as well as horses, sheep, and a small herd of cattle. The Butterfields prospered.

News of the Civil War came from people passing through on the nearby well-traveled trail. In November of 1864, Lincoln was reelected President. Soon after his second inauguration, an amendment to the constitution was submitted to the states for ratification, abolishing slavery. But not long after came word of his assassination at Ford's Theater. In addition to the terrible news, Southern resistance was already crumbling with the surrender of Robert E. Lee.

The surrender of Major General Richard Taylor ended resistance in Mississippi. Major Jefferson Davis was captured. And when General E. Kirby Smith surrendered, organized resistance ended.

The war was over, but with horrendous loss of life.

John Jay waited until the war was over to plan a trip home to Utica, New York to introduce his new family to his parents. John

Senior was still actively involved in his many business ventures. Brother Daniel was home safe from the War, where he is credited with writing Taps, the mournful bugle that to this day sounds at military funerals.

Major General Daniel Butterfield of the Army of the Potomac, with the help of the company bugler, changed the notes of the usual days end bugle call, signaling lights out for the barracks. It was then that the new version began to be played at military funerals and words were added:

> Day is done, gone the sun
> From the lake, from the hills,
> from the sky. All is well,
> safely rest, God is nigh.

Back home on the ranch, Abby was showing signs of a second child as she worked her vegetable garden on a warm spring morning. A sharp cry from above her drew her gaze to the large male golden eagle soaring along the updraft from the nearby hills. His call brought a second eagle up from a rocky draw, rising swiftly on the thermals.

As she rose toward her mate, the male folded his wings and plummeted. Abby watched in wonder as the female rolled onto her back, talons thrusting upwards. The male locked his talons with hers and together they began to spiral downward. Around and around they twirled, losing altitude in their mating dance. Finally they broke apart then sailed together toward their nesting site.

To Abby it was a sign that all was well in their valley.

ABOUT THE AUTHOR

Marian Sepulveda's writing career began in the seventh grade, in the late 1940s, when western movies were all the rage. Her favorite character, Nickie Dale, was an expert horseback rider who could yodel with the best of them. Marian was a mediocre rider, although she did yodel in a talent contest once.

Marian's interests expanded into science fiction when it became popular in the early years of television: Space Patrol, Captain Video, Tom Corbett Space Cadet. Throughout her childhood she continued to write stories in both genres. Even as an adult working for General Telephone Company she never stopped writing. At that point romance pocket books were popular. And she wrote many, unpublished.

Marian always had a love of early California history and animals. Her pets ranged from the usual cats and dogs to a ferret, a bobcat, gopher snake, and various birds, from parakeets to parrots. In early 1970s she moved to the desert in the Coachella Valley of Southern California. There she met the man who became her husband, Steve Sepulveda. She became fascinated by the history of his ancestors, who migrated from Sepulveda, Spain, to Mexico, and then California. They arrived at the Spanish presidio of San Diego in 1781.

Marian and Steve shared many traveling adventures, preferring the wild places outdoors, four-wheeling into remote canyons. On a trip to Tombstone, Arizona, they met the artist Marjorie Reed, whose life work was to paint every stage stop of the Butterfield Overland Mail. Marjorie generously gave the couple five books she had published of her paintings. And that began Marian's fascination with Butterfield history.

Years later, while Marian and Steve were visiting a remote restored stage station in Anza-Borrego, they witnessed the amazing ritual of golden eagles in courtship flight. The eagles locked talons and spiraled downward on air currents, until they finally broke apart and sailed out of sight together. Both that ritual and the Butterfield stage history appear in this story.

In the early 1990s, after Marian retired from the phone company, she and Steve became docents at the Living Desert Zoo and Botanical Gardens in Palm Desert. The zoo's outdoor habitat was home to burrowing owls, American kestrels (the smallest falcon, also known as the "sparrow hawk"), a raven, barn owl, a great horned owl, and a Harris hawk, to name a few. Her love of animals led her to animal handler's training, allowing her to introduce zoo residents personally to zoo visitors. She often held snakes, desert tortoises, chuckwallas, tarantulas, and birds of prey, which were her special interest.

Though the zoo had golden eagles, these were injured birds which were not releasable, except for one that was featured in wildlife programs. Olympia was a magnificent bird with a seven-foot wingspan. Animal shows demonstrated only natural behaviors--no parrots riding bicycles or bobcats jumping through hoops. When Olympia flew across the amphitheater and perched, the audience gasped at her majestic beauty.

All during these years Marian was writing in her spare time, learning her craft. "Where Eagles Dance" was in its infancy. Marian and Steve continued their trips into the wild places, finding traces of the Southern Emigrant Trail--also known as the Gila Trail, the Kearny Trail, and the Butterfield Stage Trail. This historic trail was used by the wagon trains and stagecoaches. They gathered any research materials they could find.

Marian lost Steve to Alzheimer's in 2003, and she lost her desire to write. She continued to work at The Living Desert. She wanted to be outdoors, hiking and enjoying the many desert gardens. And so life went on as the animals and nature sustained her. Then years later, a friend challenged her to embrace her muse. So Marian picked up the unfinished manuscript of "Where Eagles Dance" and went back to work. This was a story that insisted on being told. And now it's an e-book on Amazon.com, with a print version coming out soon.

Marian's next book will draw on her experiences at The Living Desert, with animals as characters in a story of intrigue and romance. You'll meet two adorable mountain lion kittens and a raven, among others. Beyond that, she wants to write a historical novel of the Sepulveda family's journey from Spain, during the conquest of Mexico, to California, where they were given three land grants for their service to the crown. As Marian says, "I hope you'll enjoy reading these stories as much as I will bringing them to life. I'm 78, and I'm just getting started!"

Share your comments and early California stories with author Marian Sepulveda:

WhereEaglesDance@gmail.com

Made in the USA
San Bernardino, CA
09 June 2016